Rocket Robinson™

and the
Secret of the Saint

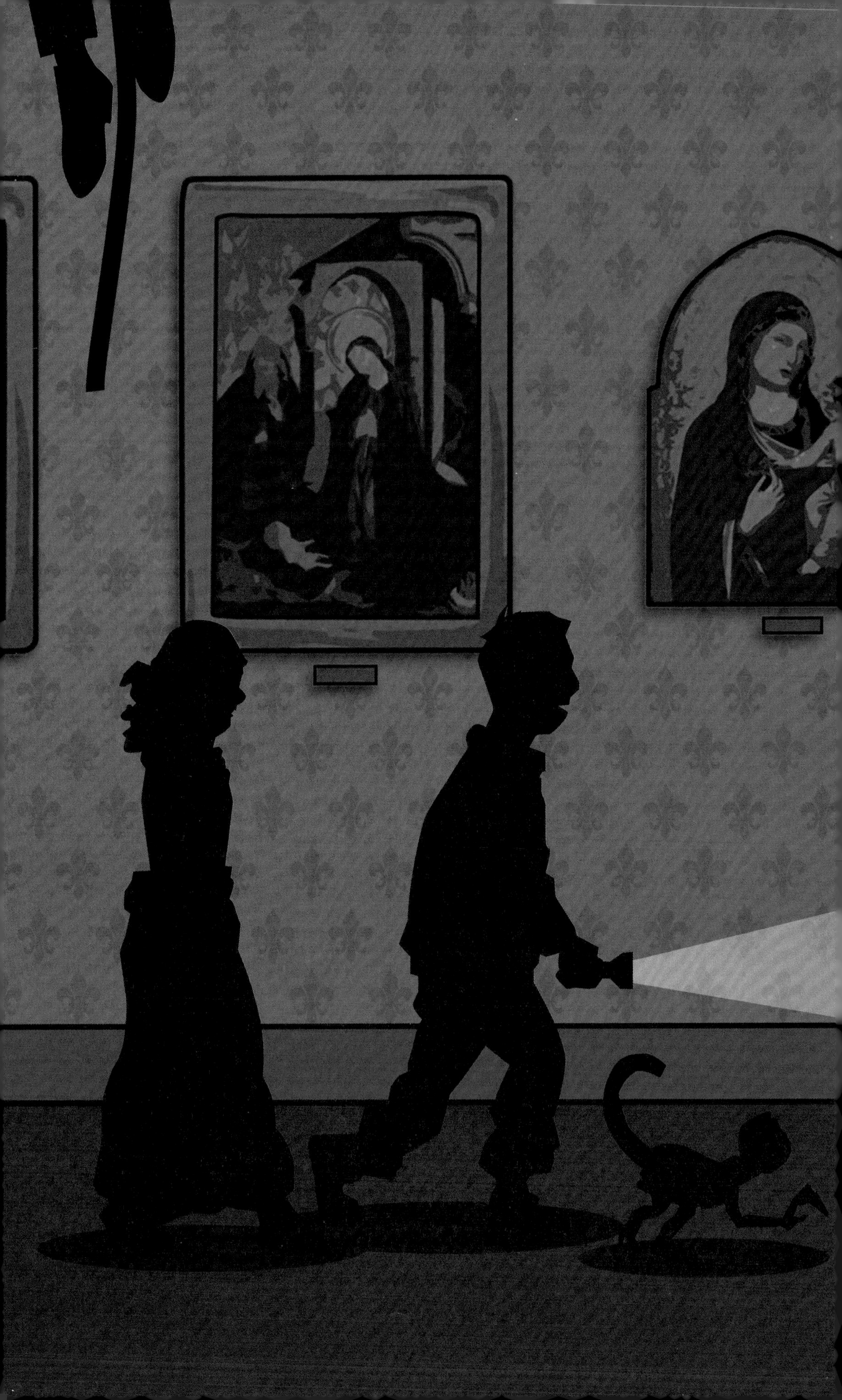

Rocket Robinson™

and the
Secret of the Saint

Written and illustrated by
SEAN O'NEILL

DARK HORSE BOOKS

President & Publisher   **MIKE RICHARDSON**

Collection Editor   **SHANTEL LaROCQUE**

Collection Assistant Editor   **BRETT ISRAEL**

Collection Designer   **CINDY CACEREZ-SPRAGUE**

Digital Art Technician   **JOSIE CHRISTENSEN**

NEIL HANKERSON Executive Vice President **TOM WEDDLE** Chief Financial Officer
RANDY STRADLEY Vice President of Publishing **NICK McWHORTER** Chief Business
Development Officer **MATT PARKINSON** Vice President of Marketing **DALE LaFOUNTAIN**
Vice President of Information Technology **CARA NIECE** Vice President of Production
and Scheduling **MARK BERNARDI** Vice President of Book Trade and Digital Sales **KEN
LIZZI** General Counsel **DAVE MARSHALL** Editor in Chief **DAVEY ESTRADA** Editorial
Director **CHRIS WARNER** Senior Books Editor **CARY GRAZZINI** Director of Specialty
Projects **LIA RIBACCHI** Art Director **VANESSA TODD-HOLMES** Director of Print Purchasing
MATT DRYER Director of Digital Art and Prepress **MICHAEL GOMBOS** Director of
International Publishing and Licensing **KARI YADRO** Director of Custom Programs

Published by Dark Horse Books
A division of Dark Horse Comics, Inc.
10956 SE Main Street
Milwaukie, OR 97222

RocketRobinson.com • DarkHorse.com

To find a comics shop in your area, visit ComicShopLocator.com.

First Dark Horse edition: September 2018
ISBN 978-1-50670-679-5

10 9 8 7 6 5 4 3 2 1
Printed in China

This book reprints *Rocket Robinson and the Secret of the Saint* previously published by BoilerRoom Studios.

Library of Congress Cataloging-in-Publication Data

Names: O'Neill, Sean, 1968- author, illustrator.
Title: Rocket Robinson and the secret of the saint / written and illustrated
  by Sean O'Neill.
Description: First Dark Horse edition. | Milwaukie, OR : Dark Horse Books,
  September 2018. | Summary: Rocket, Nuri, and Screech find themselves in
  1933 Paris, where a rare and mysterious painting has been stolen, so the
  young adventures set out on the trail of the stolen artistic treasure and
  its secrets.
Identifiers: LCCN 2018015852 | ISBN 9781506706795 (paperback)
Subjects: LCSH: Graphic novels. | CYAC: Graphic novels. | Adventure and
  adventurers--Fiction. | Art theft--Fiction. | Ciphers--Fiction. | Paris
  (France)--Fiction. | France--History--20th century--Fiction. | BISAC:
  JUVENILE FICTION / Historical / General. | JUVENILE FICTION / Action &
  Adventure / Survival Stories. | JUVENILE FICTION / Comics & Graphic Novels
  / General.
Classification: LCC PZ7.7.O55 Rok 2018 | DDC 741.5/973--dc23
LC record available at https://lccn.loc.gov/2018015852

For My Family

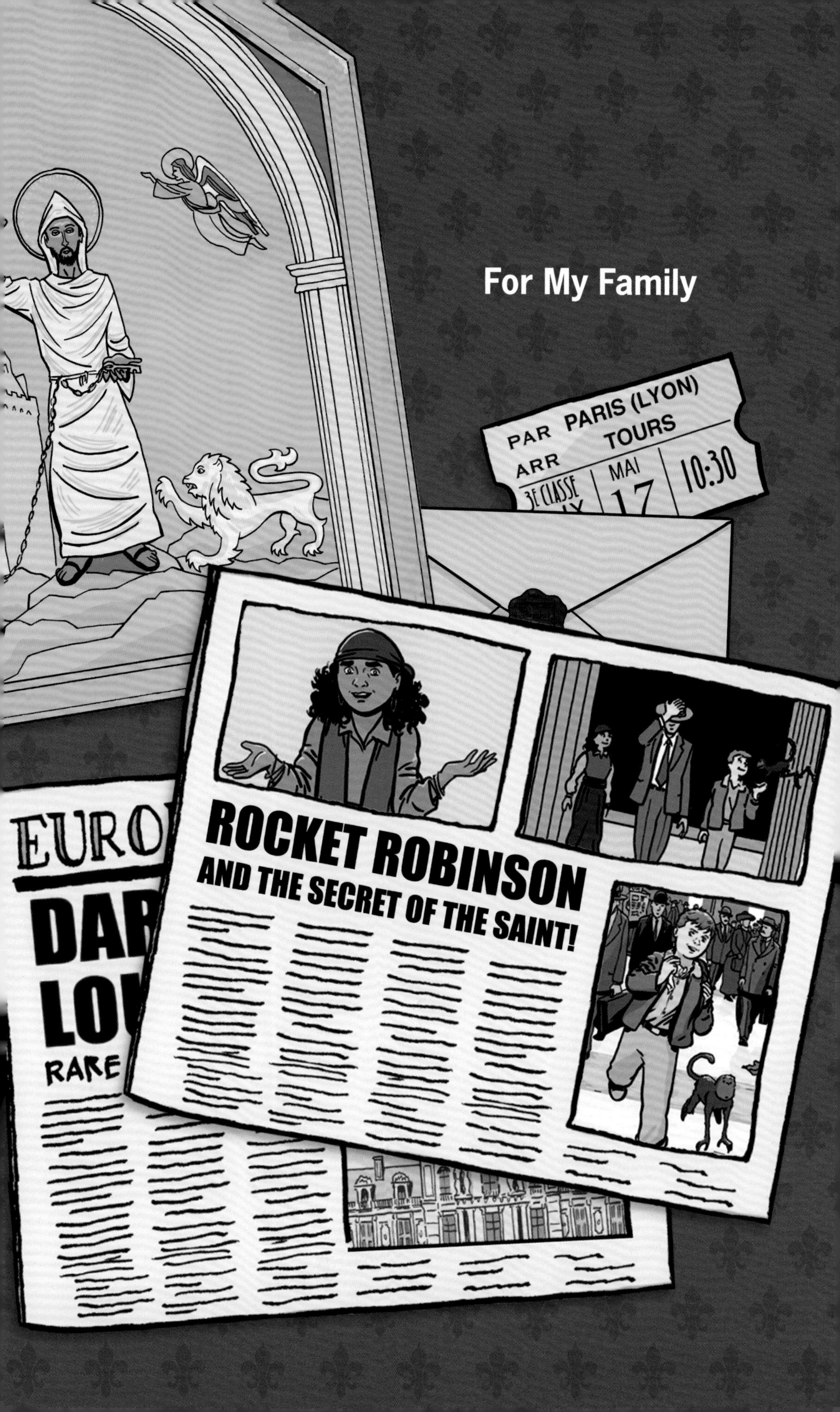
PAR PARIS (LYON)
ARR TOURS
MAI 17
10:30
ROCKET ROBINSON
AND THE SECRET OF THE SAINT!
RARE

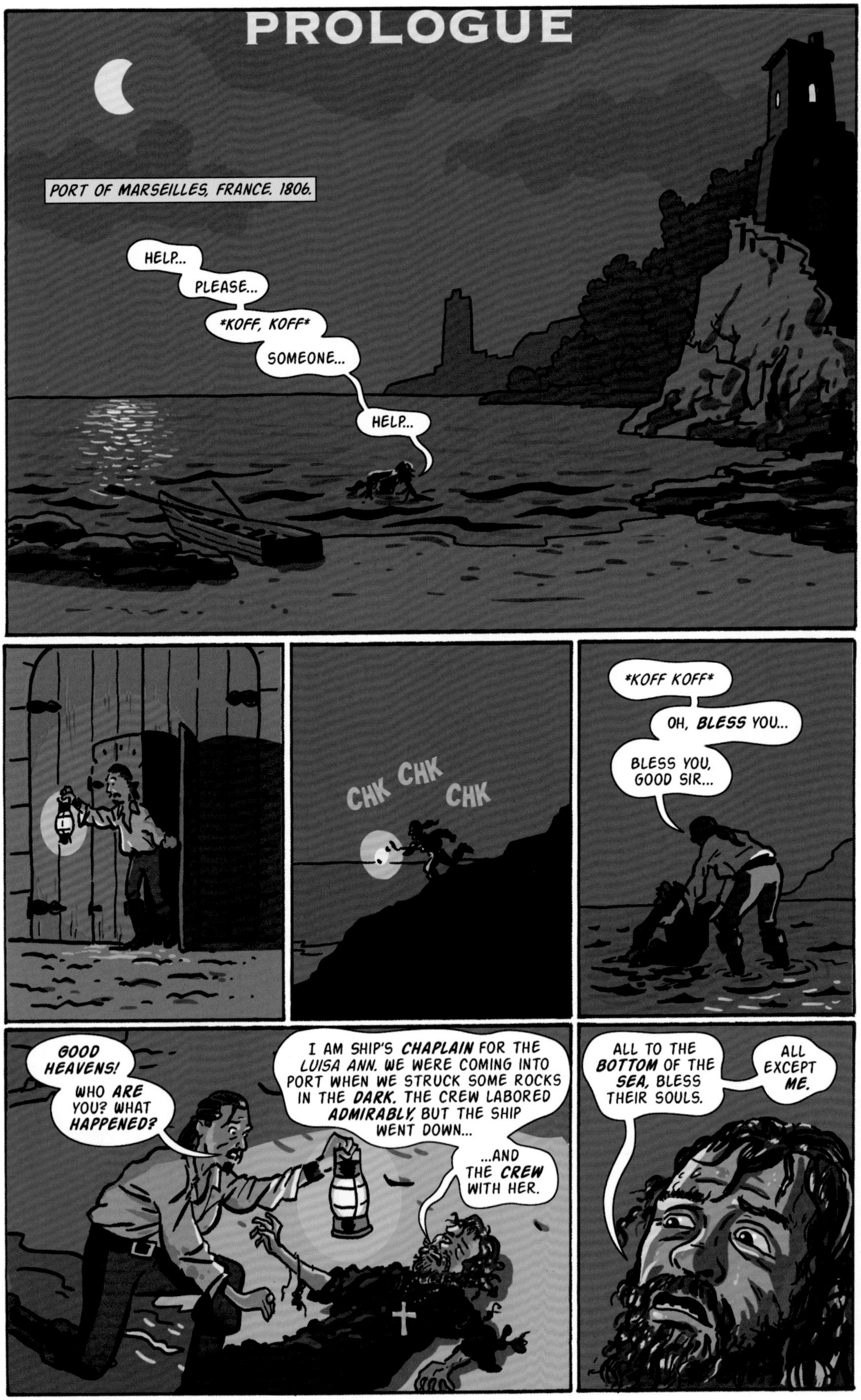
PROLOGUE
PORT OF MARSEILLES, FRANCE. 1806.
HELP...
PLEASE...
KOFF, KOFF
SOMEONE...
HELP...
CHK CHK CHK
KOFF KOFF
OH, BLESS YOU...
BLESS YOU, GOOD SIR...
GOOD HEAVENS!
WHO ARE YOU? WHAT HAPPENED?
I AM SHIP'S CHAPLAIN FOR THE LUISA ANN. WE WERE COMING INTO PORT WHEN WE STRUCK SOME ROCKS IN THE DARK. THE CREW LABORED ADMIRABLY, BUT THE SHIP WENT DOWN...
...AND THE CREW WITH HER.
ALL TO THE BOTTOM OF THE SEA, BLESS THEIR SOULS.
ALL EXCEPT ME.

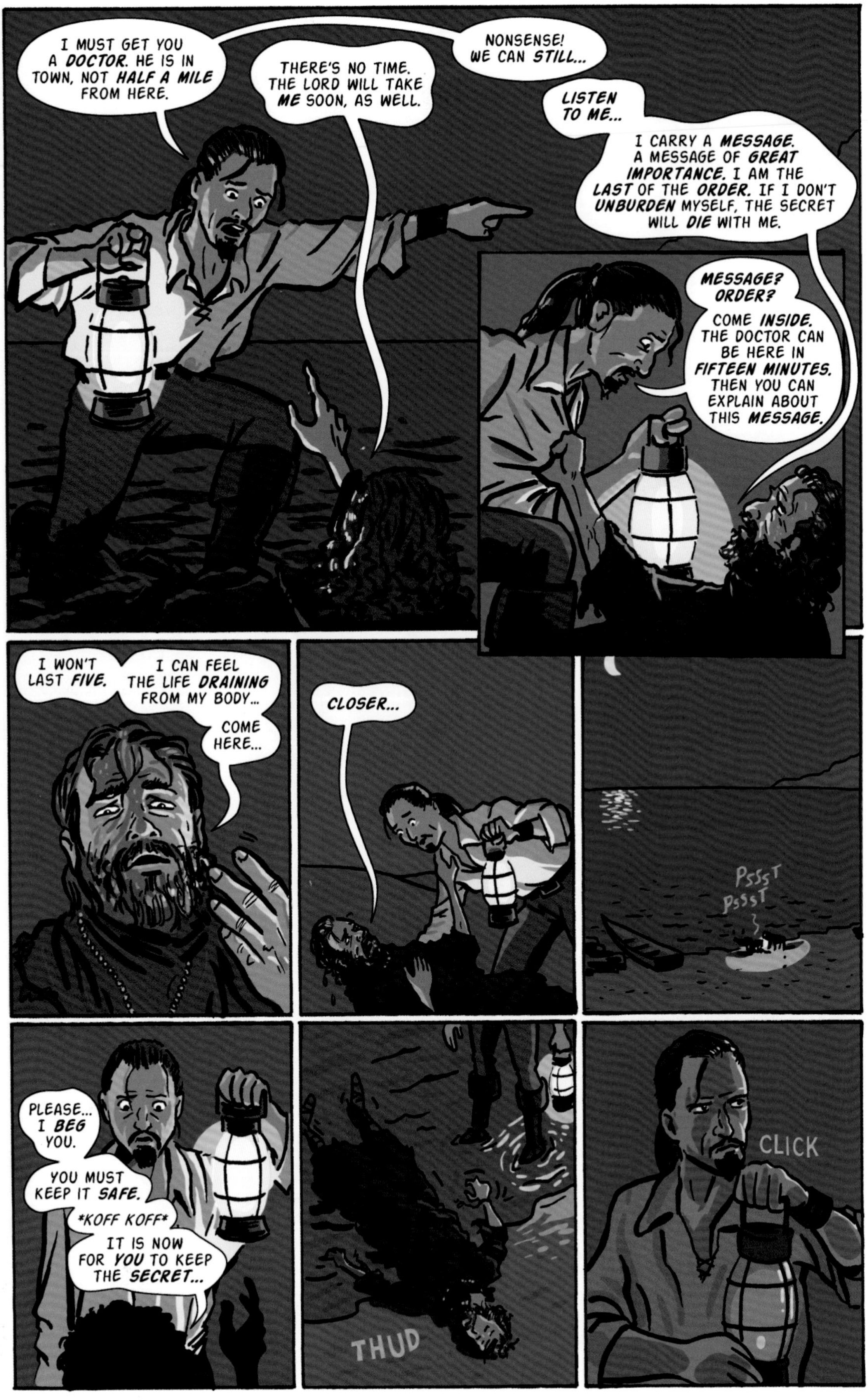
I MUST GET YOU A DOCTOR. HE IS IN TOWN, NOT HALF A MILE FROM HERE.
THERE'S NO TIME. THE LORD WILL TAKE ME SOON, AS WELL.
NONSENSE! WE CAN STILL...
LISTEN TO ME...
I CARRY A MESSAGE. A MESSAGE OF GREAT IMPORTANCE. I AM THE LAST OF THE ORDER. IF I DON'T UNBURDEN MYSELF, THE SECRET WILL DIE WITH ME.
MESSAGE? ORDER?
COME INSIDE. THE DOCTOR CAN BE HERE IN FIFTEEN MINUTES. THEN YOU CAN EXPLAIN ABOUT THIS MESSAGE.
I WON'T LAST FIVE.
I CAN FEEL THE LIFE DRAINING FROM MY BODY...
COME HERE...
CLOSER...
PSSST
PSSST
PLEASE... I BEG YOU.
YOU MUST KEEP IT SAFE.
KOFF KOFF
IT IS NOW FOR YOU TO KEEP THE SECRET...
THUD
CLICK

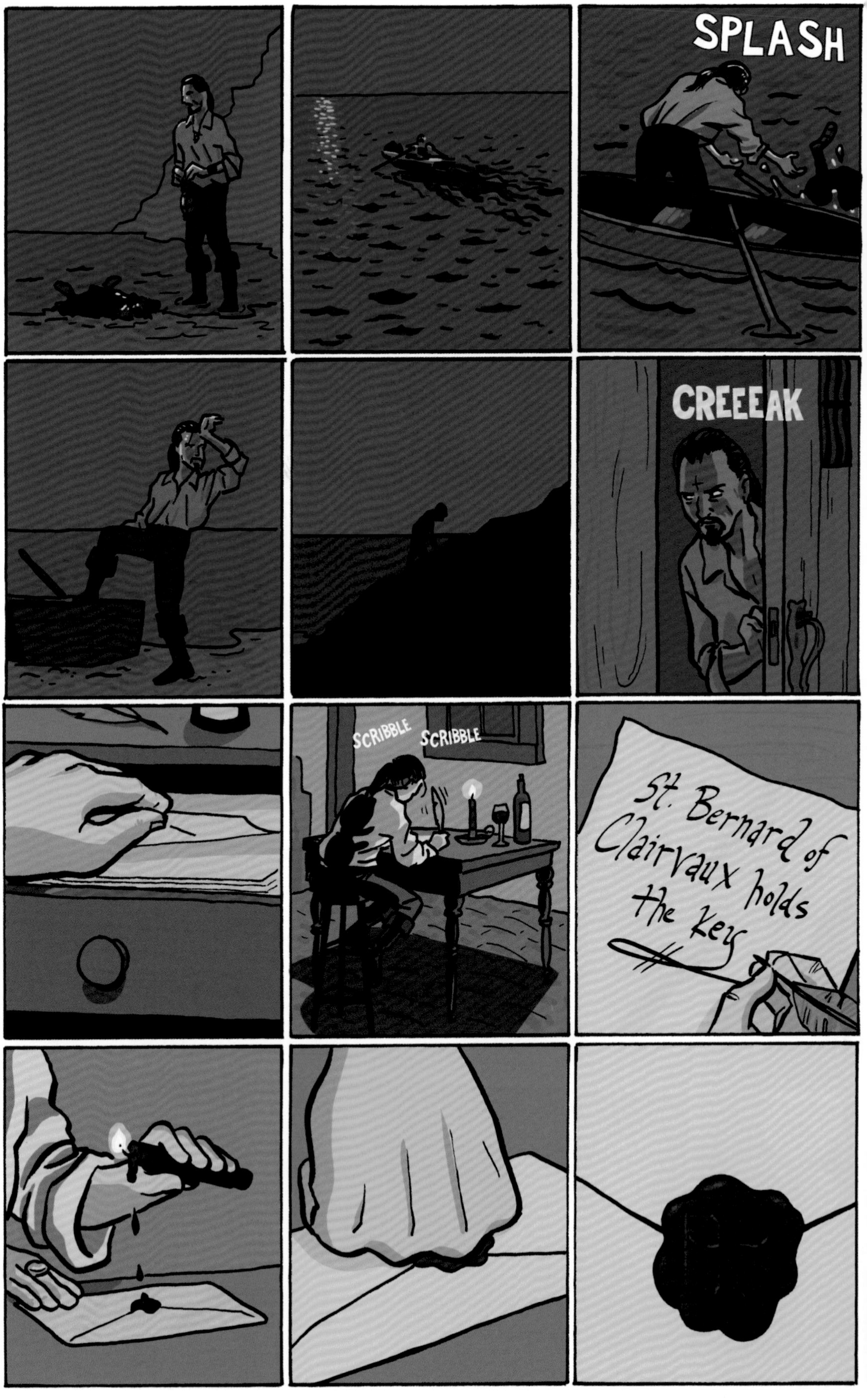
SPLASH
CREEEAK
SCRIBBLE
SCRIBBLE
St. Bernard of
Clairvaux holds
the Keys

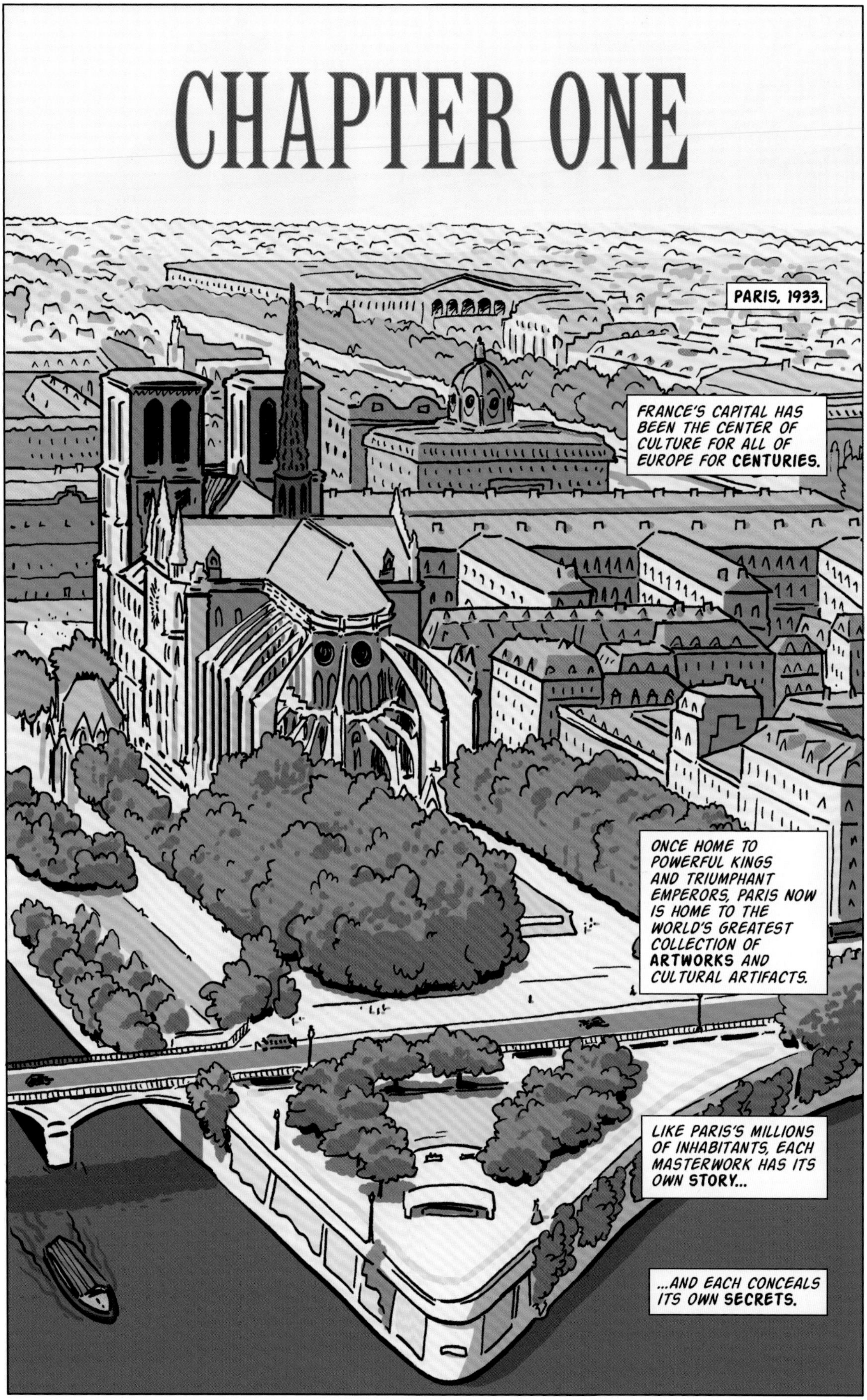
CHAPTER ONE
PARIS, 1933.
FRANCE'S CAPITAL HAS BEEN THE CENTER OF CULTURE FOR ALL OF EUROPE FOR CENTURIES.
ONCE HOME TO POWERFUL KINGS AND TRIUMPHANT EMPERORS, PARIS NOW IS HOME TO THE WORLD'S GREATEST COLLECTION OF ARTWORKS AND CULTURAL ARTIFACTS.
LIKE PARIS'S MILLIONS OF INHABITANTS, EACH MASTERWORK HAS ITS OWN STORY...
...AND EACH CONCEALS ITS OWN SECRETS.

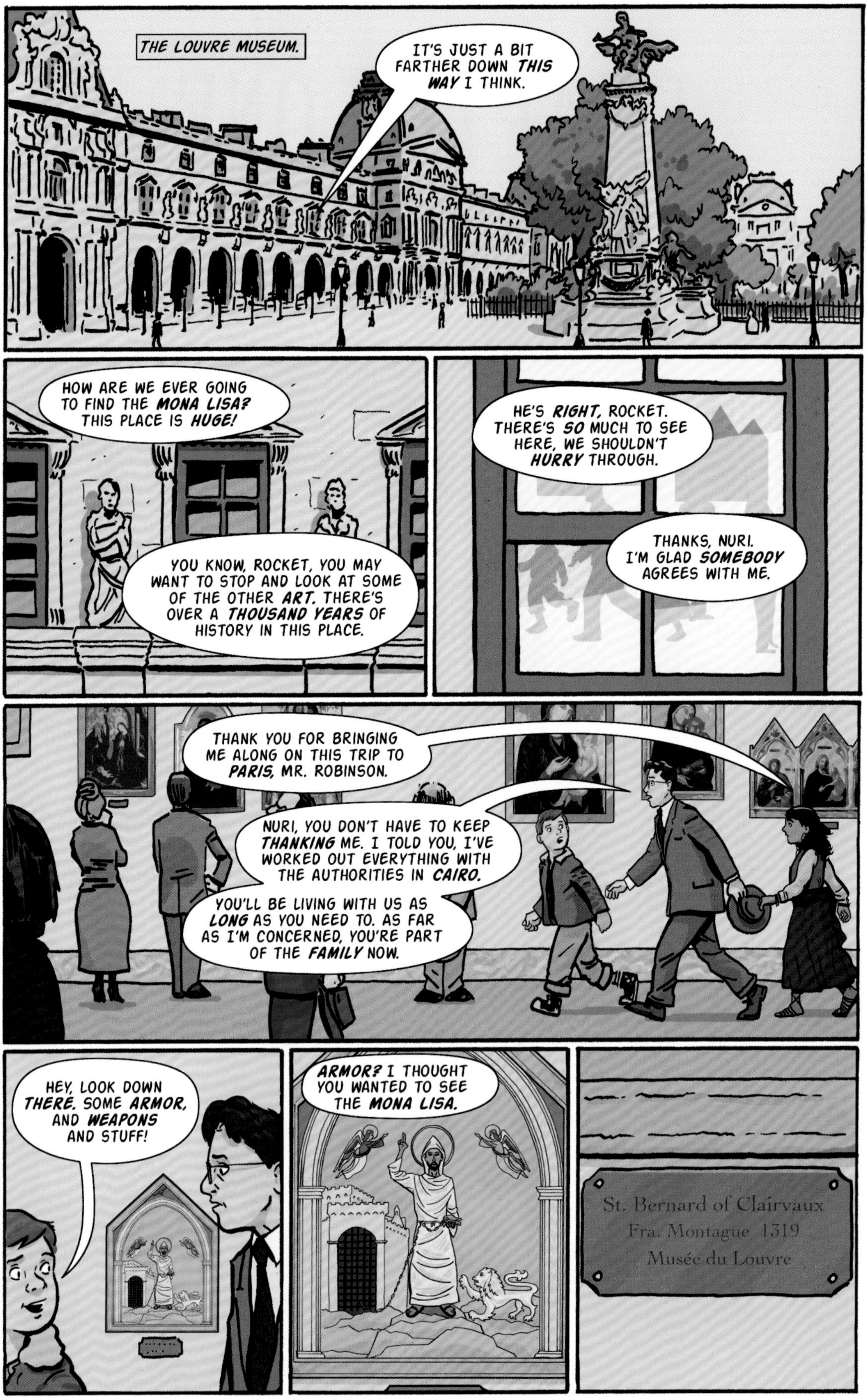
THE LOUVRE MUSEUM.
IT'S JUST A BIT FARTHER DOWN THIS WAY I THINK.
HOW ARE WE EVER GOING TO FIND THE MONA LISA? THIS PLACE IS HUGE!
YOU KNOW, ROCKET, YOU MAY WANT TO STOP AND LOOK AT SOME OF THE OTHER ART. THERE'S OVER A THOUSAND YEARS OF HISTORY IN THIS PLACE.
HE'S RIGHT, ROCKET. THERE'S SO MUCH TO SEE HERE, WE SHOULDN'T HURRY THROUGH.
THANKS, NURI. I'M GLAD SOMEBODY AGREES WITH ME.
THANK YOU FOR BRINGING ME ALONG ON THIS TRIP TO PARIS, MR. ROBINSON.
NURI, YOU DON'T HAVE TO KEEP THANKING ME. I TOLD YOU, I'VE WORKED OUT EVERYTHING WITH THE AUTHORITIES IN CAIRO.
YOU'LL BE LIVING WITH US AS LONG AS YOU NEED TO. AS FAR AS I'M CONCERNED, YOU'RE PART OF THE FAMILY NOW.
HEY, LOOK DOWN THERE. SOME ARMOR, AND WEAPONS AND STUFF!
ARMOR? I THOUGHT YOU WANTED TO SEE THE MONA LISA.
St. Bernard of Clairvaux
Fra. Montague 1319
Musée du Louvre

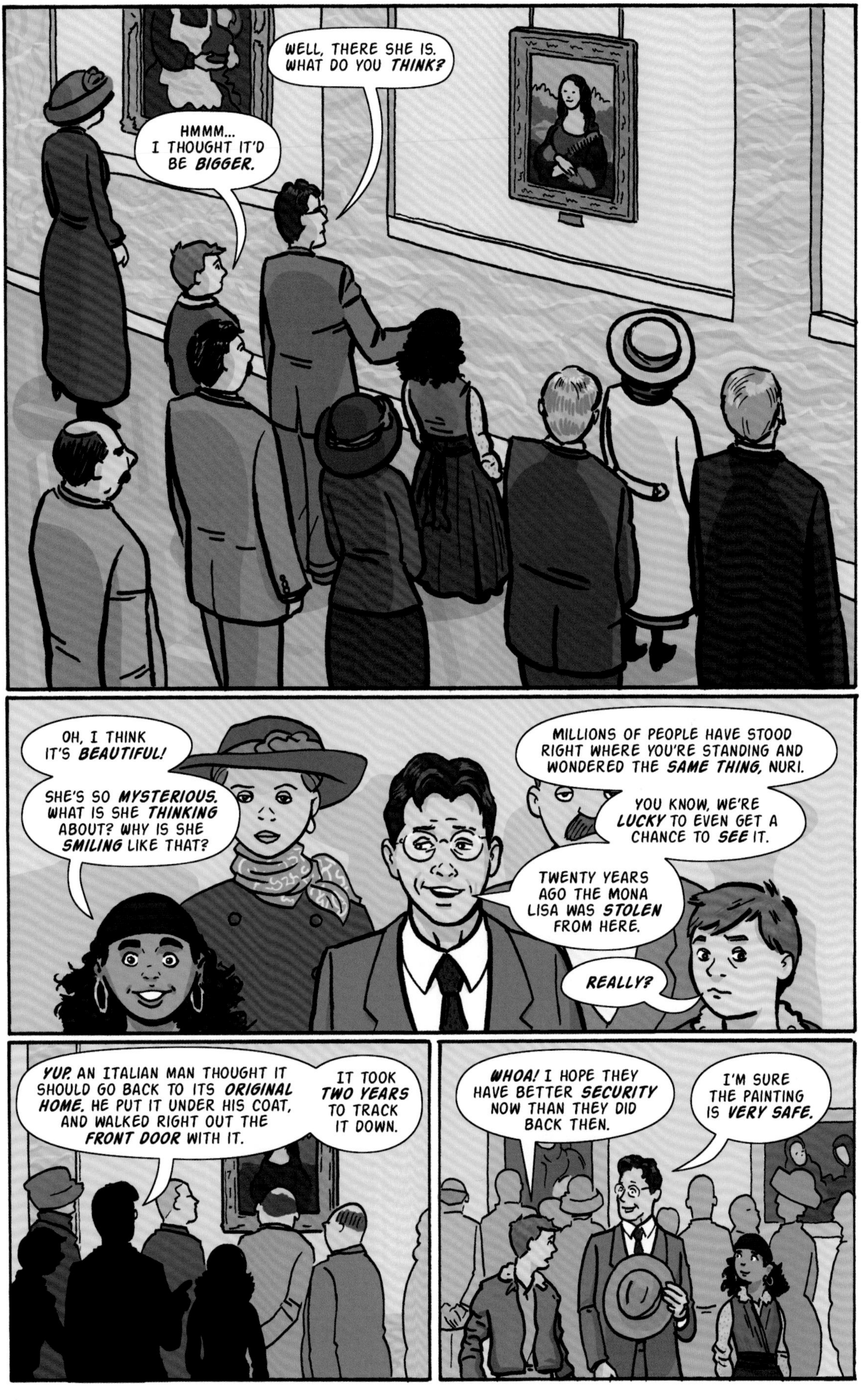

WELL, THERE SHE IS. WHAT DO YOU THINK?
HMMM... I THOUGHT IT'D BE BIGGER.
OH, I THINK IT'S BEAUTIFUL!
SHE'S SO MYSTERIOUS. WHAT IS SHE THINKING ABOUT? WHY IS SHE SMILING LIKE THAT?
MILLIONS OF PEOPLE HAVE STOOD RIGHT WHERE YOU'RE STANDING AND WONDERED THE SAME THING, NURI.
YOU KNOW, WE'RE LUCKY TO EVEN GET A CHANCE TO SEE IT.
TWENTY YEARS AGO THE MONA LISA WAS STOLEN FROM HERE.
REALLY?
YUP. AN ITALIAN MAN THOUGHT IT SHOULD GO BACK TO ITS ORIGINAL HOME. HE PUT IT UNDER HIS COAT, AND WALKED RIGHT OUT THE FRONT DOOR WITH IT.
IT TOOK TWO YEARS TO TRACK IT DOWN.
WHOA! I HOPE THEY HAVE BETTER SECURITY NOW THAN THEY DID BACK THEN.
I'M SURE THE PAINTING IS VERY SAFE.

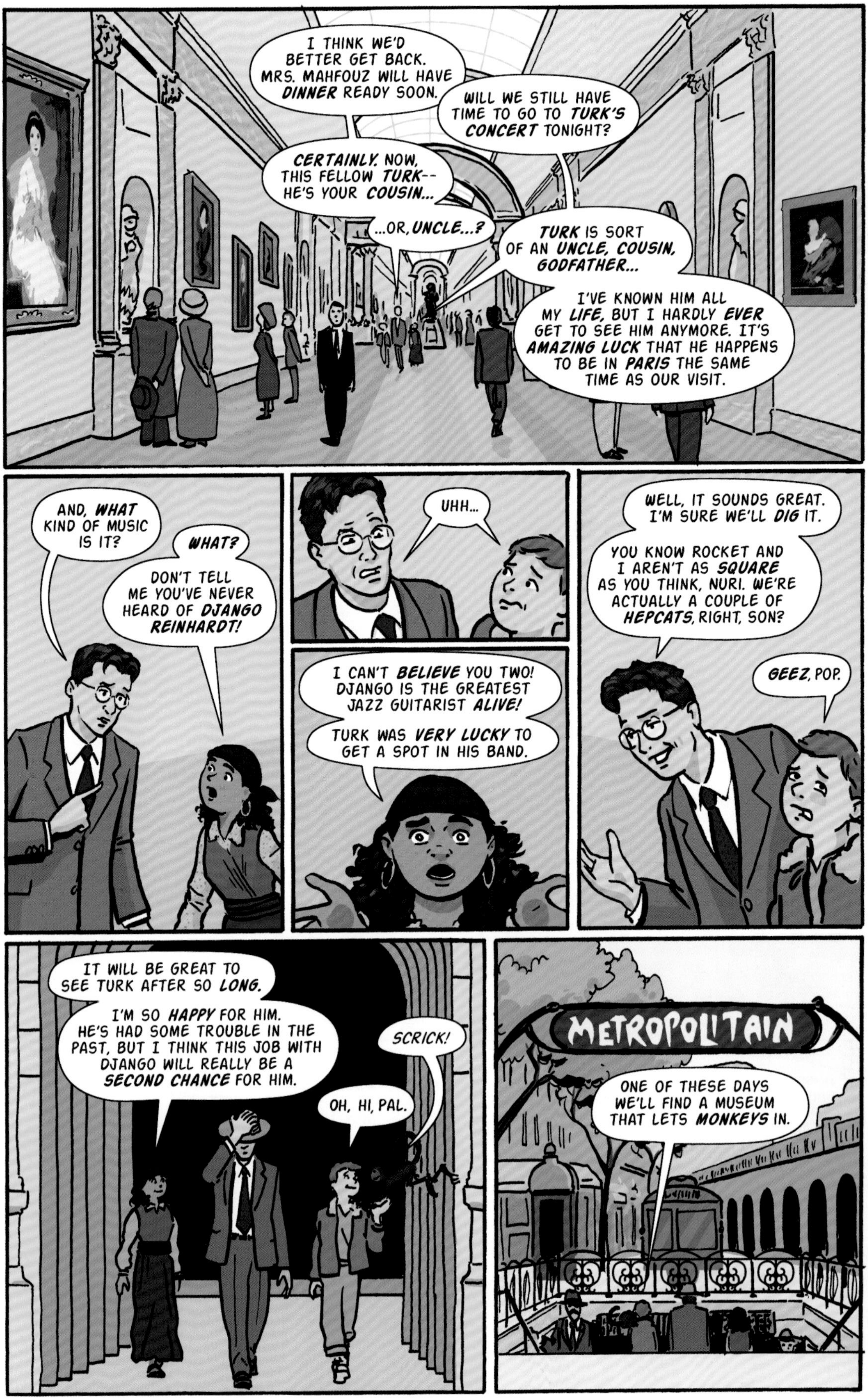
I THINK WE'D BETTER GET BACK. MRS. MAHFOUZ WILL HAVE DINNER READY SOON.
WILL WE STILL HAVE TIME TO GO TO TURK'S CONCERT TONIGHT?
CERTAINLY. NOW, THIS FELLOW TURK-- HE'S YOUR COUSIN...
...OR, UNCLE...?
TURK IS SORT OF AN UNCLE, COUSIN, GODFATHER...
I'VE KNOWN HIM ALL MY LIFE, BUT I HARDLY EVER GET TO SEE HIM ANYMORE. IT'S AMAZING LUCK THAT HE HAPPENS TO BE IN PARIS THE SAME TIME AS OUR VISIT.
AND, WHAT KIND OF MUSIC IS IT?
WHAT?
DON'T TELL ME YOU'VE NEVER HEARD OF DJANGO REINHARDT!
UHH...
I CAN'T BELIEVE YOU TWO! DJANGO IS THE GREATEST JAZZ GUITARIST ALIVE!
TURK WAS VERY LUCKY TO GET A SPOT IN HIS BAND.
WELL, IT SOUNDS GREAT. I'M SURE WE'LL DIG IT.
YOU KNOW ROCKET AND I AREN'T AS SQUARE AS YOU THINK, NURI. WE'RE ACTUALLY A COUPLE OF HEPCATS, RIGHT, SON?
GEEZ, POP.
IT WILL BE GREAT TO SEE TURK AFTER SO LONG.
I'M SO HAPPY FOR HIM. HE'S HAD SOME TROUBLE IN THE PAST, BUT I THINK THIS JOB WITH DJANGO WILL REALLY BE A SECOND CHANCE FOR HIM.
SCRICK!
OH, HI, PAL.
METROPOLITAIN
ONE OF THESE DAYS WE'LL FIND A MUSEUM THAT LETS MONKEYS IN.

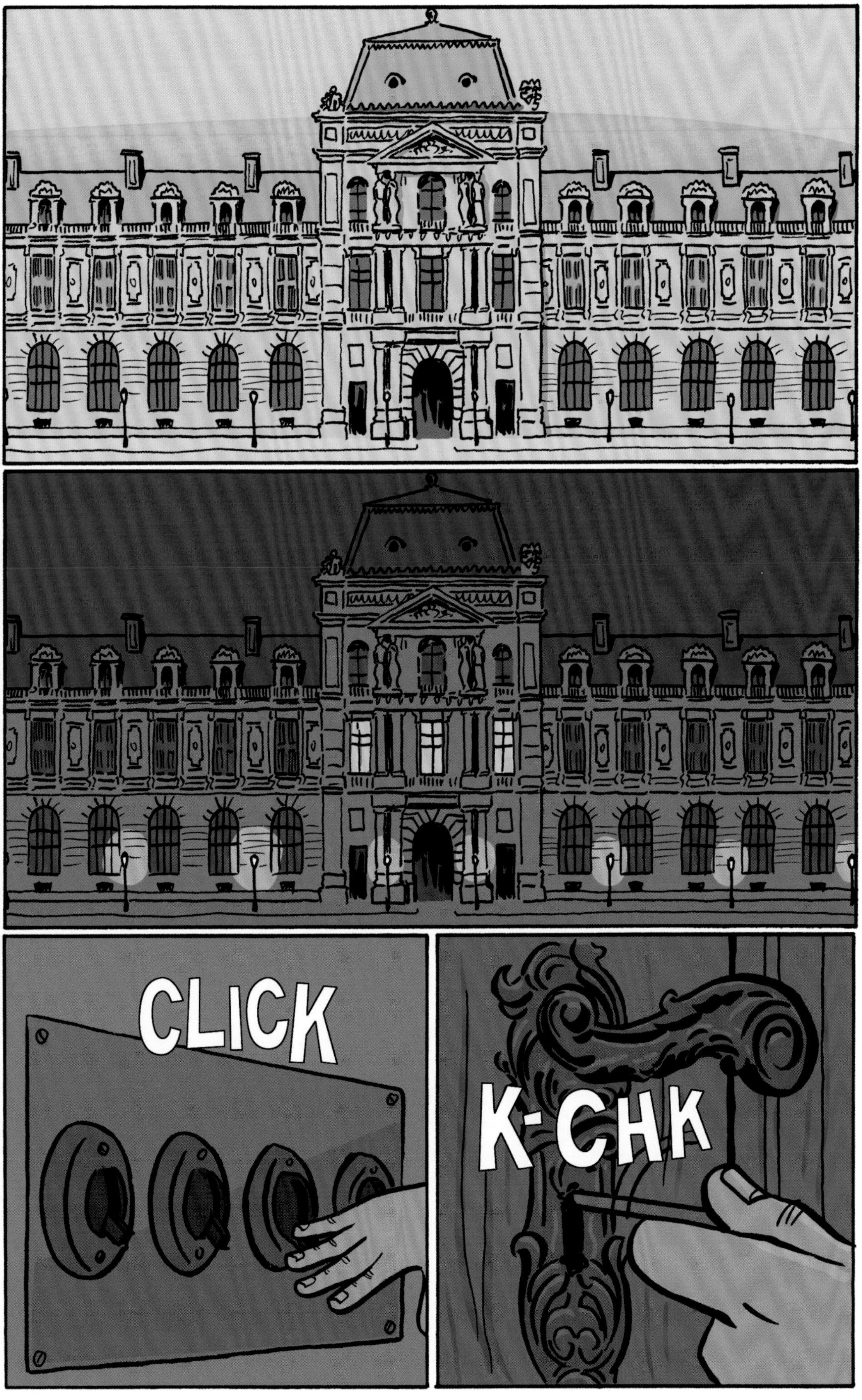
CLICK
K-CHK

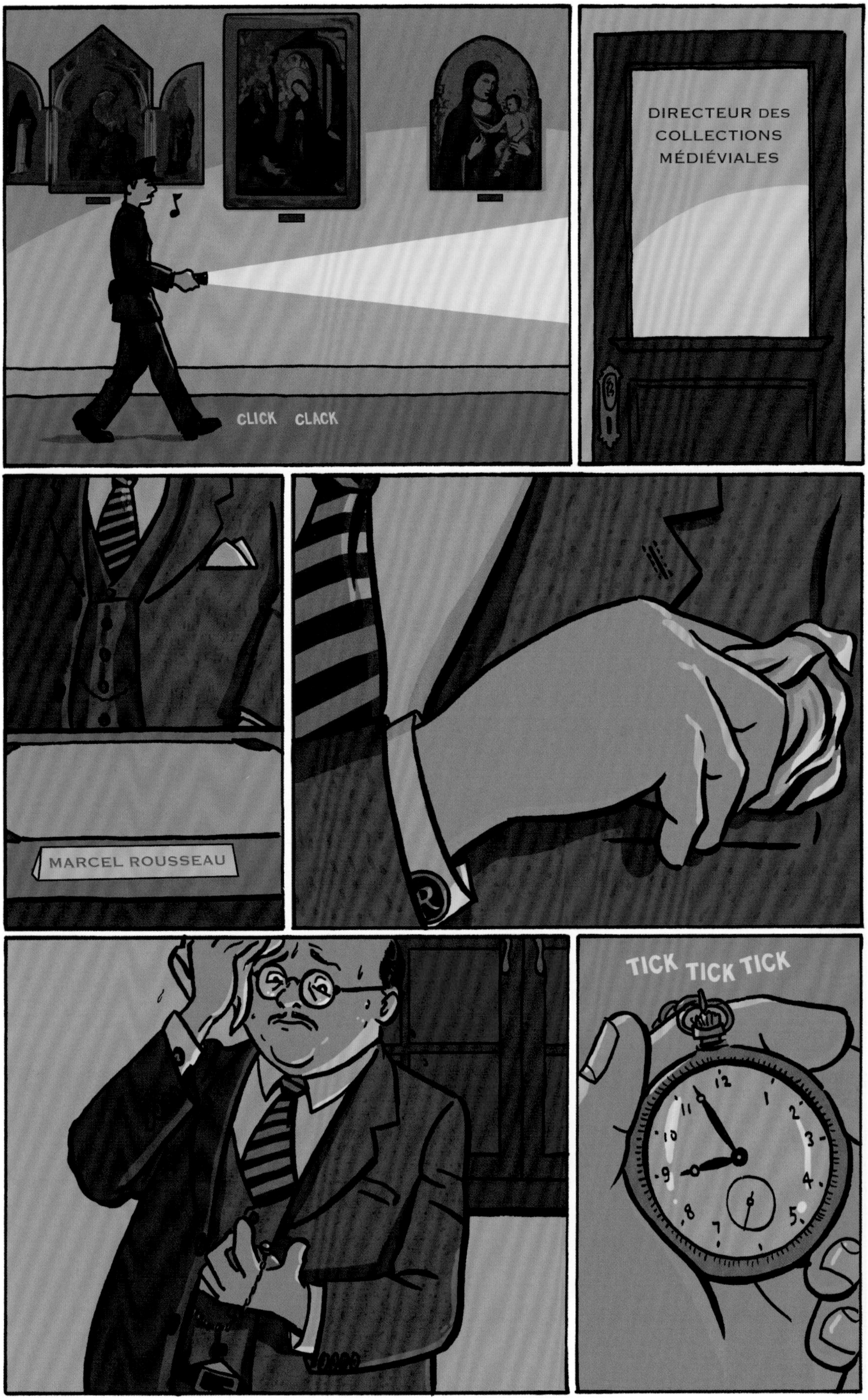
DIRECTEUR DES
COLLECTIONS
MÉDIÉVIALES
CLICK CLACK
MARCEL ROUSSEAU
TICK TICK TICK

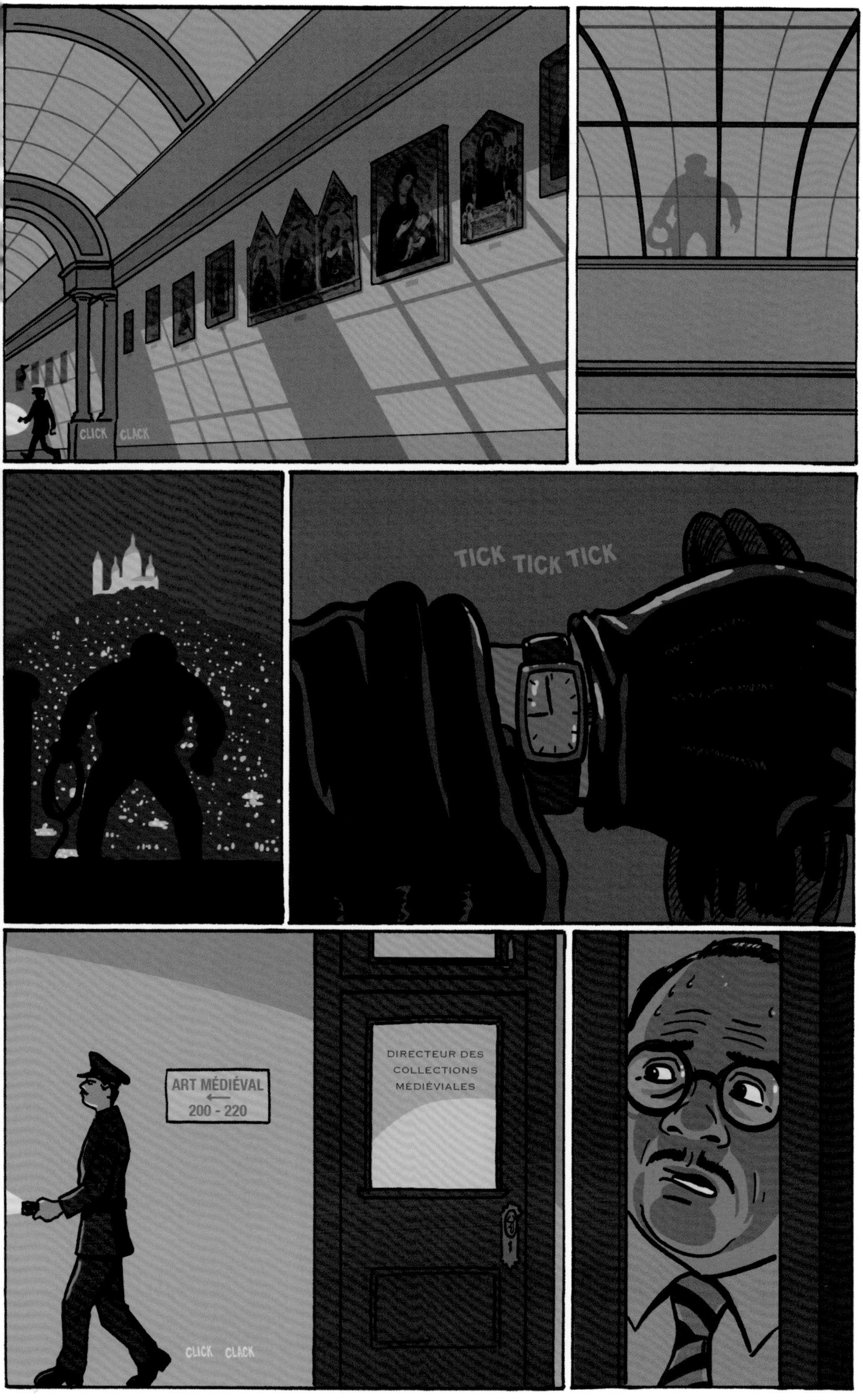

CLICK CLACK
TICK TICK TICK
ART MÉDIÉVAL
200 - 220
DIRECTEUR DES
COLLECTIONS
MÉDIÉVIALES
CLICK CLACK

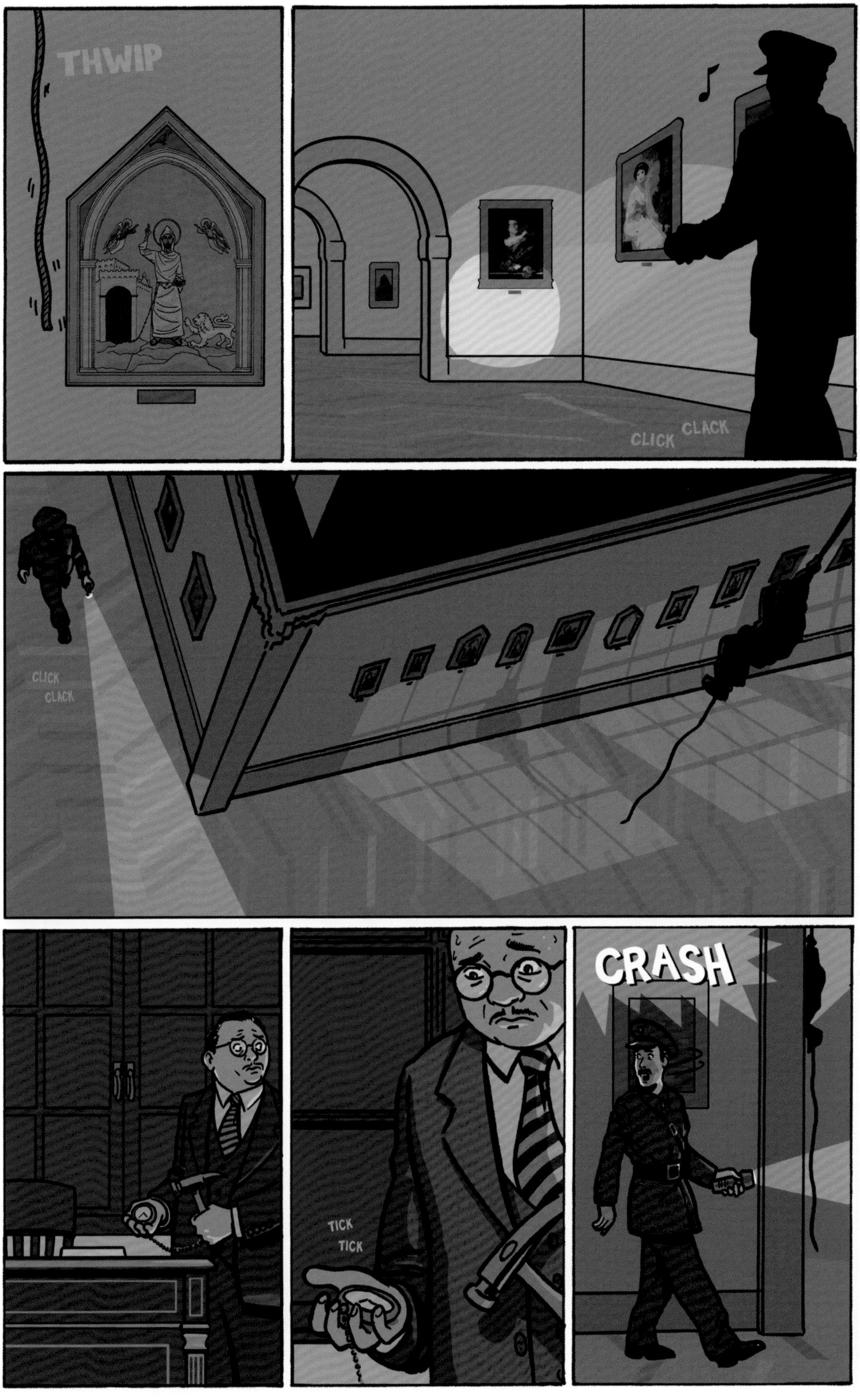
THWIP
CLICK CLACK
CLICK
CLACK
TICK
TICK
CRASH

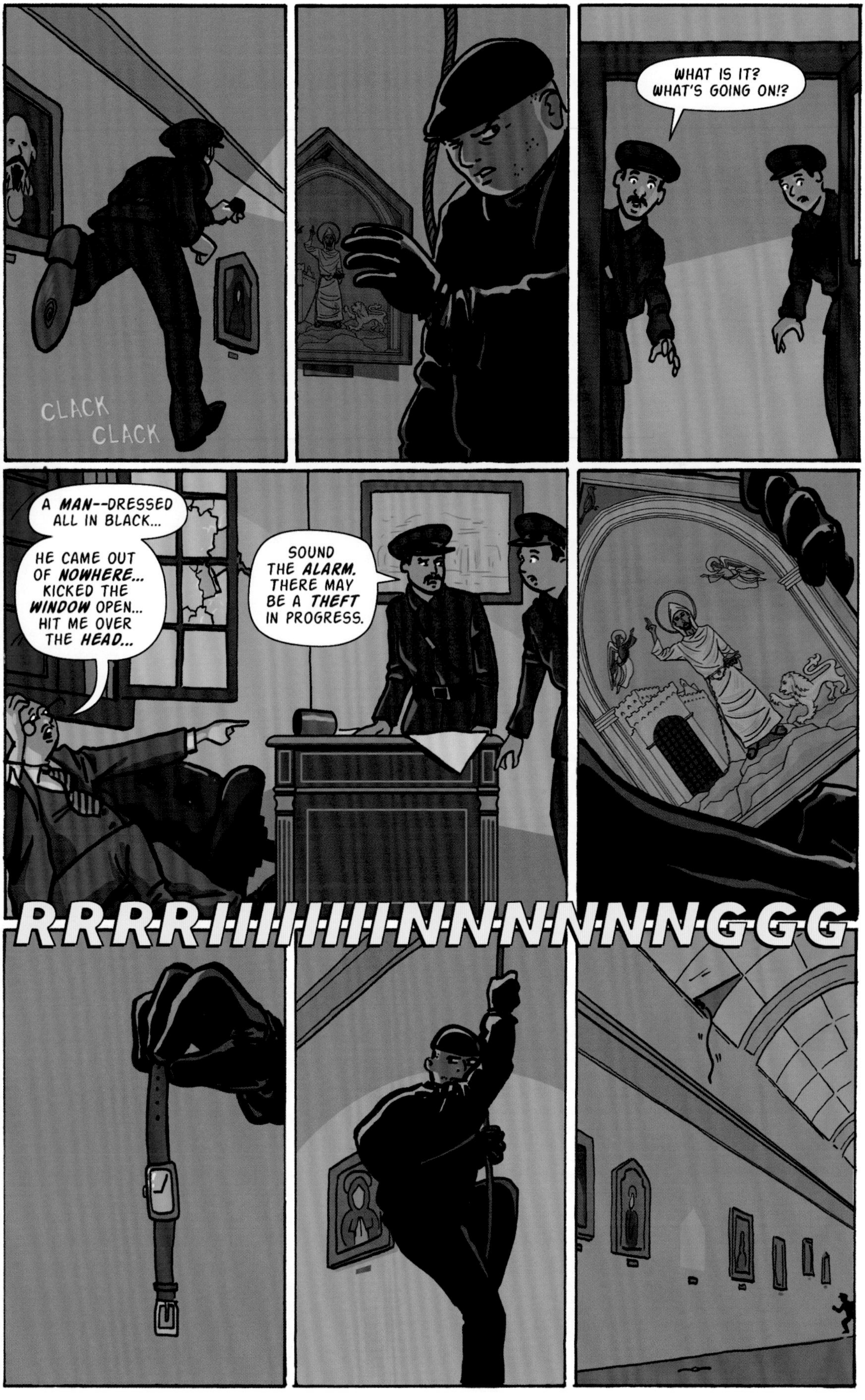
CLACK
CLACK
WHAT IS IT? WHAT'S GOING ON!?
A MAN--DRESSED ALL IN BLACK...
HE CAME OUT OF NOWHERE... KICKED THE WINDOW OPEN... HIT ME OVER THE HEAD...
SOUND THE ALARM. THERE MAY BE A THEFT IN PROGRESS.
RRRRIIIIIIIIINNNNNNNNGGG

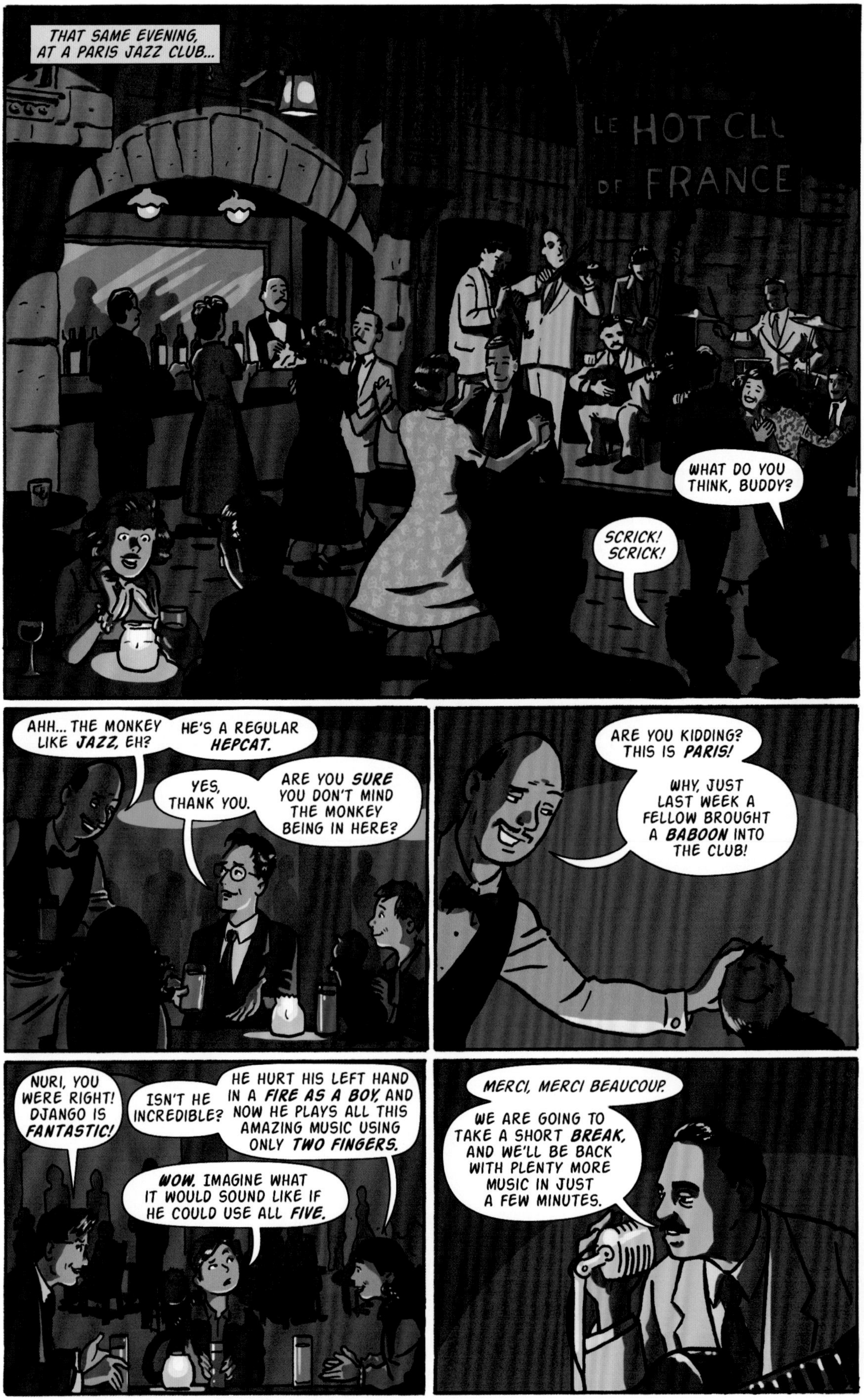
THAT SAME EVENING, AT A PARIS JAZZ CLUB...
LE HOT CLU DE FRANCE
WHAT DO YOU THINK, BUDDY?
SCRICK! SCRICK!
AHH... THE MONKEY LIKE JAZZ, EH?
HE'S A REGULAR HEPCAT.
YES, THANK YOU.
ARE YOU SURE YOU DON'T MIND THE MONKEY BEING IN HERE?
ARE YOU KIDDING? THIS IS PARIS!
WHY, JUST LAST WEEK A FELLOW BROUGHT A BABOON INTO THE CLUB!
NURI, YOU WERE RIGHT! DJANGO IS FANTASTIC!
ISN'T HE INCREDIBLE?
HE HURT HIS LEFT HAND IN A FIRE AS A BOY, AND NOW HE PLAYS ALL THIS AMAZING MUSIC USING ONLY TWO FINGERS.
WOW. IMAGINE WHAT IT WOULD SOUND LIKE IF HE COULD USE ALL FIVE.
MERCI, MERCI BEAUCOUP.
WE ARE GOING TO TAKE A SHORT BREAK, AND WE'LL BE BACK WITH PLENTY MORE MUSIC IN JUST A FEW MINUTES.

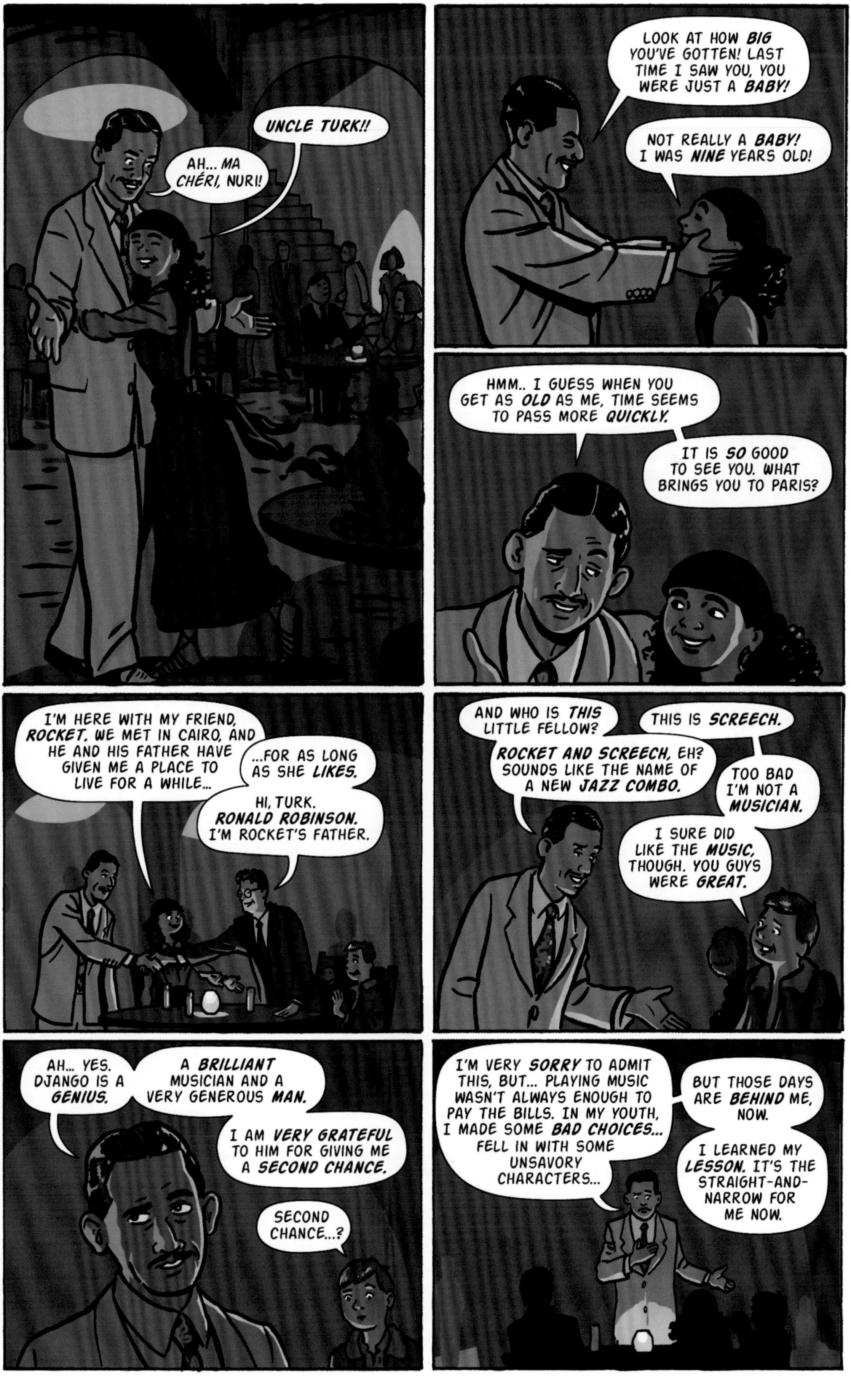
UNCLE TURK!!
AH... MA CHÉRI, NURI!
LOOK AT HOW BIG YOU'VE GOTTEN! LAST TIME I SAW YOU, YOU WERE JUST A BABY!
NOT REALLY A BABY! I WAS NINE YEARS OLD!
HMM.. I GUESS WHEN YOU GET AS OLD AS ME, TIME SEEMS TO PASS MORE QUICKLY.
IT IS SO GOOD TO SEE YOU. WHAT BRINGS YOU TO PARIS?
I'M HERE WITH MY FRIEND, ROCKET. WE MET IN CAIRO, AND HE AND HIS FATHER HAVE GIVEN ME A PLACE TO LIVE FOR A WHILE...
...FOR AS LONG AS SHE LIKES.
HI, TURK. RONALD ROBINSON. I'M ROCKET'S FATHER.
AND WHO IS THIS LITTLE FELLOW?
THIS IS SCREECH.
ROCKET AND SCREECH, EH? SOUNDS LIKE THE NAME OF A NEW JAZZ COMBO.
TOO BAD I'M NOT A MUSICIAN.
I SURE DID LIKE THE MUSIC, THOUGH. YOU GUYS WERE GREAT.
AH... YES. DJANGO IS A GENIUS.
A BRILLIANT MUSICIAN AND A VERY GENEROUS MAN.
I AM VERY GRATEFUL TO HIM FOR GIVING ME A SECOND CHANCE.
SECOND CHANCE...?
I'M VERY SORRY TO ADMIT THIS, BUT... PLAYING MUSIC WASN'T ALWAYS ENOUGH TO PAY THE BILLS. IN MY YOUTH, I MADE SOME BAD CHOICES... FELL IN WITH SOME UNSAVORY CHARACTERS...
BUT THOSE DAYS ARE BEHIND ME, NOW.
I LEARNED MY LESSON. IT'S THE STRAIGHT-AND-NARROW FOR ME NOW.

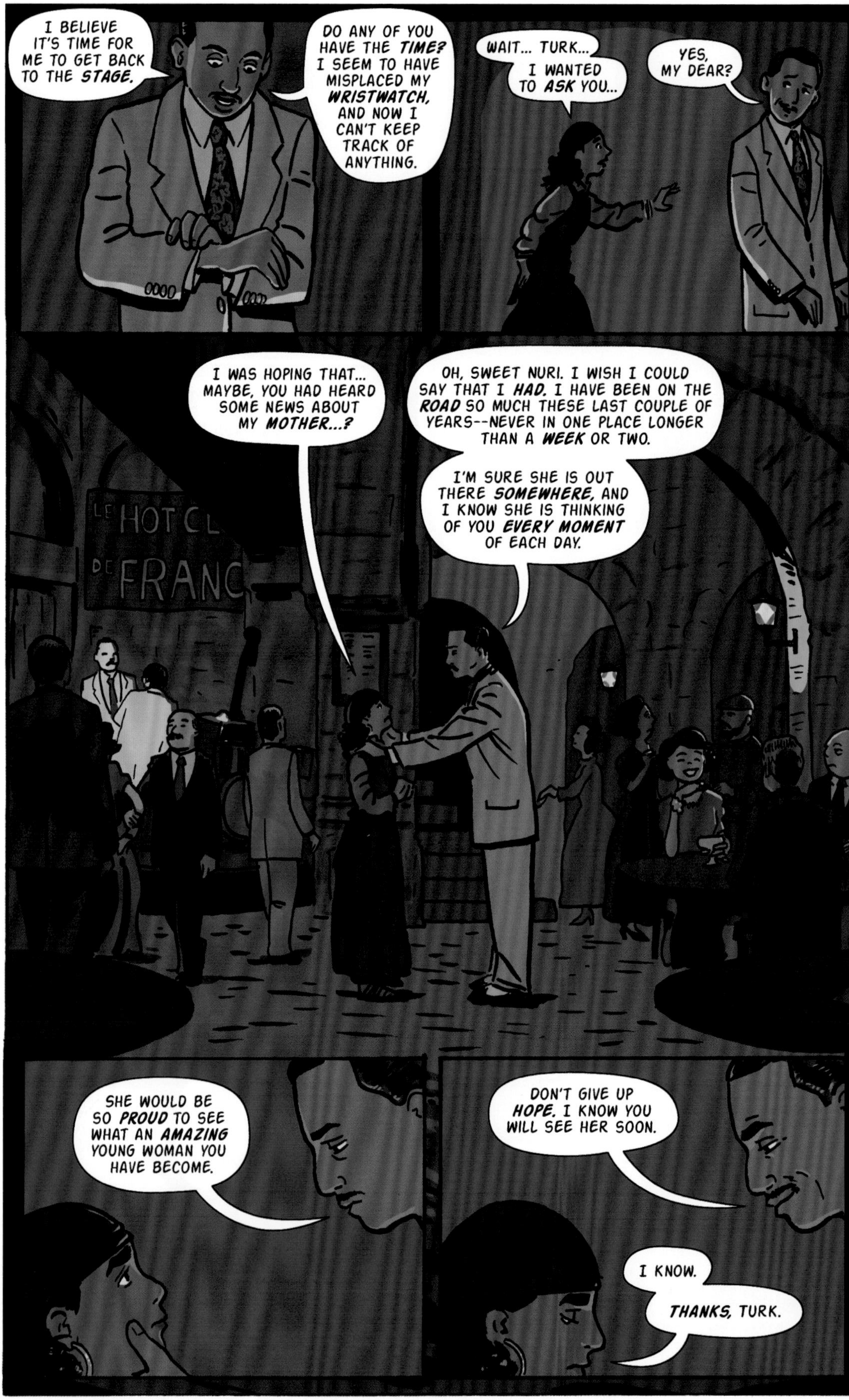
I BELIEVE IT'S TIME FOR ME TO GET BACK TO THE STAGE.
DO ANY OF YOU HAVE THE TIME? I SEEM TO HAVE MISPLACED MY WRISTWATCH, AND NOW I CAN'T KEEP TRACK OF ANYTHING.
WAIT... TURK... I WANTED TO ASK YOU...
YES, MY DEAR?
I WAS HOPING THAT... MAYBE, YOU HAD HEARD SOME NEWS ABOUT MY MOTHER...?
OH, SWEET NURI. I WISH I COULD SAY THAT I HAD. I HAVE BEEN ON THE ROAD SO MUCH THESE LAST COUPLE OF YEARS--NEVER IN ONE PLACE LONGER THAN A WEEK OR TWO.
I'M SURE SHE IS OUT THERE SOMEWHERE, AND I KNOW SHE IS THINKING OF YOU EVERY MOMENT OF EACH DAY.
LE HOT CL
DE FRANC
SHE WOULD BE SO PROUD TO SEE WHAT AN AMAZING YOUNG WOMAN YOU HAVE BECOME.
DON'T GIVE UP HOPE. I KNOW YOU WILL SEE HER SOON.
I KNOW.
THANKS, TURK.

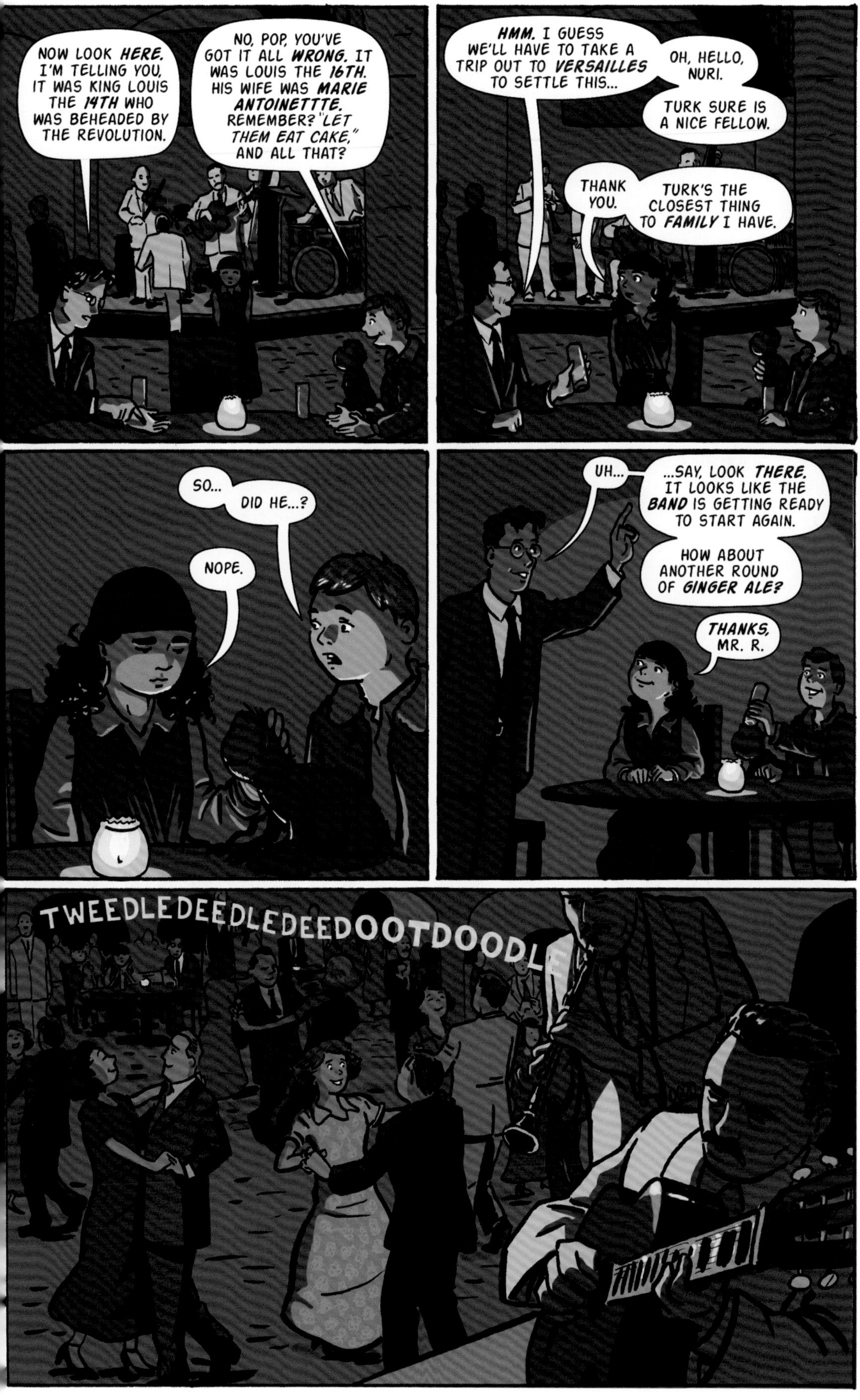
NOW LOOK *HERE.* I'M TELLING YOU, IT WAS KING LOUIS THE *14TH* WHO WAS BEHEADED BY THE REVOLUTION.
NO, POP, YOU'VE GOT IT ALL *WRONG.* IT WAS LOUIS THE *16TH.* HIS WIFE WAS *MARIE ANTOINETTTE.* REMEMBER? *"LET THEM EAT CAKE,"* AND ALL THAT?
HMM. I GUESS WE'LL HAVE TO TAKE A TRIP OUT TO *VERSAILLES* TO SETTLE THIS...
OH, HELLO, NURI.
TURK SURE IS A NICE FELLOW.
THANK YOU.
TURK'S THE CLOSEST THING TO *FAMILY* I HAVE.
SO...
DID HE...?
NOPE.
UH...
...SAY, LOOK *THERE.* IT LOOKS LIKE THE *BAND* IS GETTING READY TO START AGAIN.
HOW ABOUT ANOTHER ROUND OF *GINGER ALE?*
THANKS, MR. R.
TWEEDLEDEEDLEDEEDOOTDOODLE

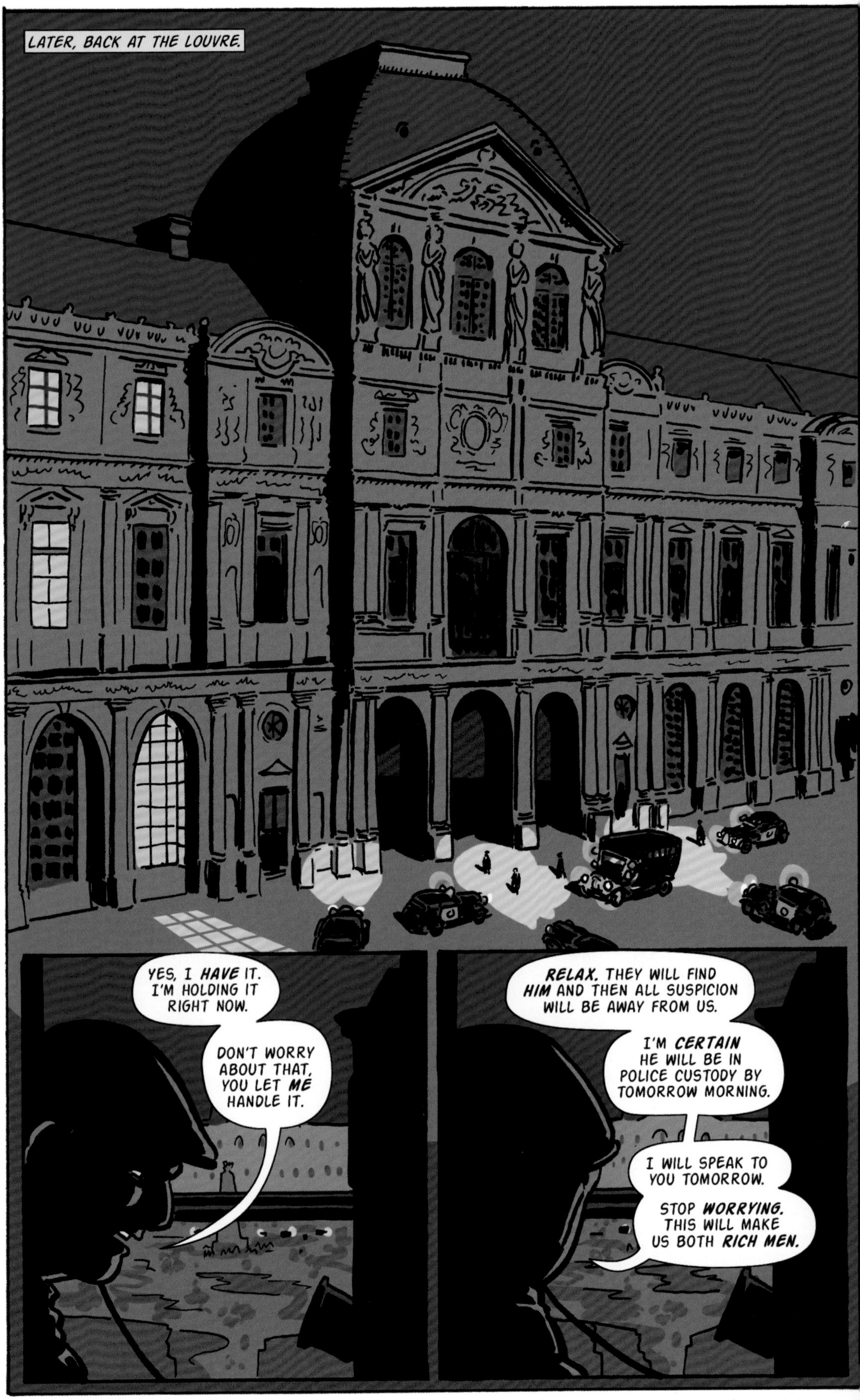
LATER, BACK AT THE LOUVRE.
YES, I HAVE IT. I'M HOLDING IT RIGHT NOW.
DON'T WORRY ABOUT THAT, YOU LET ME HANDLE IT.
RELAX. THEY WILL FIND HIM AND THEN ALL SUSPICION WILL BE AWAY FROM US.
I'M CERTAIN HE WILL BE IN POLICE CUSTODY BY TOMORROW MORNING.
I WILL SPEAK TO YOU TOMORROW.
STOP WORRYING. THIS WILL MAKE US BOTH RICH MEN.

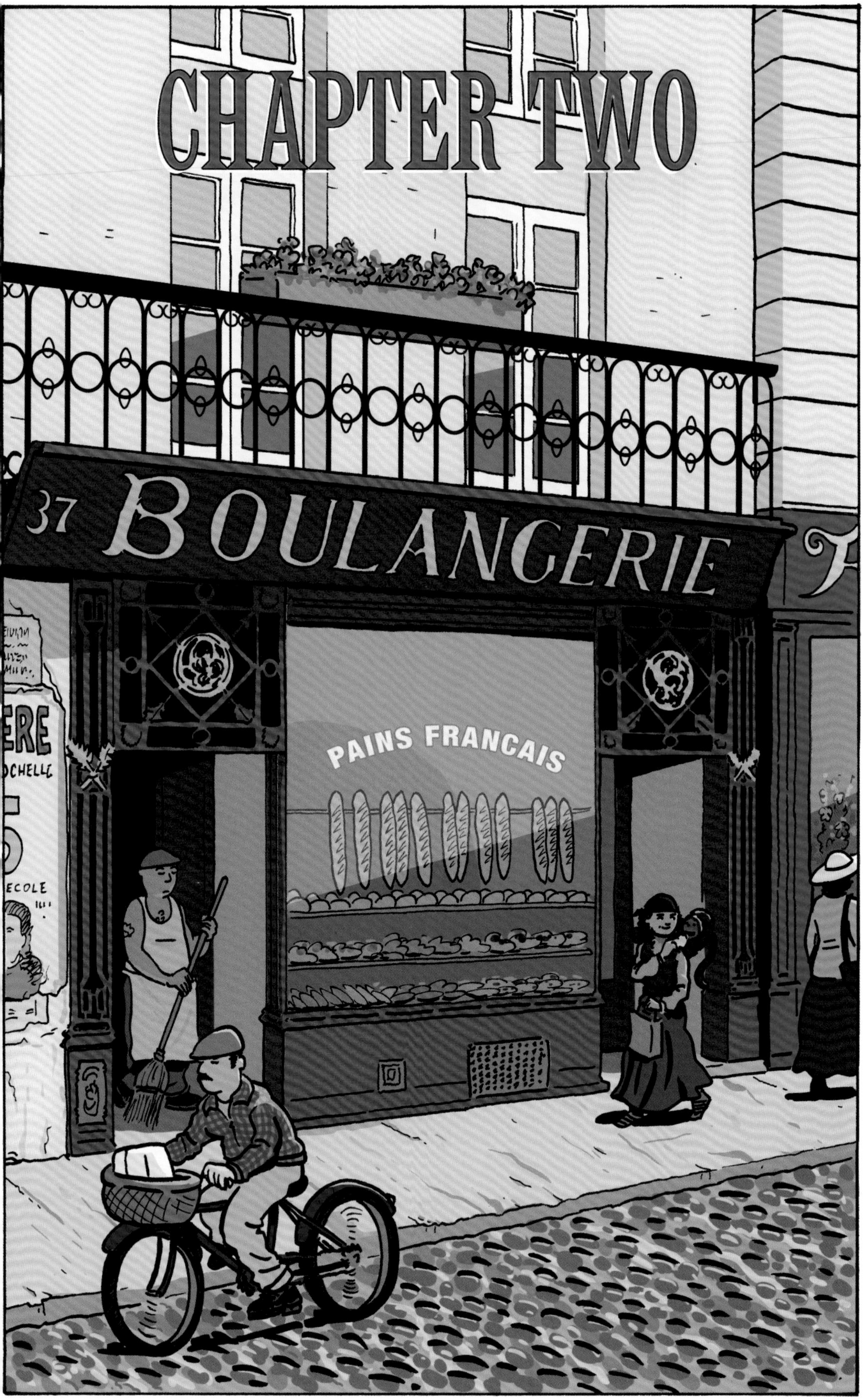
CHAPTER TWO
37 BOULANGERIE
PAINS FRANCAIS

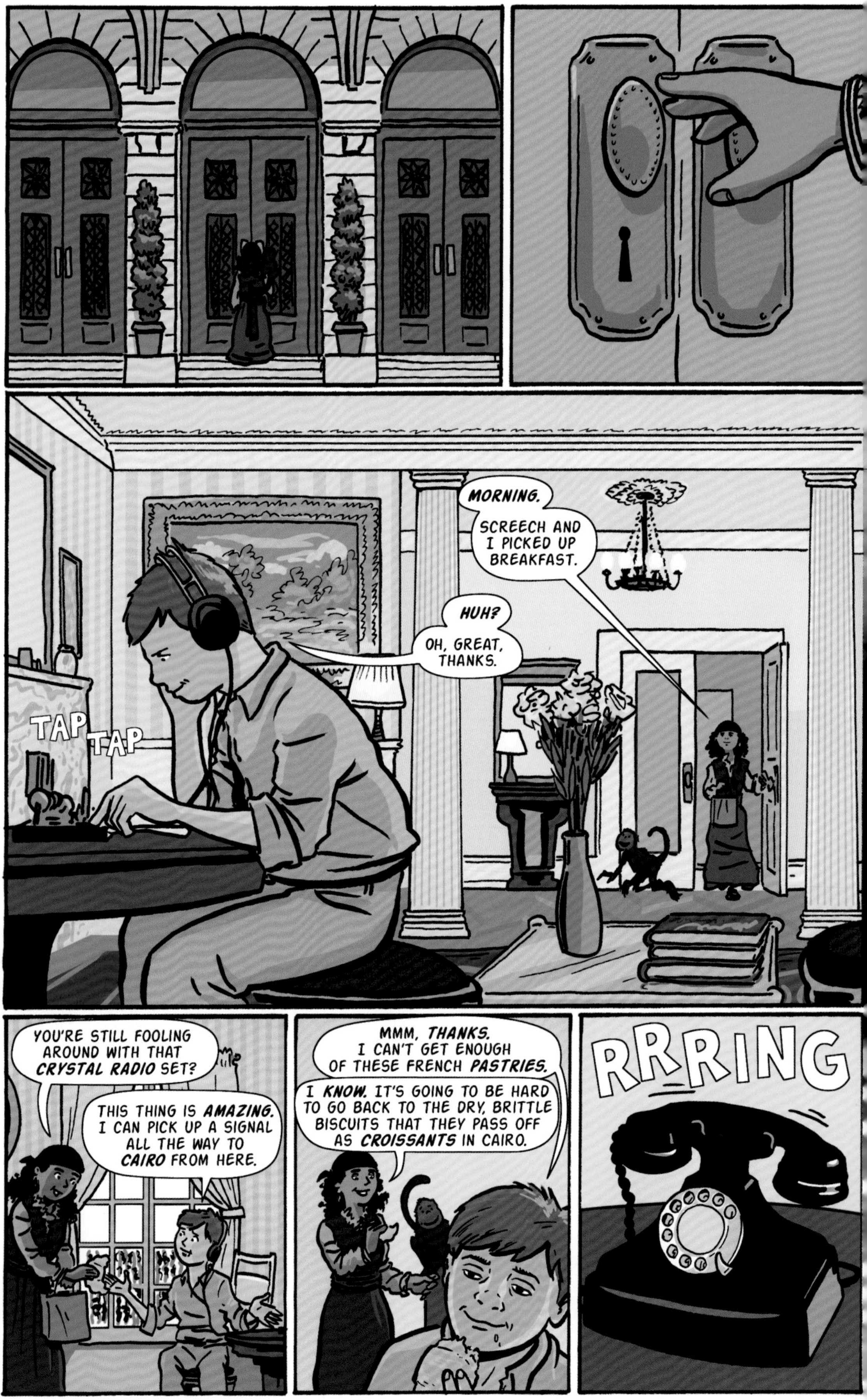

MORNING.
SCREECH AND I PICKED UP BREAKFAST.
HUH?
OH, GREAT, THANKS.
TAP TAP
YOU'RE STILL FOOLING AROUND WITH THAT CRYSTAL RADIO SET?
THIS THING IS AMAZING. I CAN PICK UP A SIGNAL ALL THE WAY TO CAIRO FROM HERE.
MMM, THANKS. I CAN'T GET ENOUGH OF THESE FRENCH PASTRIES.
I KNOW. IT'S GOING TO BE HARD TO GO BACK TO THE DRY, BRITTLE BISCUITS THAT THEY PASS OFF AS CROISSANTS IN CAIRO.
RRRING

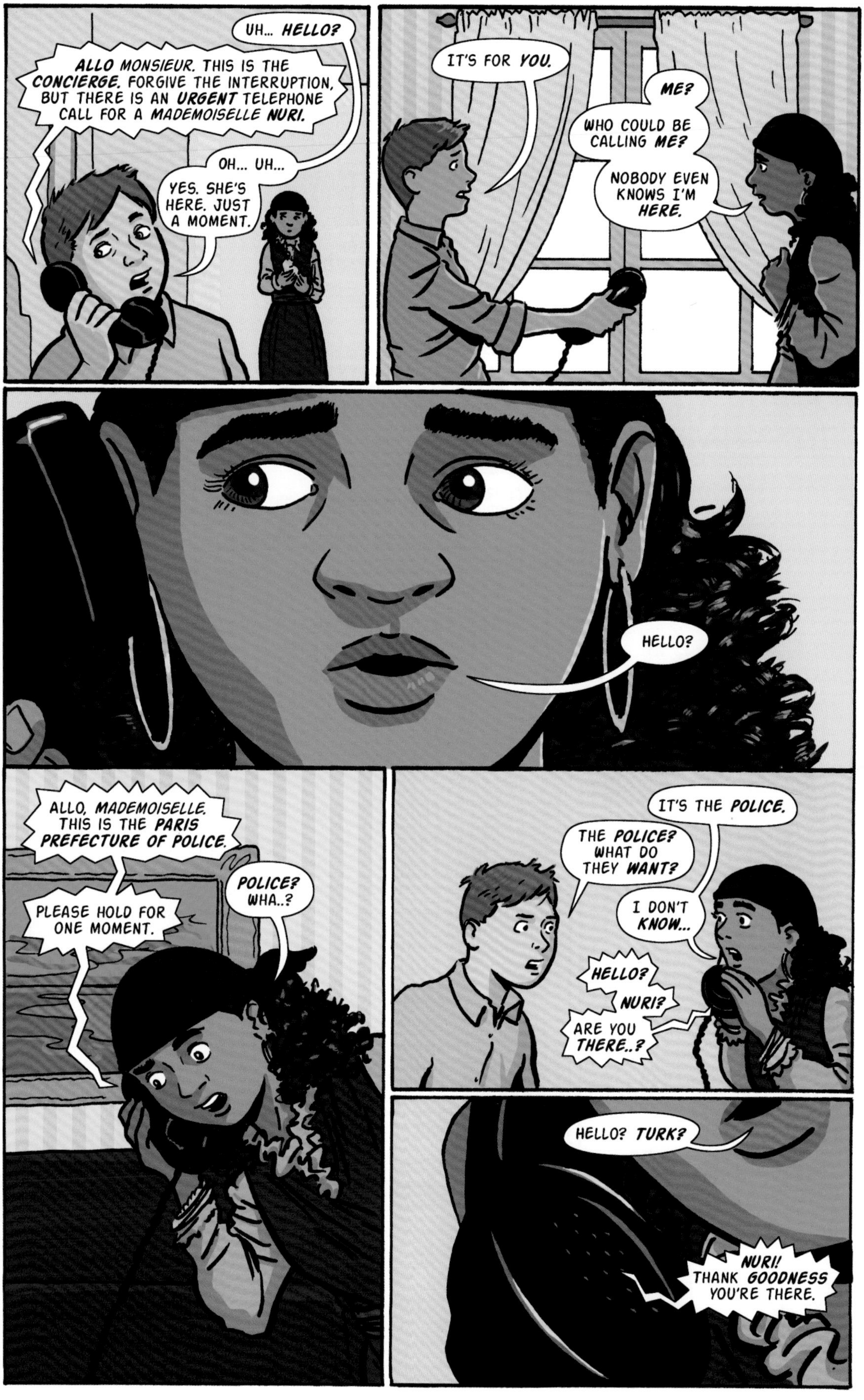

UH... HELLO?
ALLO MONSIEUR. THIS IS THE CONCIERGE. FORGIVE THE INTERRUPTION, BUT THERE IS AN URGENT TELEPHONE CALL FOR A MADEMOISELLE NURI.
OH... UH...
YES. SHE'S HERE. JUST A MOMENT.
IT'S FOR YOU.
ME?
WHO COULD BE CALLING ME?
NOBODY EVEN KNOWS I'M HERE.
HELLO?
ALLO, MADEMOISELLE. THIS IS THE PARIS PREFECTURE OF POLICE.
PLEASE HOLD FOR ONE MOMENT.
POLICE? WHA..?
IT'S THE POLICE.
THE POLICE? WHAT DO THEY WANT?
I DON'T KNOW...
HELLO?
NURI?
ARE YOU THERE..?
HELLO? TURK?
NURI! THANK GOODNESS YOU'RE THERE.

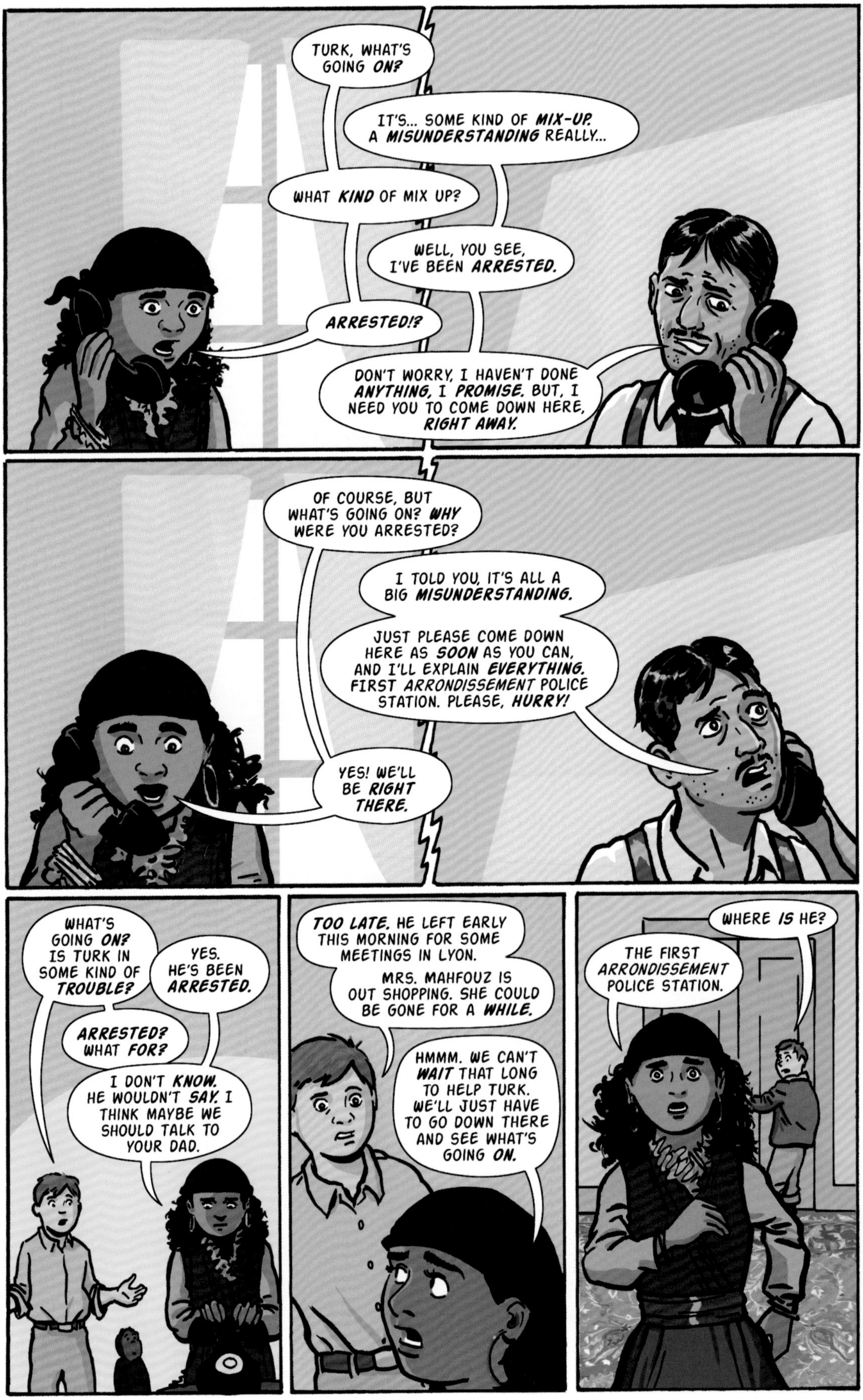
TURK, WHAT'S GOING ON?
IT'S... SOME KIND OF MIX-UP. A MISUNDERSTANDING REALLY...
WHAT KIND OF MIX UP?
WELL, YOU SEE, I'VE BEEN ARRESTED.
ARRESTED!?
DON'T WORRY, I HAVEN'T DONE ANYTHING, I PROMISE. BUT, I NEED YOU TO COME DOWN HERE, RIGHT AWAY.
OF COURSE, BUT WHAT'S GOING ON? WHY WERE YOU ARRESTED?
I TOLD YOU, IT'S ALL A BIG MISUNDERSTANDING.
JUST PLEASE COME DOWN HERE AS SOON AS YOU CAN, AND I'LL EXPLAIN EVERYTHING. FIRST ARRONDISSEMENT POLICE STATION. PLEASE, HURRY!
YES! WE'LL BE RIGHT THERE.
WHAT'S GOING ON? IS TURK IN SOME KIND OF TROUBLE?
YES. HE'S BEEN ARRESTED.
ARRESTED? WHAT FOR?
I DON'T KNOW. HE WOULDN'T SAY. I THINK MAYBE WE SHOULD TALK TO YOUR DAD.
TOO LATE. HE LEFT EARLY THIS MORNING FOR SOME MEETINGS IN LYON.
MRS. MAHFOUZ IS OUT SHOPPING. SHE COULD BE GONE FOR A WHILE.
HMMM. WE CAN'T WAIT THAT LONG TO HELP TURK. WE'LL JUST HAVE TO GO DOWN THERE AND SEE WHAT'S GOING ON.
WHERE IS HE?
THE FIRST ARRONDISSEMENT POLICE STATION.

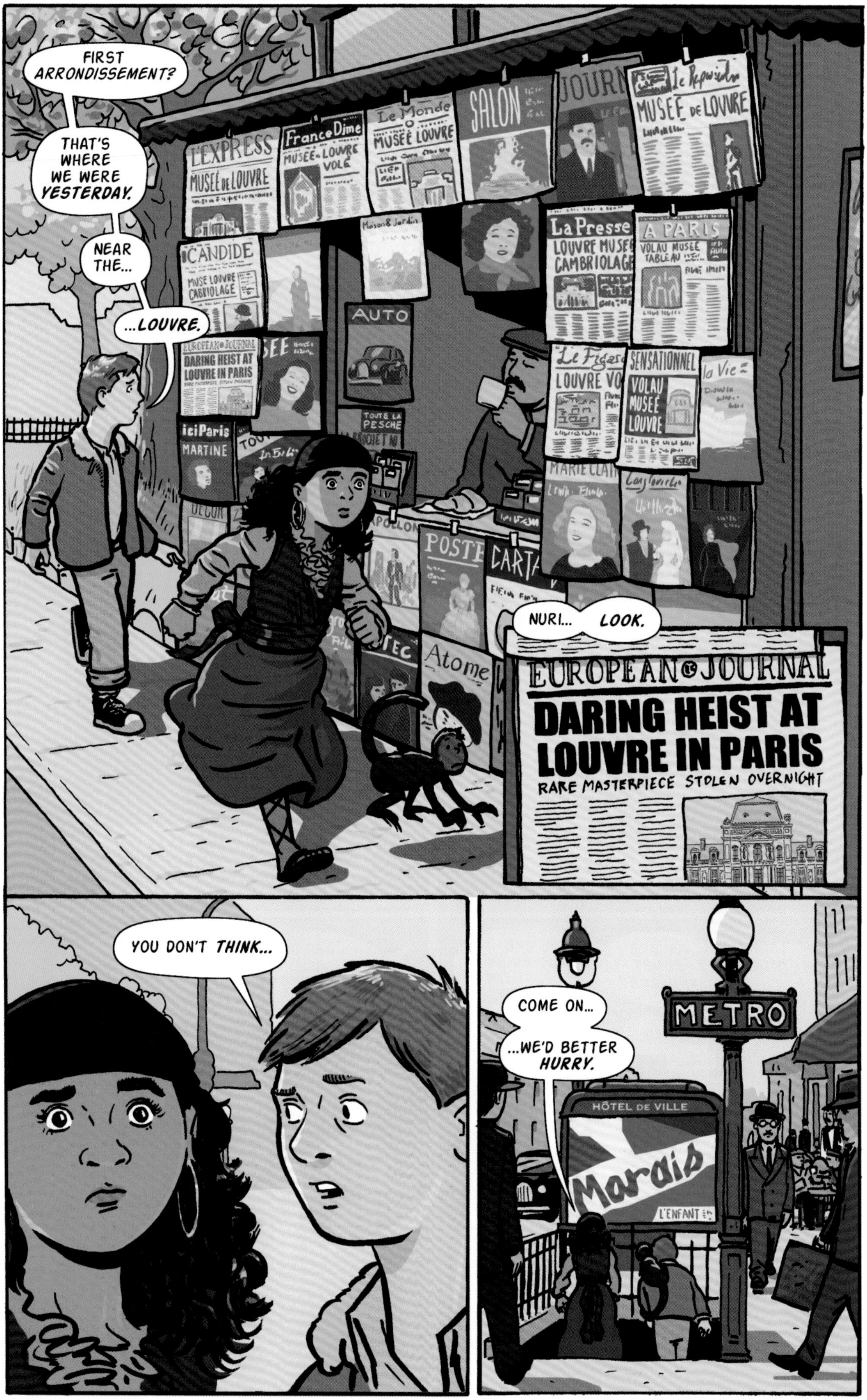
FIRST ARRONDISSEMENT?
THAT'S WHERE WE WERE YESTERDAY.
NEAR THE...
...LOUVRE.
NURI... LOOK.
EUROPEAN JOURNAL
DARING HEIST AT LOUVRE IN PARIS
RARE MASTERPIECE STOLEN OVERNIGHT
YOU DON'T THINK...
COME ON...
...WE'D BETTER HURRY.
METRO
HÔTEL DE VILLE
Marais

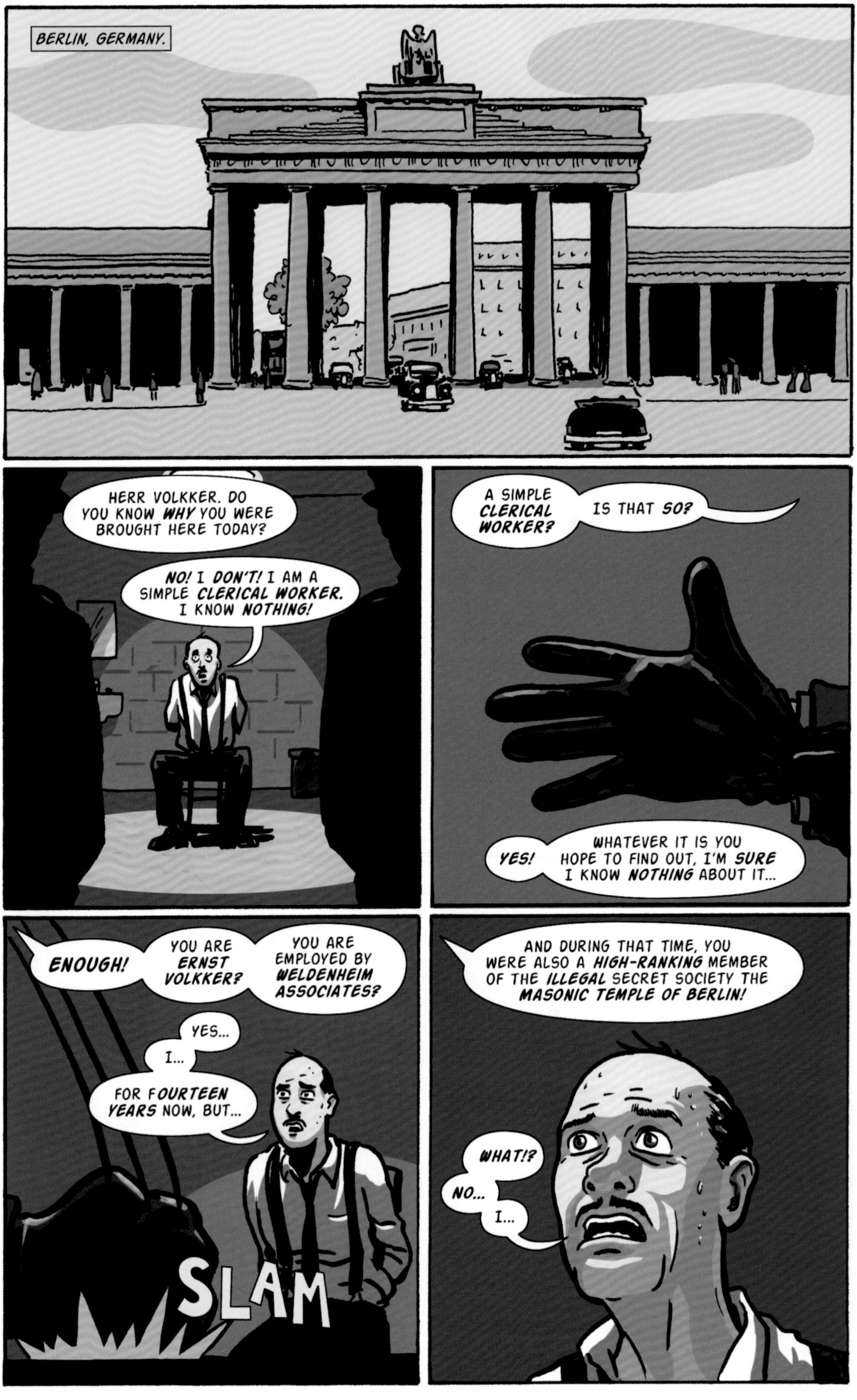
BERLIN, GERMANY.
HERR VOLKKER. DO YOU KNOW WHY YOU WERE BROUGHT HERE TODAY?
NO! I DON'T! I AM A SIMPLE CLERICAL WORKER. I KNOW NOTHING!
A SIMPLE CLERICAL WORKER?
IS THAT SO?
YES!
WHATEVER IT IS YOU HOPE TO FIND OUT, I'M SURE I KNOW NOTHING ABOUT IT...
ENOUGH!
YOU ARE ERNST VOLKKER?
YOU ARE EMPLOYED BY WELDENHEIM ASSOCIATES?
YES...
I...
FOR FOURTEEN YEARS NOW, BUT...
SLAM
AND DURING THAT TIME, YOU WERE ALSO A HIGH-RANKING MEMBER OF THE ILLEGAL SECRET SOCIETY THE MASONIC TEMPLE OF BERLIN!
WHAT!?
NO...
I...

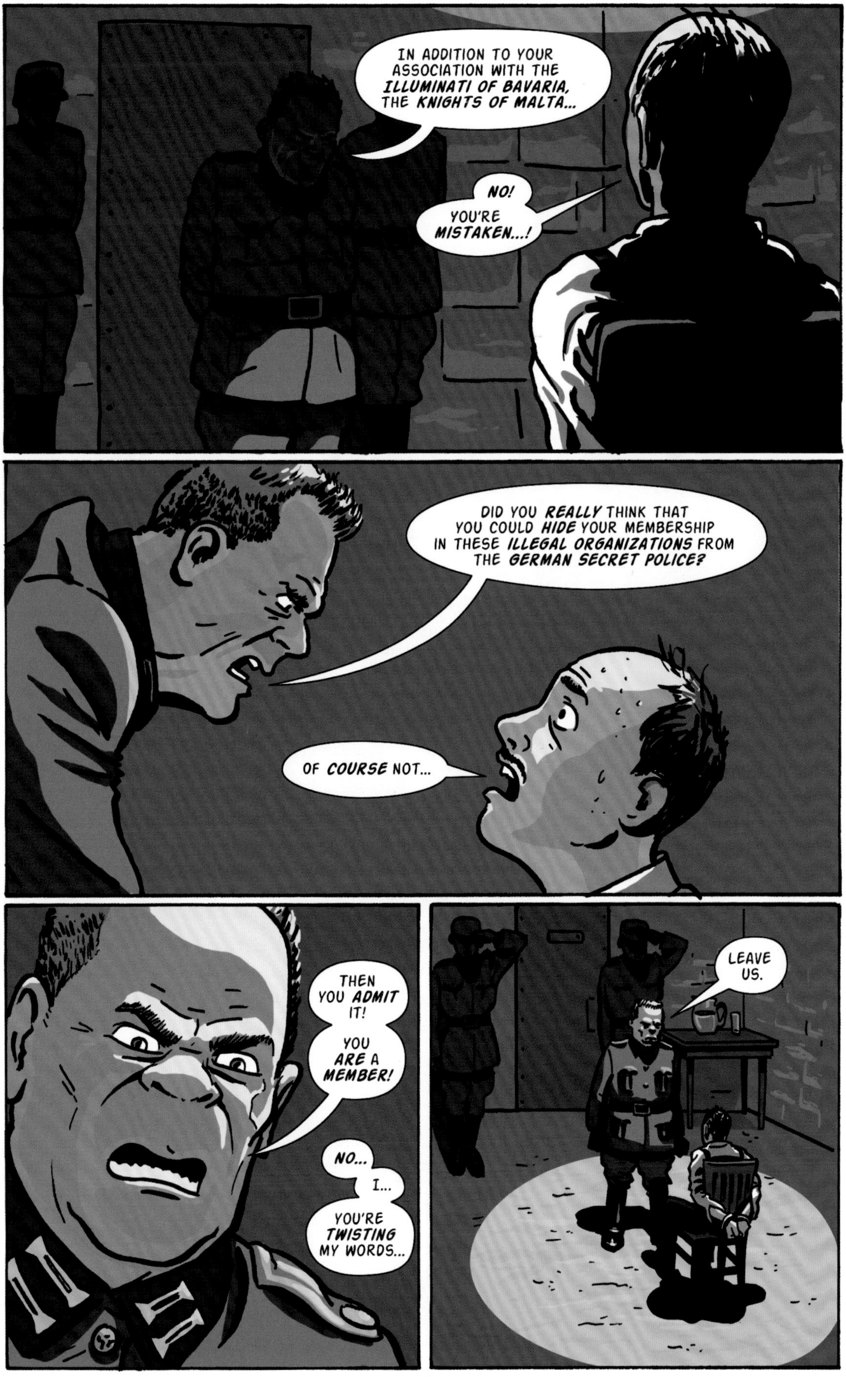
IN ADDITION TO YOUR ASSOCIATION WITH THE ILLUMINATI OF BAVARIA, THE KNIGHTS OF MALTA...
NO!
YOU'RE MISTAKEN...!
DID YOU REALLY THINK THAT YOU COULD HIDE YOUR MEMBERSHIP IN THESE ILLEGAL ORGANIZATIONS FROM THE GERMAN SECRET POLICE?
OF COURSE NOT...
THEN YOU ADMIT IT!
YOU ARE A MEMBER!
NO...
I...
YOU'RE TWISTING MY WORDS...
LEAVE US.

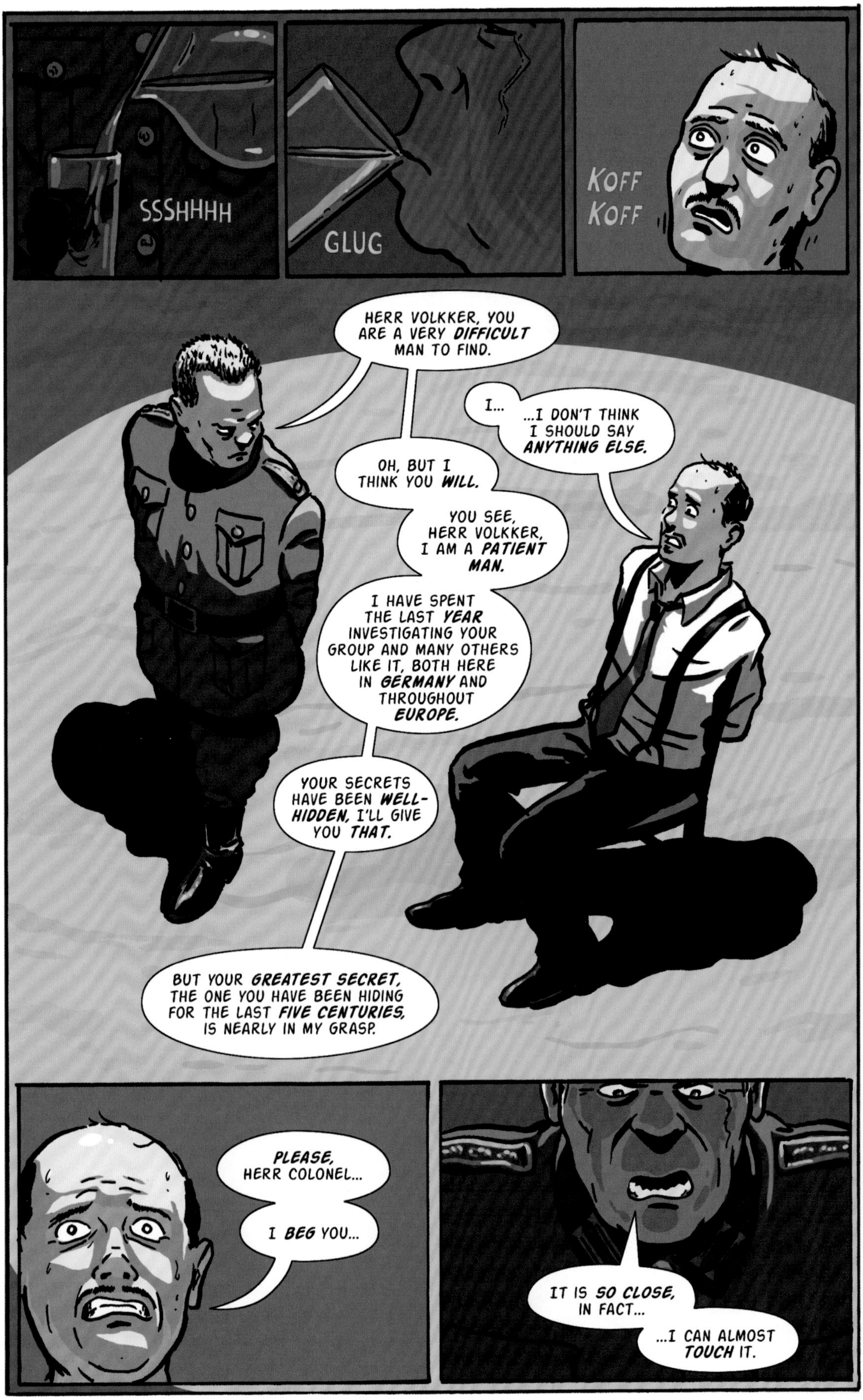
SSSHHHH
GLUG
KOFF KOFF
HERR VOLKKER, YOU ARE A VERY DIFFICULT MAN TO FIND.
I...
...I DON'T THINK I SHOULD SAY ANYTHING ELSE.
OH, BUT I THINK YOU WILL.
YOU SEE, HERR VOLKKER, I AM A PATIENT MAN.
I HAVE SPENT THE LAST YEAR INVESTIGATING YOUR GROUP AND MANY OTHERS LIKE IT, BOTH HERE IN GERMANY AND THROUGHOUT EUROPE.
YOUR SECRETS HAVE BEEN WELL-HIDDEN, I'LL GIVE YOU THAT.
BUT YOUR GREATEST SECRET, THE ONE YOU HAVE BEEN HIDING FOR THE LAST FIVE CENTURIES, IS NEARLY IN MY GRASP.
PLEASE, HERR COLONEL...
I BEG YOU...
IT IS SO CLOSE, IN FACT...
...I CAN ALMOST TOUCH IT.

KNOCK KNOCK
FORGIVE ME, SIR, BUT THE OTHER OFFICERS HAVE GATHERED AND THEY AWAIT YOUR ARRIVAL UPSTAIRS.
AH. SAVED BY THE BELL, EH, HERR VOLKKER? WELL, NOT TO WORRY. WE WILL CONTINUE OUR CONVERSATION VERY SOON.
IN THE MEANTIME, I LEAVE YOU IN THE VERY CAPABLE HANDS OF LIEUTENANT SCHNELLER HERE.
FIND OUT WHAT HE KNOWS.
IT IS OF THE UTMOST IMPORTANCE.
DO YOU UNDERSTAND?
LEAVE IT TO ME, COLONEL.

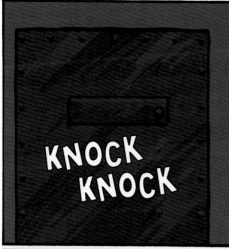

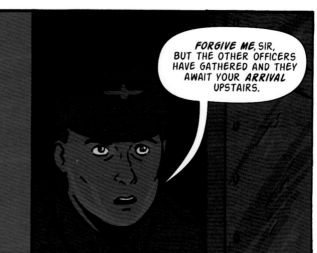

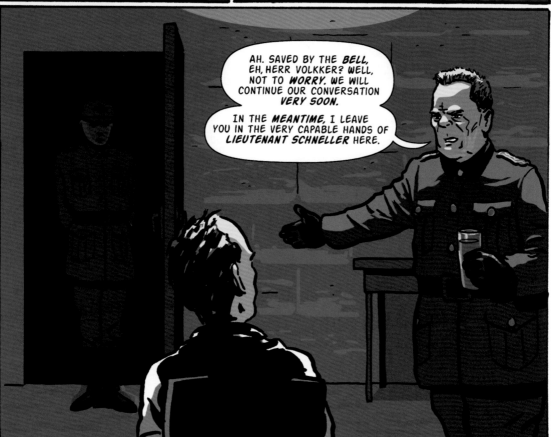

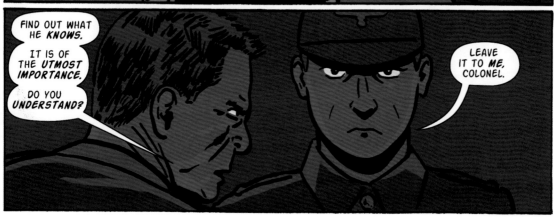

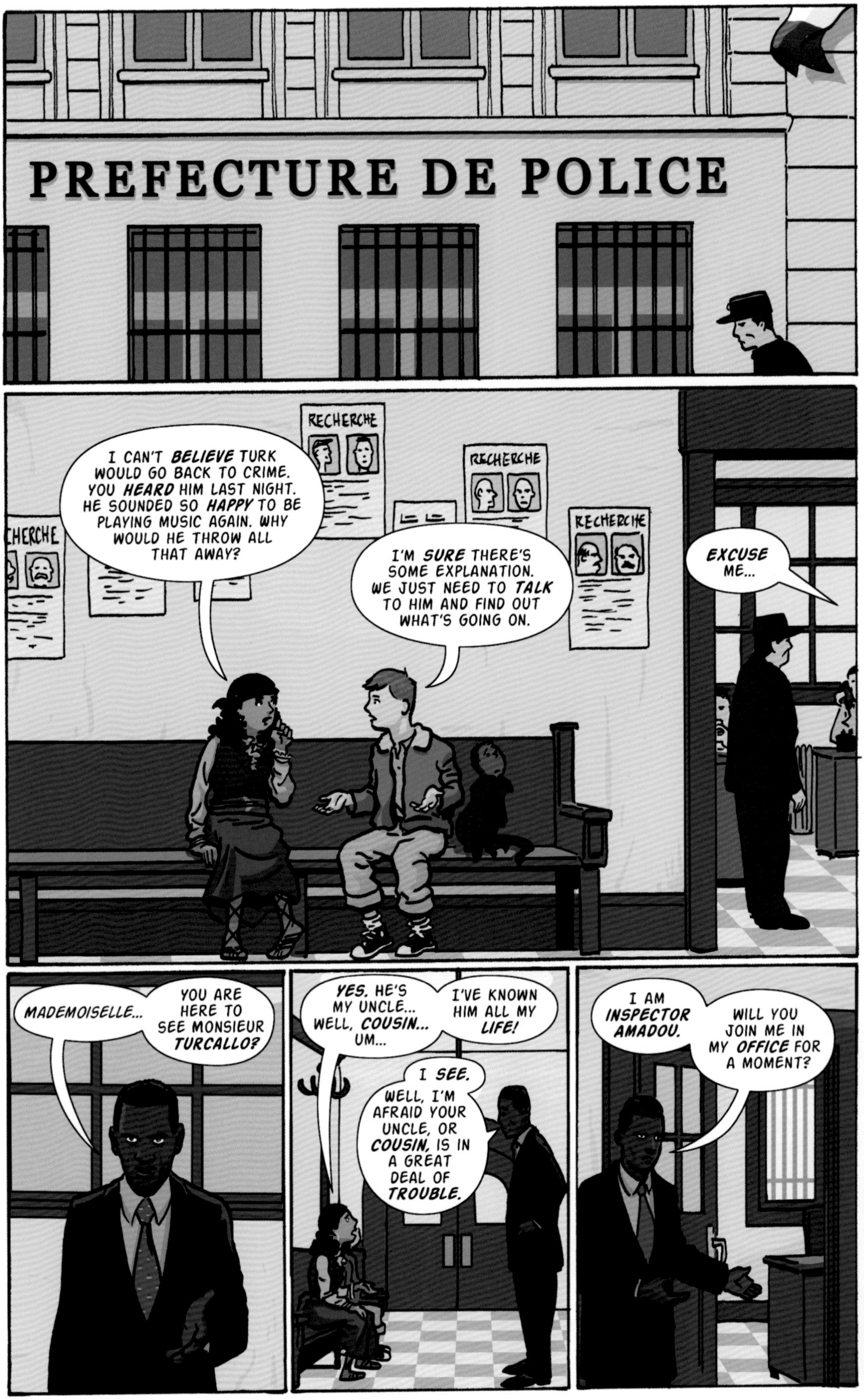
PREFECTURE DE POLICE
RECHERCHE
I CAN'T BELIEVE TURK WOULD GO BACK TO CRIME. YOU HEARD HIM LAST NIGHT. HE SOUNDED SO HAPPY TO BE PLAYING MUSIC AGAIN. WHY WOULD HE THROW ALL THAT AWAY?
I'M SURE THERE'S SOME EXPLANATION. WE JUST NEED TO TALK TO HIM AND FIND OUT WHAT'S GOING ON.
EXCUSE ME...
MADEMOISELLE...
YOU ARE HERE TO SEE MONSIEUR TURCALLO?
YES. HE'S MY UNCLE... WELL, COUSIN... UM...
I'VE KNOWN HIM ALL MY LIFE!
I SEE.
WELL, I'M AFRAID YOUR UNCLE, OR COUSIN, IS IN A GREAT DEAL OF TROUBLE.
I AM INSPECTOR AMADOU.
WILL YOU JOIN ME IN MY OFFICE FOR A MOMENT?

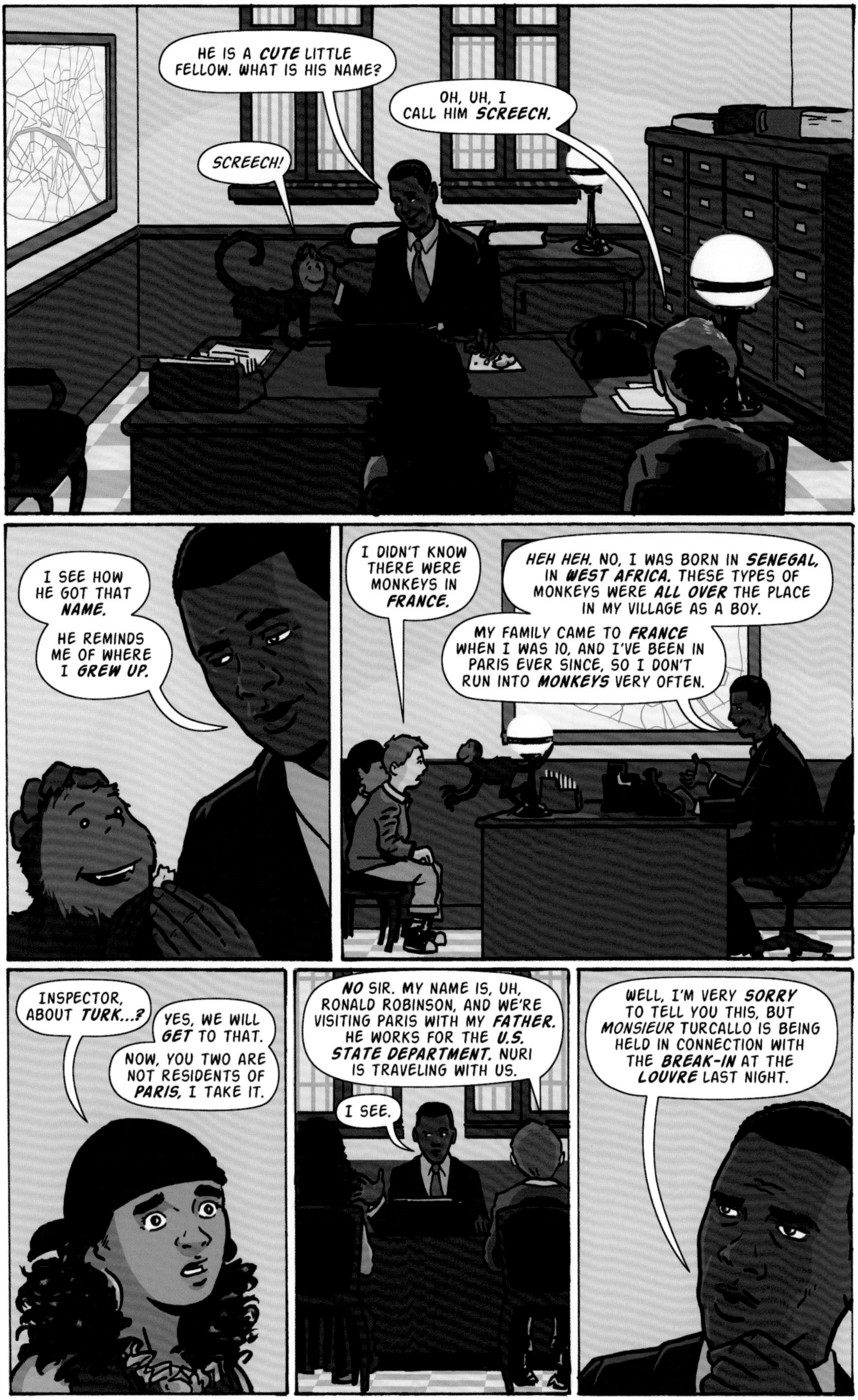
HE IS A CUTE LITTLE FELLOW. WHAT IS HIS NAME?
SCREECH!
OH, UH, I CALL HIM SCREECH.
I SEE HOW HE GOT THAT NAME.
HE REMINDS ME OF WHERE I GREW UP.
I DIDN'T KNOW THERE WERE MONKEYS IN FRANCE.
HEH HEH. NO, I WAS BORN IN SENEGAL, IN WEST AFRICA. THESE TYPES OF MONKEYS WERE ALL OVER THE PLACE IN MY VILLAGE AS A BOY.
MY FAMILY CAME TO FRANCE WHEN I WAS 10, AND I'VE BEEN IN PARIS EVER SINCE, SO I DON'T RUN INTO MONKEYS VERY OFTEN.
INSPECTOR, ABOUT TURK...?
YES, WE WILL GET TO THAT.
NOW, YOU TWO ARE NOT RESIDENTS OF PARIS, I TAKE IT.
NO SIR. MY NAME IS, UH, RONALD ROBINSON, AND WE'RE VISITING PARIS WITH MY FATHER. HE WORKS FOR THE U.S. STATE DEPARTMENT. NURI IS TRAVELING WITH US.
I SEE.
WELL, I'M VERY SORRY TO TELL YOU THIS, BUT MONSIEUR TURCALLO IS BEING HELD IN CONNECTION WITH THE BREAK-IN AT THE LOUVRE LAST NIGHT.

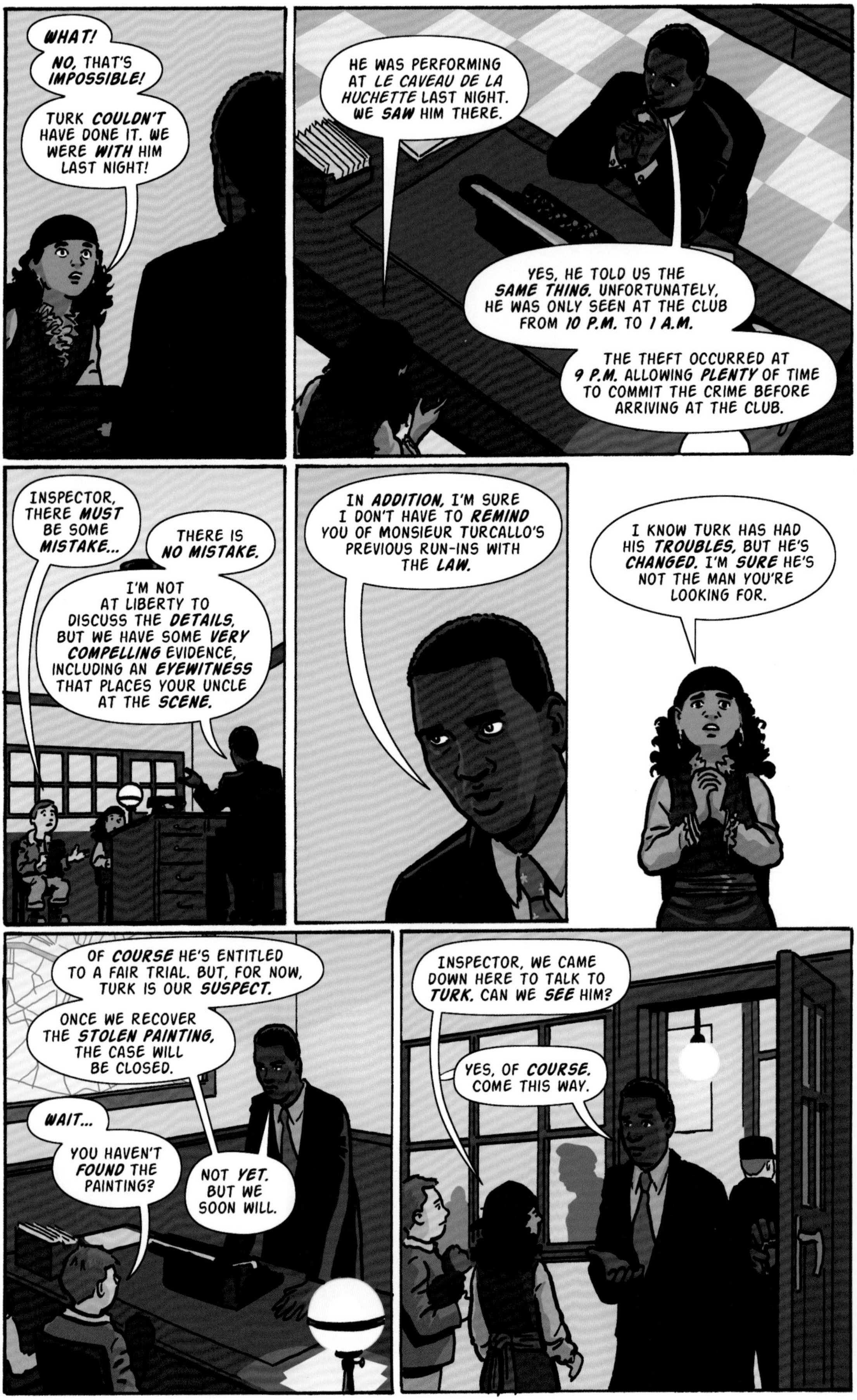
WHAT!
NO, THAT'S IMPOSSIBLE!
TURK COULDN'T HAVE DONE IT. WE WERE WITH HIM LAST NIGHT!
HE WAS PERFORMING AT LE CAVEAU DE LA HUCHETTE LAST NIGHT. WE SAW HIM THERE.
YES, HE TOLD US THE SAME THING. UNFORTUNATELY, HE WAS ONLY SEEN AT THE CLUB FROM 10 P.M. TO 1 A.M.
THE THEFT OCCURRED AT 9 P.M. ALLOWING PLENTY OF TIME TO COMMIT THE CRIME BEFORE ARRIVING AT THE CLUB.
INSPECTOR, THERE MUST BE SOME MISTAKE...
THERE IS NO MISTAKE.
I'M NOT AT LIBERTY TO DISCUSS THE DETAILS, BUT WE HAVE SOME VERY COMPELLING EVIDENCE, INCLUDING AN EYEWITNESS THAT PLACES YOUR UNCLE AT THE SCENE.
IN ADDITION, I'M SURE I DON'T HAVE TO REMIND YOU OF MONSIEUR TURCALLO'S PREVIOUS RUN-INS WITH THE LAW.
I KNOW TURK HAS HAD HIS TROUBLES, BUT HE'S CHANGED. I'M SURE HE'S NOT THE MAN YOU'RE LOOKING FOR.
OF COURSE HE'S ENTITLED TO A FAIR TRIAL. BUT, FOR NOW, TURK IS OUR SUSPECT.
ONCE WE RECOVER THE STOLEN PAINTING, THE CASE WILL BE CLOSED.
WAIT...
YOU HAVEN'T FOUND THE PAINTING?
NOT YET. BUT WE SOON WILL.
INSPECTOR, WE CAME DOWN HERE TO TALK TO TURK. CAN WE SEE HIM?
YES, OF COURSE. COME THIS WAY.

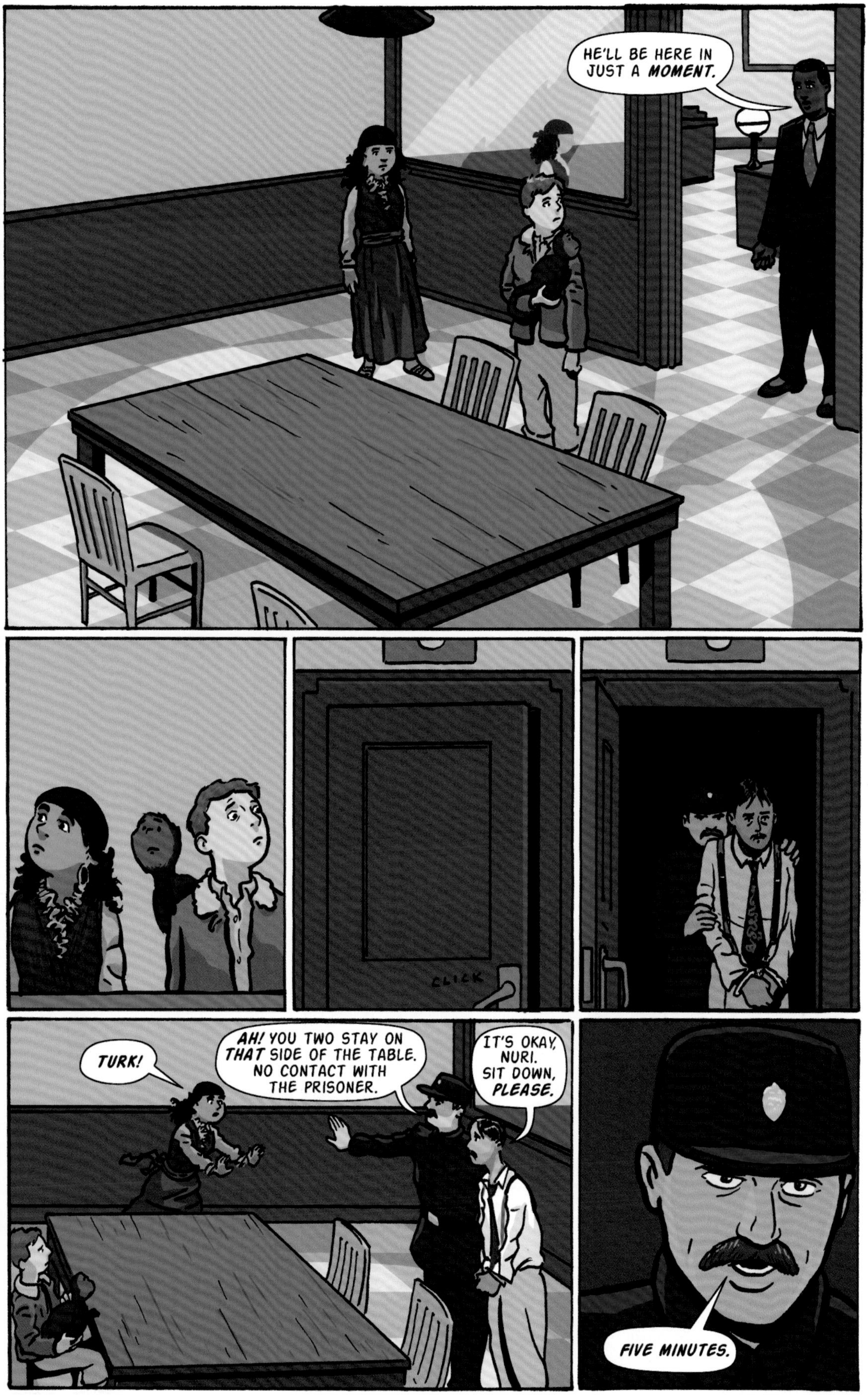
HE'LL BE HERE IN JUST A MOMENT.
CLICK
TURK!
AH! YOU TWO STAY ON THAT SIDE OF THE TABLE. NO CONTACT WITH THE PRISONER.
IT'S OKAY, NURI. SIT DOWN, PLEASE.
FIVE MINUTES.

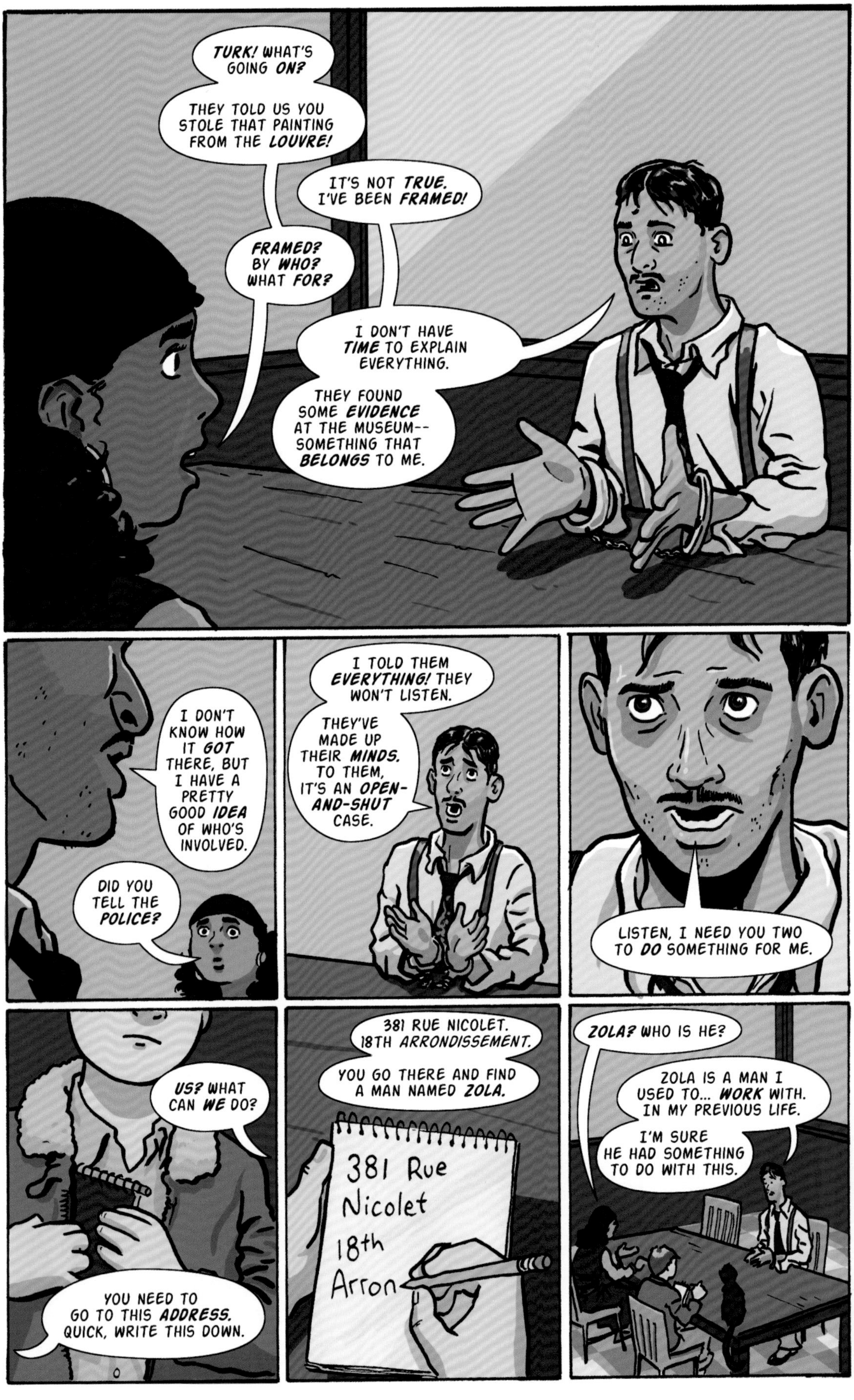
TURK! WHAT'S GOING ON?
THEY TOLD US YOU STOLE THAT PAINTING FROM THE LOUVRE!
IT'S NOT TRUE. I'VE BEEN FRAMED!
FRAMED? BY WHO? WHAT FOR?
I DON'T HAVE TIME TO EXPLAIN EVERYTHING.
THEY FOUND SOME EVIDENCE AT THE MUSEUM-- SOMETHING THAT BELONGS TO ME.
I DON'T KNOW HOW IT GOT THERE, BUT I HAVE A PRETTY GOOD IDEA OF WHO'S INVOLVED.
DID YOU TELL THE POLICE?
I TOLD THEM EVERYTHING! THEY WON'T LISTEN.
THEY'VE MADE UP THEIR MINDS. TO THEM, IT'S AN OPEN-AND-SHUT CASE.
LISTEN, I NEED YOU TWO TO DO SOMETHING FOR ME.
US? WHAT CAN WE DO?
YOU NEED TO GO TO THIS ADDRESS. QUICK, WRITE THIS DOWN.
381 RUE NICOLET. 18TH ARRONDISSEMENT.
YOU GO THERE AND FIND A MAN NAMED ZOLA.
381 Rue Nicolet 18th Arron
ZOLA? WHO IS HE?
ZOLA IS A MAN I USED TO... WORK WITH. IN MY PREVIOUS LIFE.
I'M SURE HE HAD SOMETHING TO DO WITH THIS.

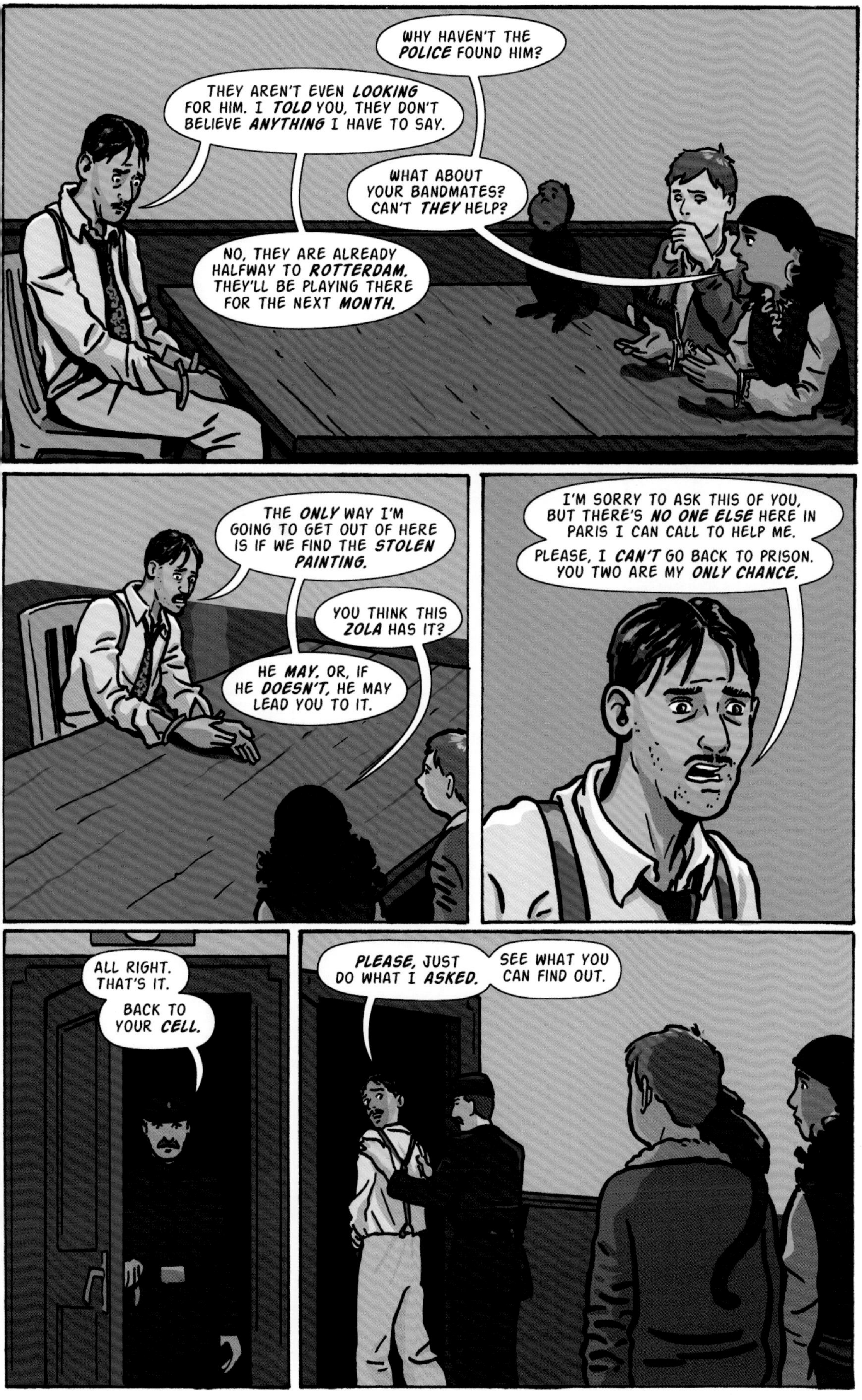
WHY HAVEN'T THE POLICE FOUND HIM?
THEY AREN'T EVEN LOOKING FOR HIM. I TOLD YOU, THEY DON'T BELIEVE ANYTHING I HAVE TO SAY.
WHAT ABOUT YOUR BANDMATES? CAN'T THEY HELP?
NO, THEY ARE ALREADY HALFWAY TO ROTTERDAM. THEY'LL BE PLAYING THERE FOR THE NEXT MONTH.
THE ONLY WAY I'M GOING TO GET OUT OF HERE IS IF WE FIND THE STOLEN PAINTING.
YOU THINK THIS ZOLA HAS IT?
HE MAY. OR, IF HE DOESN'T, HE MAY LEAD YOU TO IT.
I'M SORRY TO ASK THIS OF YOU, BUT THERE'S NO ONE ELSE HERE IN PARIS I CAN CALL TO HELP ME.
PLEASE, I CAN'T GO BACK TO PRISON. YOU TWO ARE MY ONLY CHANCE.
ALL RIGHT. THAT'S IT.
BACK TO YOUR CELL.
PLEASE, JUST DO WHAT I ASKED.
SEE WHAT YOU CAN FIND OUT.

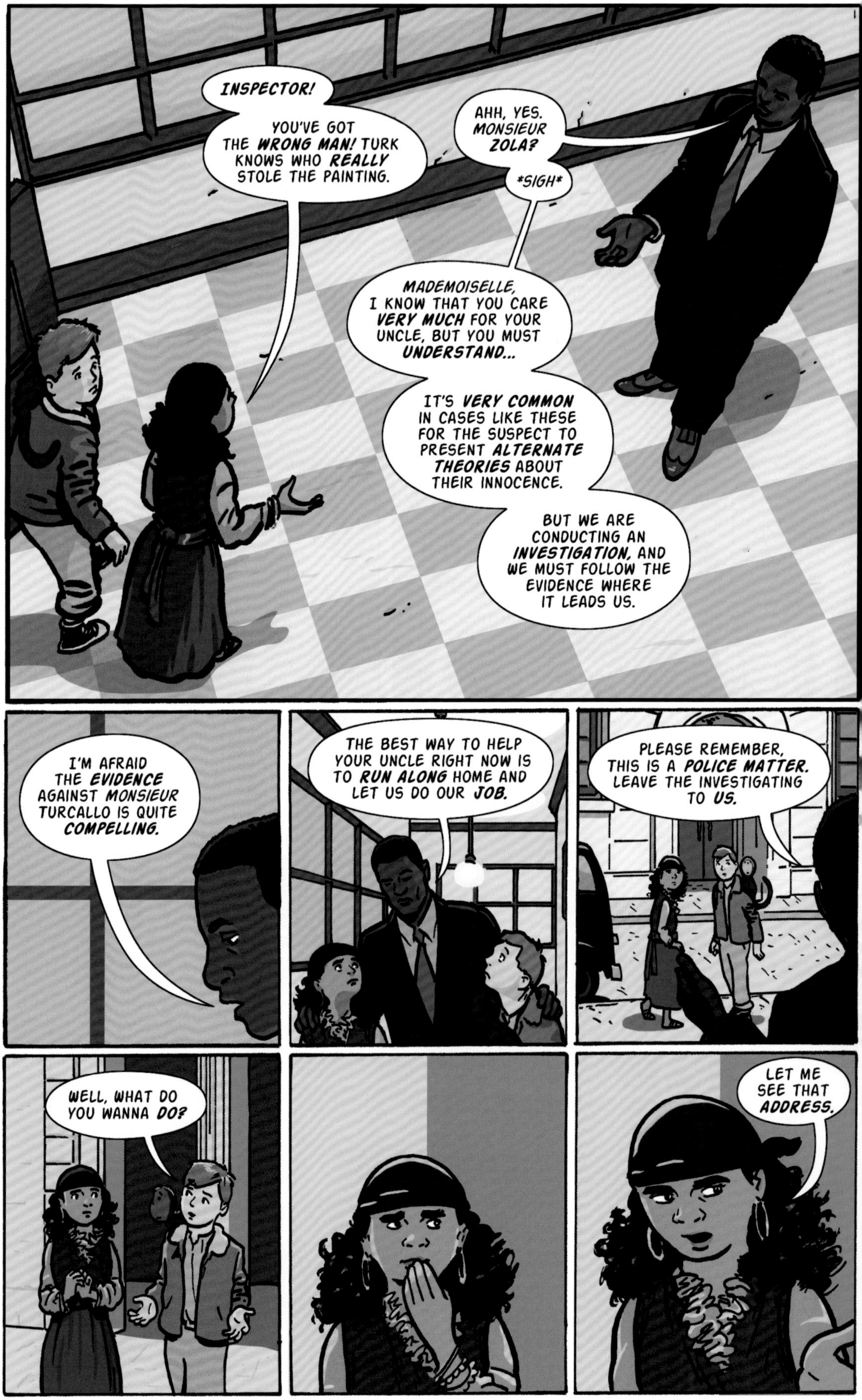
INSPECTOR!
YOU'VE GOT THE WRONG MAN! TURK KNOWS WHO REALLY STOLE THE PAINTING.
AHH, YES. MONSIEUR ZOLA?
SIGH
MADEMOISELLE, I KNOW THAT YOU CARE VERY MUCH FOR YOUR UNCLE, BUT YOU MUST UNDERSTAND...
IT'S VERY COMMON IN CASES LIKE THESE FOR THE SUSPECT TO PRESENT ALTERNATE THEORIES ABOUT THEIR INNOCENCE.
BUT WE ARE CONDUCTING AN INVESTIGATION, AND WE MUST FOLLOW THE EVIDENCE WHERE IT LEADS US.
I'M AFRAID THE EVIDENCE AGAINST MONSIEUR TURCALLO IS QUITE COMPELLING.
THE BEST WAY TO HELP YOUR UNCLE RIGHT NOW IS TO RUN ALONG HOME AND LET US DO OUR JOB.
PLEASE REMEMBER, THIS IS A POLICE MATTER. LEAVE THE INVESTIGATING TO US.
WELL, WHAT DO YOU WANNA DO?
LET ME SEE THAT ADDRESS.

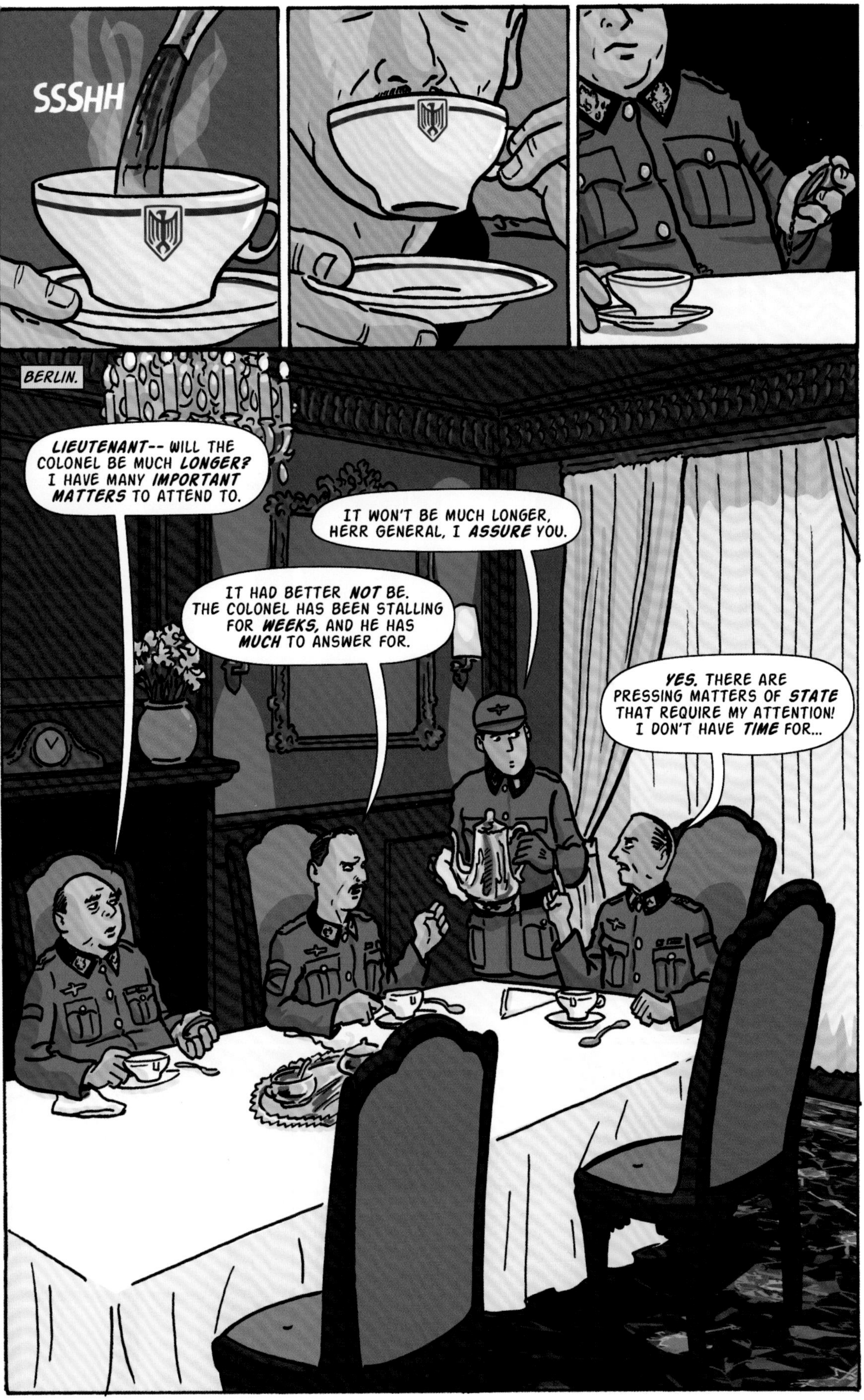
SSSHH
BERLIN.
LIEUTENANT-- WILL THE COLONEL BE MUCH LONGER? I HAVE MANY IMPORTANT MATTERS TO ATTEND TO.
IT WON'T BE MUCH LONGER, HERR GENERAL, I ASSURE YOU.
IT HAD BETTER NOT BE. THE COLONEL HAS BEEN STALLING FOR WEEKS, AND HE HAS MUCH TO ANSWER FOR.
YES. THERE ARE PRESSING MATTERS OF STATE THAT REQUIRE MY ATTENTION! I DON'T HAVE TIME FOR...

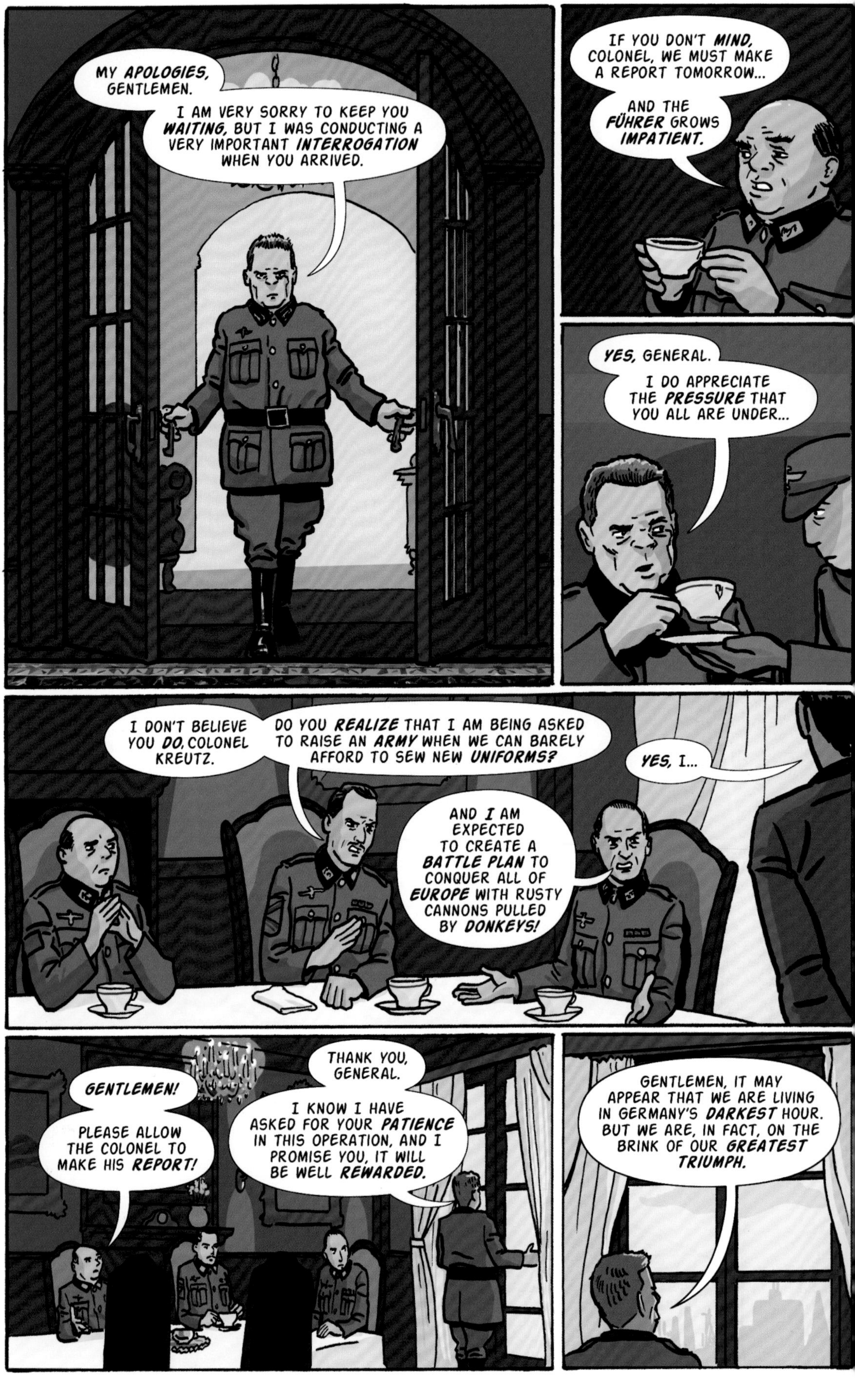
MY APOLOGIES, GENTLEMEN.
I AM VERY SORRY TO KEEP YOU WAITING, BUT I WAS CONDUCTING A VERY IMPORTANT INTERROGATION WHEN YOU ARRIVED.
IF YOU DON'T MIND, COLONEL, WE MUST MAKE A REPORT TOMORROW...
AND THE FÜHRER GROWS IMPATIENT.
YES, GENERAL.
I DO APPRECIATE THE PRESSURE THAT YOU ALL ARE UNDER...
I DON'T BELIEVE YOU DO, COLONEL KREUTZ.
DO YOU REALIZE THAT I AM BEING ASKED TO RAISE AN ARMY WHEN WE CAN BARELY AFFORD TO SEW NEW UNIFORMS?
YES, I...
AND I AM EXPECTED TO CREATE A BATTLE PLAN TO CONQUER ALL OF EUROPE WITH RUSTY CANNONS PULLED BY DONKEYS!
GENTLEMEN!
PLEASE ALLOW THE COLONEL TO MAKE HIS REPORT!
THANK YOU, GENERAL.
I KNOW I HAVE ASKED FOR YOUR PATIENCE IN THIS OPERATION, AND I PROMISE YOU, IT WILL BE WELL REWARDED.
GENTLEMEN, IT MAY APPEAR THAT WE ARE LIVING IN GERMANY'S DARKEST HOUR. BUT WE ARE, IN FACT, ON THE BRINK OF OUR GREATEST TRIUMPH.

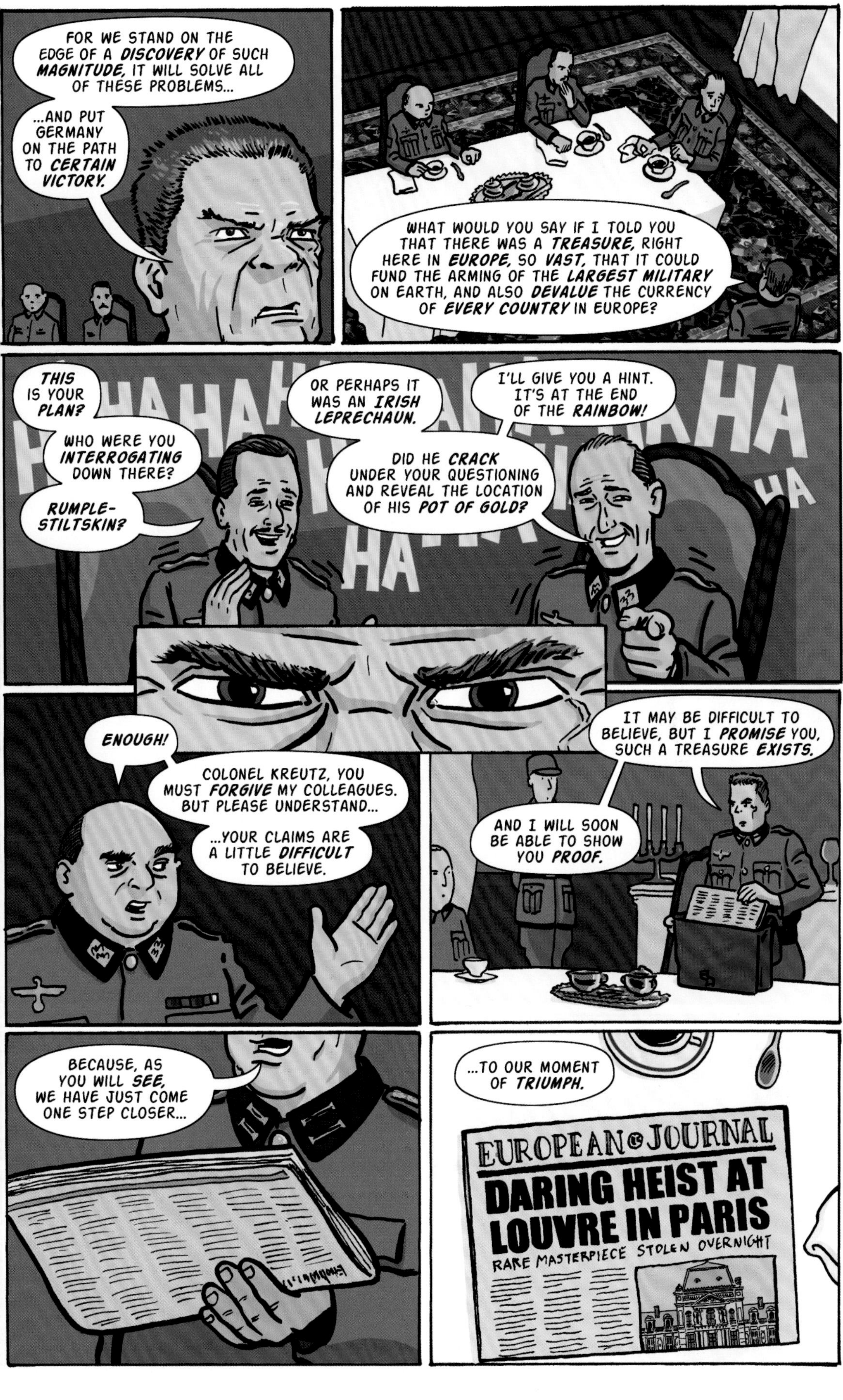
FOR WE STAND ON THE EDGE OF A DISCOVERY OF SUCH MAGNITUDE, IT WILL SOLVE ALL OF THESE PROBLEMS...
...AND PUT GERMANY ON THE PATH TO CERTAIN VICTORY.
WHAT WOULD YOU SAY IF I TOLD YOU THAT THERE WAS A TREASURE, RIGHT HERE IN EUROPE, SO VAST, THAT IT COULD FUND THE ARMING OF THE LARGEST MILITARY ON EARTH, AND ALSO DEVALUE THE CURRENCY OF EVERY COUNTRY IN EUROPE?
HAHAHAHA
THIS IS YOUR PLAN?
WHO WERE YOU INTERROGATING DOWN THERE?
RUMPLE-STILTSKIN?
OR PERHAPS IT WAS AN IRISH LEPRECHAUN.
DID HE CRACK UNDER YOUR QUESTIONING AND REVEAL THE LOCATION OF HIS POT OF GOLD?
I'LL GIVE YOU A HINT. IT'S AT THE END OF THE RAINBOW!
ENOUGH!
COLONEL KREUTZ, YOU MUST FORGIVE MY COLLEAGUES. BUT PLEASE UNDERSTAND...
...YOUR CLAIMS ARE A LITTLE DIFFICULT TO BELIEVE.
IT MAY BE DIFFICULT TO BELIEVE, BUT I PROMISE YOU, SUCH A TREASURE EXISTS.
AND I WILL SOON BE ABLE TO SHOW YOU PROOF.
BECAUSE, AS YOU WILL SEE, WE HAVE JUST COME ONE STEP CLOSER...
...TO OUR MOMENT OF TRIUMPH.
EUROPEAN JOURNAL
DARING HEIST AT LOUVRE IN PARIS
RARE MASTERPIECE STOLEN OVERNIGHT

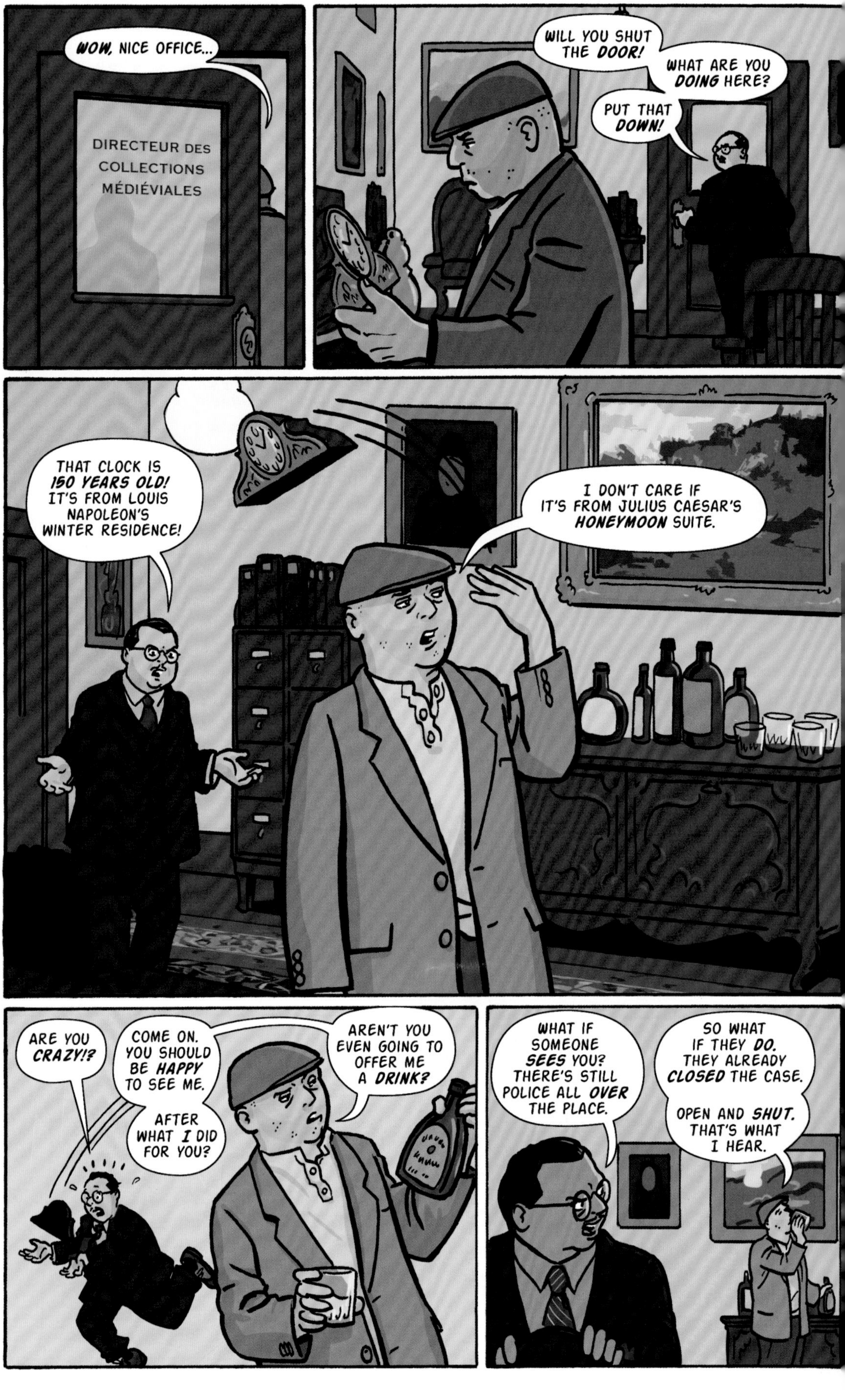
WOW, NICE OFFICE...
DIRECTEUR DES COLLECTIONS MÉDIÉVIALES
WILL YOU SHUT THE DOOR!
WHAT ARE YOU DOING HERE?
PUT THAT DOWN!
THAT CLOCK IS 150 YEARS OLD! IT'S FROM LOUIS NAPOLEON'S WINTER RESIDENCE!
I DON'T CARE IF IT'S FROM JULIUS CAESAR'S HONEYMOON SUITE.
ARE YOU CRAZY!?
COME ON. YOU SHOULD BE HAPPY TO SEE ME.
AFTER WHAT I DID FOR YOU?
AREN'T YOU EVEN GOING TO OFFER ME A DRINK?
WHAT IF SOMEONE SEES YOU? THERE'S STILL POLICE ALL OVER THE PLACE.
SO WHAT IF THEY DO. THEY ALREADY CLOSED THE CASE.
OPEN AND SHUT. THAT'S WHAT I HEAR.

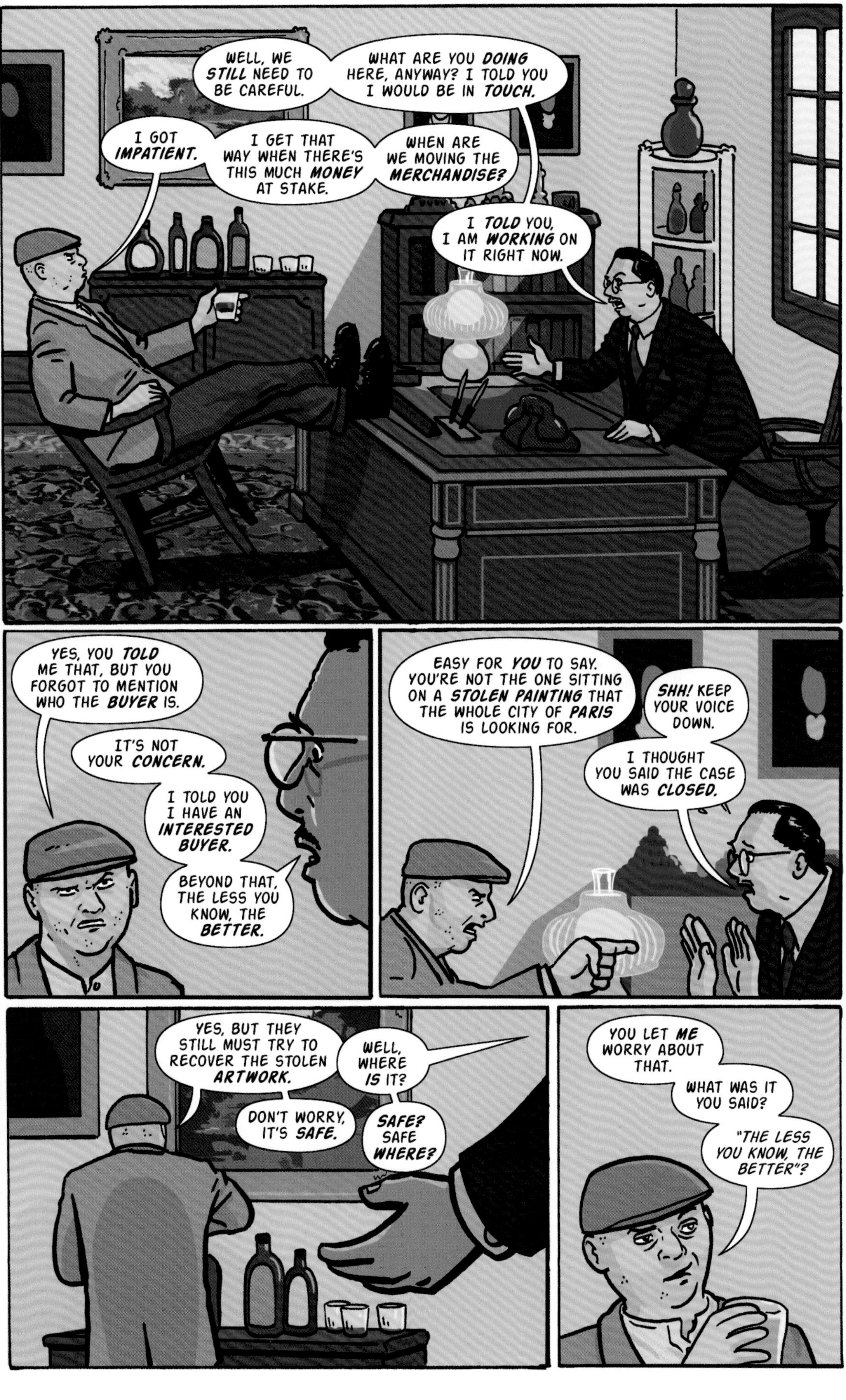
I GOT IMPATIENT.
I GET THAT WAY WHEN THERE'S THIS MUCH MONEY AT STAKE.
WELL, WE STILL NEED TO BE CAREFUL.
WHAT ARE YOU DOING HERE, ANYWAY? I TOLD YOU I WOULD BE IN TOUCH.
WHEN ARE WE MOVING THE MERCHANDISE?
I TOLD YOU, I AM WORKING ON IT RIGHT NOW.
YES, YOU TOLD ME THAT, BUT YOU FORGOT TO MENTION WHO THE BUYER IS.
IT'S NOT YOUR CONCERN.
I TOLD YOU I HAVE AN INTERESTED BUYER.
BEYOND THAT, THE LESS YOU KNOW, THE BETTER.
EASY FOR YOU TO SAY. YOU'RE NOT THE ONE SITTING ON A STOLEN PAINTING THAT THE WHOLE CITY OF PARIS IS LOOKING FOR.
SHH! KEEP YOUR VOICE DOWN.
I THOUGHT YOU SAID THE CASE WAS CLOSED.
YES, BUT THEY STILL MUST TRY TO RECOVER THE STOLEN ARTWORK.
WELL, WHERE IS IT?
DON'T WORRY, IT'S SAFE.
SAFE? SAFE WHERE?
YOU LET ME WORRY ABOUT THAT.
WHAT WAS IT YOU SAID?
"THE LESS YOU KNOW, THE BETTER"?

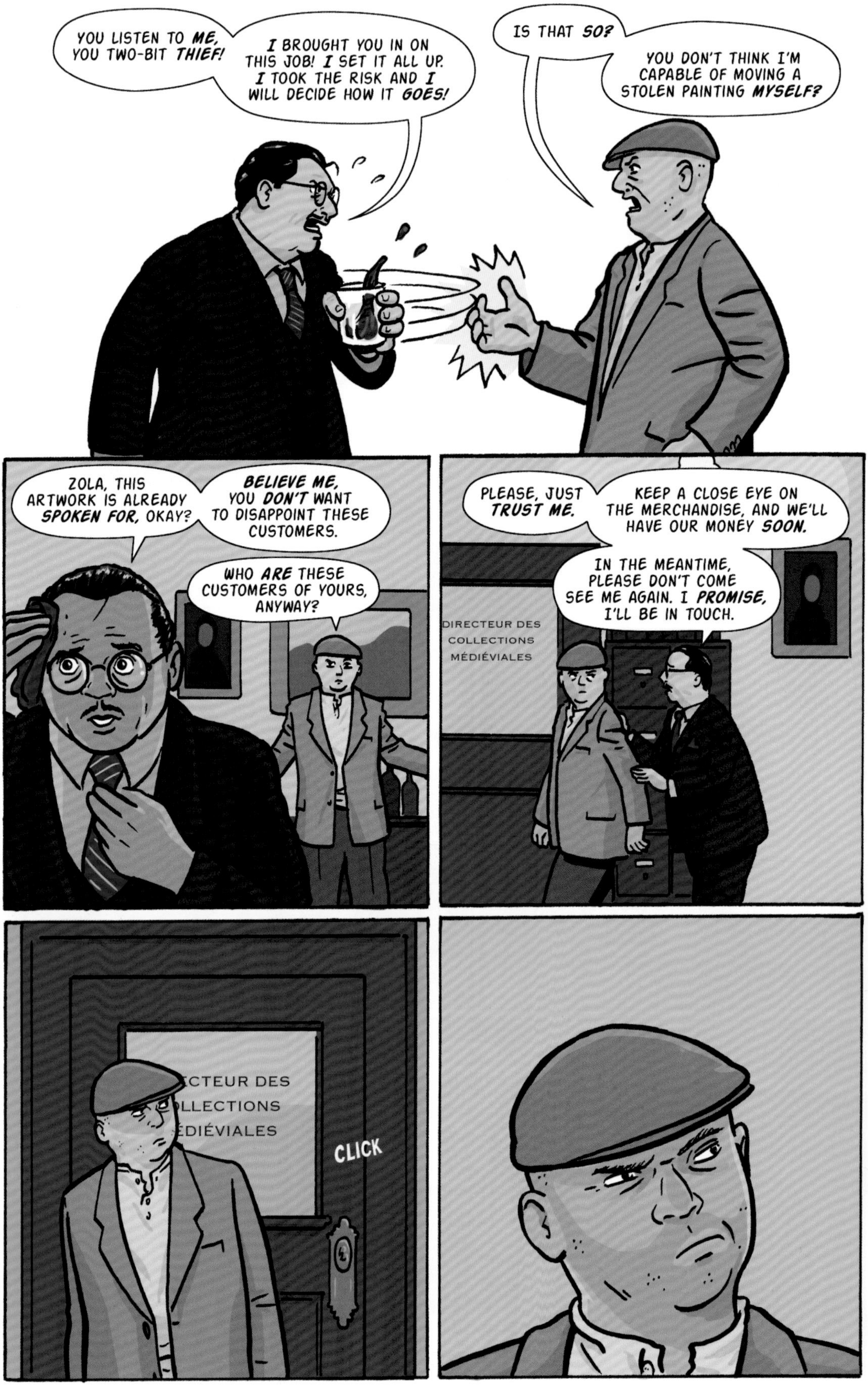
YOU LISTEN TO ME, YOU TWO-BIT THIEF!
I BROUGHT YOU IN ON THIS JOB! I SET IT ALL UP. I TOOK THE RISK AND I WILL DECIDE HOW IT GOES!
IS THAT SO?
YOU DON'T THINK I'M CAPABLE OF MOVING A STOLEN PAINTING MYSELF?
ZOLA, THIS ARTWORK IS ALREADY SPOKEN FOR, OKAY?
BELIEVE ME, YOU DON'T WANT TO DISAPPOINT THESE CUSTOMERS.
WHO ARE THESE CUSTOMERS OF YOURS, ANYWAY?
PLEASE, JUST TRUST ME.
KEEP A CLOSE EYE ON THE MERCHANDISE, AND WE'LL HAVE OUR MONEY SOON.
IN THE MEANTIME, PLEASE DON'T COME SEE ME AGAIN. I PROMISE, I'LL BE IN TOUCH.
DIRECTEUR DES COLLECTIONS MÉDIÉVIALES
CLICK

CHAPTER THREE

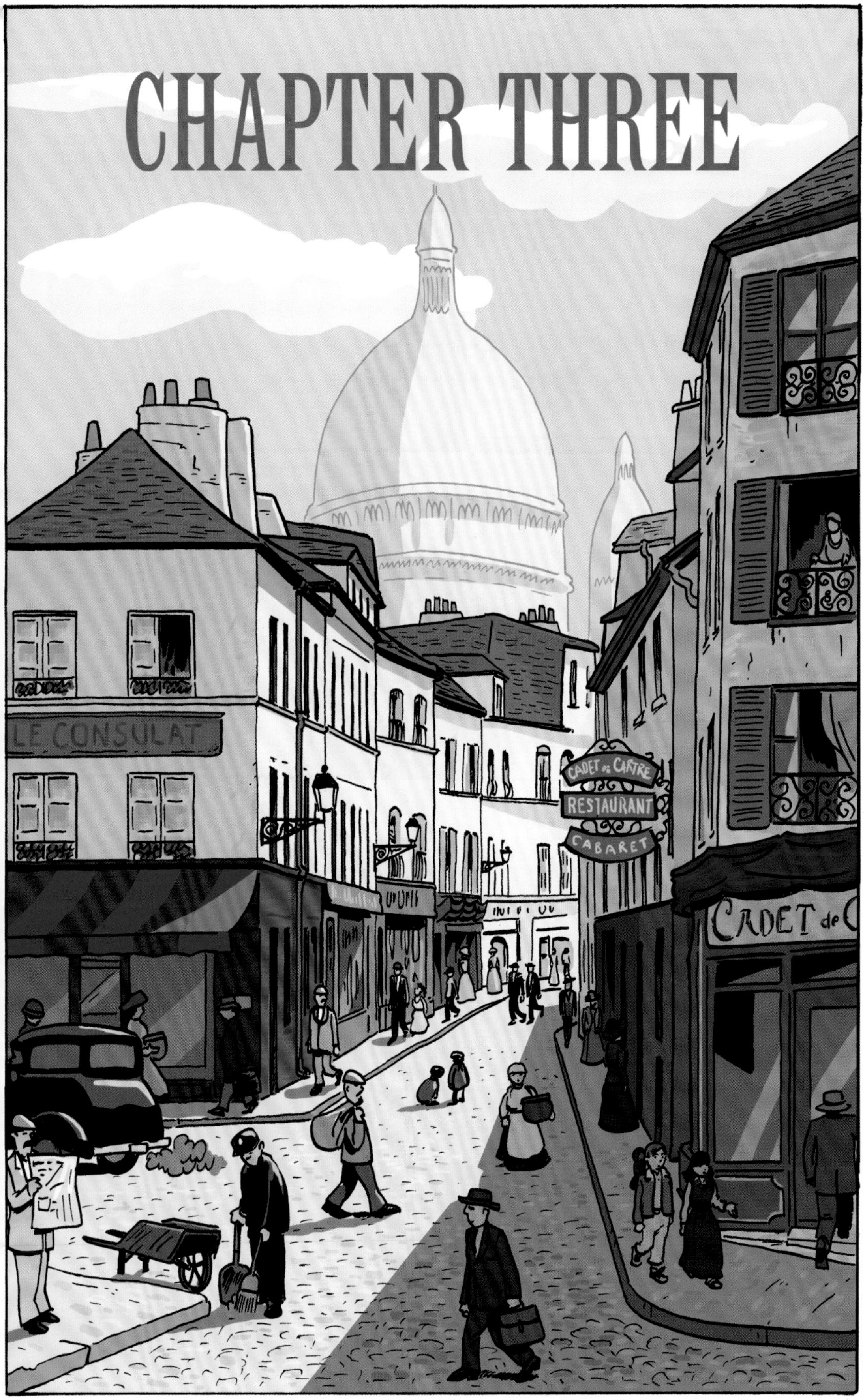
LE CONSULAT
CADET de CARTRE
RESTAURANT
CABARET

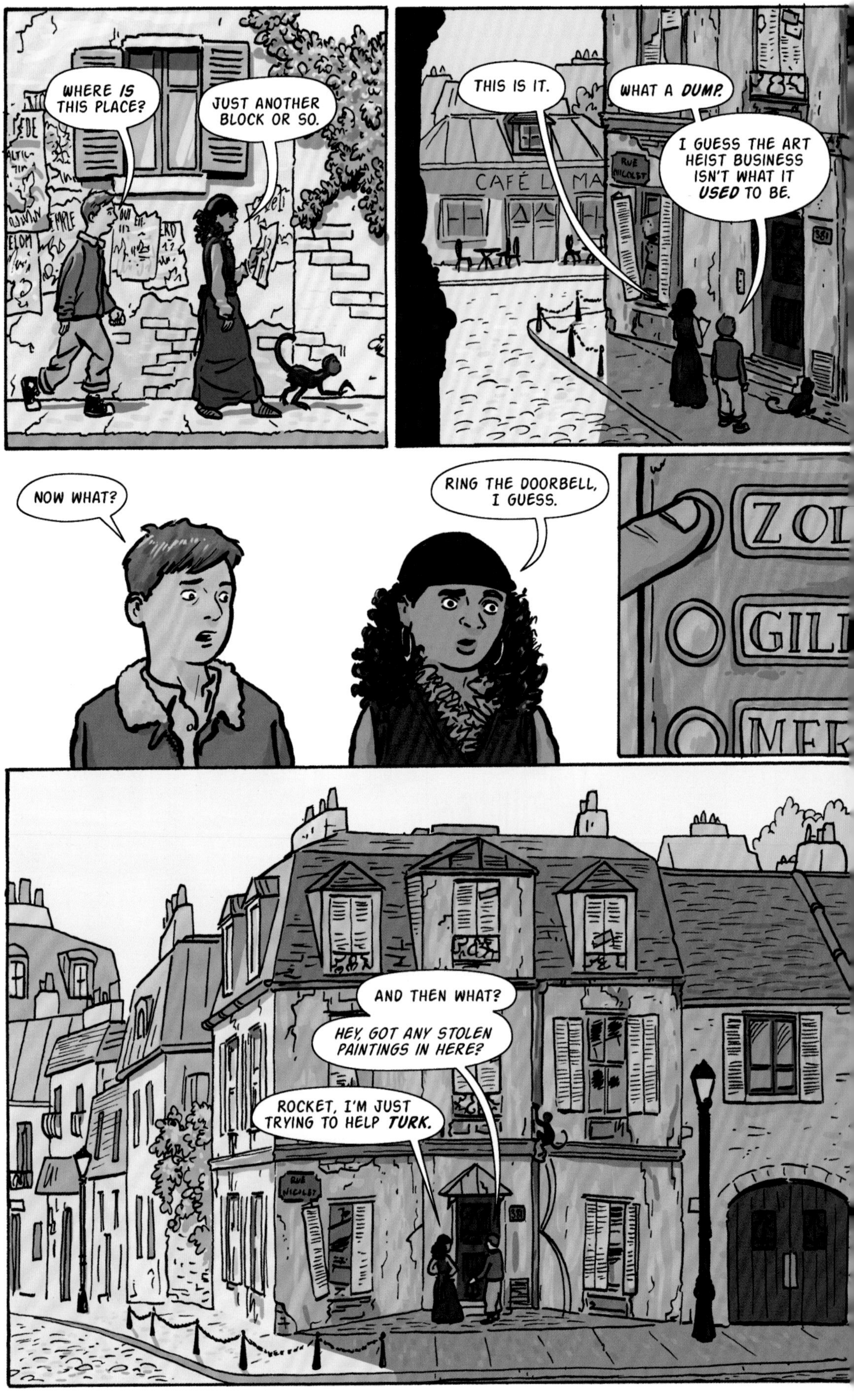
WHERE *IS* THIS PLACE?
JUST ANOTHER BLOCK OR SO.
THIS IS IT.
WHAT A ***DUMP.***
I GUESS THE ART HEIST BUSINESS ISN'T WHAT IT ***USED*** TO BE.
CAFÉ LA MA
RUE NICOLET
NOW WHAT?
RING THE DOORBELL, I GUESS.
AND THEN WHAT?
HEY, GOT ANY STOLEN PAINTINGS IN HERE?
ROCKET, I'M JUST TRYING TO HELP ***TURK.***

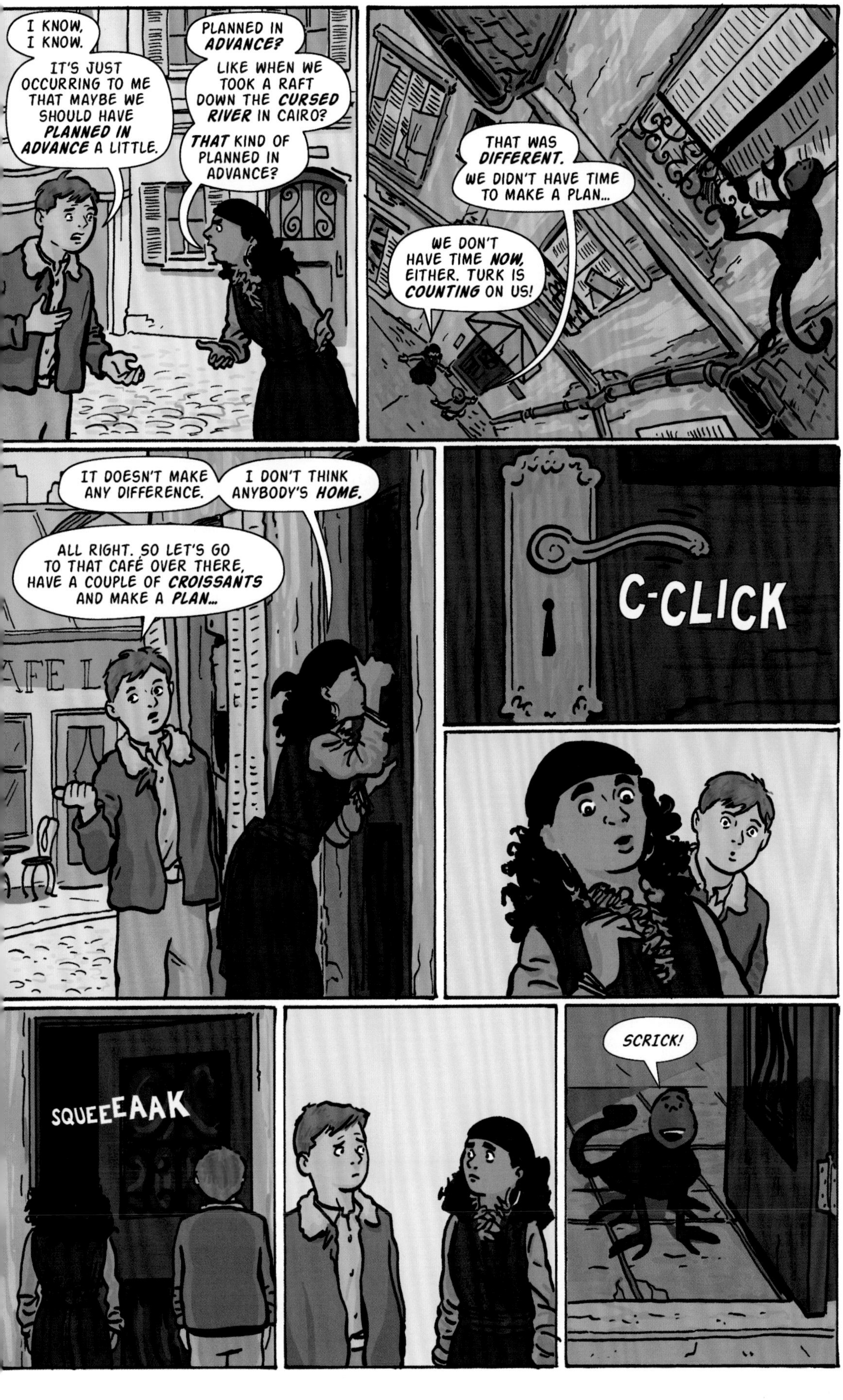
I KNOW, I KNOW.
IT'S JUST OCCURRING TO ME THAT MAYBE WE SHOULD HAVE PLANNED IN ADVANCE A LITTLE.
PLANNED IN ADVANCE?
LIKE WHEN WE TOOK A RAFT DOWN THE CURSED RIVER IN CAIRO?
THAT KIND OF PLANNED IN ADVANCE?
THAT WAS DIFFERENT.
WE DIDN'T HAVE TIME TO MAKE A PLAN...
WE DON'T HAVE TIME NOW, EITHER. TURK IS COUNTING ON US!
IT DOESN'T MAKE ANY DIFFERENCE.
I DON'T THINK ANYBODY'S HOME.
ALL RIGHT. SO LET'S GO TO THAT CAFÉ OVER THERE, HAVE A COUPLE OF CROISSANTS AND MAKE A PLAN...
AFE L
C-CLICK
SQUEEEAAK
SCRICK!

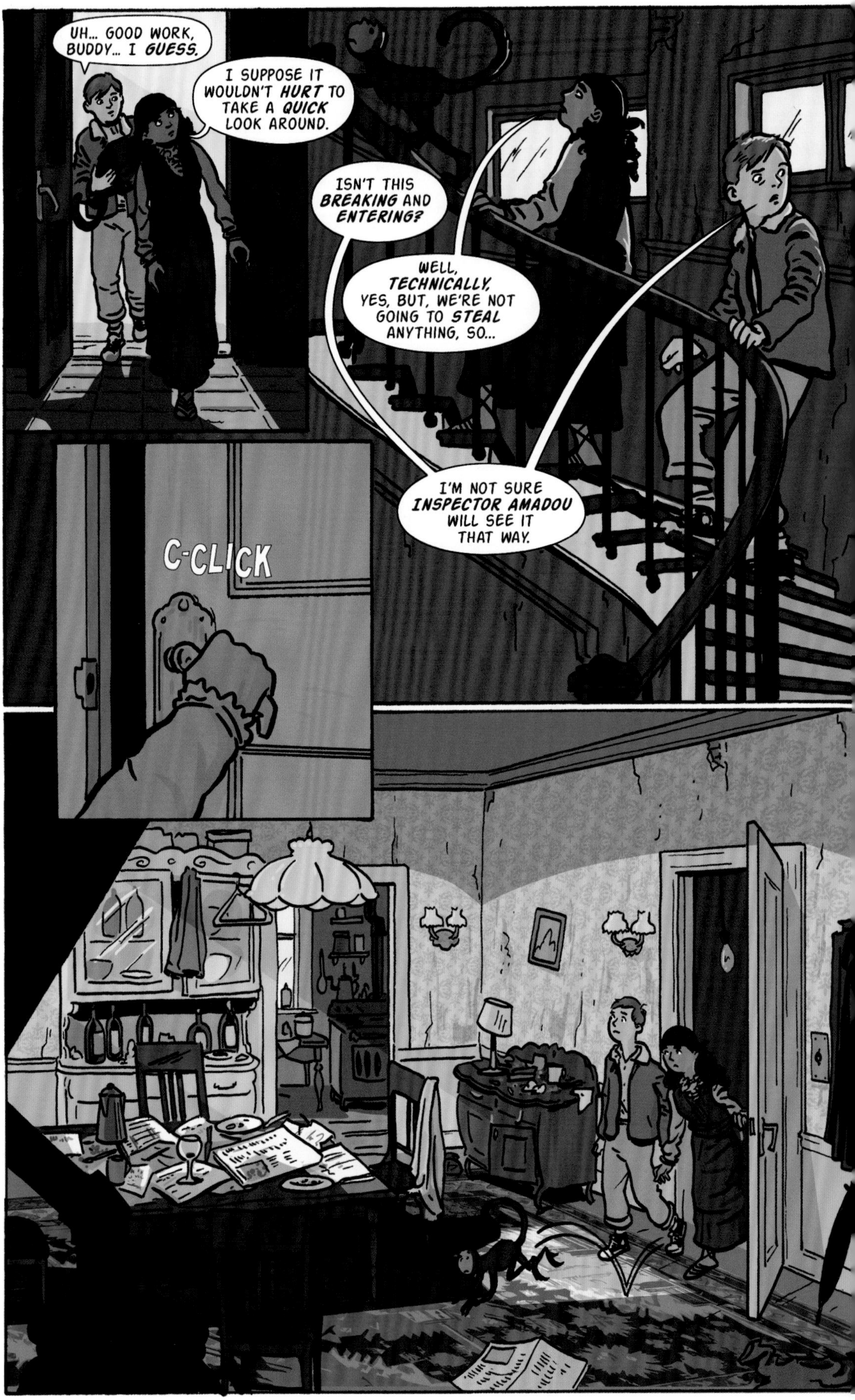
UH... GOOD WORK, BUDDY... I GUESS.
I SUPPOSE IT WOULDN'T HURT TO TAKE A QUICK LOOK AROUND.
ISN'T THIS BREAKING AND ENTERING?
WELL, TECHNICALLY, YES, BUT, WE'RE NOT GOING TO STEAL ANYTHING, SO...
I'M NOT SURE INSPECTOR AMADOU WILL SEE IT THAT WAY.
C-CLICK

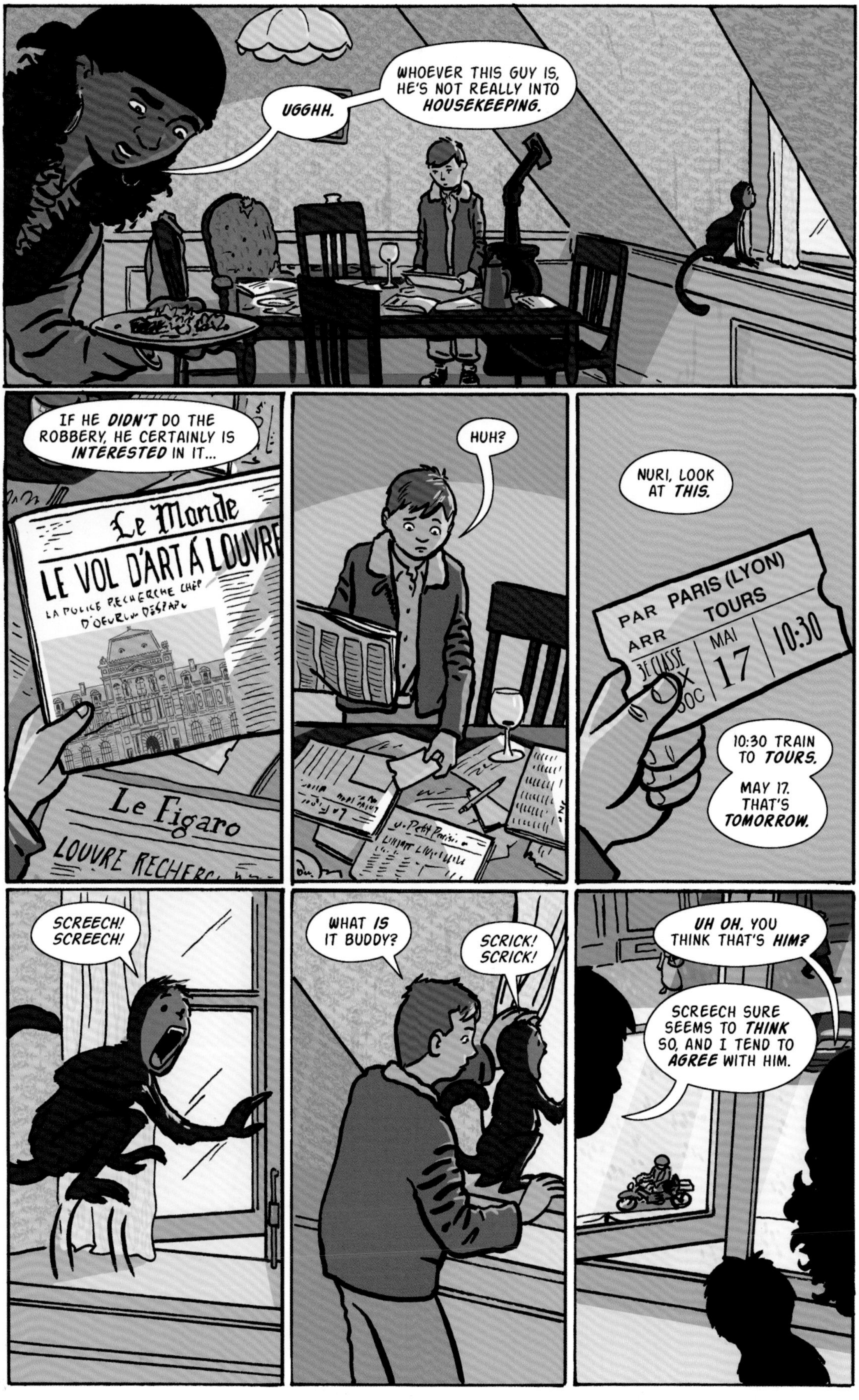
UGGHH.
WHOEVER THIS GUY IS, HE'S NOT REALLY INTO HOUSEKEEPING.
IF HE DIDN'T DO THE ROBBERY, HE CERTAINLY IS INTERESTED IN IT...
Le Monde
LE VOL D'ART Á LOUVRE
Le Figaro
HUH?
NURI, LOOK AT THIS.
PAR PARIS (LYON)
ARR TOURS
MAI 17
10:30
10:30 TRAIN TO TOURS.
MAY 17. THAT'S TOMORROW.
SCREECH! SCREECH!
WHAT IS IT BUDDY?
SCRICK! SCRICK!
UH OH. YOU THINK THAT'S HIM?
SCREECH SURE SEEMS TO THINK SO, AND I TEND TO AGREE WITH HIM.

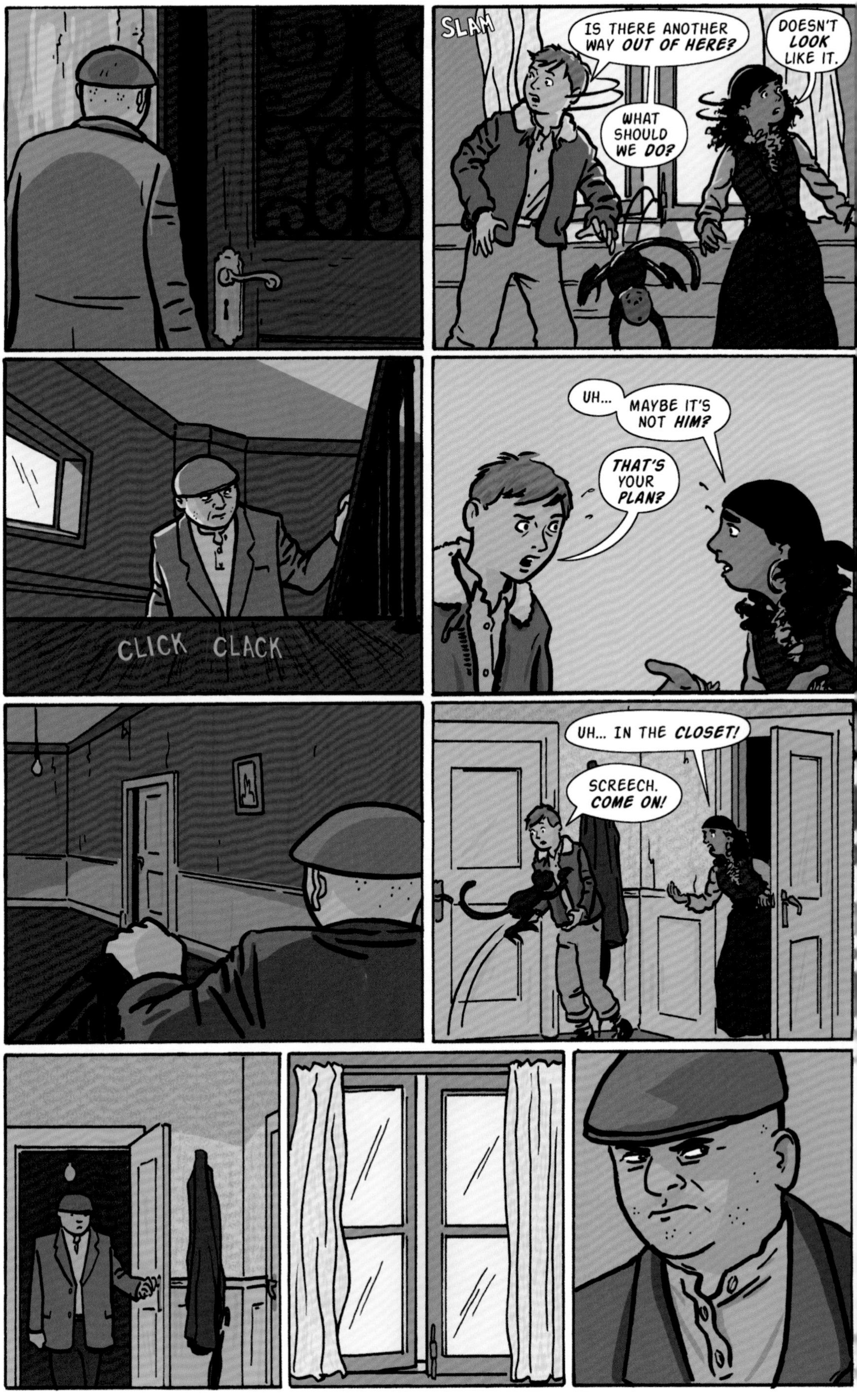
SLAM
IS THERE ANOTHER WAY OUT OF HERE?
WHAT SHOULD WE DO?
DOESN'T LOOK LIKE IT.
CLICK CLACK
UH...
MAYBE IT'S NOT HIM?
THAT'S YOUR PLAN?
UH... IN THE CLOSET!
SCREECH. COME ON!

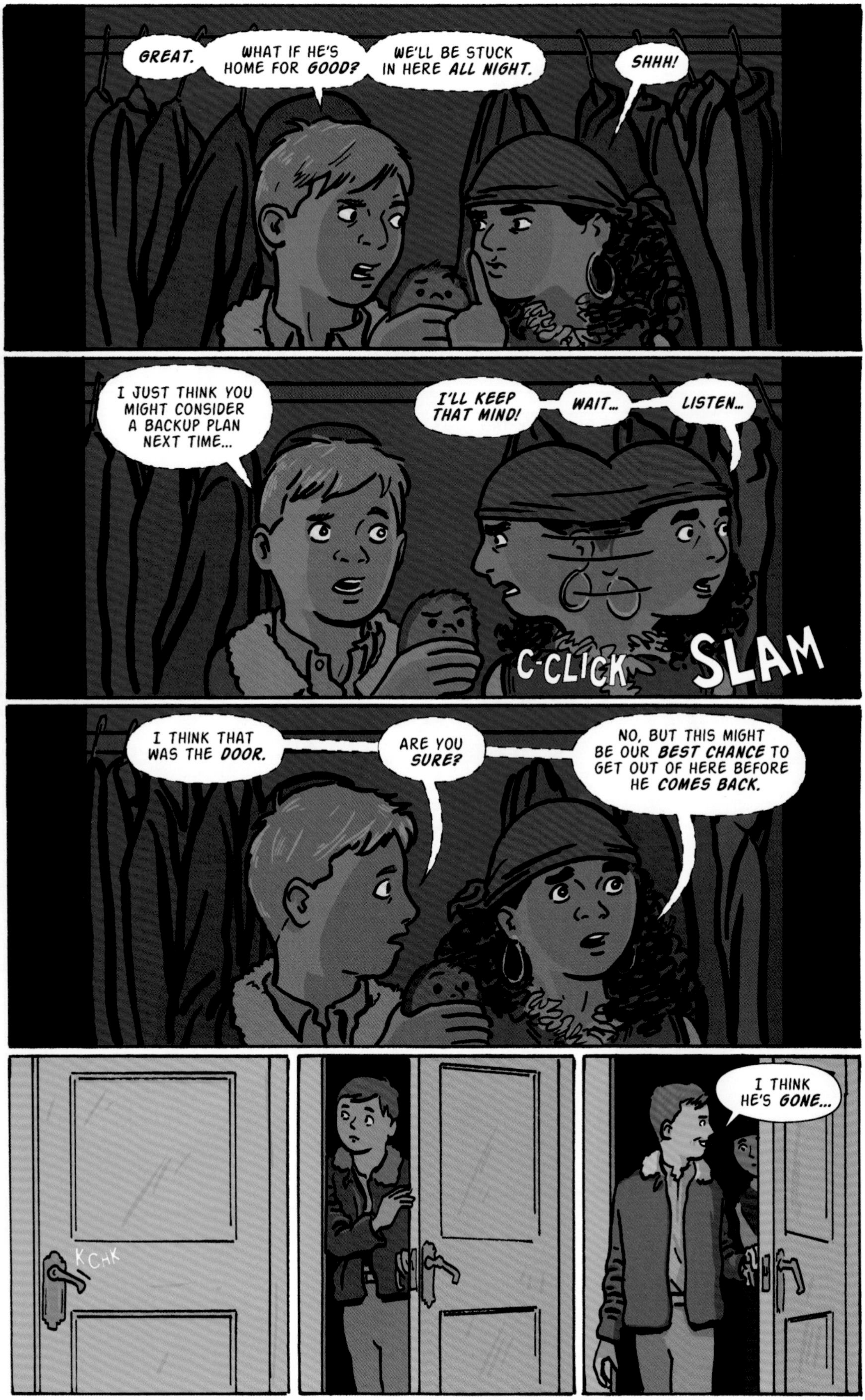
GREAT.
WHAT IF HE'S HOME FOR GOOD?
WE'LL BE STUCK IN HERE ALL NIGHT.
SHHH!
I JUST THINK YOU MIGHT CONSIDER A BACKUP PLAN NEXT TIME...
I'LL KEEP THAT MIND!
WAIT...
LISTEN...
C-CLICK
SLAM
I THINK THAT WAS THE DOOR.
ARE YOU SURE?
NO, BUT THIS MIGHT BE OUR BEST CHANCE TO GET OUT OF HERE BEFORE HE COMES BACK.
KCHK
I THINK HE'S GONE...

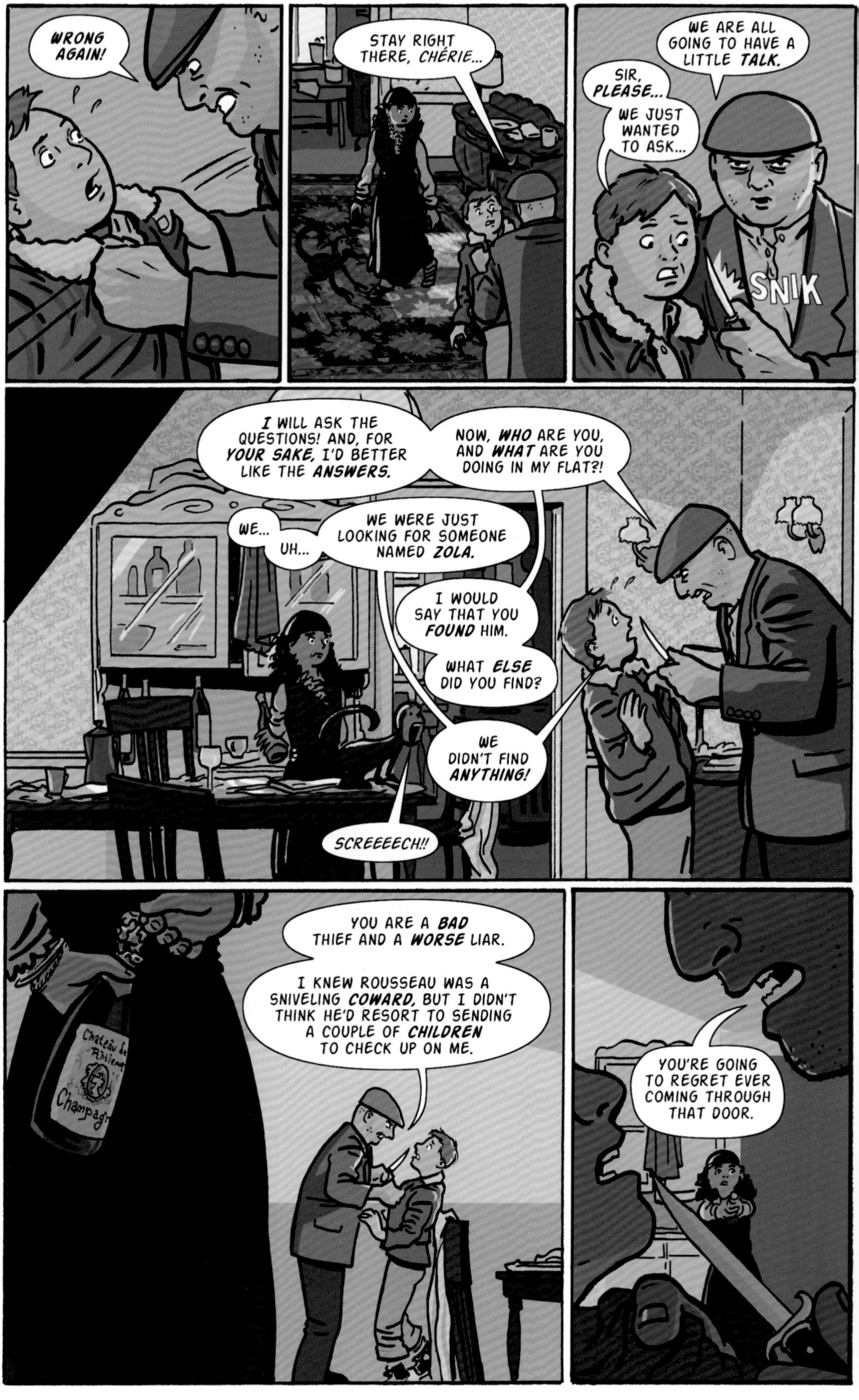
WRONG AGAIN!
STAY RIGHT THERE, CHÉRIE...
WE ARE ALL GOING TO HAVE A LITTLE TALK.
SIR, PLEASE...
WE JUST WANTED TO ASK...
SNIK
I WILL ASK THE QUESTIONS! AND, FOR YOUR SAKE, I'D BETTER LIKE THE ANSWERS.
NOW, WHO ARE YOU, AND WHAT ARE YOU DOING IN MY FLAT?!
WE... UH...
WE WERE JUST LOOKING FOR SOMEONE NAMED ZOLA.
I WOULD SAY THAT YOU FOUND HIM.
WHAT ELSE DID YOU FIND?
WE DIDN'T FIND ANYTHING!
SCREEEECH!!
YOU ARE A BAD THIEF AND A WORSE LIAR.
I KNEW ROUSSEAU WAS A SNIVELING COWARD, BUT I DIDN'T THINK HE'D RESORT TO SENDING A COUPLE OF CHILDREN TO CHECK UP ON ME.
YOU'RE GOING TO REGRET EVER COMING THROUGH THAT DOOR.

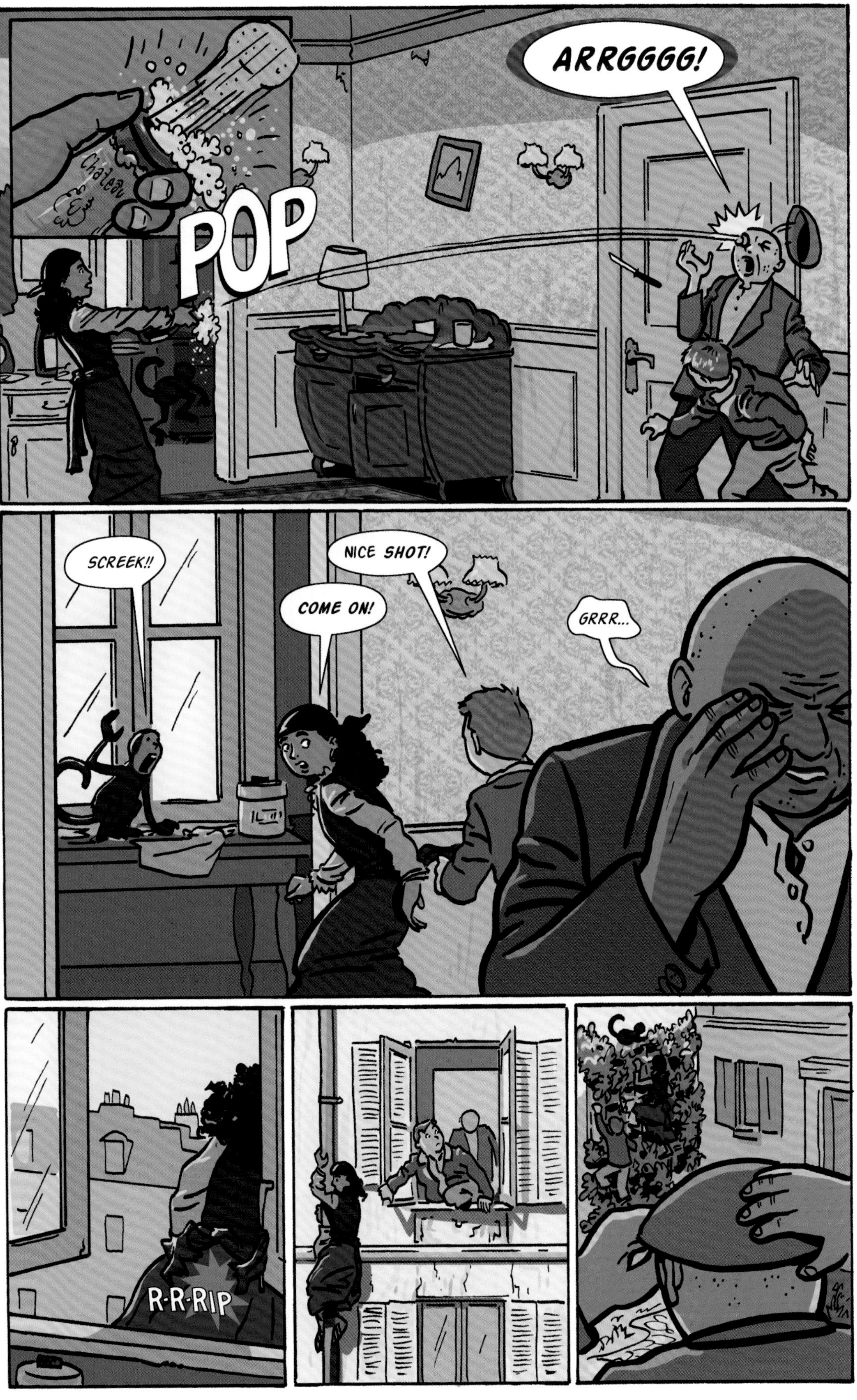
Chateau
POP
ARRGGGG!
SCREEK!!
COME ON!
NICE SHOT!
GRRR...
R-R-RIP

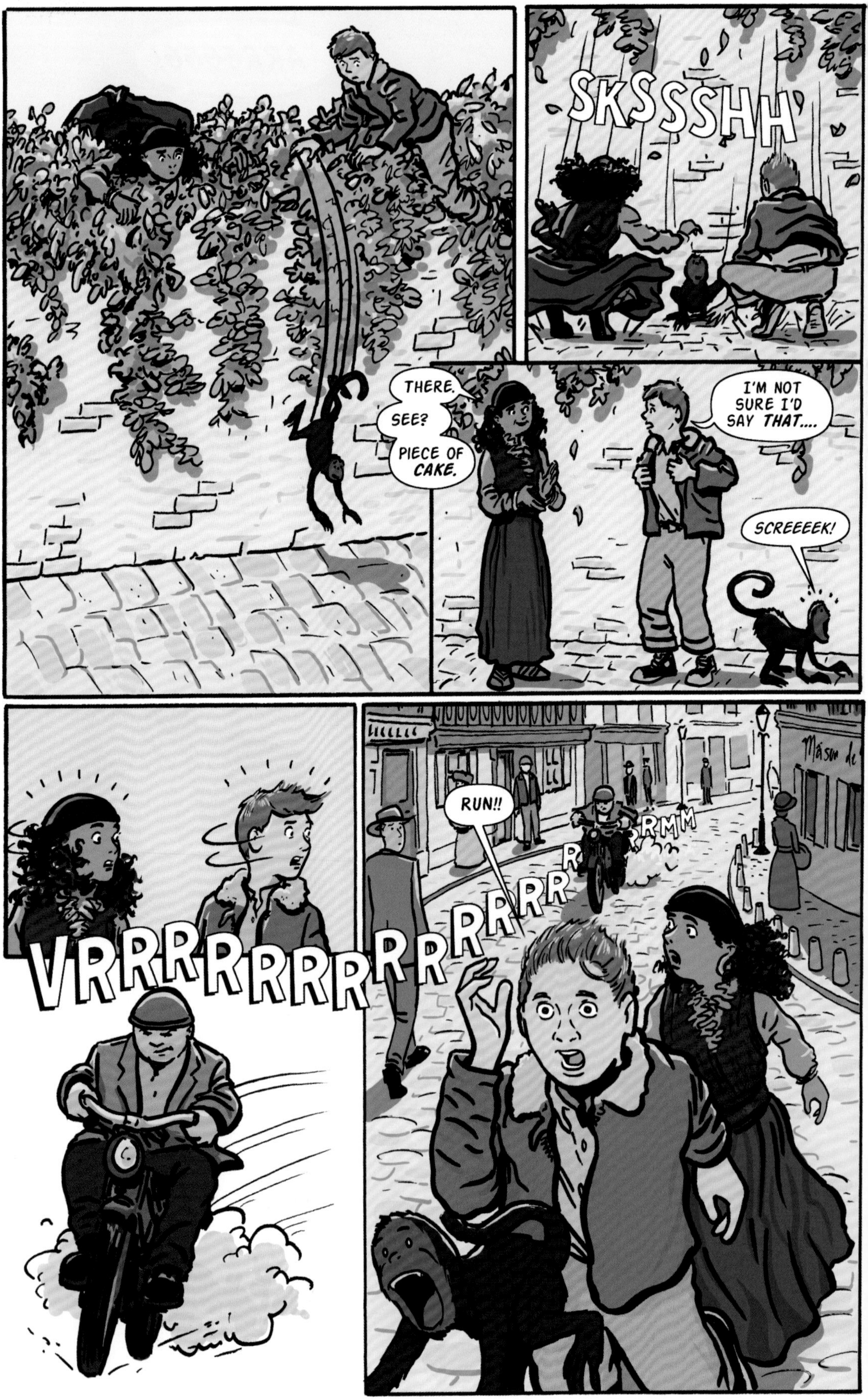
SKSSSHH
THERE.
SEE?
PIECE OF CAKE.
I'M NOT SURE I'D SAY THAT....
SCREEEEK!
VRRRRRRRRRRRRRRRRR
RUN!!
RRMM
Mâison de

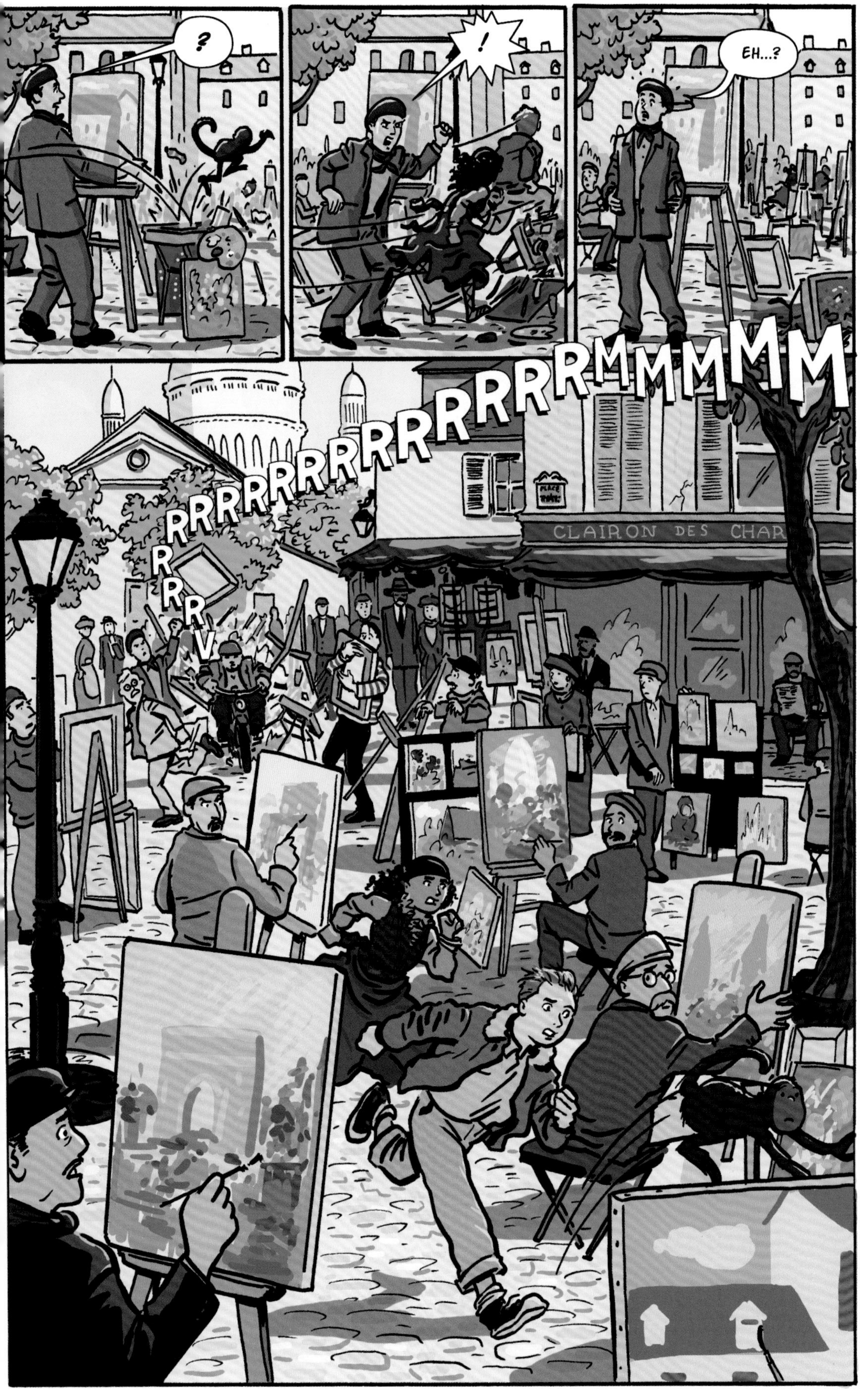
?
!
EH...?
RRRRRRRRRRRRRRRRRRRMMMMM
RRRRV
PLACE
CLAIRON DES CHAR

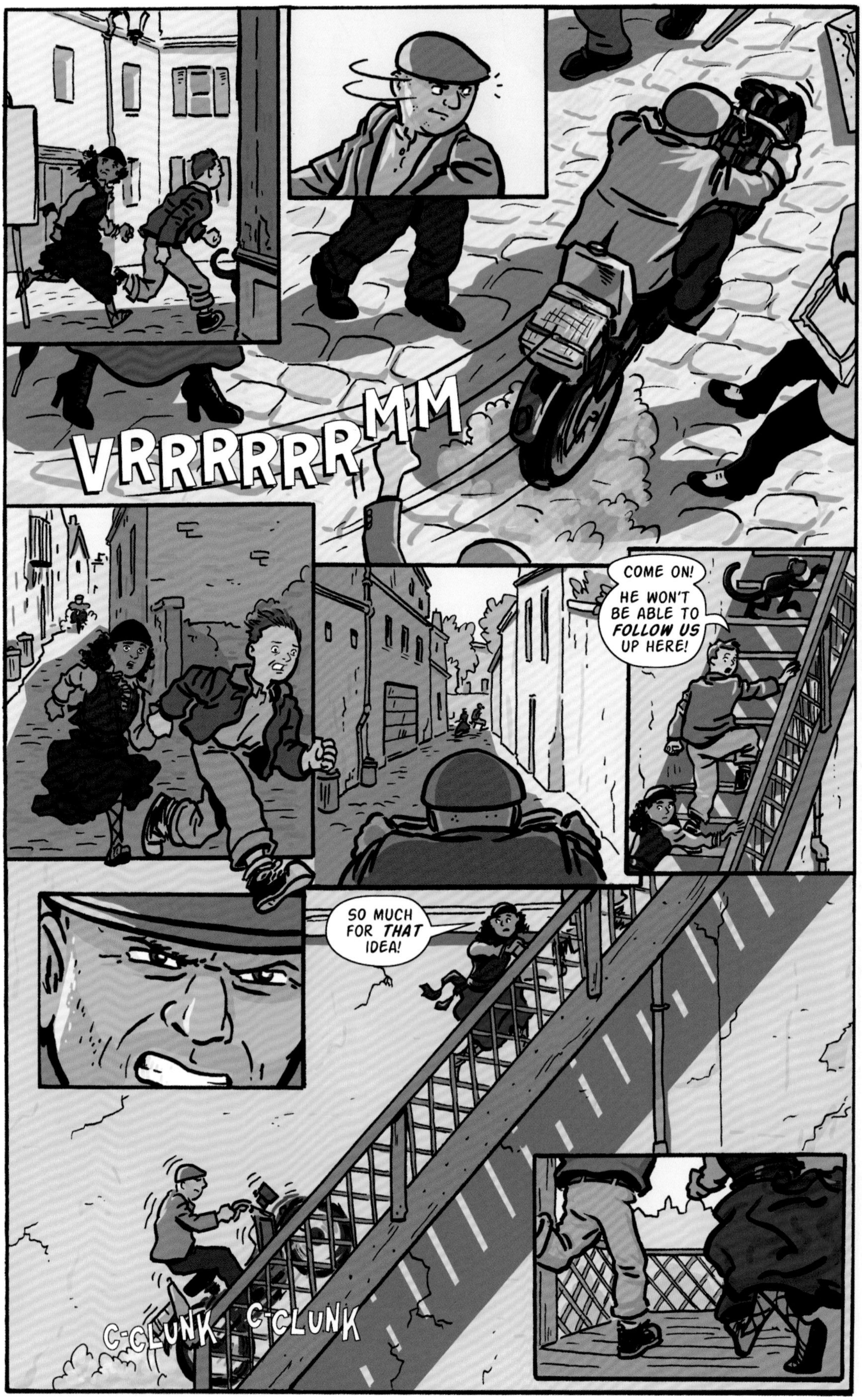
VRRRRRRMM
COME ON! HE WON'T BE ABLE TO *FOLLOW US* UP HERE!
SO MUCH FOR *THAT* IDEA!
C-CLUNK C-CLUNK

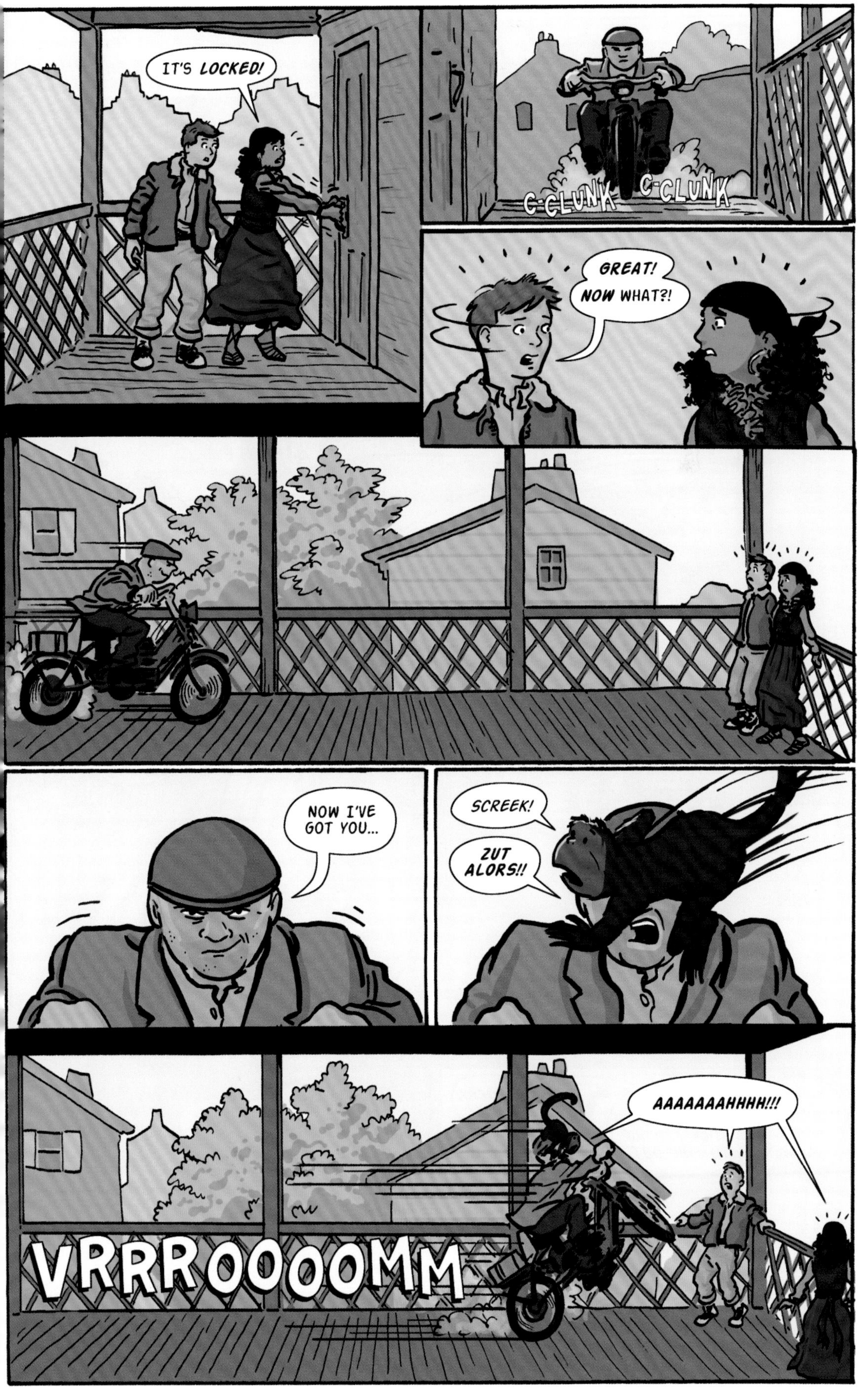
IT'S LOCKED!
C-CLUNK C-CLUNK
GREAT!
NOW WHAT?!
NOW I'VE GOT YOU...
SCREEK!
ZUT ALORS!!
AAAAAAAHHHH!!!
VRRROOOOMM

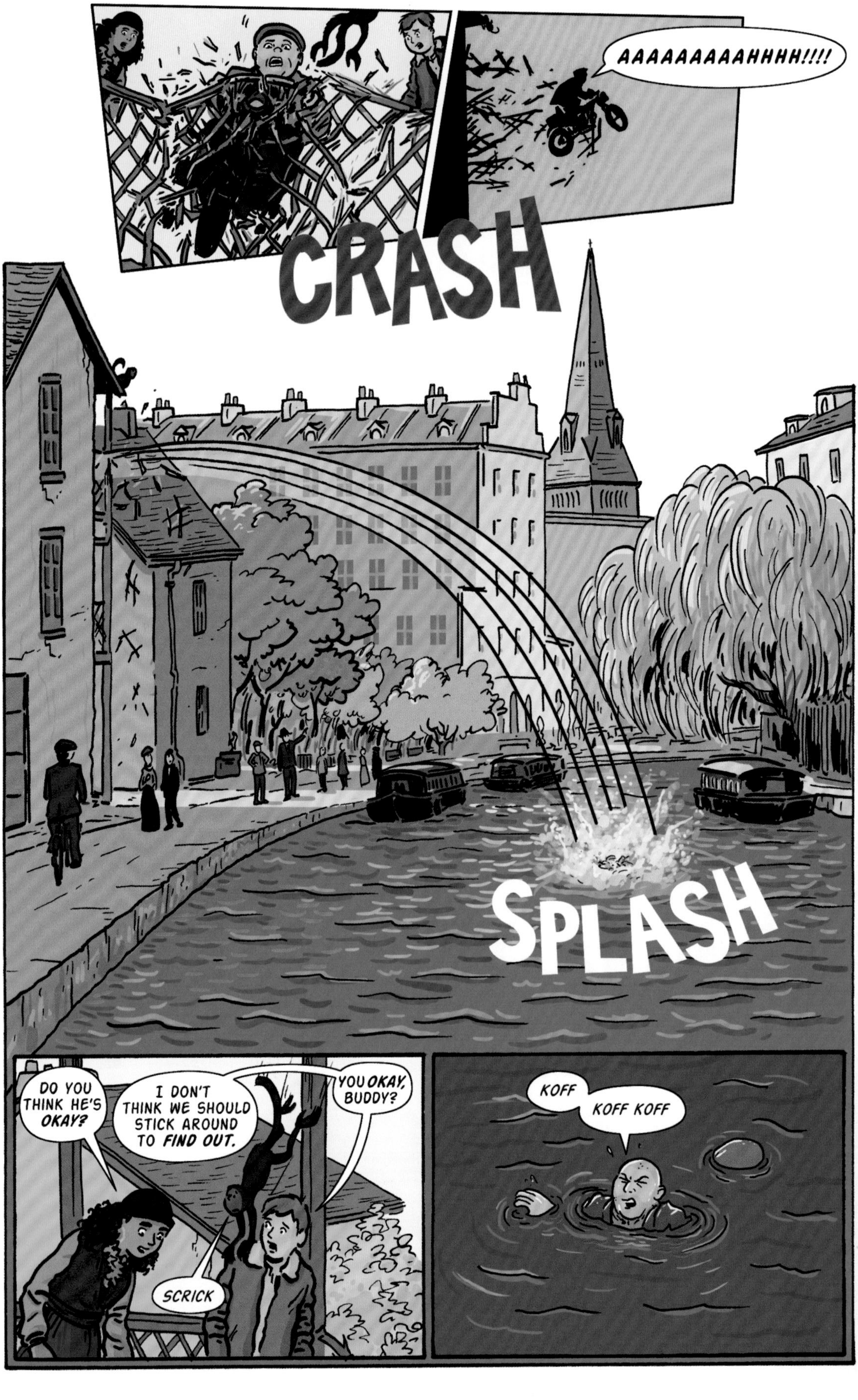
AAAAAAAAAHHHH!!!!
CRASH
SPLASH
DO YOU THINK HE'S OKAY?
I DON'T THINK WE SHOULD STICK AROUND TO FIND OUT.
YOU OKAY, BUDDY?
SCRICK
KOFF
KOFF KOFF

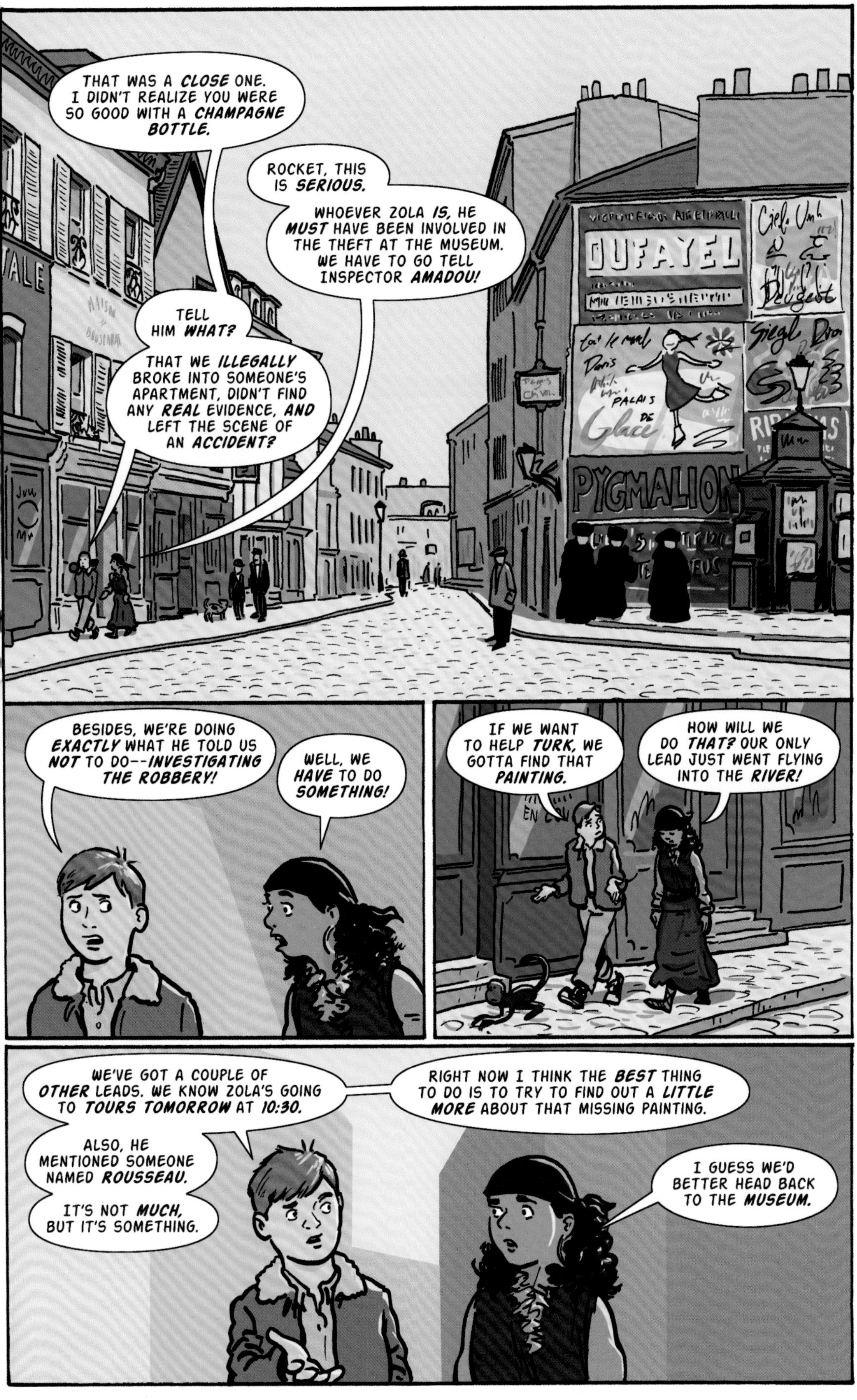
THAT WAS A CLOSE ONE. I DIDN'T REALIZE YOU WERE SO GOOD WITH A CHAMPAGNE BOTTLE.
ROCKET, THIS IS SERIOUS.
WHOEVER ZOLA IS, HE MUST HAVE BEEN INVOLVED IN THE THEFT AT THE MUSEUM. WE HAVE TO GO TELL INSPECTOR AMADOU!
TELL HIM WHAT?
THAT WE ILLEGALLY BROKE INTO SOMEONE'S APARTMENT, DIDN'T FIND ANY REAL EVIDENCE, AND LEFT THE SCENE OF AN ACCIDENT?
DUFAYEL
PYGMALION
PALAIS DE Glace
BESIDES, WE'RE DOING EXACTLY WHAT HE TOLD US NOT TO DO--INVESTIGATING THE ROBBERY!
WELL, WE HAVE TO DO SOMETHING!
IF WE WANT TO HELP TURK, WE GOTTA FIND THAT PAINTING.
HOW WILL WE DO THAT? OUR ONLY LEAD JUST WENT FLYING INTO THE RIVER!
WE'VE GOT A COUPLE OF OTHER LEADS. WE KNOW ZOLA'S GOING TO TOURS TOMORROW AT 10:30.
ALSO, HE MENTIONED SOMEONE NAMED ROUSSEAU.
IT'S NOT MUCH, BUT IT'S SOMETHING.
RIGHT NOW I THINK THE BEST THING TO DO IS TO TRY TO FIND OUT A LITTLE MORE ABOUT THAT MISSING PAINTING.
I GUESS WE'D BETTER HEAD BACK TO THE MUSEUM.

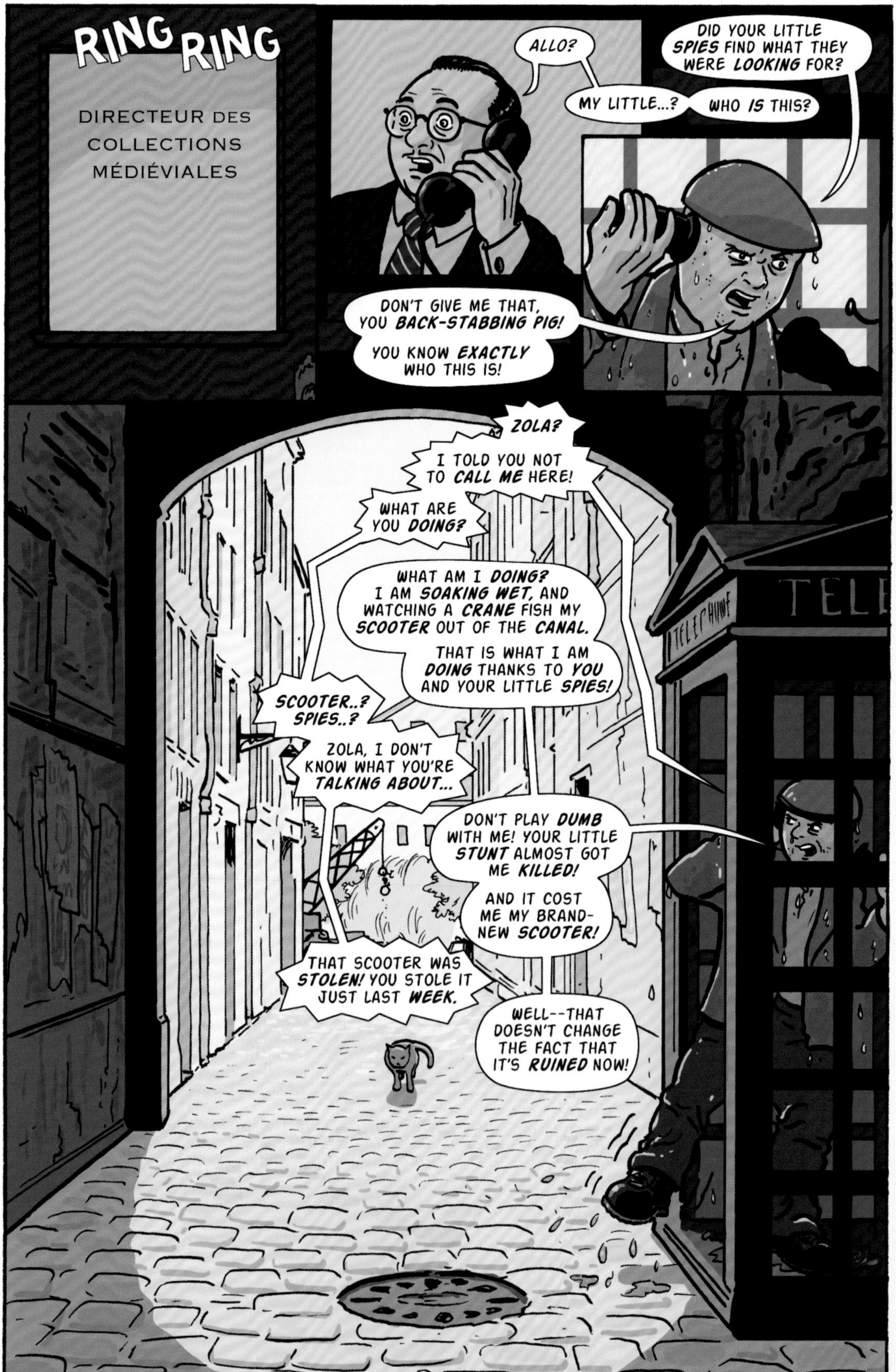
RING RING
DIRECTEUR DES COLLECTIONS MÉDIÉVIALES
ALLO?
DID YOUR LITTLE SPIES FIND WHAT THEY WERE LOOKING FOR?
MY LITTLE...?
WHO IS THIS?
DON'T GIVE ME THAT, YOU BACK-STABBING PIG!
YOU KNOW EXACTLY WHO THIS IS!
ZOLA?
I TOLD YOU NOT TO CALL ME HERE!
WHAT ARE YOU DOING?
WHAT AM I DOING? I AM SOAKING WET, AND WATCHING A CRANE FISH MY SCOOTER OUT OF THE CANAL.
THAT IS WHAT I AM DOING THANKS TO YOU AND YOUR LITTLE SPIES!
TELE
SCOOTER..? SPIES..?
ZOLA, I DON'T KNOW WHAT YOU'RE TALKING ABOUT...
DON'T PLAY DUMB WITH ME! YOUR LITTLE STUNT ALMOST GOT ME KILLED!
AND IT COST ME MY BRAND-NEW SCOOTER!
THAT SCOOTER WAS STOLEN! YOU STOLE IT JUST LAST WEEK.
WELL--THAT DOESN'T CHANGE THE FACT THAT IT'S RUINED NOW!

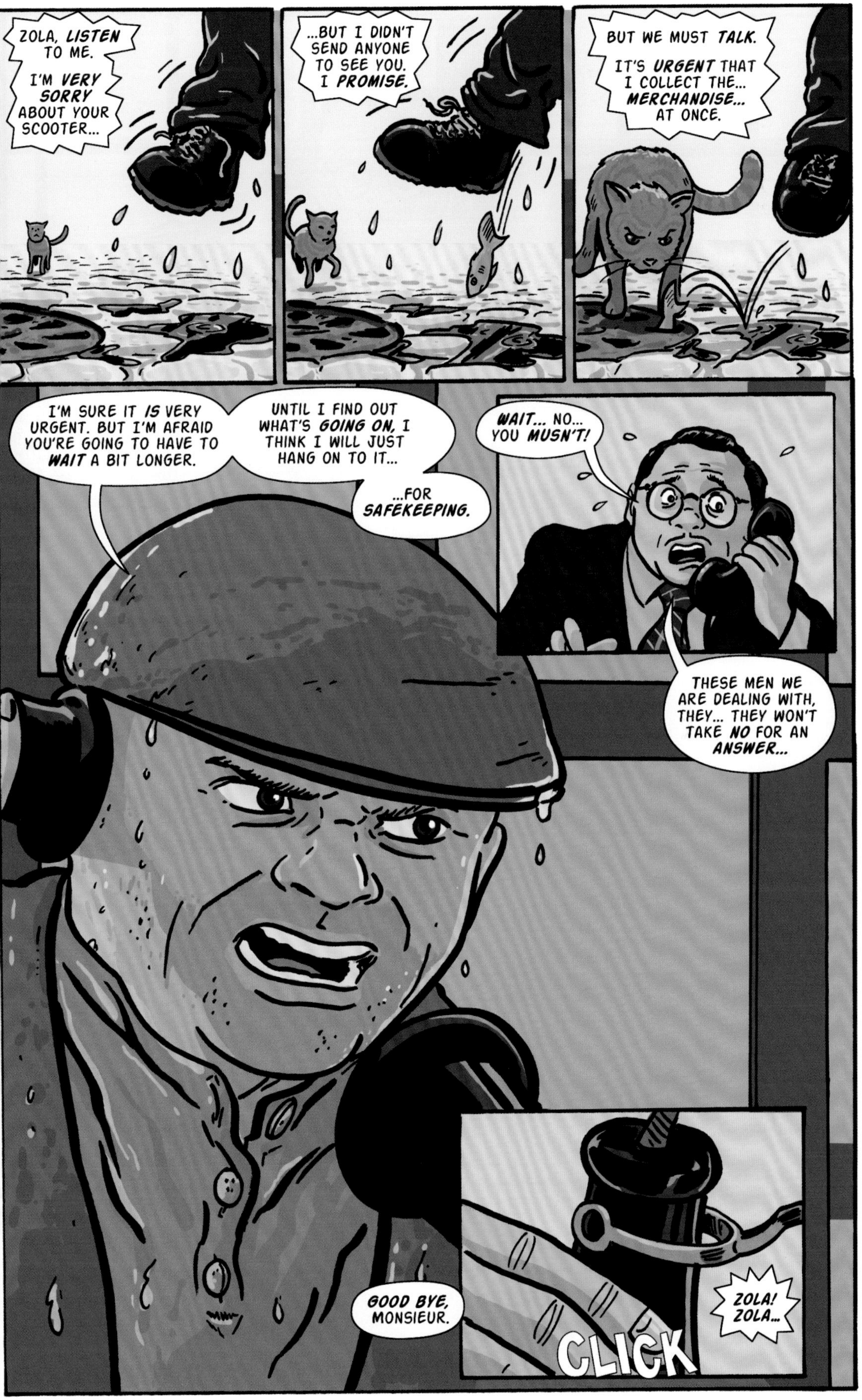
ZOLA, LISTEN TO ME.
I'M VERY SORRY ABOUT YOUR SCOOTER...
...BUT I DIDN'T SEND ANYONE TO SEE YOU. I PROMISE.
BUT WE MUST TALK.
IT'S URGENT THAT I COLLECT THE... MERCHANDISE... AT ONCE.
I'M SURE IT IS VERY URGENT. BUT I'M AFRAID YOU'RE GOING TO HAVE TO WAIT A BIT LONGER.
UNTIL I FIND OUT WHAT'S GOING ON, I THINK I WILL JUST HANG ON TO IT...
...FOR SAFEKEEPING.
WAIT... NO... YOU MUSN'T!
THESE MEN WE ARE DEALING WITH, THEY... THEY WON'T TAKE NO FOR AN ANSWER...
GOOD BYE, MONSIEUR.
CLICK
ZOLA! ZOLA...

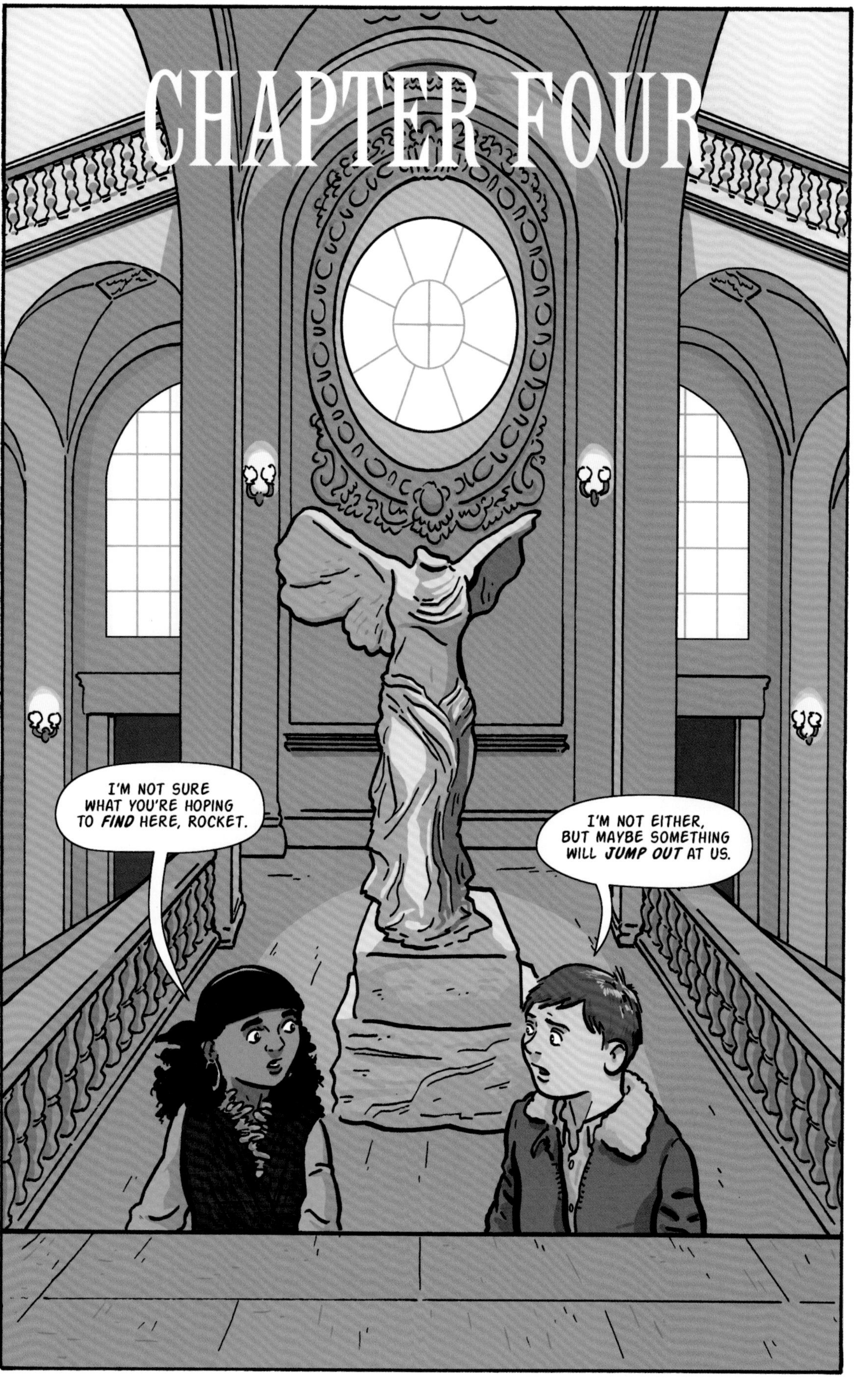
CHAPTER FOUR
I'M NOT SURE WHAT YOU'RE HOPING TO FIND HERE, ROCKET.
I'M NOT EITHER, BUT MAYBE SOMETHING WILL JUMP OUT AT US.

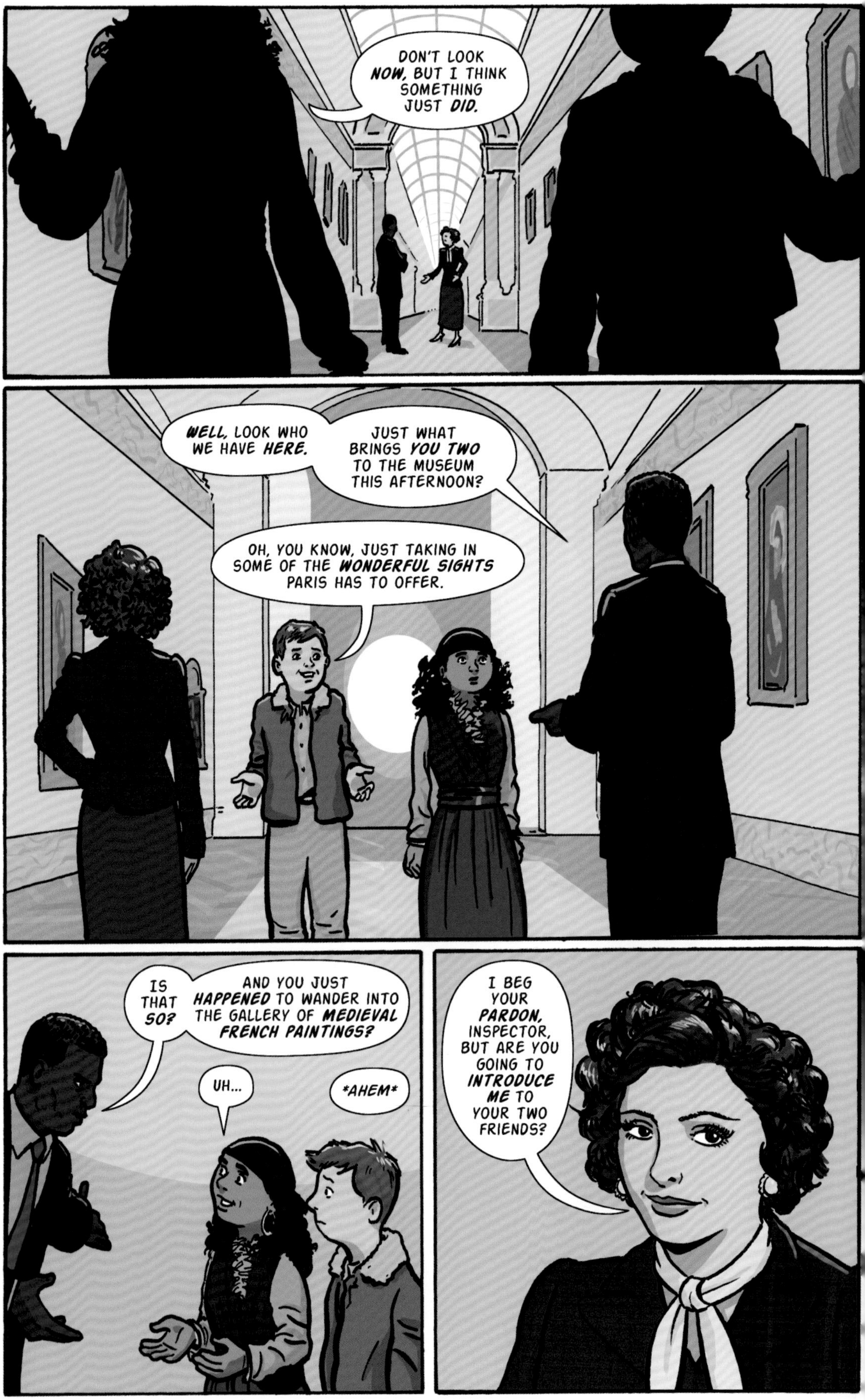
DON'T LOOK NOW, BUT I THINK SOMETHING JUST DID.
WELL, LOOK WHO WE HAVE HERE.
JUST WHAT BRINGS YOU TWO TO THE MUSEUM THIS AFTERNOON?
OH, YOU KNOW, JUST TAKING IN SOME OF THE WONDERFUL SIGHTS PARIS HAS TO OFFER.
IS THAT SO?
AND YOU JUST HAPPENED TO WANDER INTO THE GALLERY OF MEDIEVAL FRENCH PAINTINGS?
UH...
AHEM
I BEG YOUR PARDON, INSPECTOR, BUT ARE YOU GOING TO INTRODUCE ME TO YOUR TWO FRIENDS?

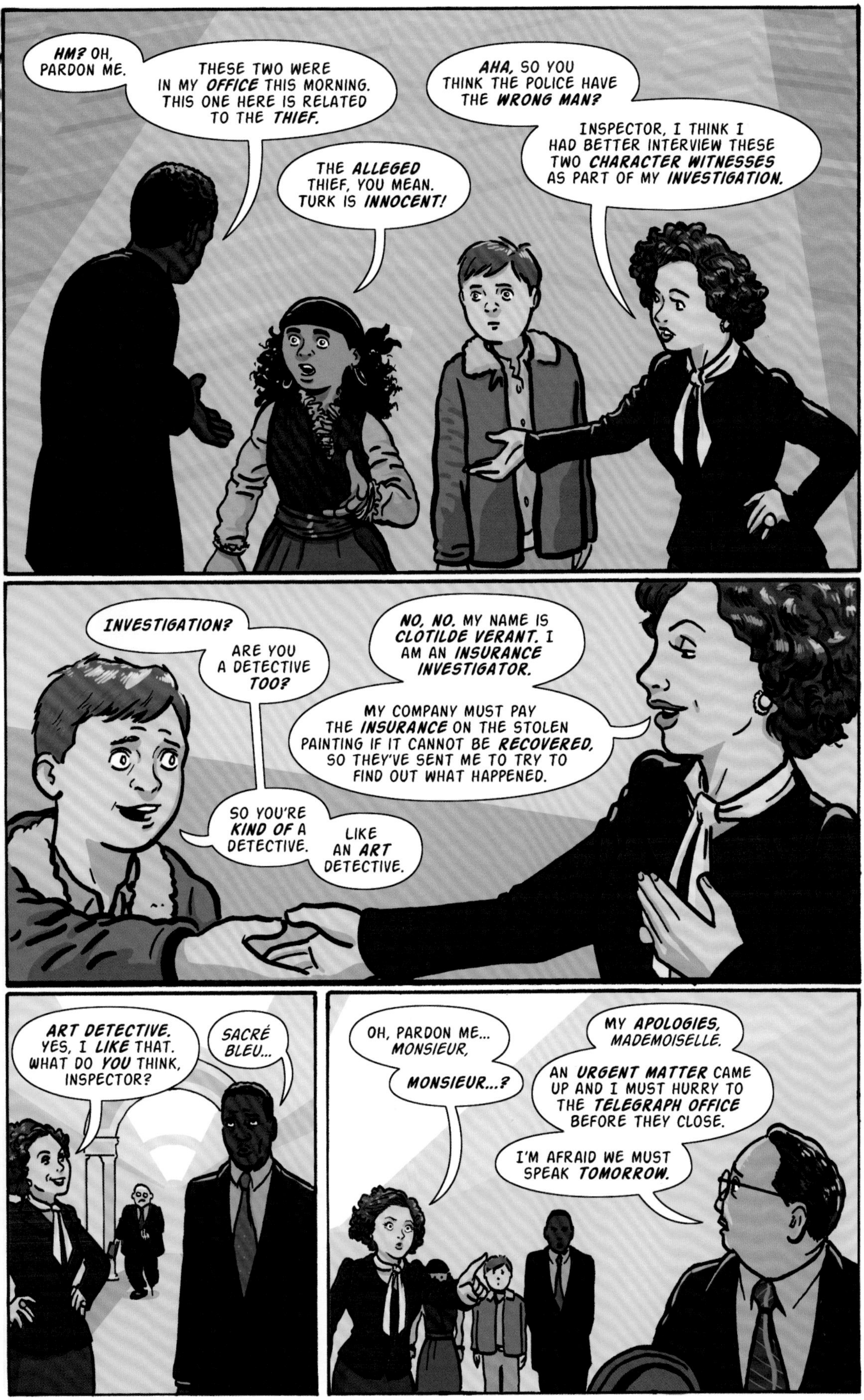
HM? OH, PARDON ME.
THESE TWO WERE IN MY OFFICE THIS MORNING. THIS ONE HERE IS RELATED TO THE THIEF.
THE ALLEGED THIEF, YOU MEAN. TURK IS INNOCENT!
AHA, SO YOU THINK THE POLICE HAVE THE WRONG MAN?
INSPECTOR, I THINK I HAD BETTER INTERVIEW THESE TWO CHARACTER WITNESSES AS PART OF MY INVESTIGATION.
INVESTIGATION?
ARE YOU A DETECTIVE TOO?
NO, NO. MY NAME IS CLOTILDE VERANT. I AM AN INSURANCE INVESTIGATOR.
MY COMPANY MUST PAY THE INSURANCE ON THE STOLEN PAINTING IF IT CANNOT BE RECOVERED, SO THEY'VE SENT ME TO TRY TO FIND OUT WHAT HAPPENED.
SO YOU'RE KIND OF A DETECTIVE.
LIKE AN ART DETECTIVE.
ART DETECTIVE. YES, I LIKE THAT. WHAT DO YOU THINK, INSPECTOR?
SACRÉ BLEU...
OH, PARDON ME... MONSIEUR,
MONSIEUR...?
MY APOLOGIES, MADEMOISELLE.
AN URGENT MATTER CAME UP AND I MUST HURRY TO THE TELEGRAPH OFFICE BEFORE THEY CLOSE.
I'M AFRAID WE MUST SPEAK TOMORROW.

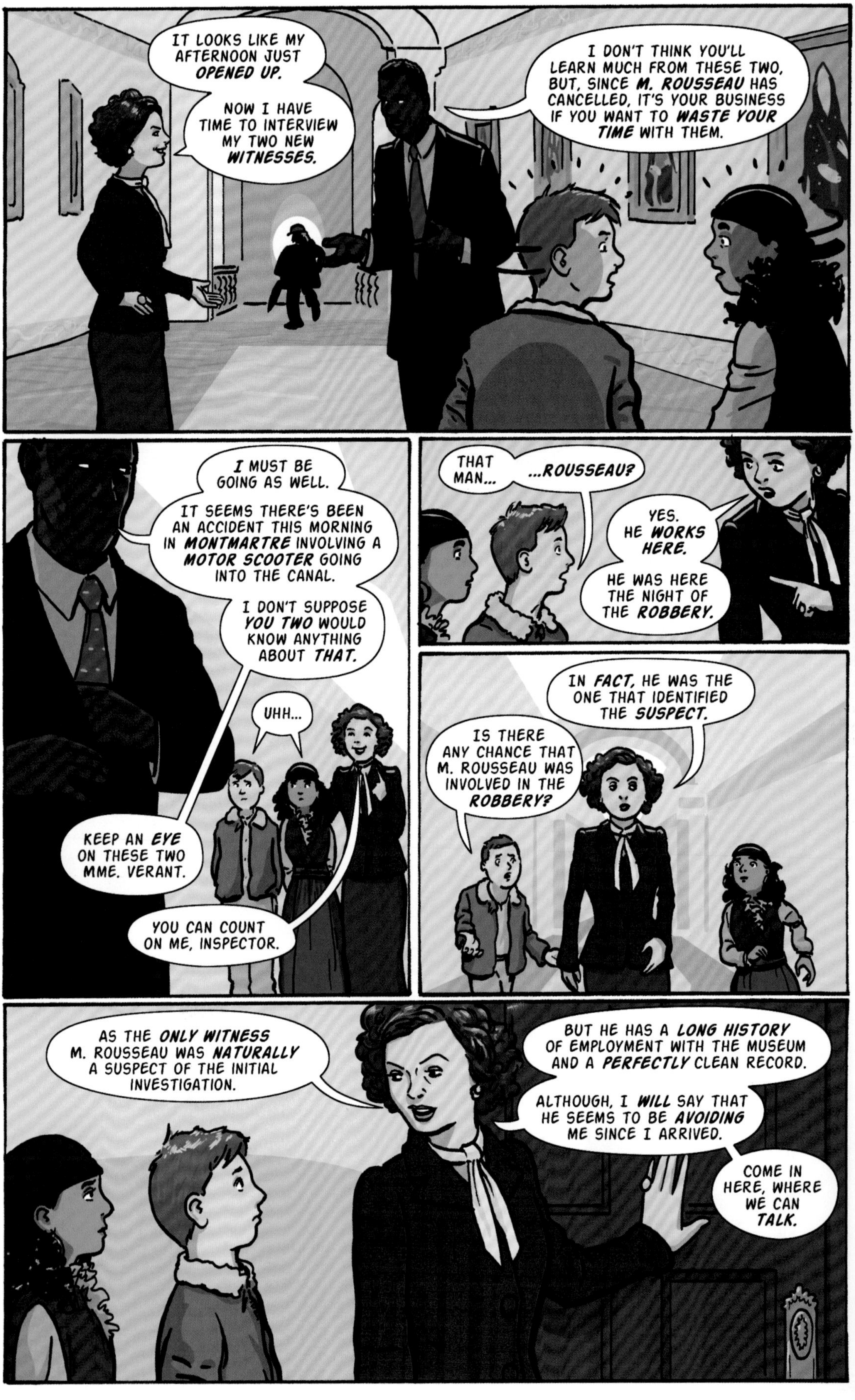
IT LOOKS LIKE MY AFTERNOON JUST OPENED UP.
NOW I HAVE TIME TO INTERVIEW MY TWO NEW WITNESSES.
I DON'T THINK YOU'LL LEARN MUCH FROM THESE TWO, BUT, SINCE M. ROUSSEAU HAS CANCELLED, IT'S YOUR BUSINESS IF YOU WANT TO WASTE YOUR TIME WITH THEM.
I MUST BE GOING AS WELL.
IT SEEMS THERE'S BEEN AN ACCIDENT THIS MORNING IN MONTMARTRE INVOLVING A MOTOR SCOOTER GOING INTO THE CANAL.
I DON'T SUPPOSE YOU TWO WOULD KNOW ANYTHING ABOUT THAT.
UHH...
KEEP AN EYE ON THESE TWO MME. VERANT.
YOU CAN COUNT ON ME, INSPECTOR.
THAT MAN...
...ROUSSEAU?
YES. HE WORKS HERE.
HE WAS HERE THE NIGHT OF THE ROBBERY.
IN FACT, HE WAS THE ONE THAT IDENTIFIED THE SUSPECT.
IS THERE ANY CHANCE THAT M. ROUSSEAU WAS INVOLVED IN THE ROBBERY?
AS THE ONLY WITNESS M. ROUSSEAU WAS NATURALLY A SUSPECT OF THE INITIAL INVESTIGATION.
BUT HE HAS A LONG HISTORY OF EMPLOYMENT WITH THE MUSEUM AND A PERFECTLY CLEAN RECORD.
ALTHOUGH, I WILL SAY THAT HE SEEMS TO BE AVOIDING ME SINCE I ARRIVED.
COME IN HERE, WHERE WE CAN TALK.

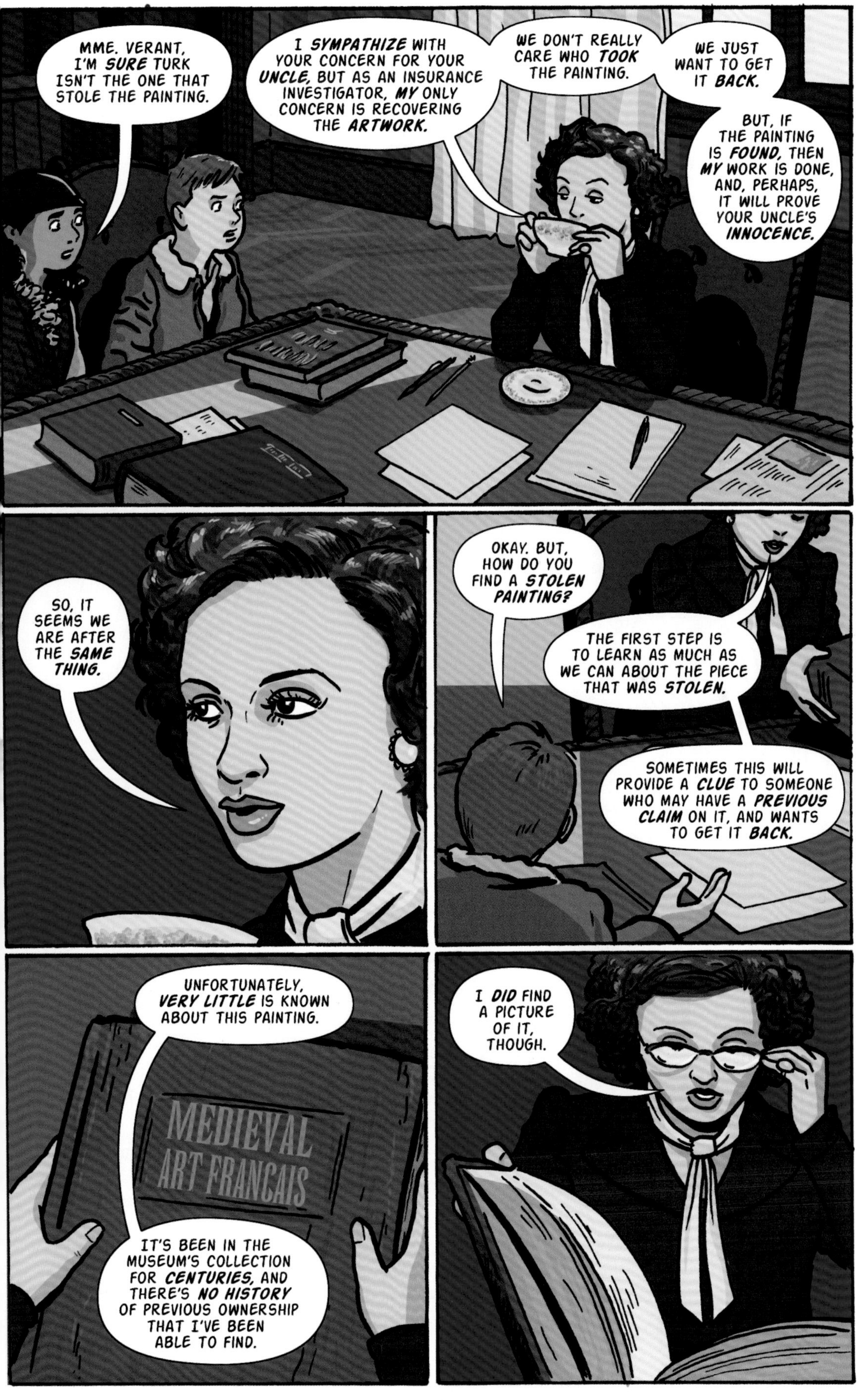

MME. VERANT, I'M SURE TURK ISN'T THE ONE THAT STOLE THE PAINTING.
I SYMPATHIZE WITH YOUR CONCERN FOR YOUR UNCLE, BUT AS AN INSURANCE INVESTIGATOR, MY ONLY CONCERN IS RECOVERING THE ARTWORK.
WE DON'T REALLY CARE WHO TOOK THE PAINTING.
WE JUST WANT TO GET IT BACK.
BUT, IF THE PAINTING IS FOUND, THEN MY WORK IS DONE, AND, PERHAPS, IT WILL PROVE YOUR UNCLE'S INNOCENCE.
SO, IT SEEMS WE ARE AFTER THE SAME THING.
OKAY. BUT, HOW DO YOU FIND A STOLEN PAINTING?
THE FIRST STEP IS TO LEARN AS MUCH AS WE CAN ABOUT THE PIECE THAT WAS STOLEN.
SOMETIMES THIS WILL PROVIDE A CLUE TO SOMEONE WHO MAY HAVE A PREVIOUS CLAIM ON IT, AND WANTS TO GET IT BACK.
UNFORTUNATELY, VERY LITTLE IS KNOWN ABOUT THIS PAINTING.
MEDIEVAL ART FRANCAIS
IT'S BEEN IN THE MUSEUM'S COLLECTION FOR CENTURIES, AND THERE'S NO HISTORY OF PREVIOUS OWNERSHIP THAT I'VE BEEN ABLE TO FIND.
I DID FIND A PICTURE OF IT, THOUGH.

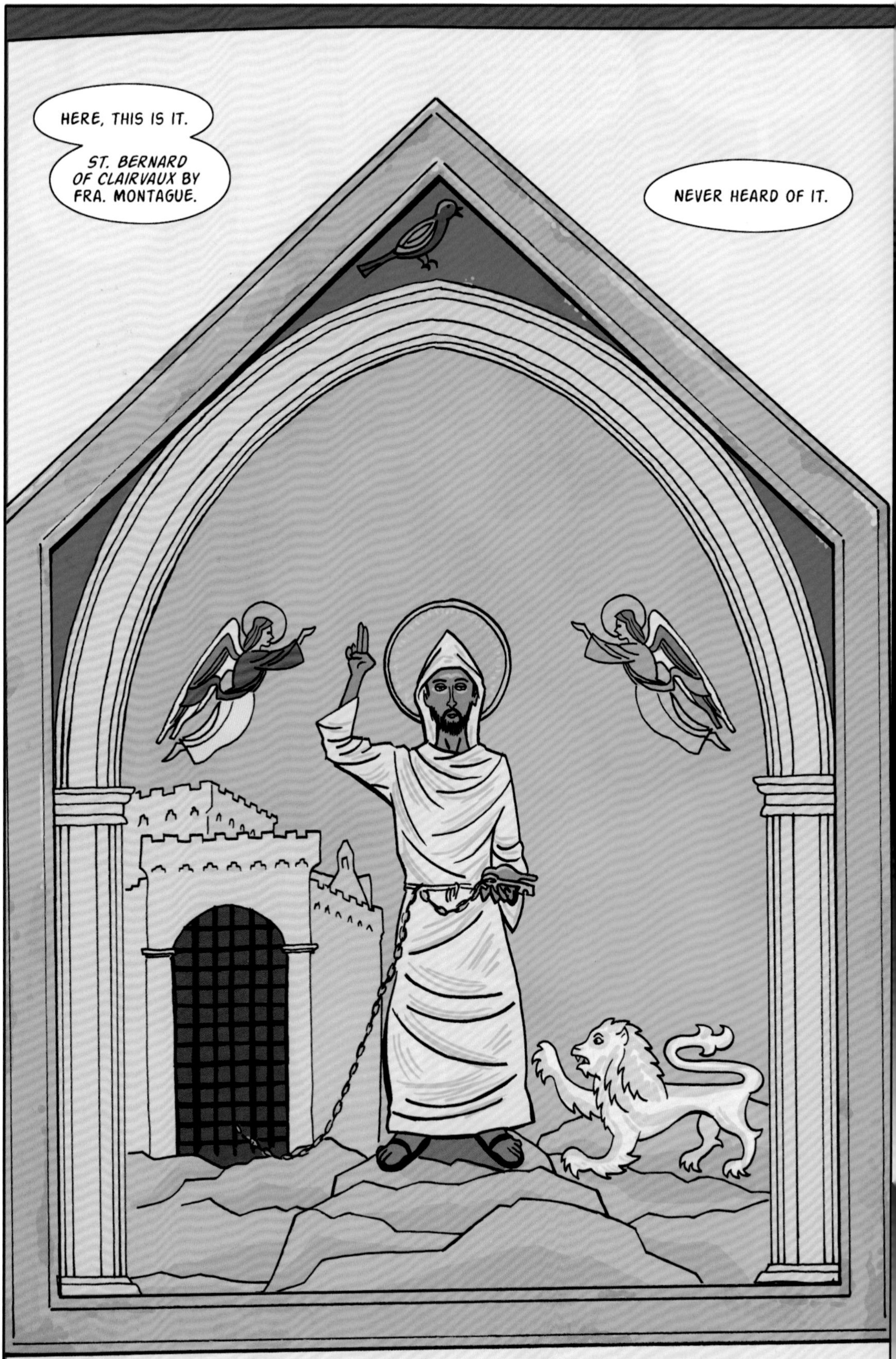
HERE, THIS IS IT.
ST. BERNARD OF CLAIRVAUX BY FRA. MONTAGUE.
NEVER HEARD OF IT.

St. Bernard of Clairvaux, Fra. Montague, 1319 MUSÉE DE LOUVRE, PARIS

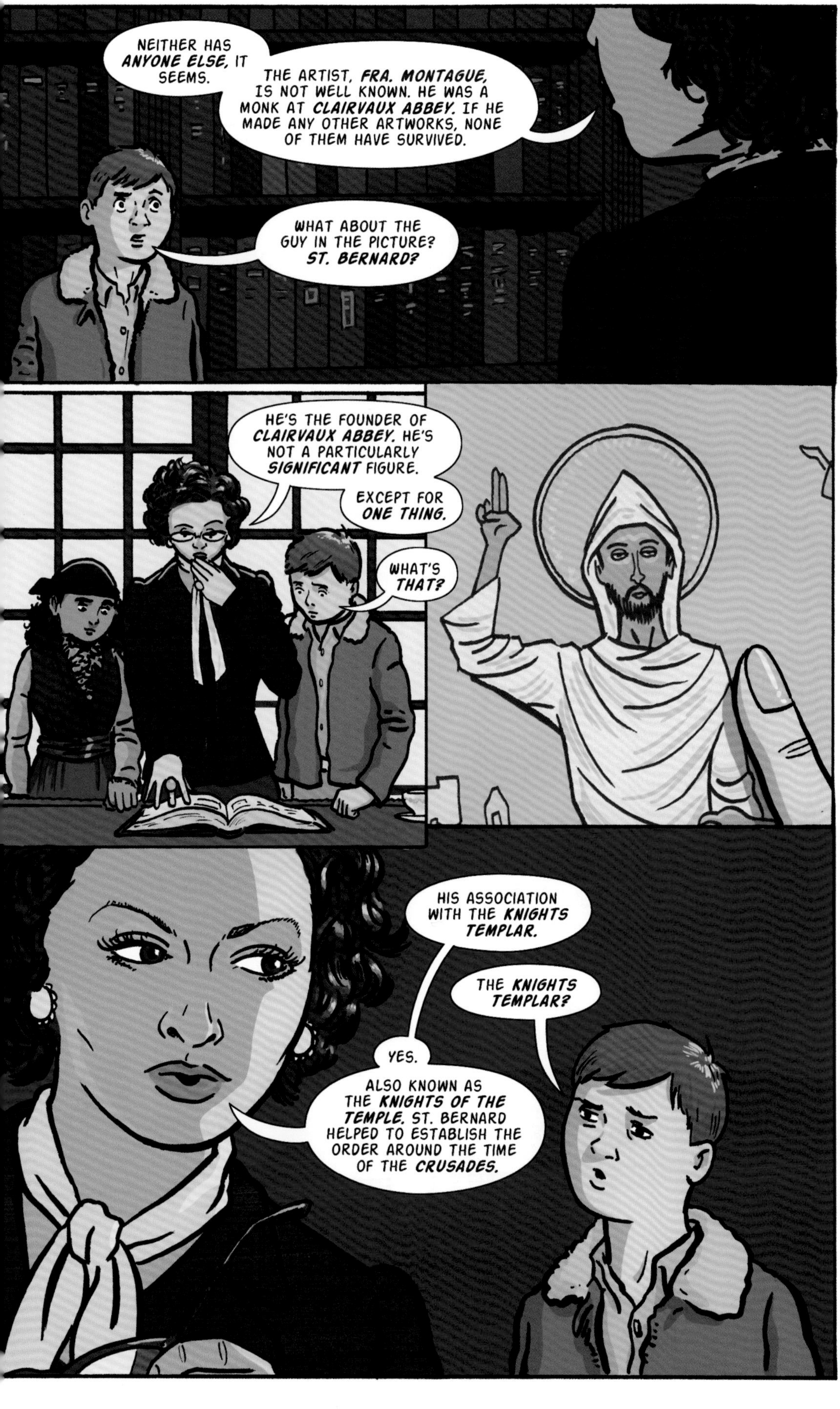
NEITHER HAS ANYONE ELSE, IT SEEMS.
THE ARTIST, FRA. MONTAGUE, IS NOT WELL KNOWN. HE WAS A MONK AT CLAIRVAUX ABBEY. IF HE MADE ANY OTHER ARTWORKS, NONE OF THEM HAVE SURVIVED.
WHAT ABOUT THE GUY IN THE PICTURE? ST. BERNARD?
HE'S THE FOUNDER OF CLAIRVAUX ABBEY. HE'S NOT A PARTICULARLY SIGNIFICANT FIGURE.
EXCEPT FOR ONE THING.
WHAT'S THAT?
HIS ASSOCIATION WITH THE KNIGHTS TEMPLAR.
THE KNIGHTS TEMPLAR?
YES.
ALSO KNOWN AS THE KNIGHTS OF THE TEMPLE. ST. BERNARD HELPED TO ESTABLISH THE ORDER AROUND THE TIME OF THE CRUSADES.

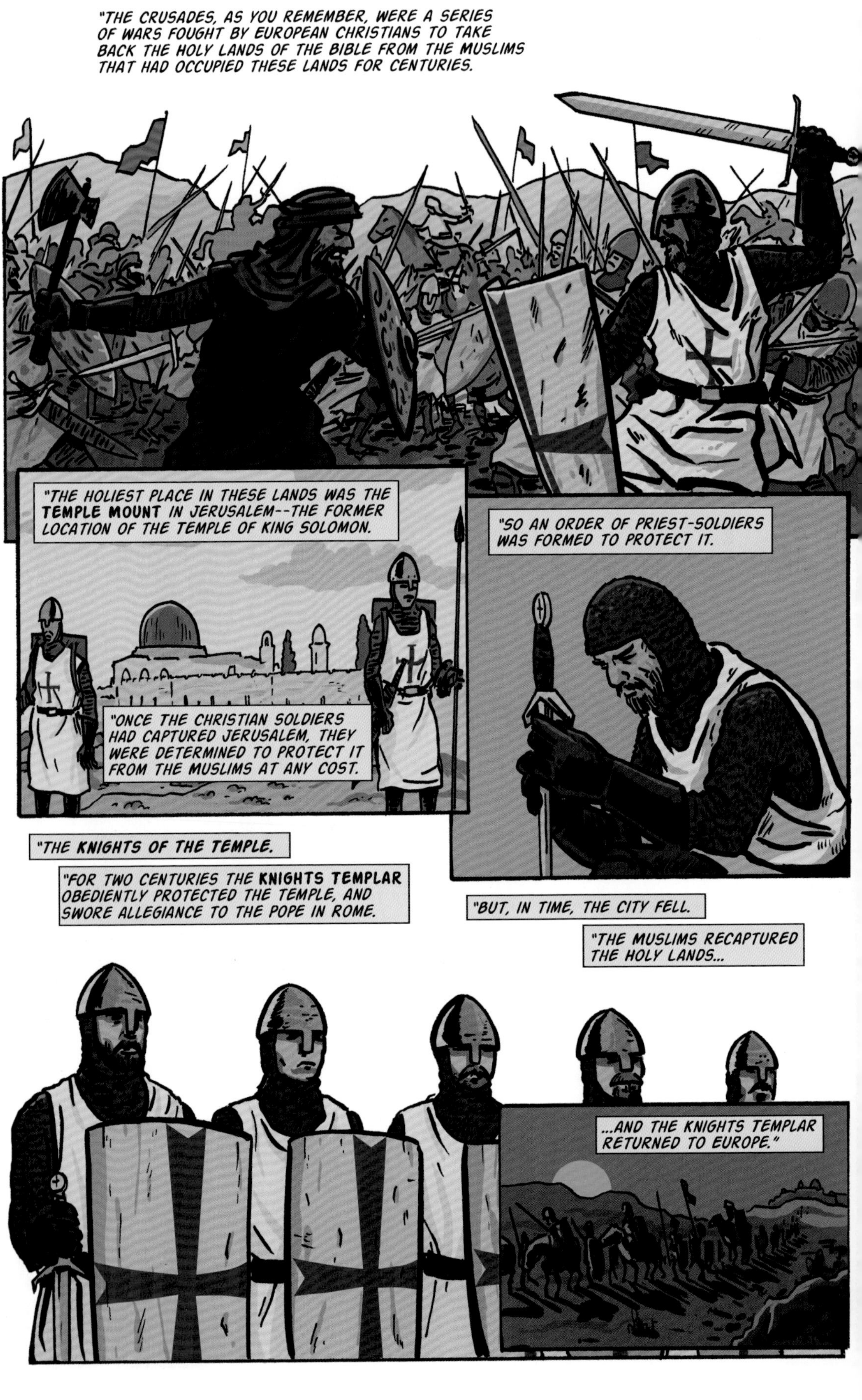
"THE CRUSADES, AS YOU REMEMBER, WERE A SERIES OF WARS FOUGHT BY EUROPEAN CHRISTIANS TO TAKE BACK THE HOLY LANDS OF THE BIBLE FROM THE MUSLIMS THAT HAD OCCUPIED THESE LANDS FOR CENTURIES.
"THE HOLIEST PLACE IN THESE LANDS WAS THE TEMPLE MOUNT IN JERUSALEM--THE FORMER LOCATION OF THE TEMPLE OF KING SOLOMON.
"ONCE THE CHRISTIAN SOLDIERS HAD CAPTURED JERUSALEM, THEY WERE DETERMINED TO PROTECT IT FROM THE MUSLIMS AT ANY COST.
"SO AN ORDER OF PRIEST-SOLDIERS WAS FORMED TO PROTECT IT.
"THE KNIGHTS OF THE TEMPLE.
"FOR TWO CENTURIES THE KNIGHTS TEMPLAR OBEDIENTLY PROTECTED THE TEMPLE, AND SWORE ALLEGIANCE TO THE POPE IN ROME.
"BUT, IN TIME, THE CITY FELL.
"THE MUSLIMS RECAPTURED THE HOLY LANDS...
...AND THE KNIGHTS TEMPLAR RETURNED TO EUROPE."

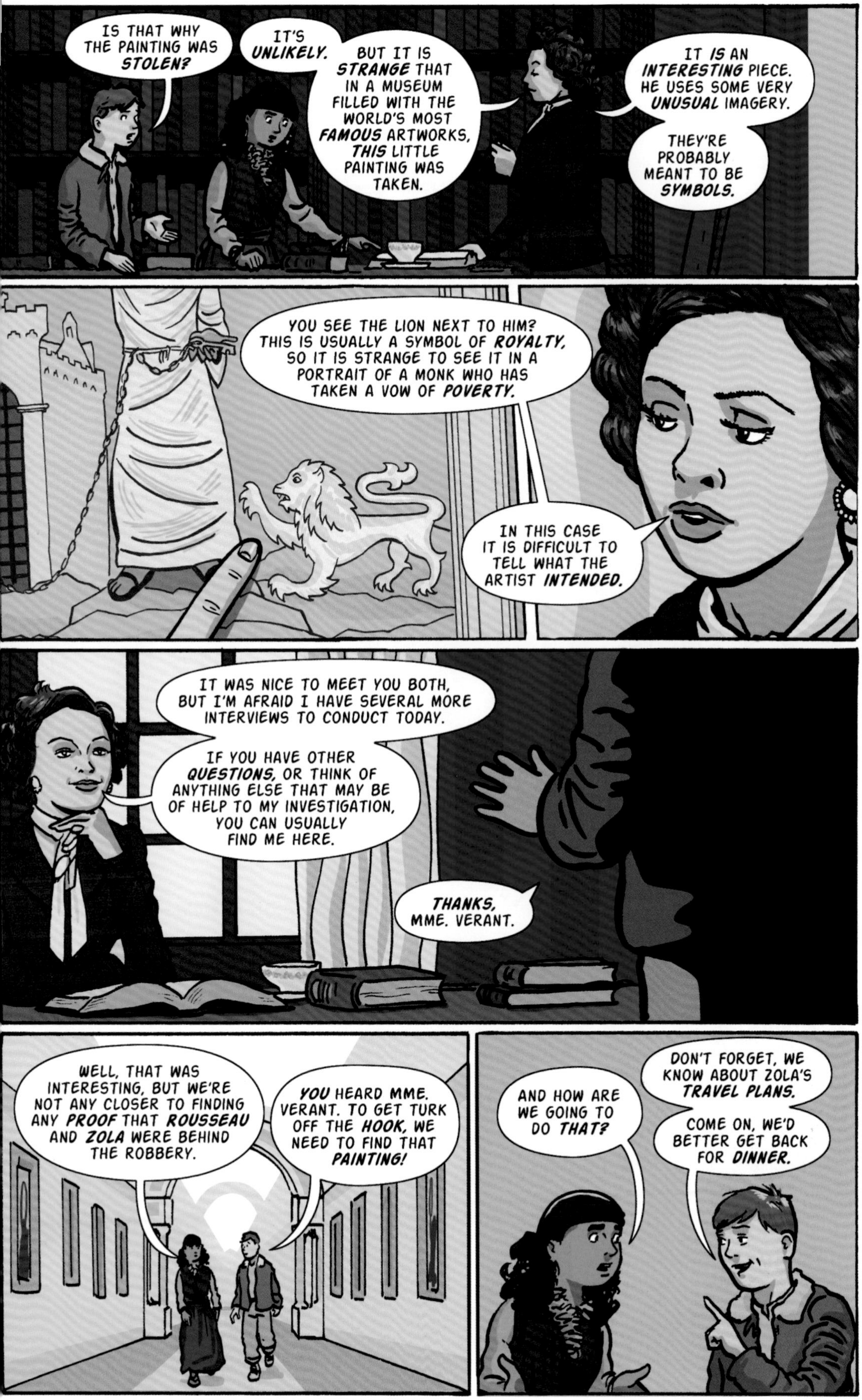

IS THAT WHY THE PAINTING WAS STOLEN?
IT'S UNLIKELY.
BUT IT IS STRANGE THAT IN A MUSEUM FILLED WITH THE WORLD'S MOST FAMOUS ARTWORKS, THIS LITTLE PAINTING WAS TAKEN.
IT IS AN INTERESTING PIECE. HE USES SOME VERY UNUSUAL IMAGERY.
THEY'RE PROBABLY MEANT TO BE SYMBOLS.
YOU SEE THE LION NEXT TO HIM? THIS IS USUALLY A SYMBOL OF ROYALTY, SO IT IS STRANGE TO SEE IT IN A PORTRAIT OF A MONK WHO HAS TAKEN A VOW OF POVERTY.
IN THIS CASE IT IS DIFFICULT TO TELL WHAT THE ARTIST INTENDED.
IT WAS NICE TO MEET YOU BOTH, BUT I'M AFRAID I HAVE SEVERAL MORE INTERVIEWS TO CONDUCT TODAY.
IF YOU HAVE OTHER QUESTIONS, OR THINK OF ANYTHING ELSE THAT MAY BE OF HELP TO MY INVESTIGATION, YOU CAN USUALLY FIND ME HERE.
THANKS, MME. VERANT.
WELL, THAT WAS INTERESTING, BUT WE'RE NOT ANY CLOSER TO FINDING ANY PROOF THAT ROUSSEAU AND ZOLA WERE BEHIND THE ROBBERY.
YOU HEARD MME. VERANT. TO GET TURK OFF THE HOOK, WE NEED TO FIND THAT PAINTING!
AND HOW ARE WE GOING TO DO THAT?
DON'T FORGET, WE KNOW ABOUT ZOLA'S TRAVEL PLANS.
COME ON, WE'D BETTER GET BACK FOR DINNER.

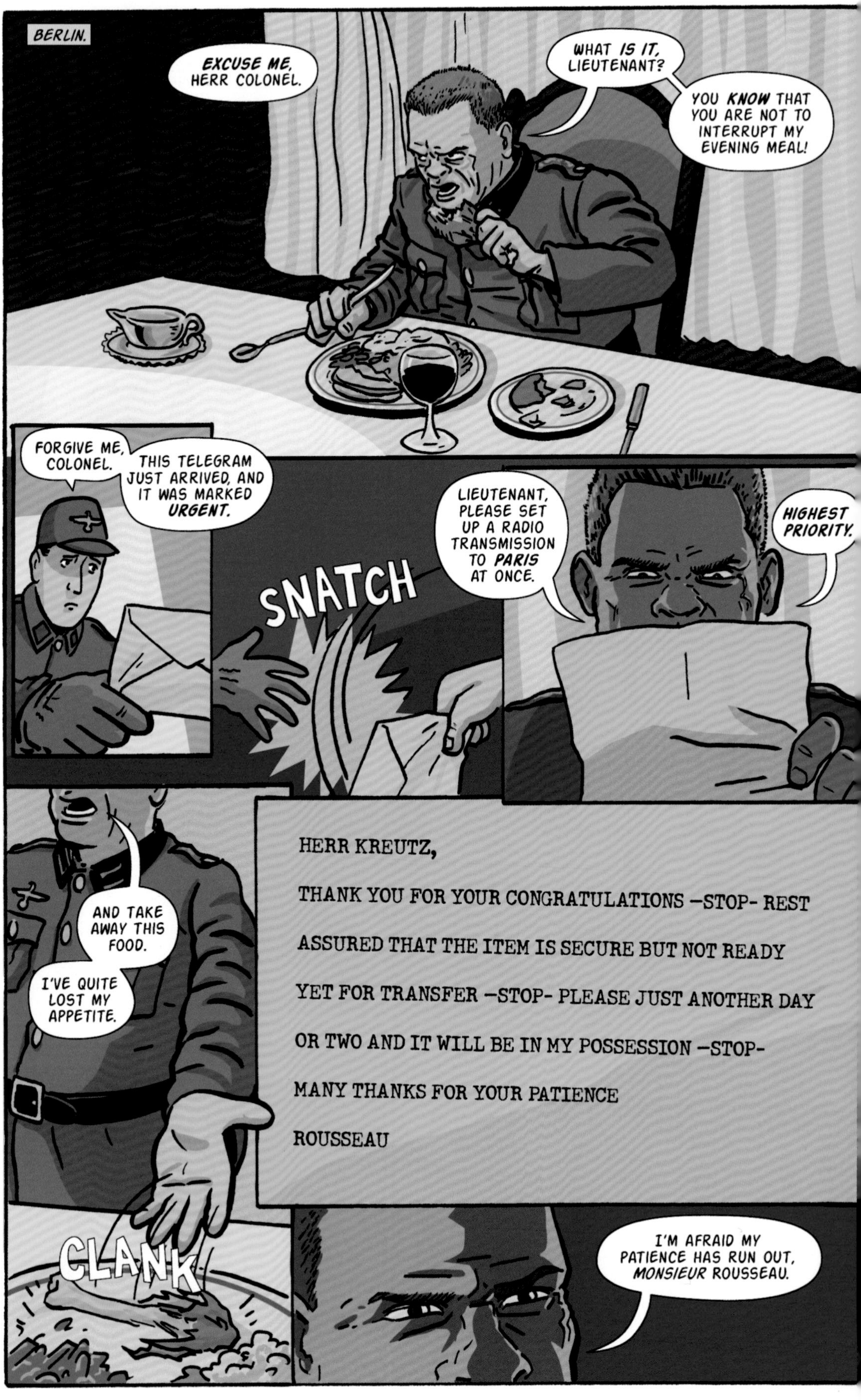
BERLIN.
EXCUSE ME, HERR COLONEL.
WHAT IS IT, LIEUTENANT?
YOU KNOW THAT YOU ARE NOT TO INTERRUPT MY EVENING MEAL!
FORGIVE ME, COLONEL.
THIS TELEGRAM JUST ARRIVED, AND IT WAS MARKED URGENT.
SNATCH
LIEUTENANT, PLEASE SET UP A RADIO TRANSMISSION TO PARIS AT ONCE.
HIGHEST PRIORITY.
AND TAKE AWAY THIS FOOD.
I'VE QUITE LOST MY APPETITE.
HERR KREUTZ,
THANK YOU FOR YOUR CONGRATULATIONS —STOP— REST ASSURED THAT THE ITEM IS SECURE BUT NOT READY YET FOR TRANSFER —STOP— PLEASE JUST ANOTHER DAY OR TWO AND IT WILL BE IN MY POSSESSION —STOP—
MANY THANKS FOR YOUR PATIENCE
ROUSSEAU
CLANK
I'M AFRAID MY PATIENCE HAS RUN OUT, MONSIEUR ROUSSEAU.

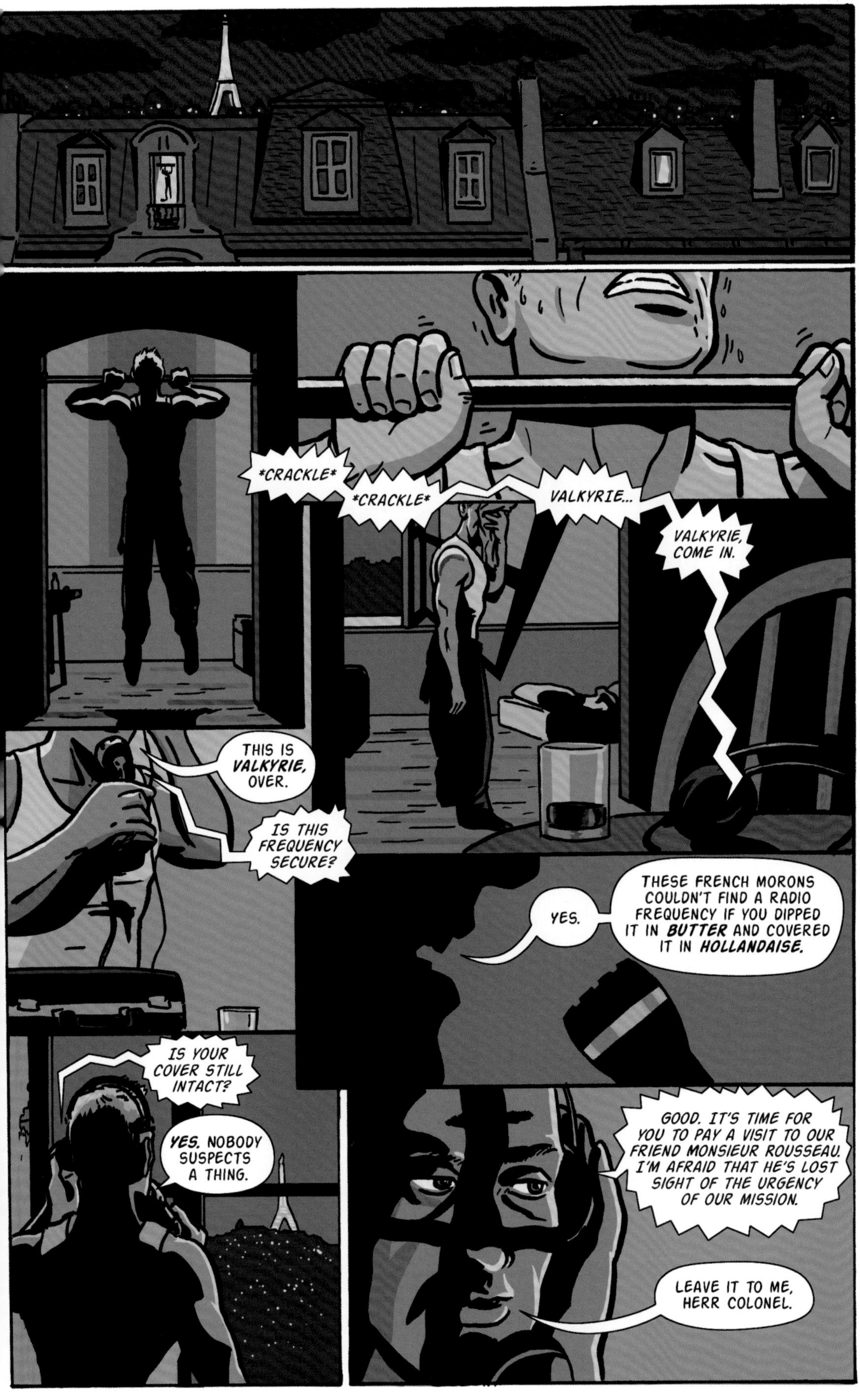
CRACKLE
CRACKLE
VALKYRIE...
VALKYRIE, COME IN.
THIS IS VALKYRIE, OVER.
IS THIS FREQUENCY SECURE?
YES.
THESE FRENCH MORONS COULDN'T FIND A RADIO FREQUENCY IF YOU DIPPED IT IN BUTTER AND COVERED IT IN HOLLANDAISE.
IS YOUR COVER STILL INTACT?
YES. NOBODY SUSPECTS A THING.
GOOD. IT'S TIME FOR YOU TO PAY A VISIT TO OUR FRIEND MONSIEUR ROUSSEAU. I'M AFRAID THAT HE'S LOST SIGHT OF THE URGENCY OF OUR MISSION.
LEAVE IT TO ME, HERR COLONEL.

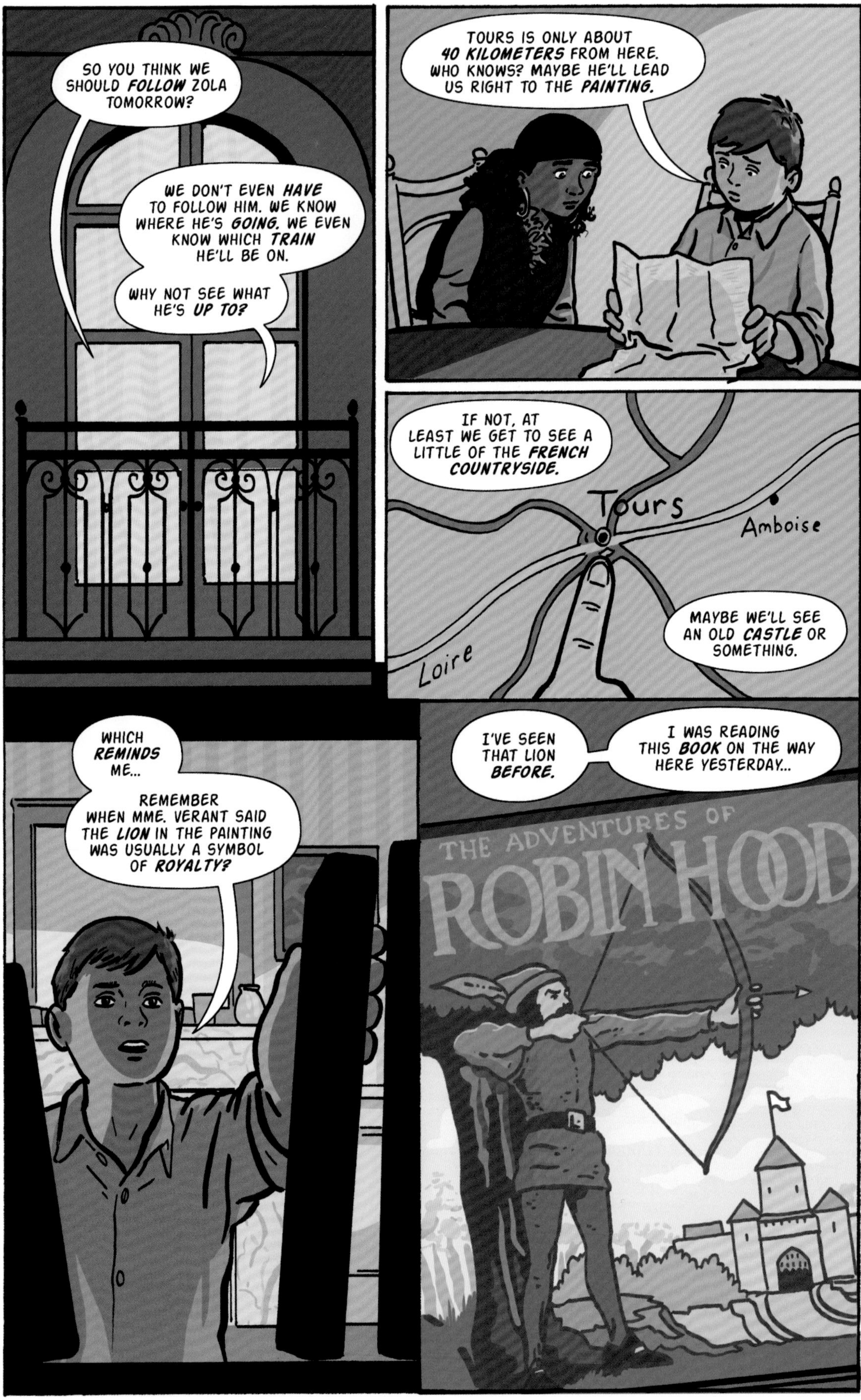
SO YOU THINK WE SHOULD FOLLOW ZOLA TOMORROW?
WE DON'T EVEN HAVE TO FOLLOW HIM. WE KNOW WHERE HE'S GOING. WE EVEN KNOW WHICH TRAIN HE'LL BE ON.
WHY NOT SEE WHAT HE'S UP TO?
TOURS IS ONLY ABOUT 40 KILOMETERS FROM HERE. WHO KNOWS? MAYBE HE'LL LEAD US RIGHT TO THE PAINTING.
IF NOT, AT LEAST WE GET TO SEE A LITTLE OF THE FRENCH COUNTRYSIDE.
Tours
Amboise
Loire
MAYBE WE'LL SEE AN OLD CASTLE OR SOMETHING.
WHICH REMINDS ME...
REMEMBER WHEN MME. VERANT SAID THE LION IN THE PAINTING WAS USUALLY A SYMBOL OF ROYALTY?
I'VE SEEN THAT LION BEFORE.
I WAS READING THIS BOOK ON THE WAY HERE YESTERDAY...
THE ADVENTURES OF
ROBIN HOOD

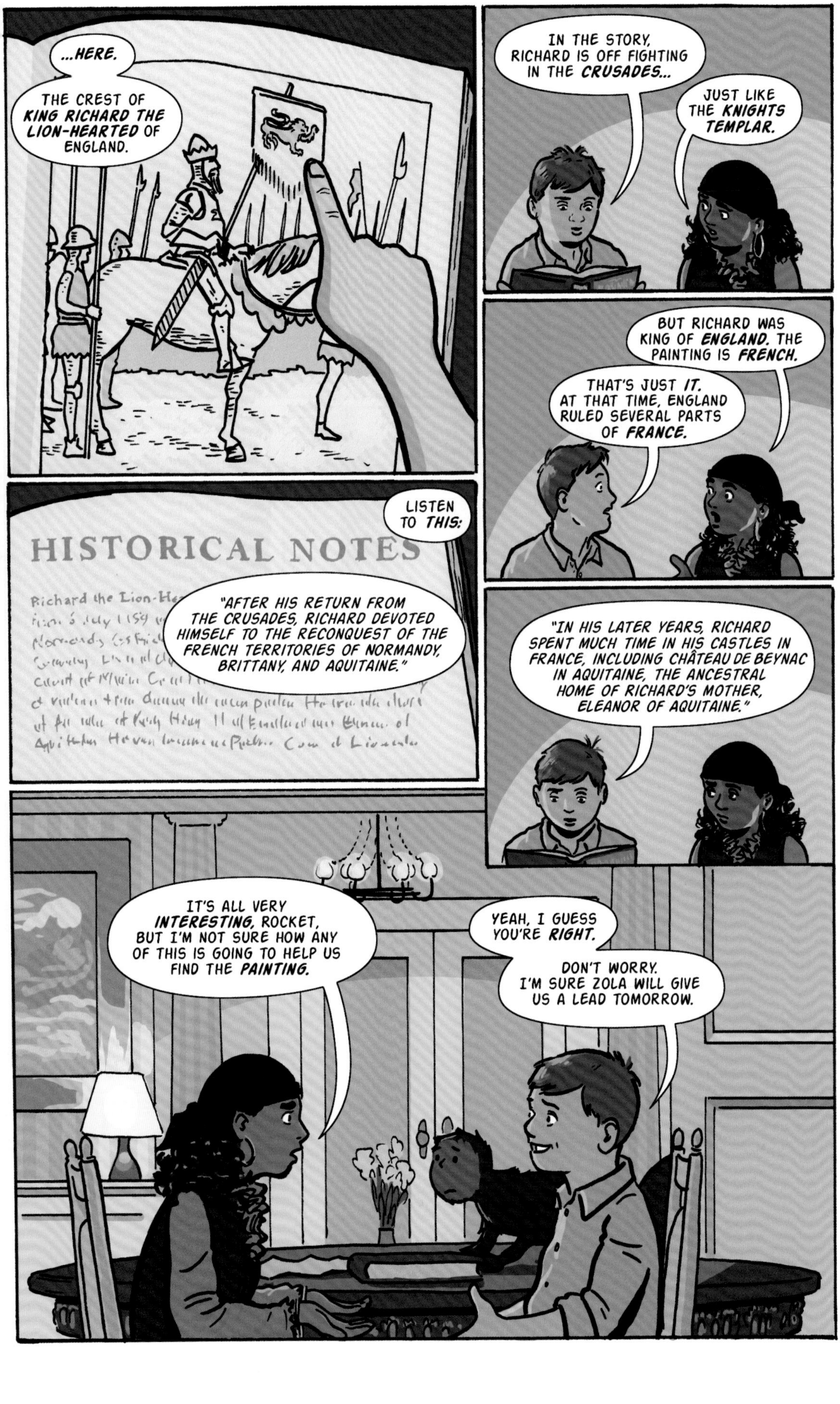

...HERE.
THE CREST OF KING RICHARD THE LION-HEARTED OF ENGLAND.
IN THE STORY, RICHARD IS OFF FIGHTING IN THE CRUSADES...
JUST LIKE THE KNIGHTS TEMPLAR.
BUT RICHARD WAS KING OF ENGLAND. THE PAINTING IS FRENCH.
THAT'S JUST IT. AT THAT TIME, ENGLAND RULED SEVERAL PARTS OF FRANCE.
LISTEN TO THIS:
HISTORICAL NOTES
"AFTER HIS RETURN FROM THE CRUSADES, RICHARD DEVOTED HIMSELF TO THE RECONQUEST OF THE FRENCH TERRITORIES OF NORMANDY, BRITTANY, AND AQUITAINE."
"IN HIS LATER YEARS, RICHARD SPENT MUCH TIME IN HIS CASTLES IN FRANCE, INCLUDING CHÂTEAU DE BEYNAC IN AQUITAINE, THE ANCESTRAL HOME OF RICHARD'S MOTHER, ELEANOR OF AQUITAINE."
IT'S ALL VERY INTERESTING, ROCKET, BUT I'M NOT SURE HOW ANY OF THIS IS GOING TO HELP US FIND THE PAINTING.
YEAH, I GUESS YOU'RE RIGHT.
DON'T WORRY. I'M SURE ZOLA WILL GIVE US A LEAD TOMORROW.

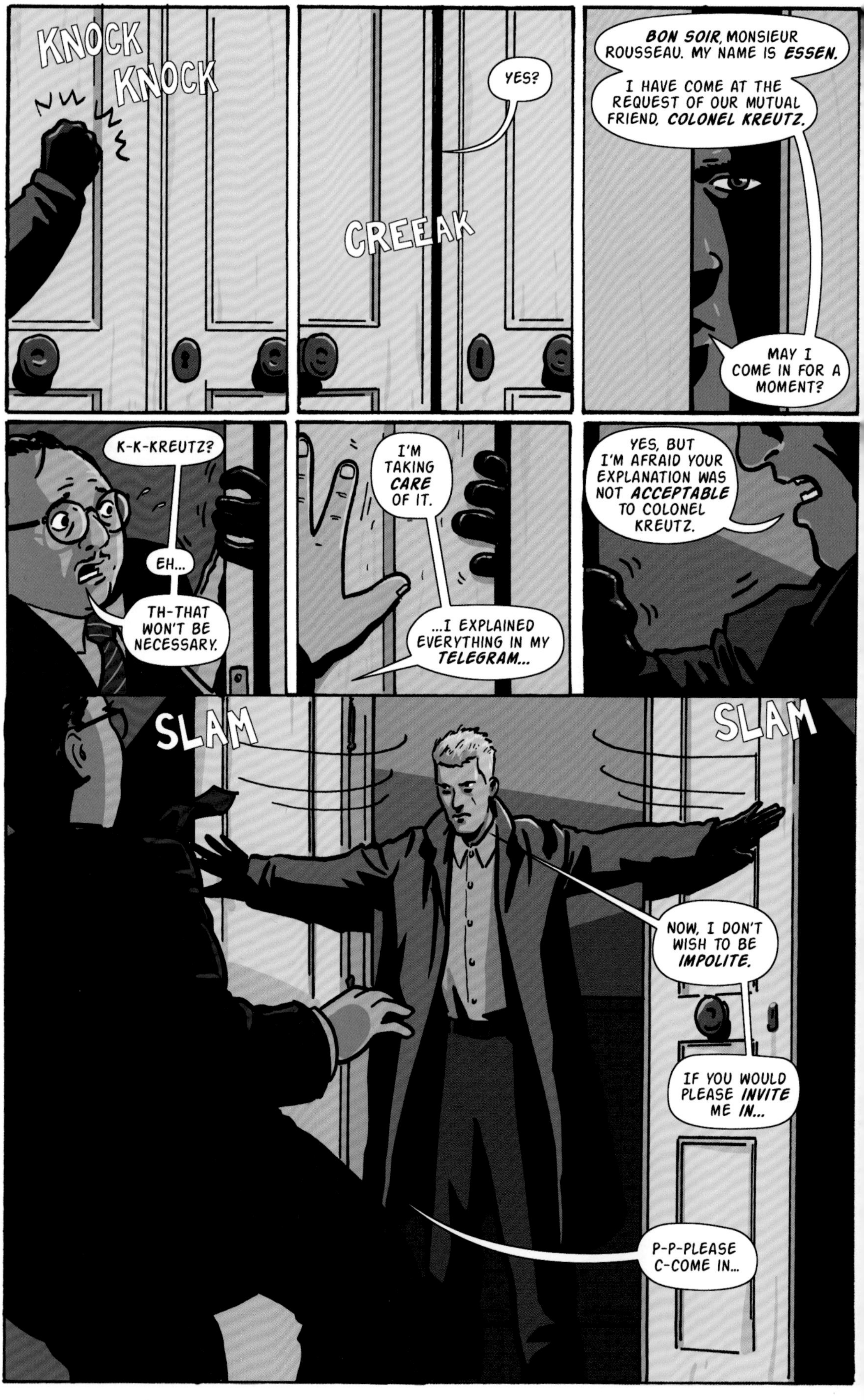
KNOCK KNOCK
YES?
CREEAK
BON SOIR, MONSIEUR ROUSSEAU. MY NAME IS ESSEN.
I HAVE COME AT THE REQUEST OF OUR MUTUAL FRIEND, COLONEL KREUTZ.
MAY I COME IN FOR A MOMENT?
K-K-KREUTZ?
EH...
TH-THAT WON'T BE NECESSARY.
I'M TAKING CARE OF IT.
...I EXPLAINED EVERYTHING IN MY TELEGRAM...
YES, BUT I'M AFRAID YOUR EXPLANATION WAS NOT ACCEPTABLE TO COLONEL KREUTZ.
SLAM
SLAM
NOW, I DON'T WISH TO BE IMPOLITE.
IF YOU WOULD PLEASE INVITE ME IN...
P-P-PLEASE C-COME IN...

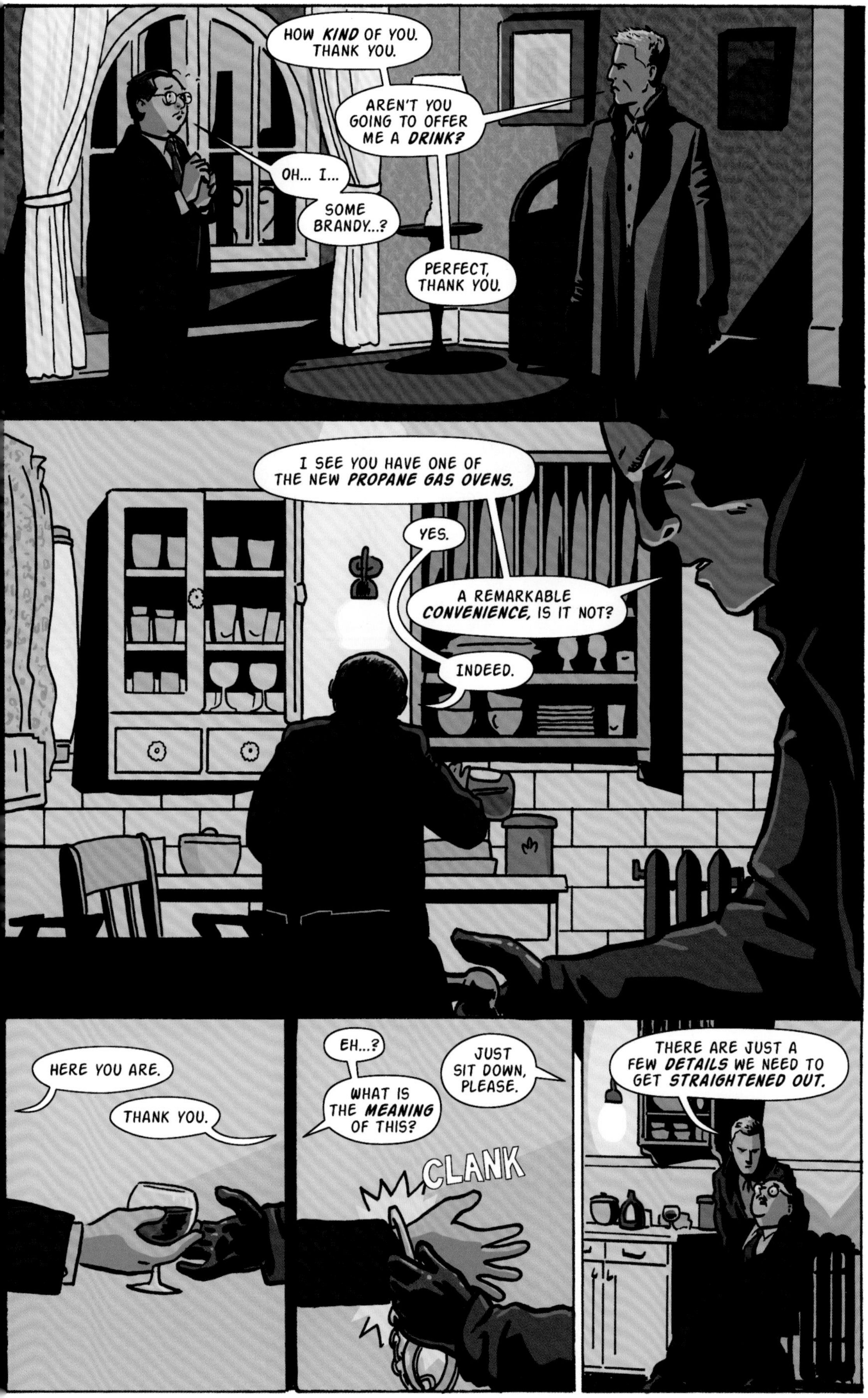

HOW KIND OF YOU. THANK YOU.
AREN'T YOU GOING TO OFFER ME A DRINK?
OH... I...
SOME BRANDY...?
PERFECT, THANK YOU.
I SEE YOU HAVE ONE OF THE NEW PROPANE GAS OVENS.
YES.
A REMARKABLE CONVENIENCE, IS IT NOT?
INDEED.
HERE YOU ARE.
THANK YOU.
EH...?
WHAT IS THE MEANING OF THIS?
JUST SIT DOWN, PLEASE.
CLANK
THERE ARE JUST A FEW DETAILS WE NEED TO GET STRAIGHTENED OUT.

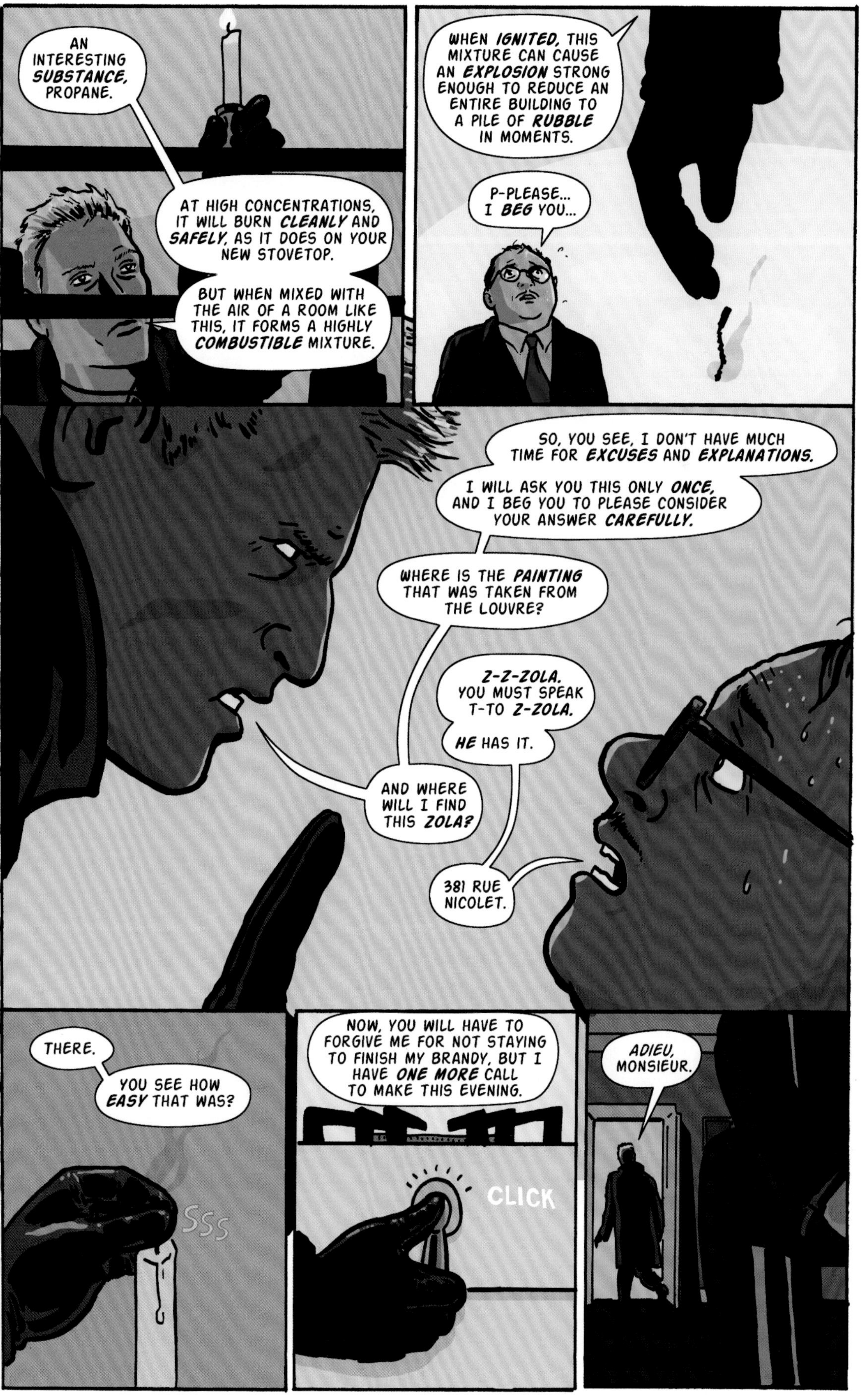
AN INTERESTING SUBSTANCE, PROPANE.
AT HIGH CONCENTRATIONS, IT WILL BURN CLEANLY AND SAFELY, AS IT DOES ON YOUR NEW STOVETOP.
BUT WHEN MIXED WITH THE AIR OF A ROOM LIKE THIS, IT FORMS A HIGHLY COMBUSTIBLE MIXTURE.
WHEN IGNITED, THIS MIXTURE CAN CAUSE AN EXPLOSION STRONG ENOUGH TO REDUCE AN ENTIRE BUILDING TO A PILE OF RUBBLE IN MOMENTS.
P-PLEASE... I BEG YOU...
SO, YOU SEE, I DON'T HAVE MUCH TIME FOR EXCUSES AND EXPLANATIONS.
I WILL ASK YOU THIS ONLY ONCE, AND I BEG YOU TO PLEASE CONSIDER YOUR ANSWER CAREFULLY.
WHERE IS THE PAINTING THAT WAS TAKEN FROM THE LOUVRE?
Z-Z-ZOLA. YOU MUST SPEAK T-TO Z-ZOLA.
HE HAS IT.
AND WHERE WILL I FIND THIS ZOLA?
381 RUE NICOLET.
THERE.
YOU SEE HOW EASY THAT WAS?
SSS
NOW, YOU WILL HAVE TO FORGIVE ME FOR NOT STAYING TO FINISH MY BRANDY, BUT I HAVE ONE MORE CALL TO MAKE THIS EVENING.
CLICK
ADIEU, MONSIEUR.

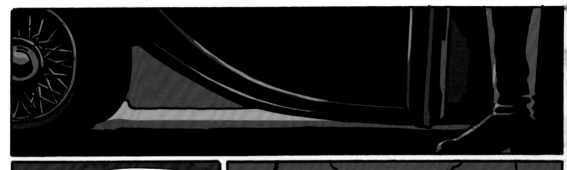

THIS WAY, GENERAL.

I STILL DON'T UNDERSTAND WHY ALL OF THIS *CLOAK AND DAGGER* BUSINESS IS NECESSARY.

PLEASE ACCEPT MY *SINCEREST* APOLOGIES, GENERAL, BUT COLONEL KREUTZ IS VERY...

...CAREFUL, SHALL WE SAY.

KNOCK KNOCK

SSSHHK

GENERAL.

WELCOME.

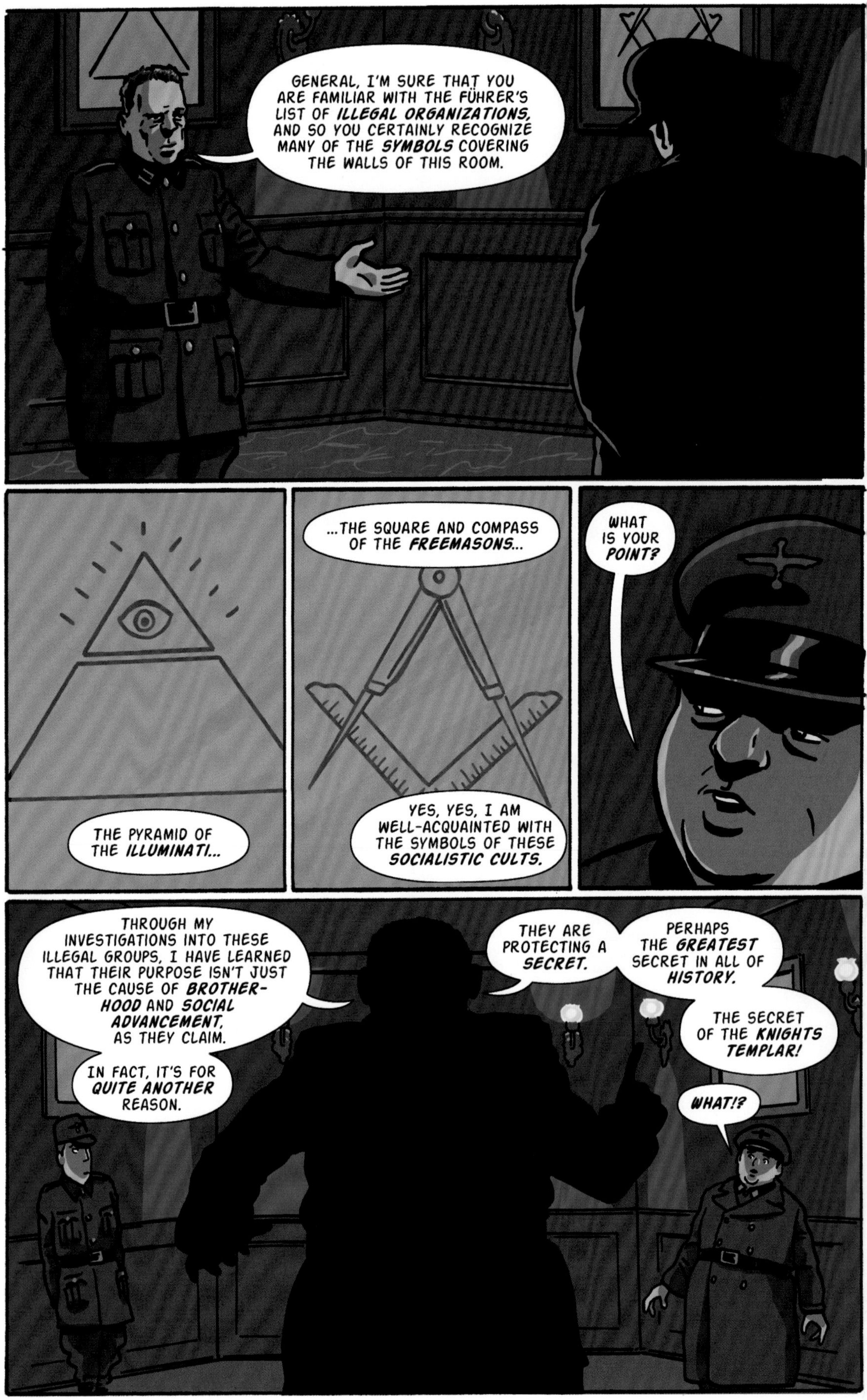
GENERAL, I'M SURE THAT YOU ARE FAMILIAR WITH THE FÜHRER'S LIST OF ILLEGAL ORGANIZATIONS, AND SO YOU CERTAINLY RECOGNIZE MANY OF THE SYMBOLS COVERING THE WALLS OF THIS ROOM.
THE PYRAMID OF THE ILLUMINATI...
...THE SQUARE AND COMPASS OF THE FREEMASONS...
YES, YES, I AM WELL-ACQUAINTED WITH THE SYMBOLS OF THESE SOCIALISTIC CULTS.
WHAT IS YOUR POINT?
THROUGH MY INVESTIGATIONS INTO THESE ILLEGAL GROUPS, I HAVE LEARNED THAT THEIR PURPOSE ISN'T JUST THE CAUSE OF BROTHER-HOOD AND SOCIAL ADVANCEMENT, AS THEY CLAIM.
IN FACT, IT'S FOR QUITE ANOTHER REASON.
THEY ARE PROTECTING A SECRET.
PERHAPS THE GREATEST SECRET IN ALL OF HISTORY.
THE SECRET OF THE KNIGHTS TEMPLAR!
WHAT!?

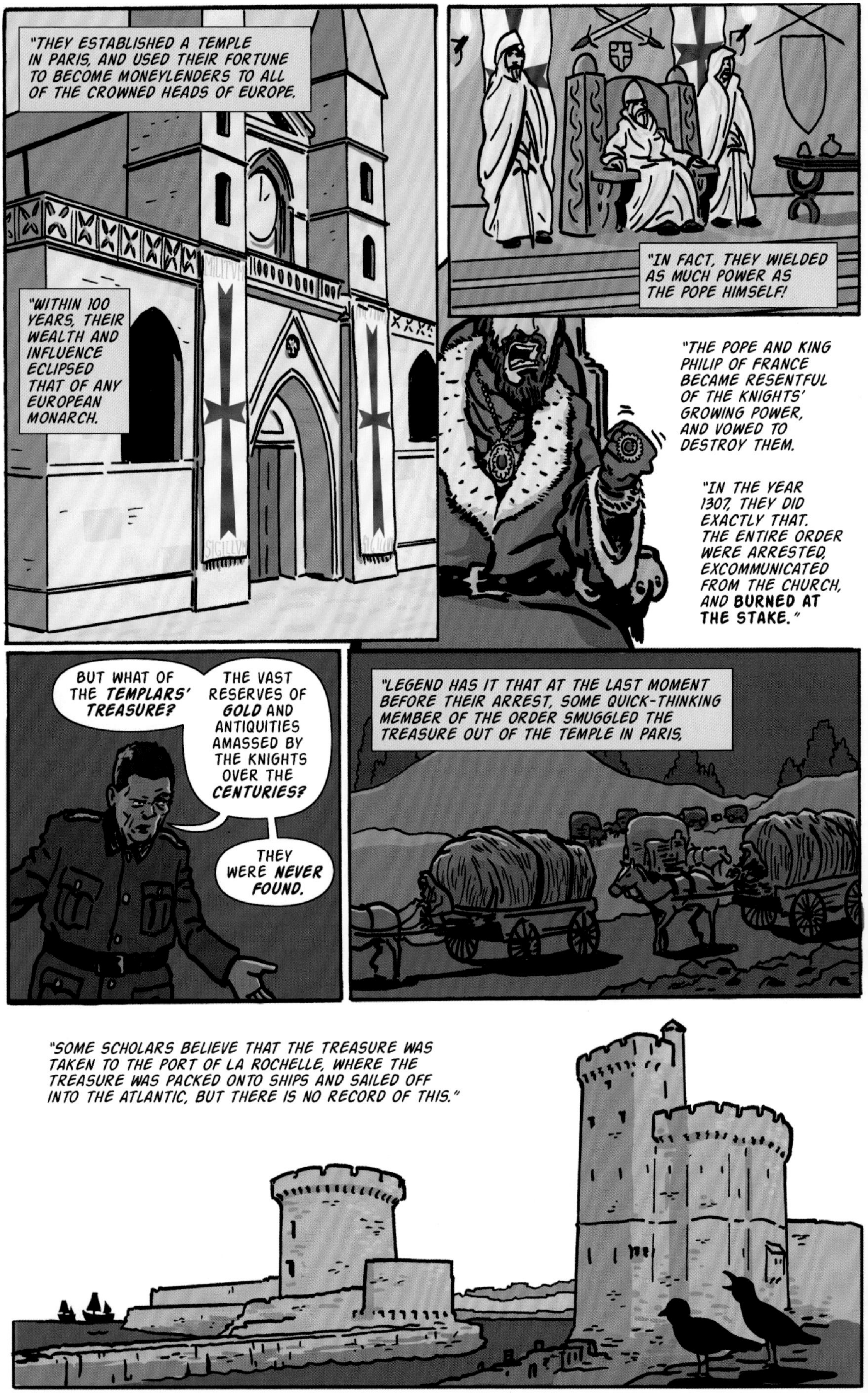
"THEY ESTABLISHED A TEMPLE IN PARIS, AND USED THEIR FORTUNE TO BECOME MONEYLENDERS TO ALL OF THE CROWNED HEADS OF EUROPE.
"WITHIN 100 YEARS, THEIR WEALTH AND INFLUENCE ECLIPSED THAT OF ANY EUROPEAN MONARCH.
"IN FACT, THEY WIELDED AS MUCH POWER AS THE POPE HIMSELF!
"THE POPE AND KING PHILIP OF FRANCE BECAME RESENTFUL OF THE KNIGHTS' GROWING POWER, AND VOWED TO DESTROY THEM.
"IN THE YEAR 1307, THEY DID EXACTLY THAT. THE ENTIRE ORDER WERE ARRESTED, EXCOMMUNICATED FROM THE CHURCH, AND **BURNED AT THE STAKE.**"
BUT WHAT OF THE ***TEMPLARS' TREASURE?***
THE VAST RESERVES OF ***GOLD*** AND ANTIQUITIES AMASSED BY THE KNIGHTS OVER THE ***CENTURIES?***
THEY WERE ***NEVER FOUND.***
"LEGEND HAS IT THAT AT THE LAST MOMENT BEFORE THEIR ARREST, SOME QUICK-THINKING MEMBER OF THE ORDER SMUGGLED THE TREASURE OUT OF THE TEMPLE IN PARIS,
"SOME SCHOLARS BELIEVE THAT THE TREASURE WAS TAKEN TO THE PORT OF LA ROCHELLE, WHERE THE TREASURE WAS PACKED ONTO SHIPS AND SAILED OFF INTO THE ATLANTIC, BUT THERE IS NO RECORD OF THIS."

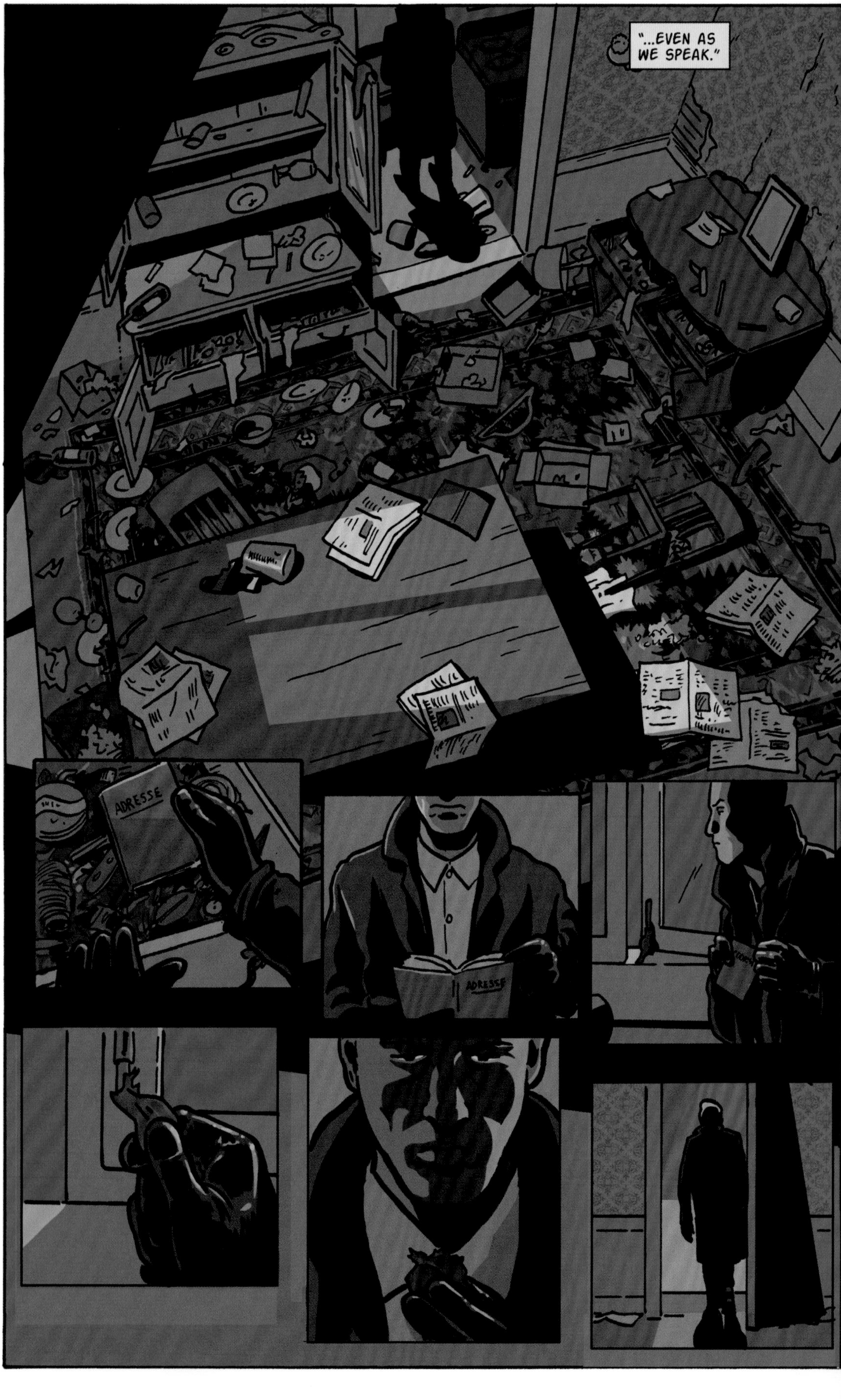
"...EVEN AS WE SPEAK."
ADRESSE
ADRESSE

CHAPTER FIVE

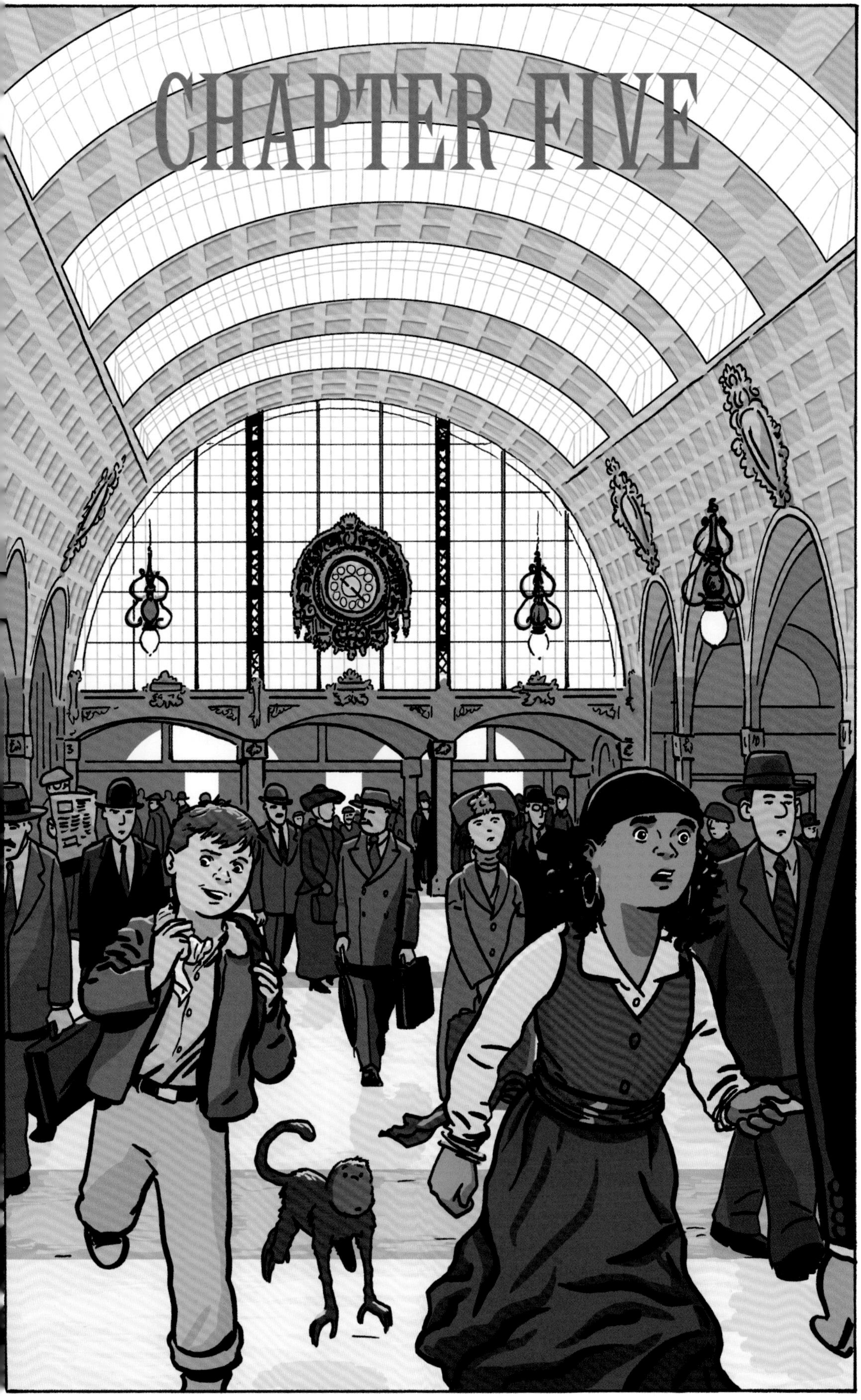

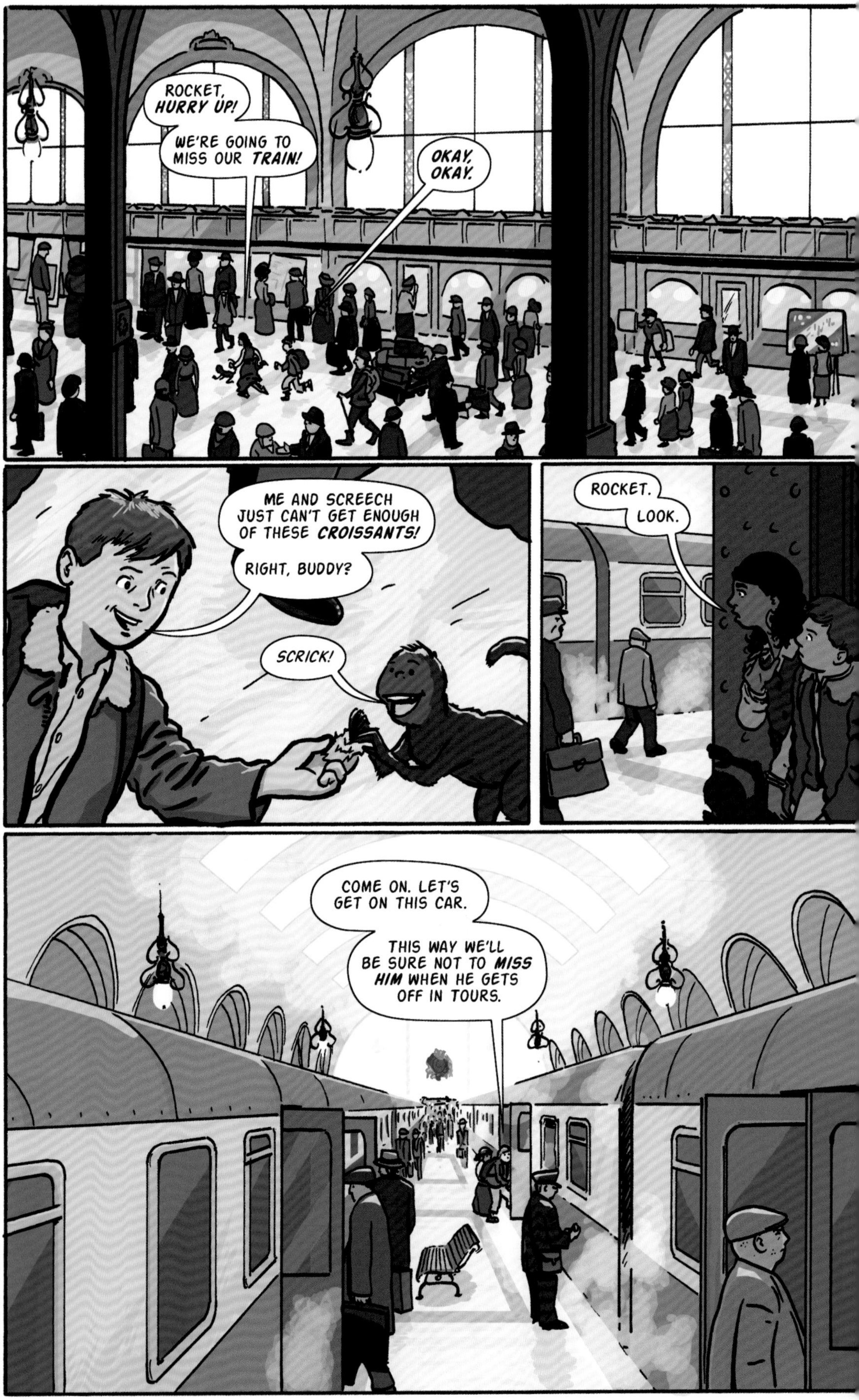
ROCKET, HURRY UP!
WE'RE GOING TO MISS OUR TRAIN!
OKAY, OKAY.
ME AND SCREECH JUST CAN'T GET ENOUGH OF THESE CROISSANTS!
RIGHT, BUDDY?
SCRICK!
ROCKET.
LOOK.
COME ON. LET'S GET ON THIS CAR.
THIS WAY WE'LL BE SURE NOT TO MISS HIM WHEN HE GETS OFF IN TOURS.

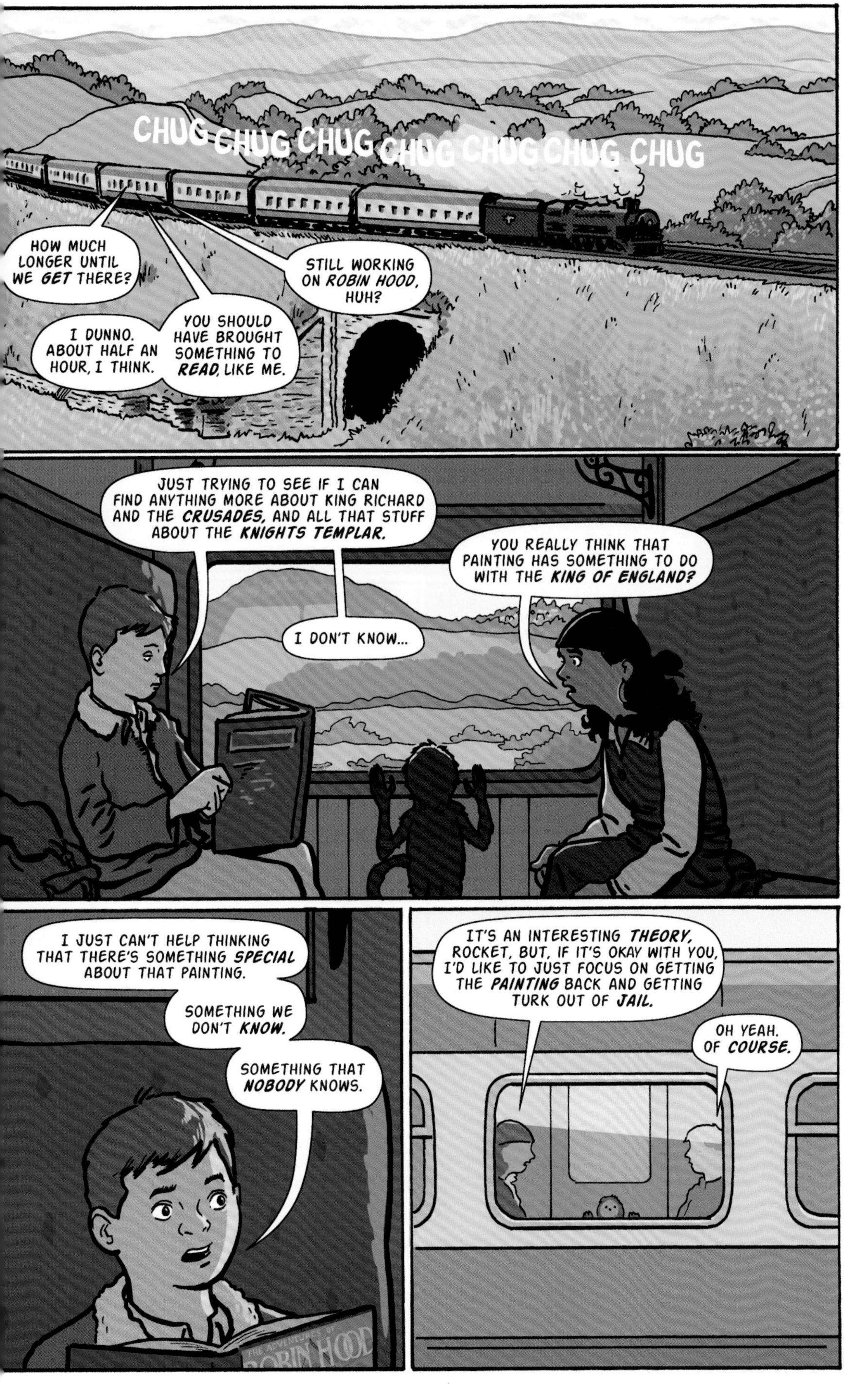
CHUG CHUG CHUG CHUG CHUG CHUG CHUG
HOW MUCH LONGER UNTIL WE *GET* THERE?
I DUNNO. ABOUT HALF AN HOUR, I THINK.
YOU SHOULD HAVE BROUGHT SOMETHING TO *READ*, LIKE ME.
STILL WORKING ON *ROBIN HOOD*, HUH?
JUST TRYING TO SEE IF I CAN FIND ANYTHING MORE ABOUT KING RICHARD AND THE *CRUSADES*, AND ALL THAT STUFF ABOUT THE *KNIGHTS TEMPLAR*.
I DON'T KNOW...
YOU REALLY THINK THAT PAINTING HAS SOMETHING TO DO WITH THE *KING OF ENGLAND?*
I JUST CAN'T HELP THINKING THAT THERE'S SOMETHING *SPECIAL* ABOUT THAT PAINTING.
SOMETHING WE DON'T *KNOW*.
SOMETHING THAT *NOBODY* KNOWS.
IT'S AN INTERESTING *THEORY*, ROCKET, BUT, IF IT'S OKAY WITH YOU, I'D LIKE TO JUST FOCUS ON GETTING THE *PAINTING* BACK AND GETTING TURK OUT OF *JAIL*.
OH YEAH. OF *COURSE*.

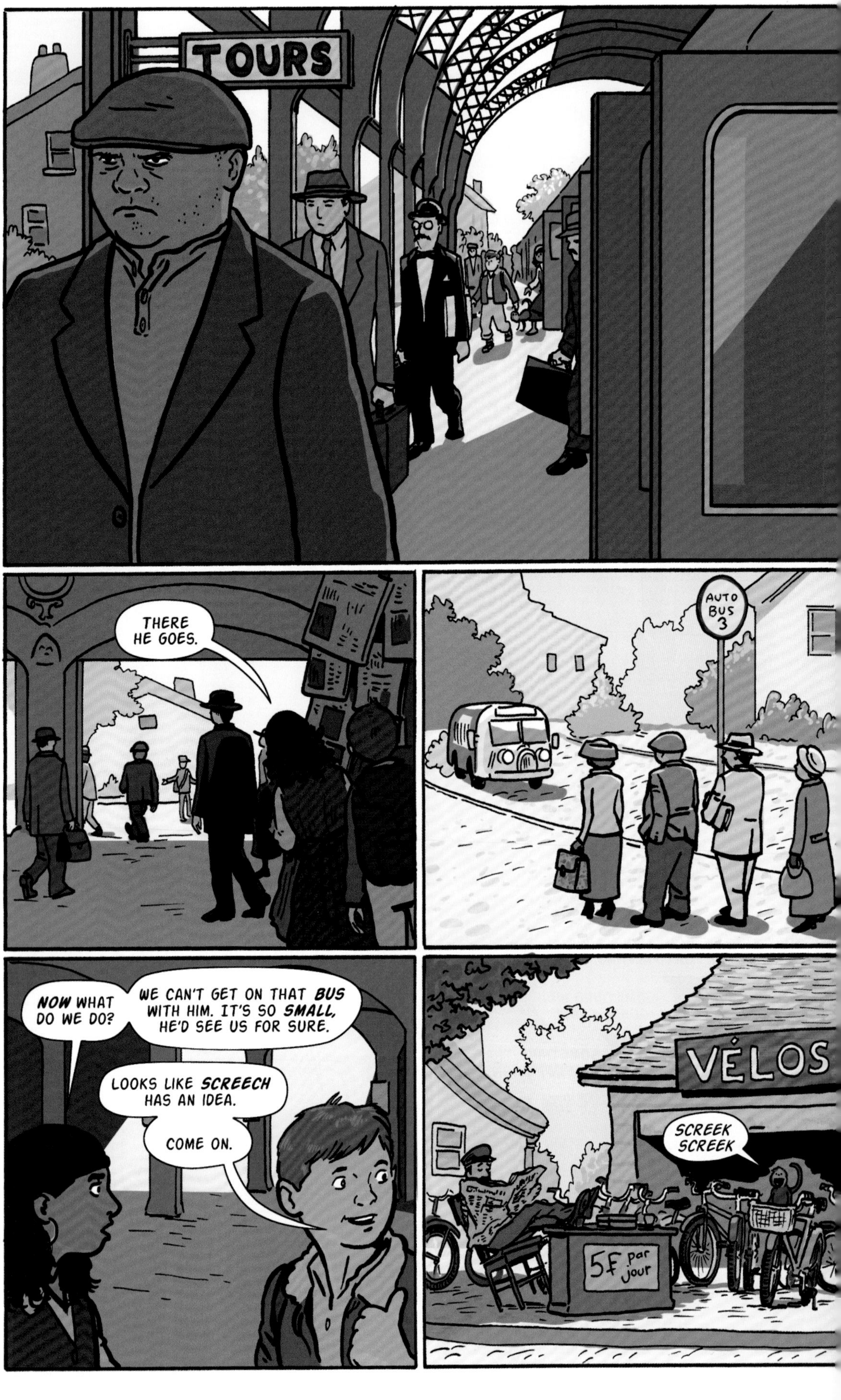

TOURS
THERE HE GOES.
AUTO BUS 3
NOW WHAT DO WE DO?
WE CAN'T GET ON THAT BUS WITH HIM. IT'S SO SMALL, HE'D SEE US FOR SURE.
LOOKS LIKE SCREECH HAS AN IDEA.
COME ON.
VÉLOS
SCREEK SCREEK
5F par jour

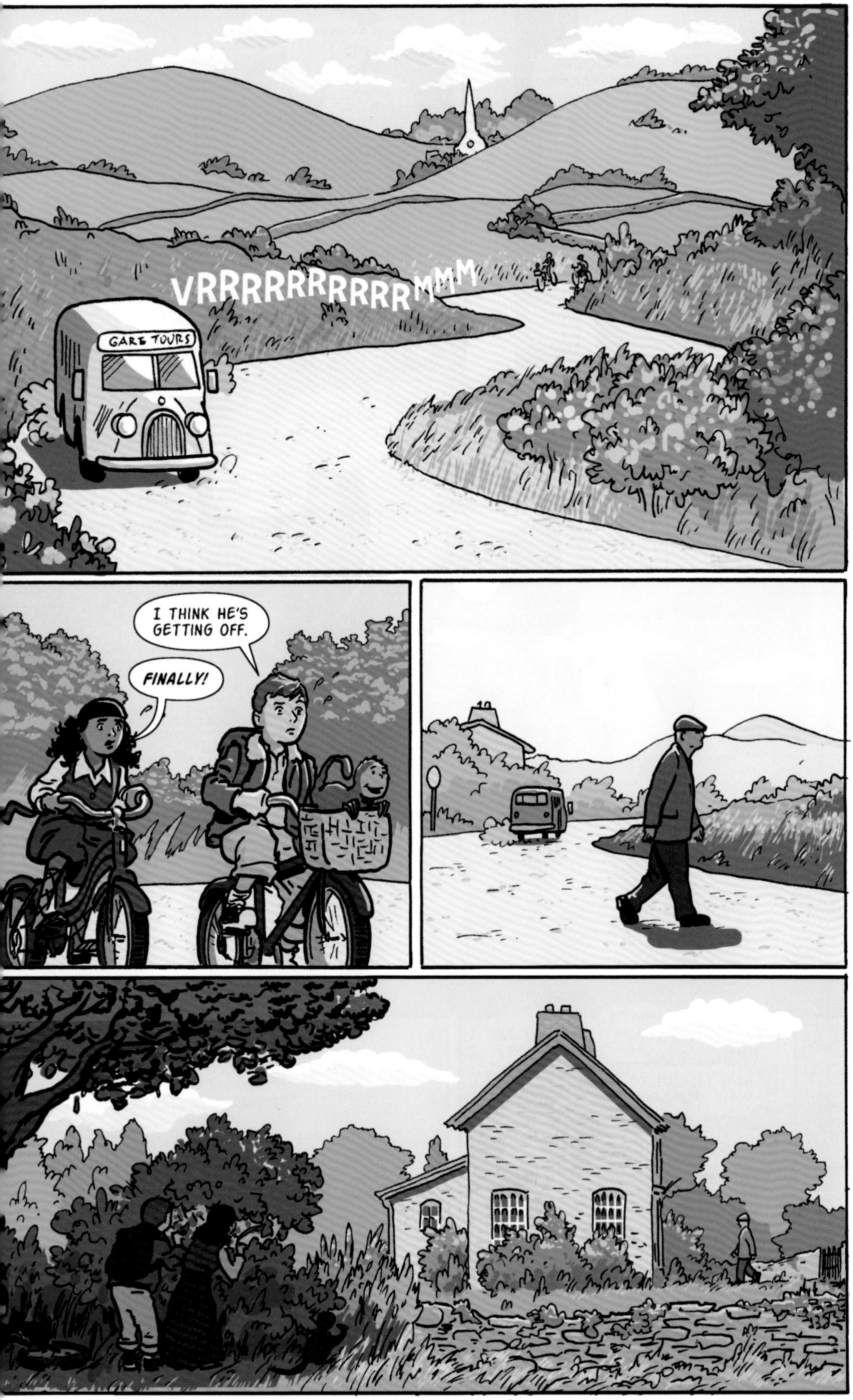
VRRRRRRRRRRRMMM
GARE TOURS
I THINK HE'S GETTING OFF.
FINALLY!

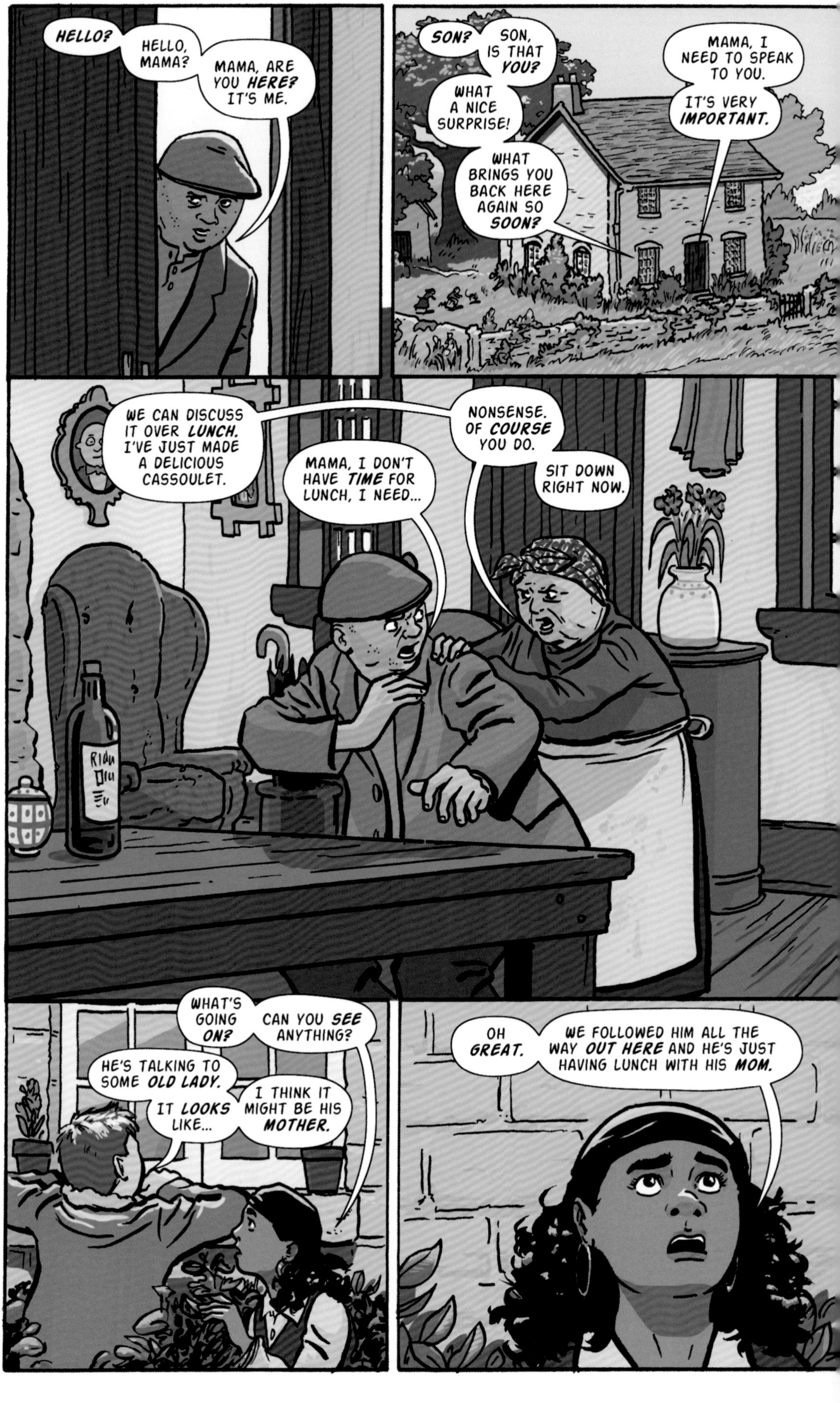
HELLO?
HELLO, MAMA?
MAMA, ARE YOU HERE? IT'S ME.
SON?
SON, IS THAT YOU?
WHAT A NICE SURPRISE!
WHAT BRINGS YOU BACK HERE AGAIN SO SOON?
MAMA, I NEED TO SPEAK TO YOU.
IT'S VERY IMPORTANT.
WE CAN DISCUSS IT OVER LUNCH. I'VE JUST MADE A DELICIOUS CASSOULET.
MAMA, I DON'T HAVE TIME FOR LUNCH, I NEED...
NONSENSE. OF COURSE YOU DO.
SIT DOWN RIGHT NOW.
WHAT'S GOING ON?
CAN YOU SEE ANYTHING?
HE'S TALKING TO SOME OLD LADY.
IT LOOKS LIKE...
I THINK IT MIGHT BE HIS MOTHER.
OH GREAT.
WE FOLLOWED HIM ALL THE WAY OUT HERE AND HE'S JUST HAVING LUNCH WITH HIS MOM.

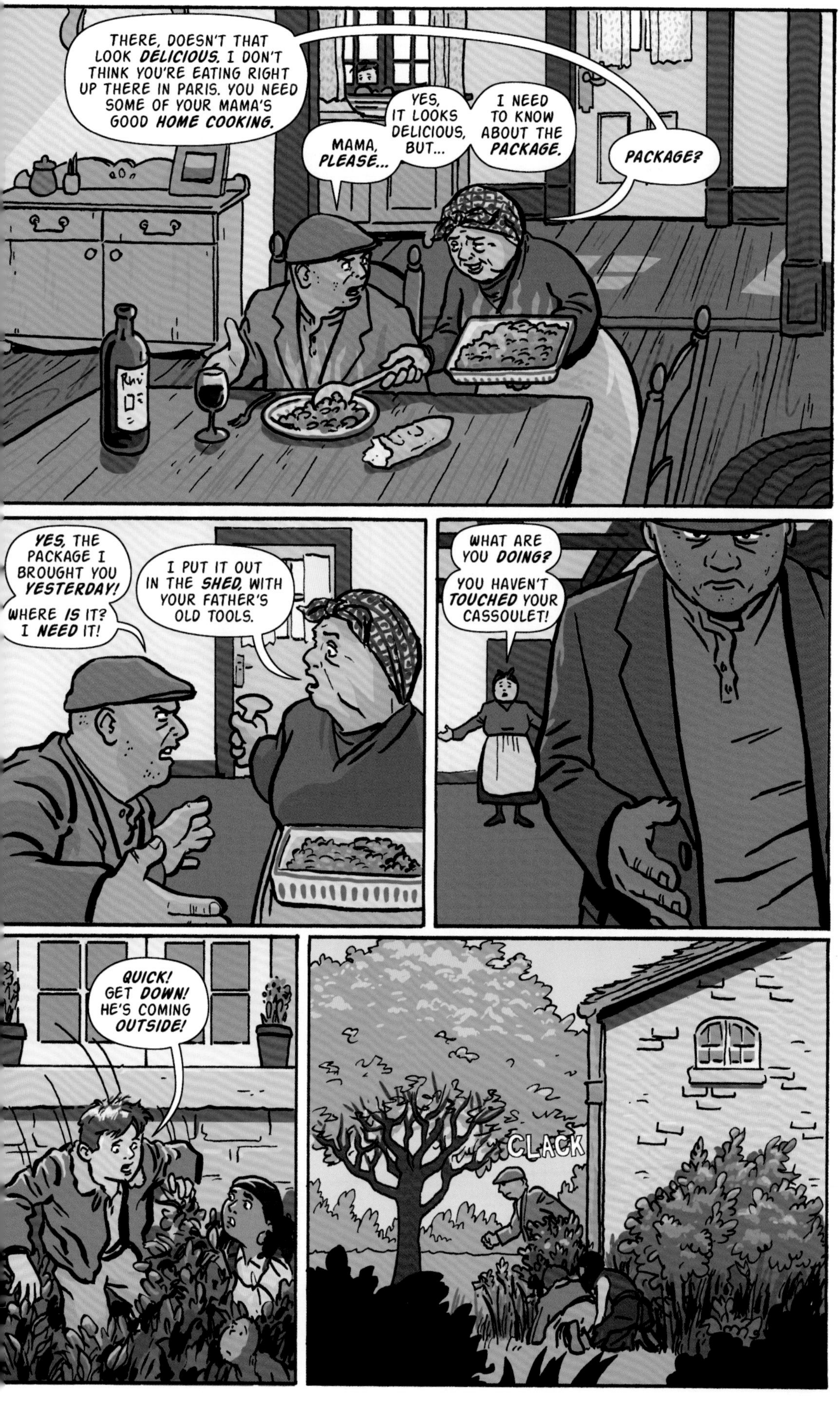

THERE, DOESN'T THAT LOOK DELICIOUS. I DON'T THINK YOU'RE EATING RIGHT UP THERE IN PARIS. YOU NEED SOME OF YOUR MAMA'S GOOD HOME COOKING.
MAMA, PLEASE...
YES, IT LOOKS DELICIOUS, BUT...
I NEED TO KNOW ABOUT THE PACKAGE.
PACKAGE?
YES, THE PACKAGE I BROUGHT YOU YESTERDAY!
WHERE IS IT? I NEED IT!
I PUT IT OUT IN THE SHED, WITH YOUR FATHER'S OLD TOOLS.
WHAT ARE YOU DOING?
YOU HAVEN'T TOUCHED YOUR CASSOULET!
QUICK! GET DOWN! HE'S COMING OUTSIDE!
CLACK

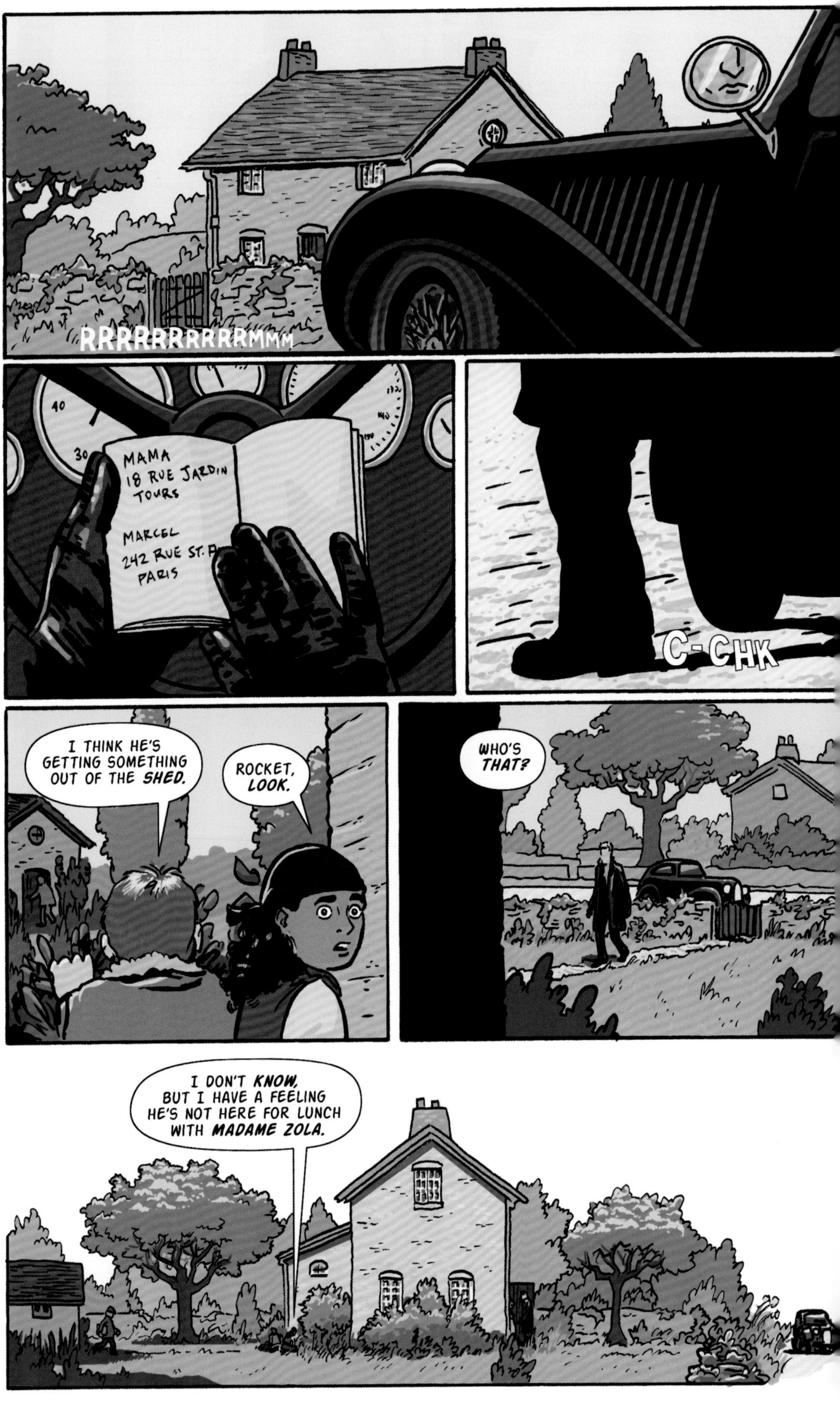
RRRRRRRRRRRMMM
MAMA
18 RUE JARDIN
TOURS
MARCEL
242 RUE ST. P
PARIS
C-CHK
I THINK HE'S GETTING SOMETHING OUT OF THE SHED.
ROCKET, LOOK.
WHO'S THAT?
I DON'T KNOW, BUT I HAVE A FEELING HE'S NOT HERE FOR LUNCH WITH MADAME ZOLA.

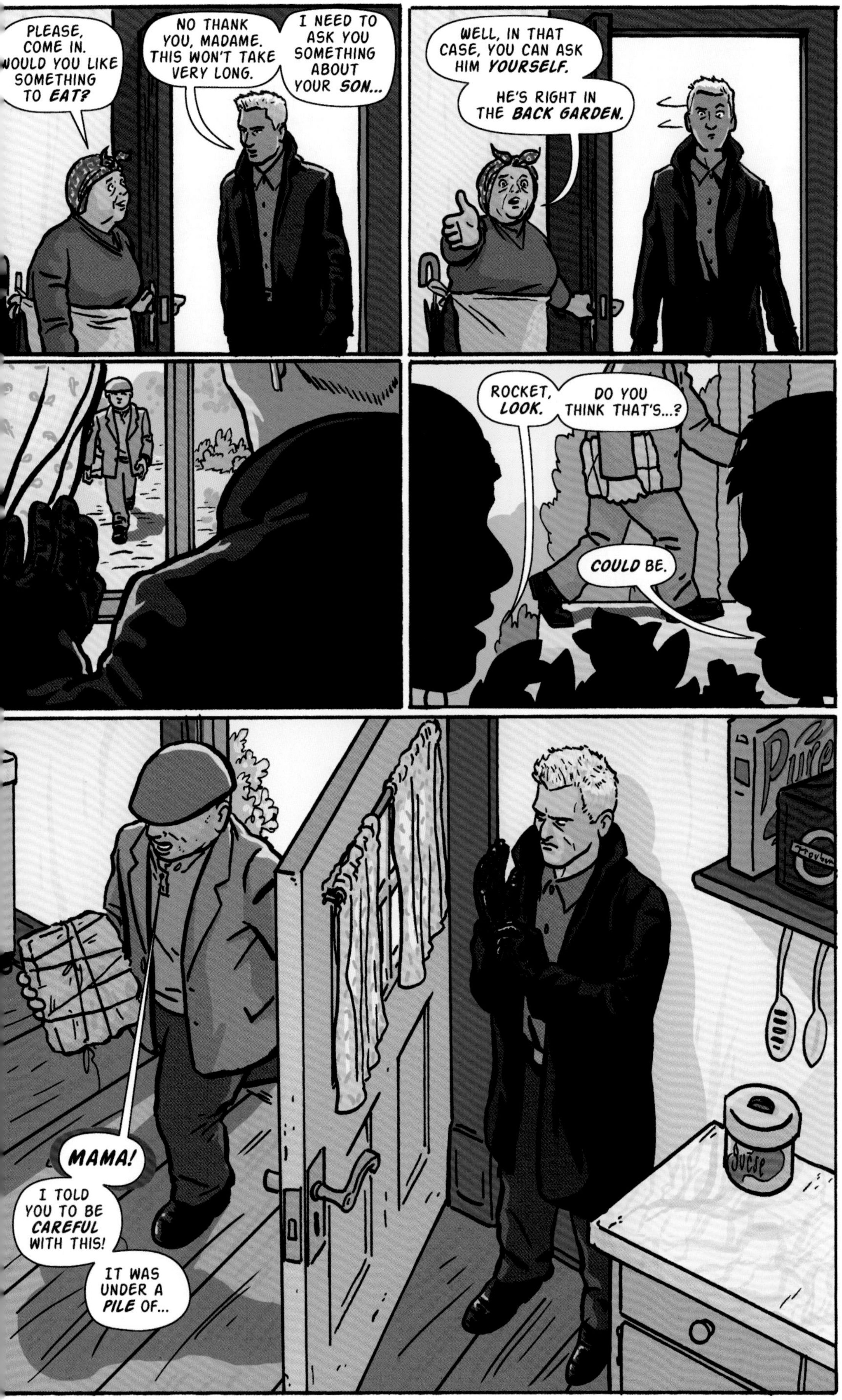
PLEASE, COME IN. WOULD YOU LIKE SOMETHING TO EAT?
NO THANK YOU, MADAME. THIS WON'T TAKE VERY LONG.
I NEED TO ASK YOU SOMETHING ABOUT YOUR SON...
WELL, IN THAT CASE, YOU CAN ASK HIM YOURSELF.
HE'S RIGHT IN THE BACK GARDEN.
ROCKET, LOOK.
DO YOU THINK THAT'S...?
COULD BE.
MAMA!
I TOLD YOU TO BE CAREFUL WITH THIS!
IT WAS UNDER A PILE OF...

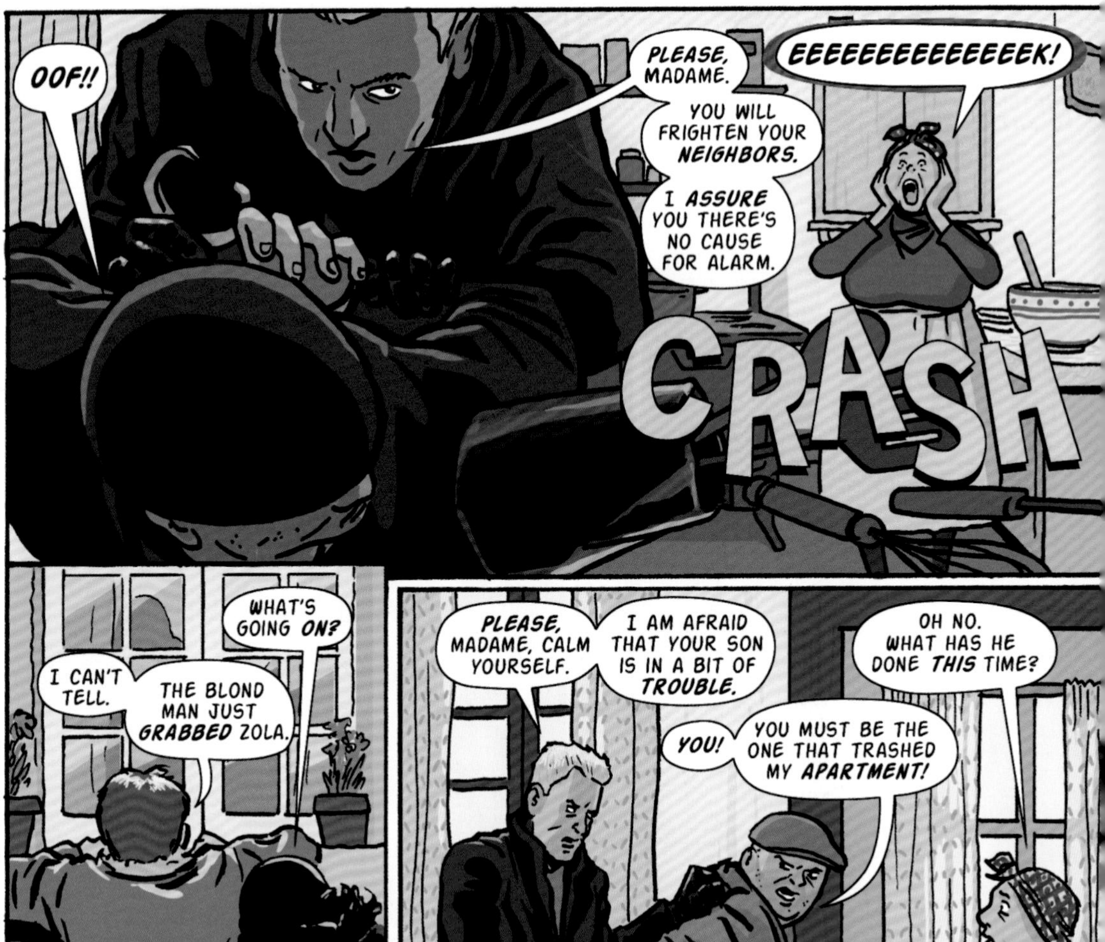
OOF!!
PLEASE, MADAME.
YOU WILL FRIGHTEN YOUR NEIGHBORS.
I ASSURE YOU THERE'S NO CAUSE FOR ALARM.
EEEEEEEEEEEEEEK!
CRASH
WHAT'S GOING ON?
I CAN'T TELL.
THE BLOND MAN JUST GRABBED ZOLA.
PLEASE, MADAME, CALM YOURSELF.
I AM AFRAID THAT YOUR SON IS IN A BIT OF TROUBLE.
OH NO. WHAT HAS HE DONE THIS TIME?
YOU!
YOU MUST BE THE ONE THAT TRASHED MY APARTMENT!
IT IS A SMALL MATTER, MADAME.
I AM SURE HE WILL COOPERATE, AND THERE WILL BE NO FURTHER TROUBLE.
ISN'T THAT RIGHT, MONSIEUR ZOLA?
IT WOULD BE A SHAME IF I HAD TO COME BACK HERE AND DISTURB YOUR POOR MOTHER AGAIN.

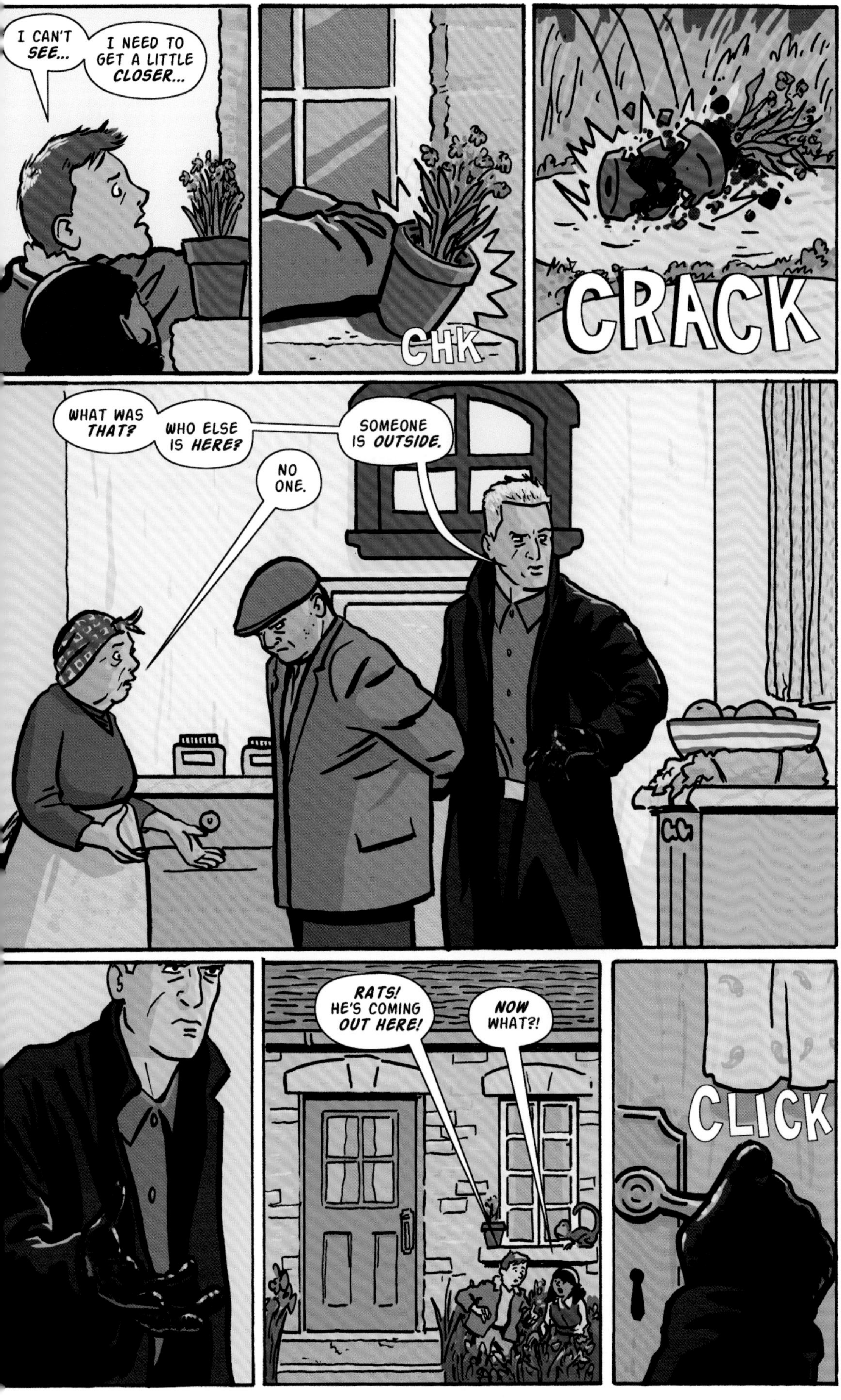
I CAN'T SEE...
I NEED TO GET A LITTLE CLOSER...
CHK
CRACK
WHAT WAS THAT?
WHO ELSE IS HERE?
SOMEONE IS OUTSIDE.
NO ONE.
RATS! HE'S COMING OUT HERE!
NOW WHAT?!
CLICK

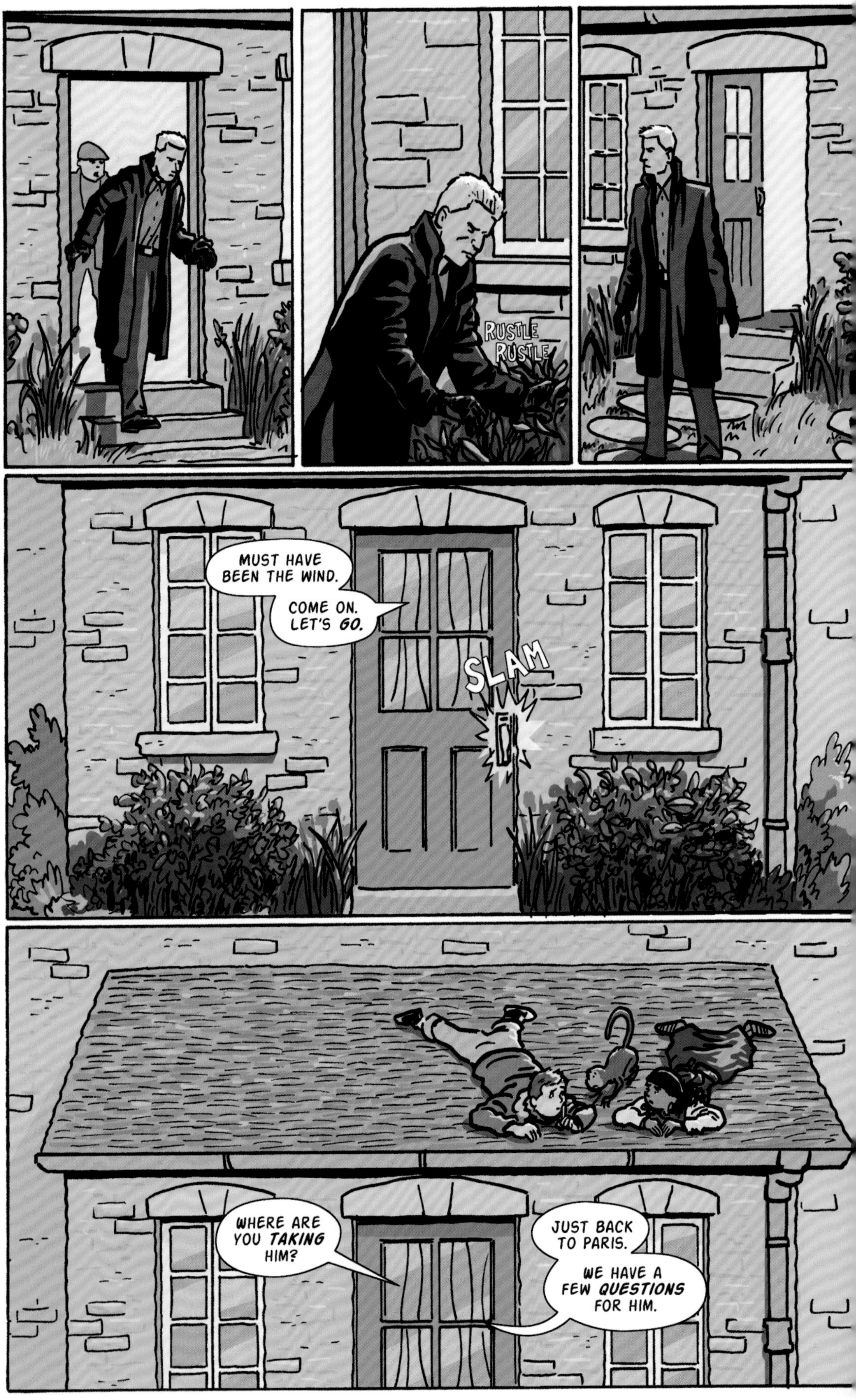
RUSTLE RUSTLE
MUST HAVE BEEN THE WIND.
COME ON. LET'S *GO.*
SLAM
WHERE ARE YOU *TAKING* HIM?
JUST BACK TO PARIS.
WE HAVE A FEW *QUESTIONS* FOR HIM.

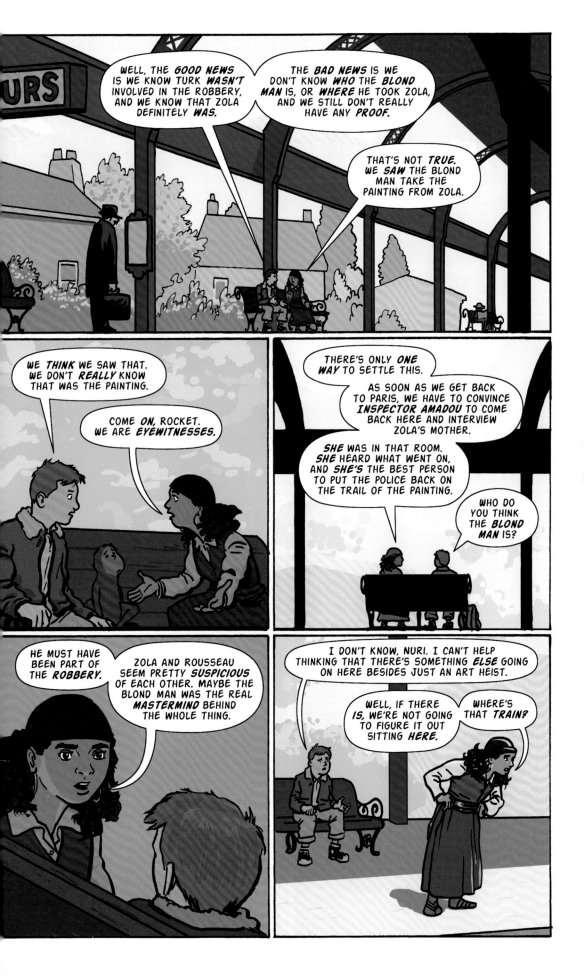

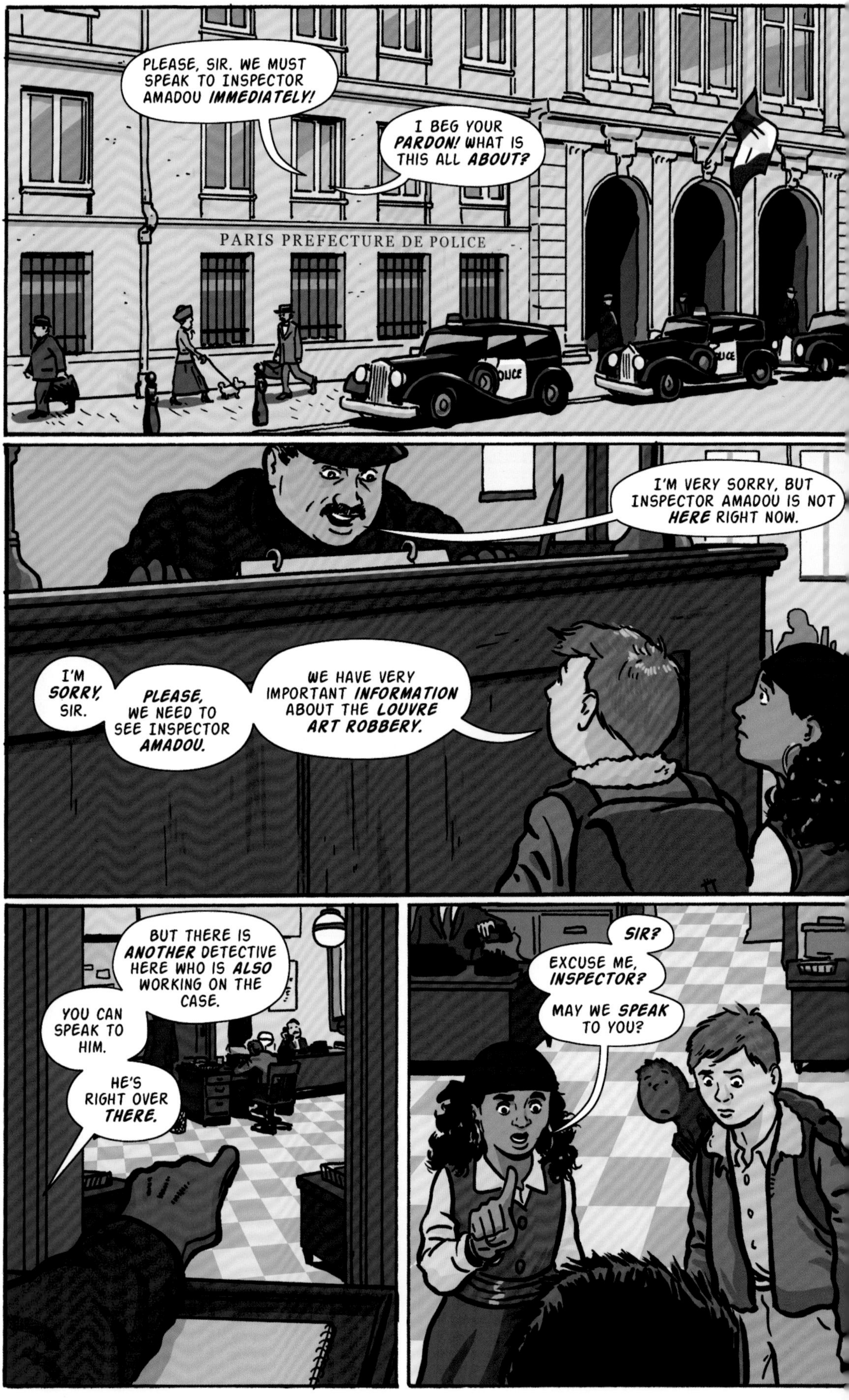

PLEASE, SIR. WE MUST SPEAK TO INSPECTOR AMADOU IMMEDIATELY!
I BEG YOUR PARDON! WHAT IS THIS ALL ABOUT?
PARIS PREFECTURE DE POLICE
I'M VERY SORRY, BUT INSPECTOR AMADOU IS NOT HERE RIGHT NOW.
I'M SORRY, SIR.
PLEASE, WE NEED TO SEE INSPECTOR AMADOU.
WE HAVE VERY IMPORTANT INFORMATION ABOUT THE LOUVRE ART ROBBERY.
BUT THERE IS ANOTHER DETECTIVE HERE WHO IS ALSO WORKING ON THE CASE.
YOU CAN SPEAK TO HIM.
HE'S RIGHT OVER THERE.
SIR?
EXCUSE ME, INSPECTOR?
MAY WE SPEAK TO YOU?

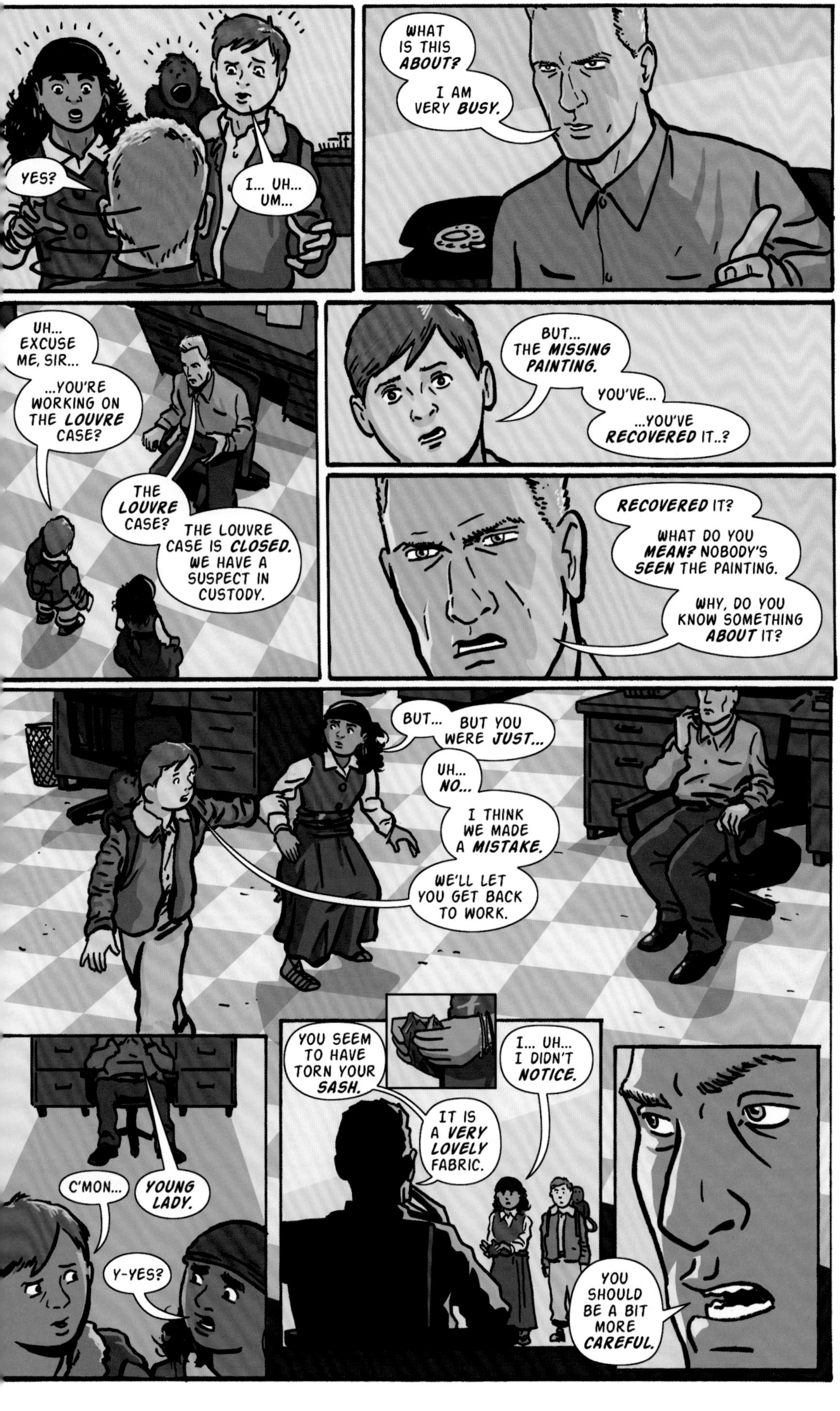
YES?
I... UH... UM...
WHAT IS THIS ABOUT?
I AM VERY BUSY.
UH... EXCUSE ME, SIR...
...YOU'RE WORKING ON THE LOUVRE CASE?
THE LOUVRE CASE?
THE LOUVRE CASE IS CLOSED. WE HAVE A SUSPECT IN CUSTODY.
BUT... THE MISSING PAINTING.
YOU'VE...
...YOU'VE RECOVERED IT..?
RECOVERED IT?
WHAT DO YOU MEAN? NOBODY'S SEEN THE PAINTING.
WHY, DO YOU KNOW SOMETHING ABOUT IT?
BUT... BUT YOU WERE JUST...
UH... NO...
I THINK WE MADE A MISTAKE.
WE'LL LET YOU GET BACK TO WORK.
C'MON...
YOUNG LADY.
Y-YES?
YOU SEEM TO HAVE TORN YOUR SASH.
IT IS A VERY LOVELY FABRIC.
I... UH... I DIDN'T NOTICE.
YOU SHOULD BE A BIT MORE CAREFUL.

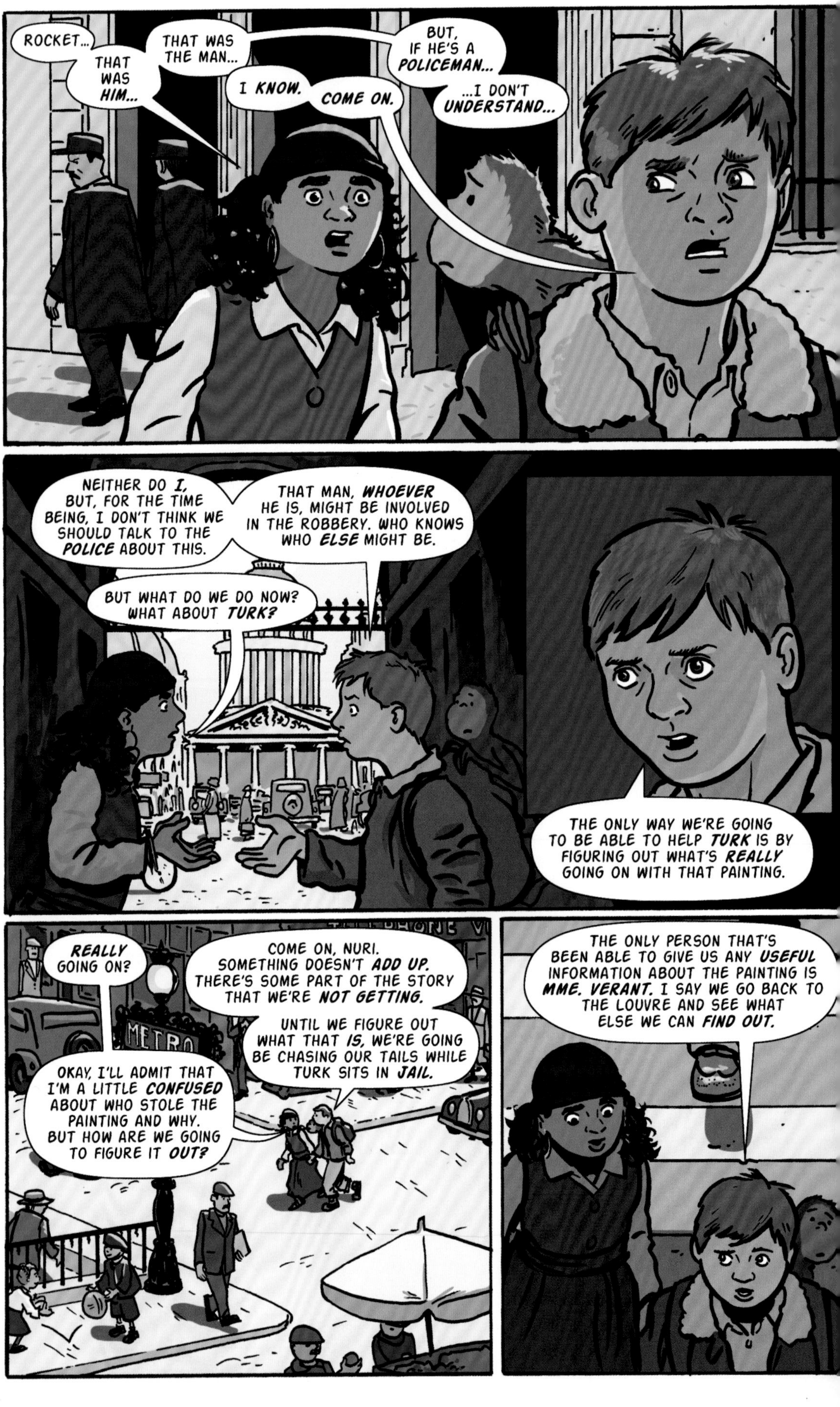
ROCKET...
THAT WAS HIM...
THAT WAS THE MAN...
I KNOW.
COME ON.
BUT, IF HE'S A POLICEMAN...
...I DON'T UNDERSTAND...
NEITHER DO I, BUT, FOR THE TIME BEING, I DON'T THINK WE SHOULD TALK TO THE POLICE ABOUT THIS.
THAT MAN, WHOEVER HE IS, MIGHT BE INVOLVED IN THE ROBBERY. WHO KNOWS WHO ELSE MIGHT BE.
BUT WHAT DO WE DO NOW? WHAT ABOUT TURK?
THE ONLY WAY WE'RE GOING TO BE ABLE TO HELP TURK IS BY FIGURING OUT WHAT'S REALLY GOING ON WITH THAT PAINTING.
REALLY GOING ON?
OKAY, I'LL ADMIT THAT I'M A LITTLE CONFUSED ABOUT WHO STOLE THE PAINTING AND WHY. BUT HOW ARE WE GOING TO FIGURE IT OUT?
METRO
COME ON, NURI. SOMETHING DOESN'T ADD UP. THERE'S SOME PART OF THE STORY THAT WE'RE NOT GETTING.
UNTIL WE FIGURE OUT WHAT THAT IS, WE'RE GOING BE CHASING OUR TAILS WHILE TURK SITS IN JAIL.
THE ONLY PERSON THAT'S BEEN ABLE TO GIVE US ANY USEFUL INFORMATION ABOUT THE PAINTING IS MME. VERANT. I SAY WE GO BACK TO THE LOUVRE AND SEE WHAT ELSE WE CAN FIND OUT.

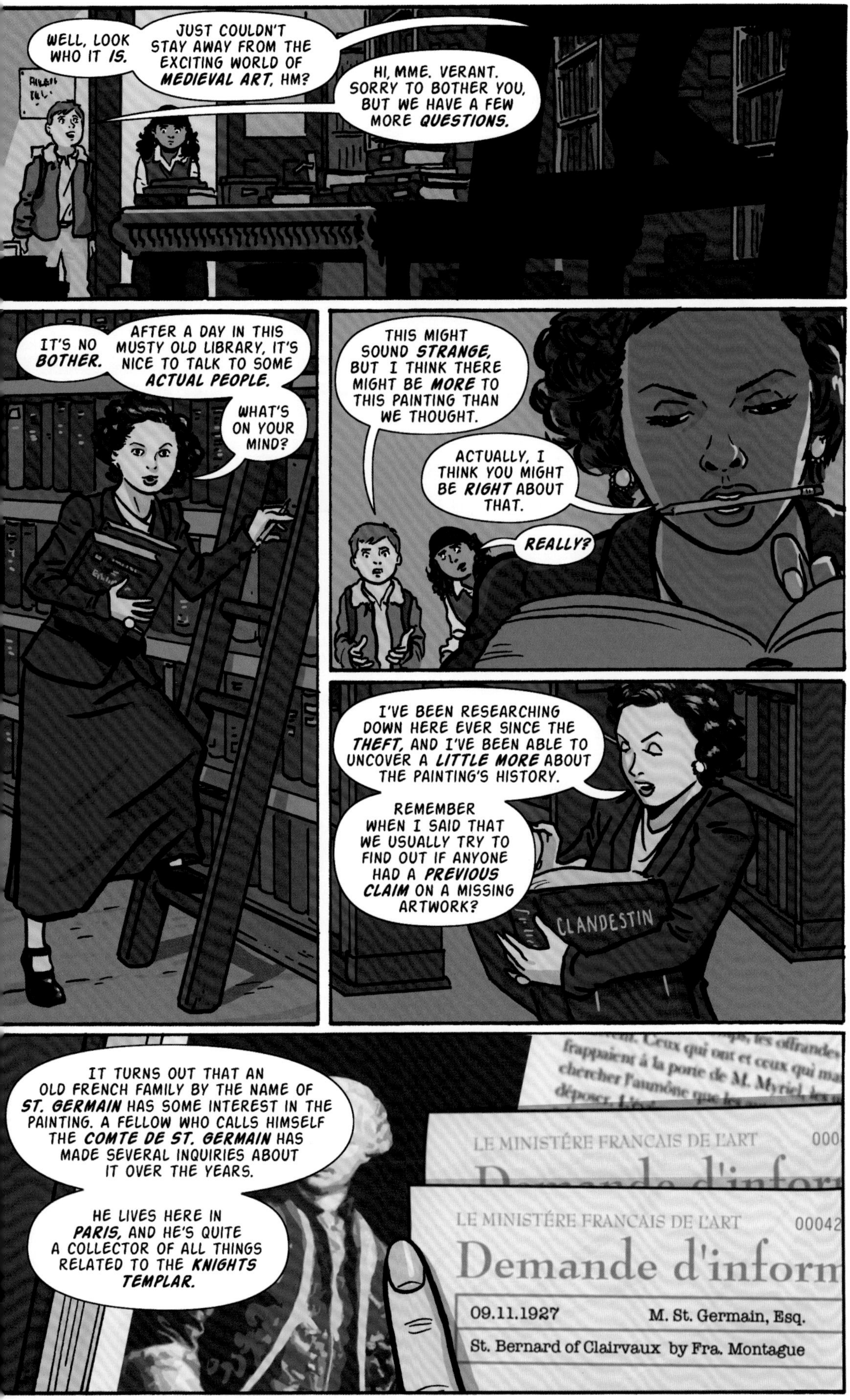

WELL, LOOK WHO IT *IS.*
JUST COULDN'T STAY AWAY FROM THE EXCITING WORLD OF *MEDIEVAL ART*, HM?
HI, MME. VERANT. SORRY TO BOTHER YOU, BUT WE HAVE A FEW MORE *QUESTIONS.*
IT'S NO *BOTHER.*
AFTER A DAY IN THIS MUSTY OLD LIBRARY, IT'S NICE TO TALK TO SOME *ACTUAL PEOPLE.*
WHAT'S ON YOUR MIND?
THIS MIGHT SOUND *STRANGE,* BUT I THINK THERE MIGHT BE *MORE* TO THIS PAINTING THAN WE THOUGHT.
ACTUALLY, I THINK YOU MIGHT BE *RIGHT* ABOUT THAT.
REALLY?
I'VE BEEN RESEARCHING DOWN HERE EVER SINCE THE *THEFT,* AND I'VE BEEN ABLE TO UNCOVER A *LITTLE MORE* ABOUT THE PAINTING'S HISTORY.
REMEMBER WHEN I SAID THAT WE USUALLY TRY TO FIND OUT IF ANYONE HAD A *PREVIOUS CLAIM* ON A MISSING ARTWORK?
CLANDESTIN
IT TURNS OUT THAT AN OLD FRENCH FAMILY BY THE NAME OF *ST. GERMAIN* HAS SOME INTEREST IN THE PAINTING. A FELLOW WHO CALLS HIMSELF THE *COMTE DE ST. GERMAIN* HAS MADE SEVERAL INQUIRIES ABOUT IT OVER THE YEARS.
HE LIVES HERE IN *PARIS,* AND HE'S QUITE A COLLECTOR OF ALL THINGS RELATED TO THE *KNIGHTS TEMPLAR.*
LE MINISTÉRE FRANCAIS DE L'ART
LE MINISTÉRE FRANCAIS DE L'ART 00042
Demande d'inform
09.11.1927 M. St. Germain, Esq.
St. Bernard of Clairvaux by Fra. Montague

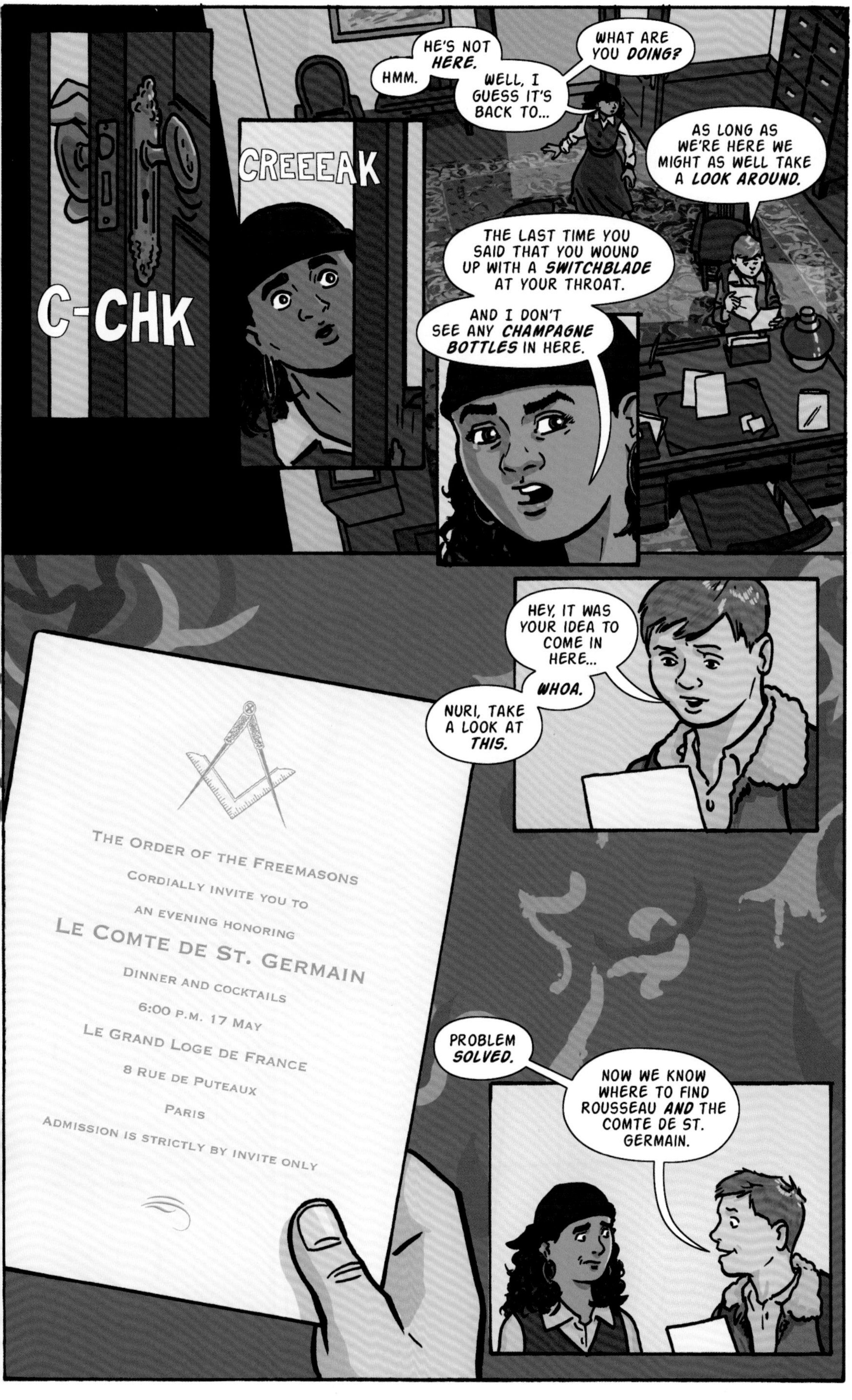
C-CHK
CREEEAK
HMM.
HE'S NOT HERE.
WELL, I GUESS IT'S BACK TO...
WHAT ARE YOU DOING?
AS LONG AS WE'RE HERE WE MIGHT AS WELL TAKE A LOOK AROUND.
THE LAST TIME YOU SAID THAT YOU WOUND UP WITH A SWITCHBLADE AT YOUR THROAT.
AND I DON'T SEE ANY CHAMPAGNE BOTTLES IN HERE.
HEY, IT WAS YOUR IDEA TO COME IN HERE...
WHOA.
NURI, TAKE A LOOK AT THIS.
THE ORDER OF THE FREEMASONS
CORDIALLY INVITE YOU TO
AN EVENING HONORING
LE COMTE DE ST. GERMAIN
DINNER AND COCKTAILS
6:00 P.M. 17 MAY
LE GRAND LOGE DE FRANCE
8 RUE DE PUTEAUX
PARIS
ADMISSION IS STRICTLY BY INVITE ONLY
PROBLEM SOLVED.
NOW WE KNOW WHERE TO FIND ROUSSEAU AND THE COMTE DE ST. GERMAIN.

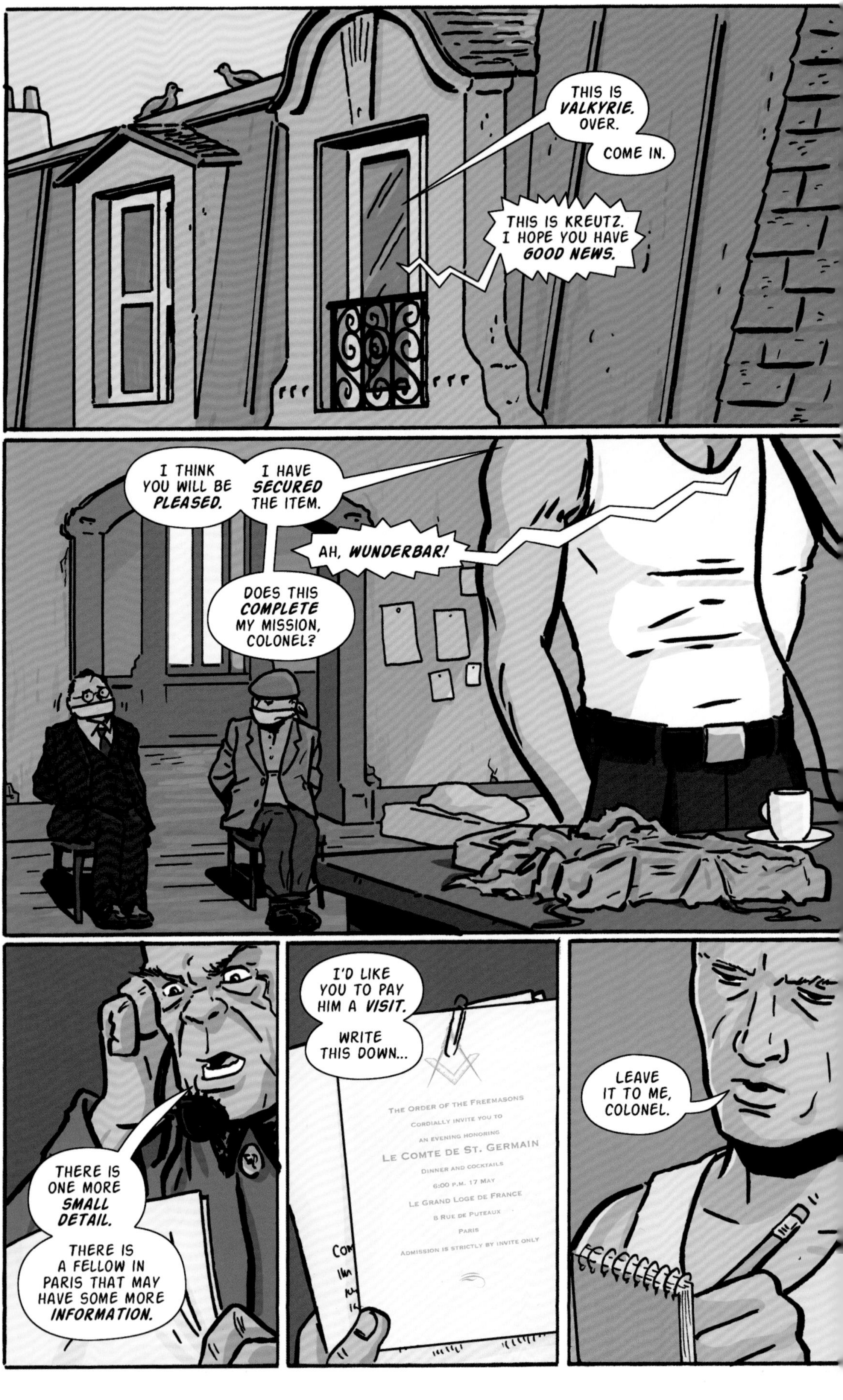
THIS IS *VALKYRIE.* OVER.
COME IN.
THIS IS KREUTZ. I HOPE YOU HAVE *GOOD NEWS.*
I THINK YOU WILL BE *PLEASED.*
I HAVE *SECURED* THE ITEM.
AH, *WUNDERBAR!*
DOES THIS *COMPLETE* MY MISSION, COLONEL?
THERE IS ONE MORE *SMALL DETAIL.*
THERE IS A FELLOW IN PARIS THAT MAY HAVE SOME MORE *INFORMATION.*
I'D LIKE YOU TO PAY HIM A *VISIT.*
WRITE THIS DOWN...
The Order of the Freemasons
Cordially invite you to
an evening honoring
Le Comte de St. Germain
Dinner and cocktails
6:00 p.m. 17 May
Le Grand Loge de France
8 Rue de Puteaux
Paris
Admission is strictly by invite only
LEAVE IT TO ME, COLONEL.

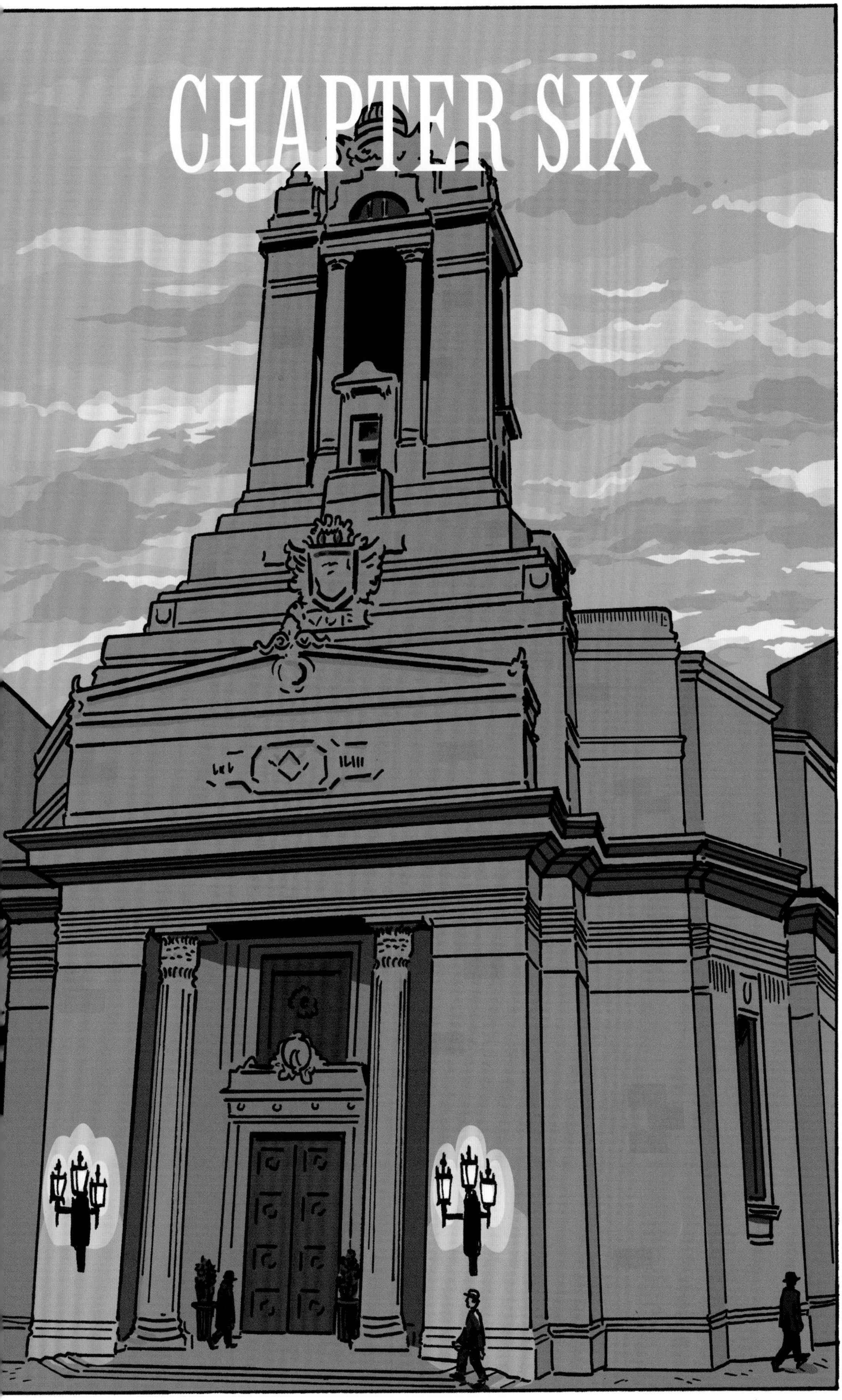
CHAPTER SIX

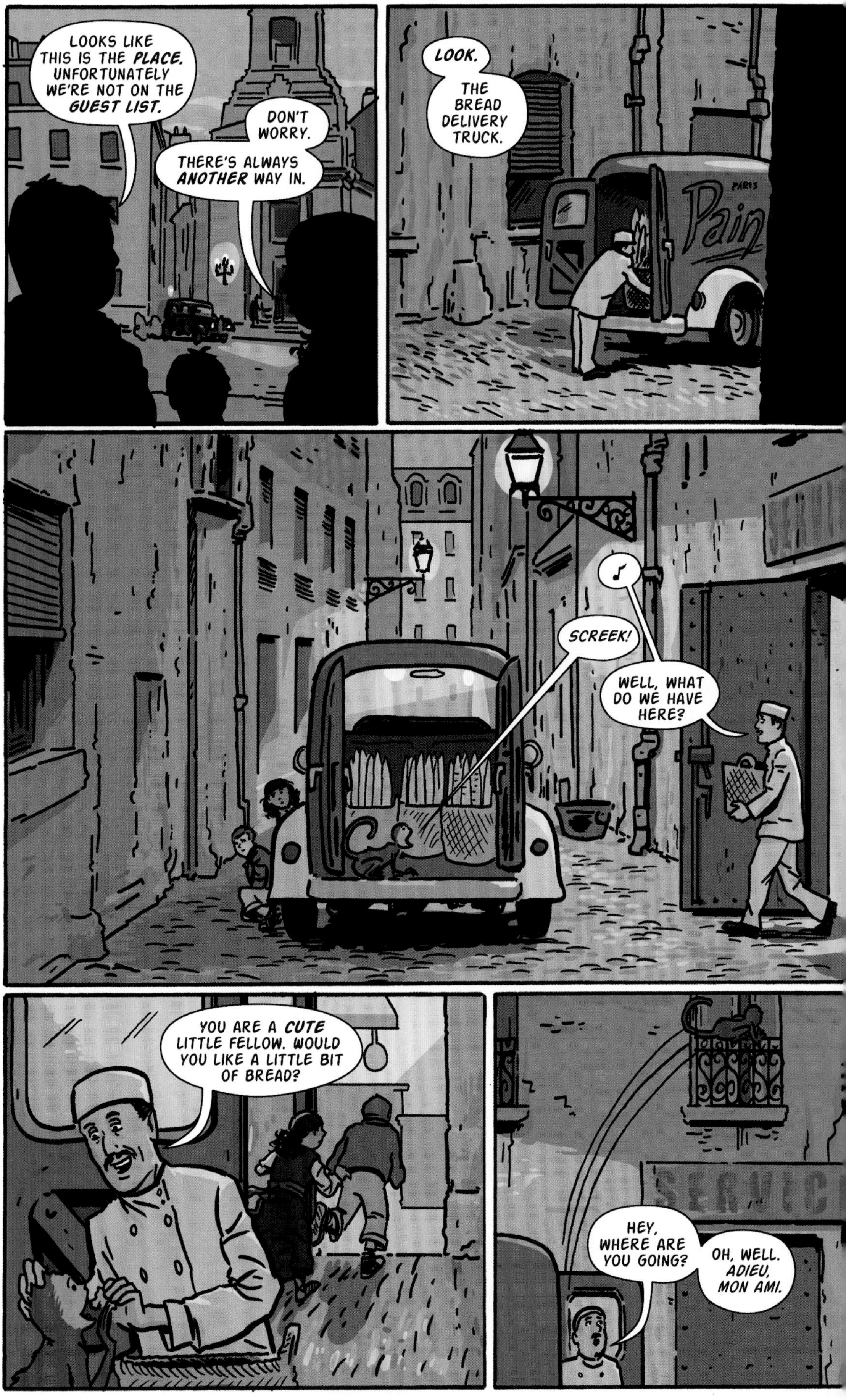
LOOKS LIKE THIS IS THE *PLACE.* UNFORTUNATELY WE'RE NOT ON THE *GUEST LIST.*
DON'T WORRY.
THERE'S ALWAYS *ANOTHER* WAY IN.
LOOK.
THE BREAD DELIVERY TRUCK.
PARIS
Pain
SCREEK!
WELL, WHAT DO WE HAVE HERE?
YOU ARE A *CUTE* LITTLE FELLOW. WOULD YOU LIKE A LITTLE BIT OF BREAD?
SERVIC
HEY, WHERE ARE YOU GOING?
OH, WELL. *ADIEU, MON AMI.*

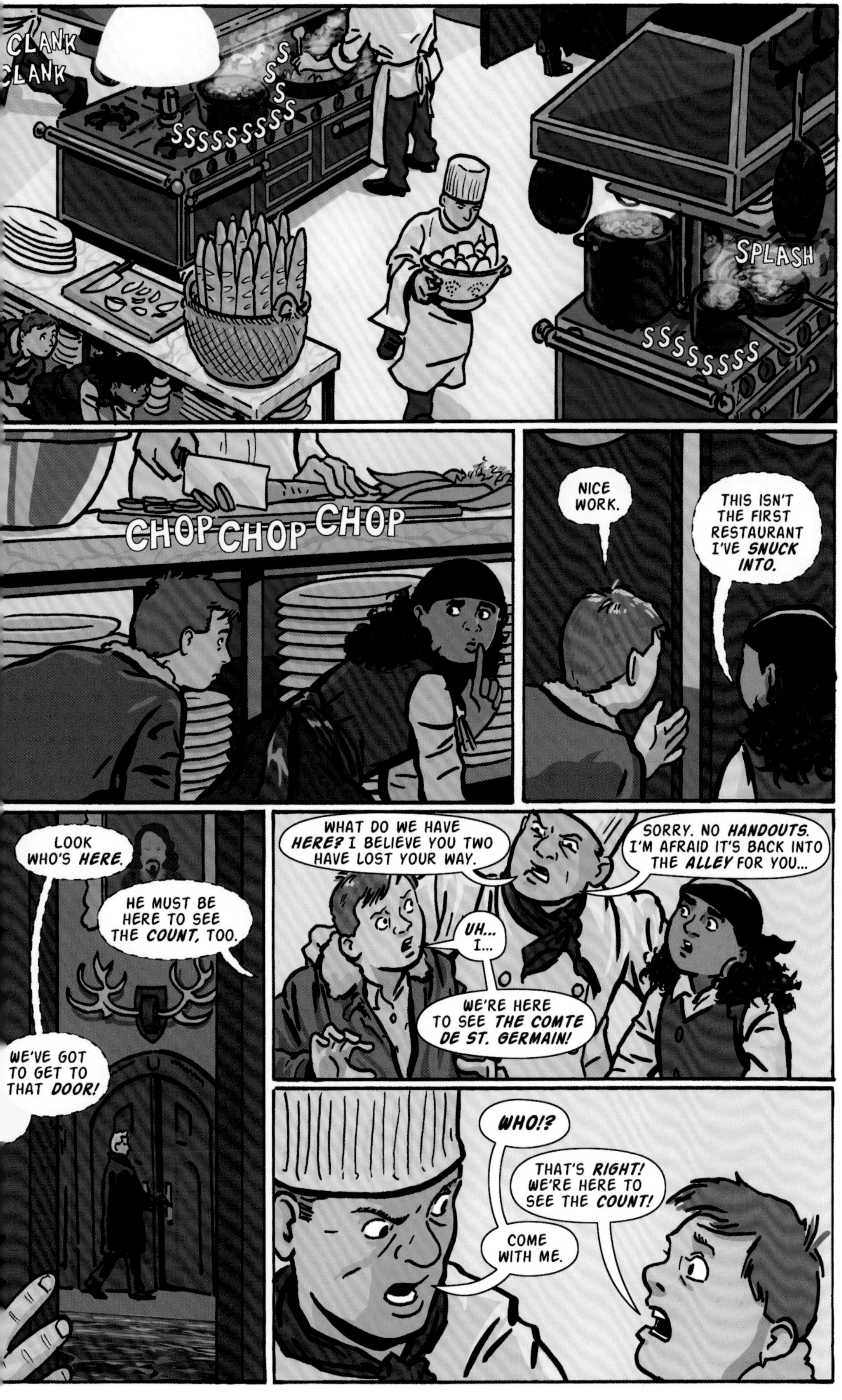
CLANK
CLANK
S S S S SSSSSSSS
SPLASH
SSSSSSSS
CHOP CHOP CHOP
NICE WORK.
THIS ISN'T THE FIRST RESTAURANT I'VE SNUCK INTO.
LOOK WHO'S HERE.
HE MUST BE HERE TO SEE THE COUNT, TOO.
WE'VE GOT TO GET TO THAT DOOR!
WHAT DO WE HAVE HERE? I BELIEVE YOU TWO HAVE LOST YOUR WAY.
SORRY. NO HANDOUTS. I'M AFRAID IT'S BACK INTO THE ALLEY FOR YOU...
UH... I...
WE'RE HERE TO SEE THE COMTE DE ST. GERMAIN!
WHO!?
THAT'S RIGHT! WE'RE HERE TO SEE THE COUNT!
COME WITH ME.

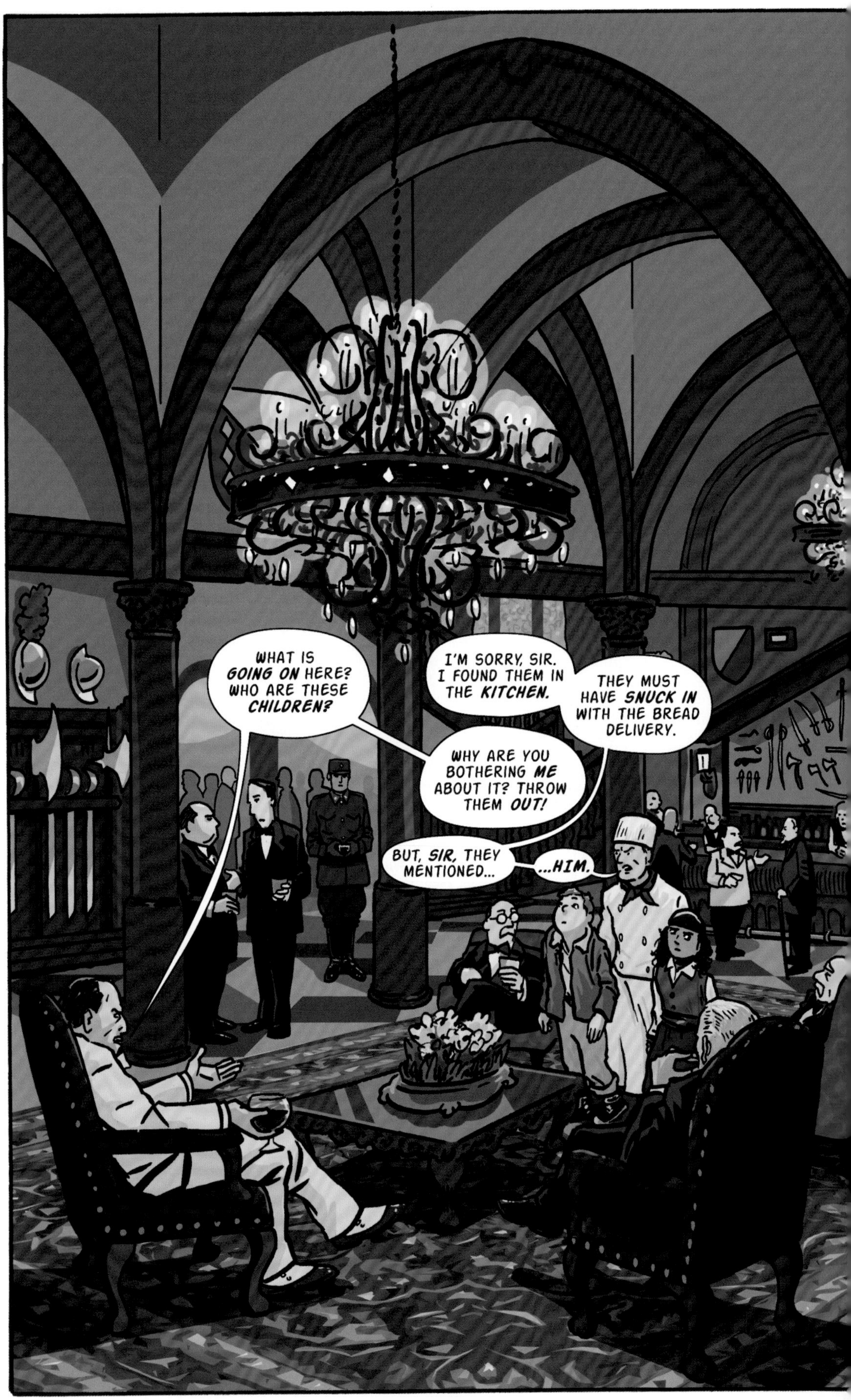
WHAT IS GOING ON HERE? WHO ARE THESE CHILDREN?
I'M SORRY, SIR. I FOUND THEM IN THE KITCHEN.
THEY MUST HAVE SNUCK IN WITH THE BREAD DELIVERY.
WHY ARE YOU BOTHERING ME ABOUT IT? THROW THEM OUT!
BUT, SIR, THEY MENTIONED...
...HIM.

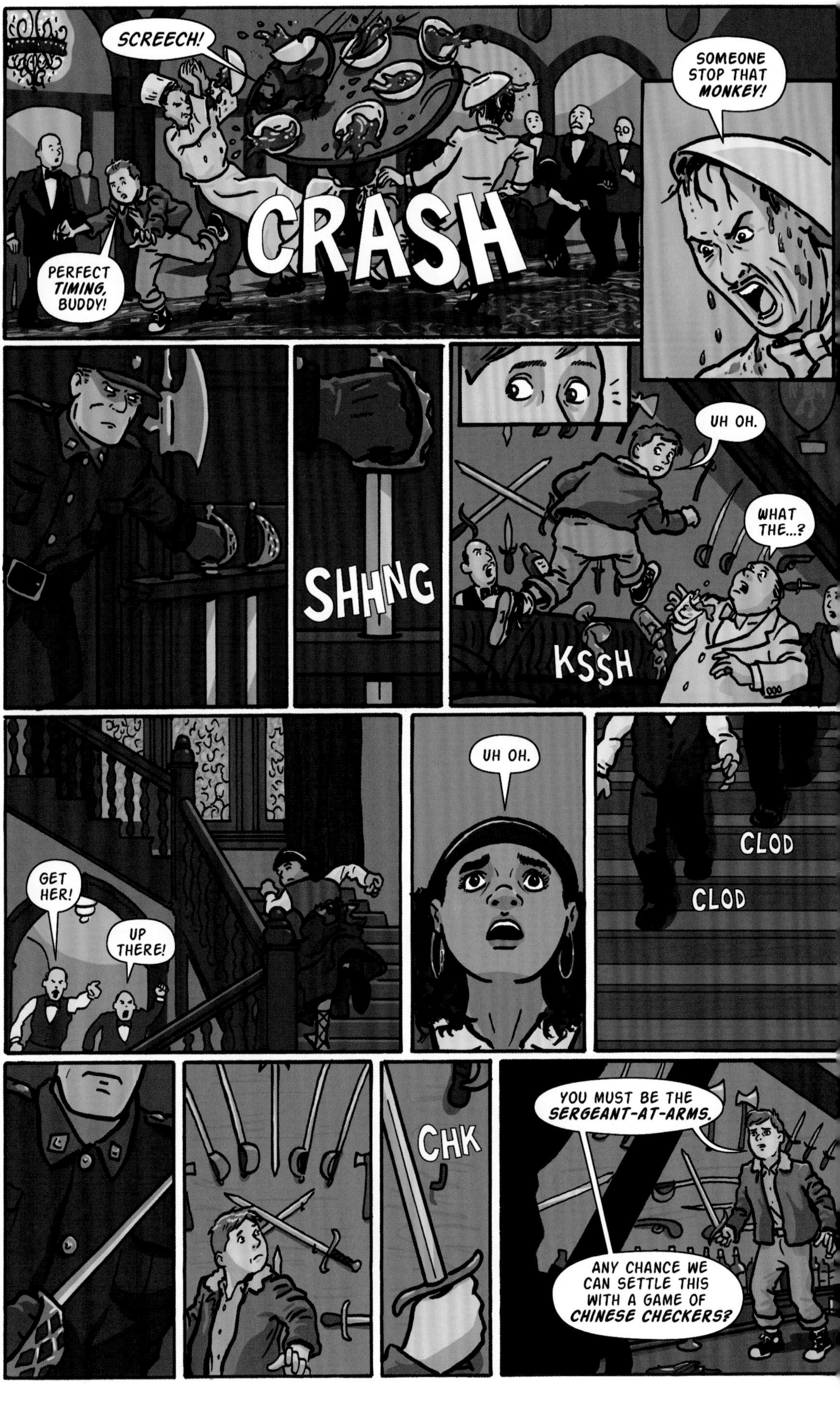
SCREECH!
SOMEONE STOP THAT MONKEY!
CRASH
PERFECT TIMING, BUDDY!
SHHNG
UH OH.
WHAT THE...?
KSSH
UH OH.
CLOD
CLOD
GET HER!
UP THERE!
CHK
YOU MUST BE THE SERGEANT-AT-ARMS.
ANY CHANCE WE CAN SETTLE THIS WITH A GAME OF CHINESE CHECKERS?

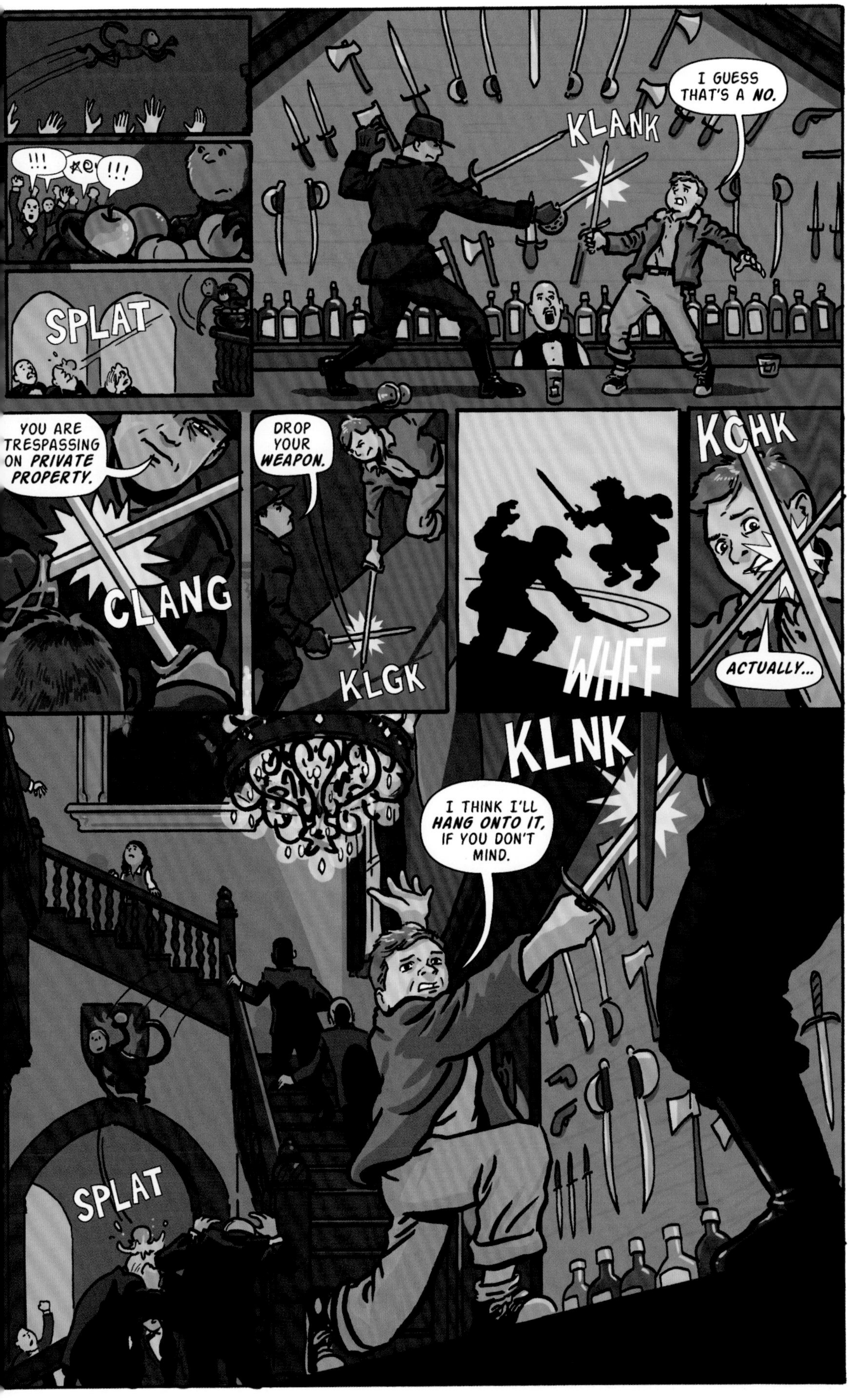

!!!
!!!
SPLAT
KLANK
I GUESS THAT'S A NO.
YOU ARE TRESPASSING ON PRIVATE PROPERTY.
CLANG
DROP YOUR WEAPON.
KLGK
WHFF
KCHK
ACTUALLY...
KLNK
I THINK I'LL HANG ONTO IT, IF YOU DON'T MIND.
SPLAT

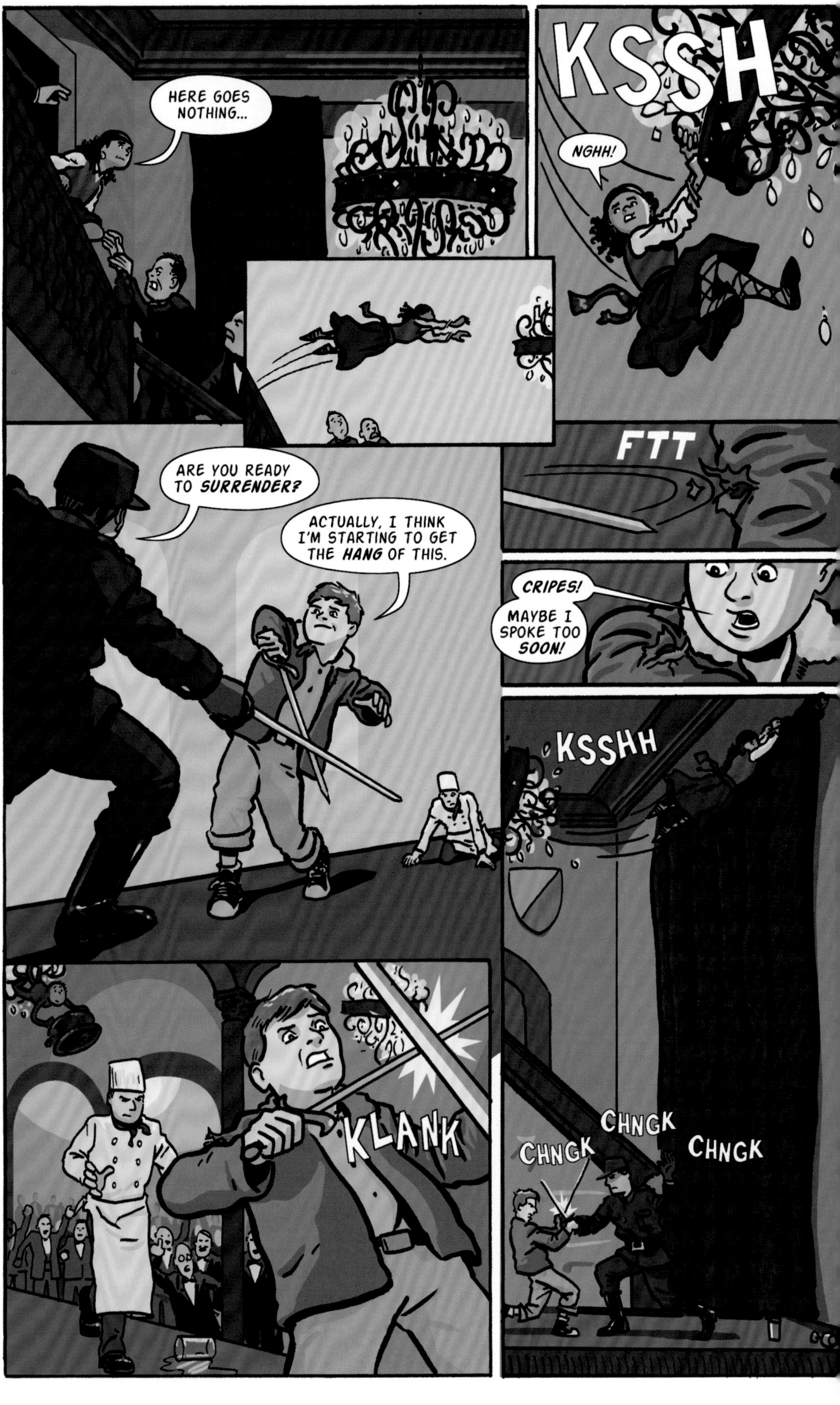
HERE GOES NOTHING...
KSSH
NGHH!
ARE YOU READY TO SURRENDER?
ACTUALLY, I THINK I'M STARTING TO GET THE HANG OF THIS.
FTT
CRIPES!
MAYBE I SPOKE TOO SOON!
KSSHH
KLANK
CHNGK
CHNGK
CHNGK

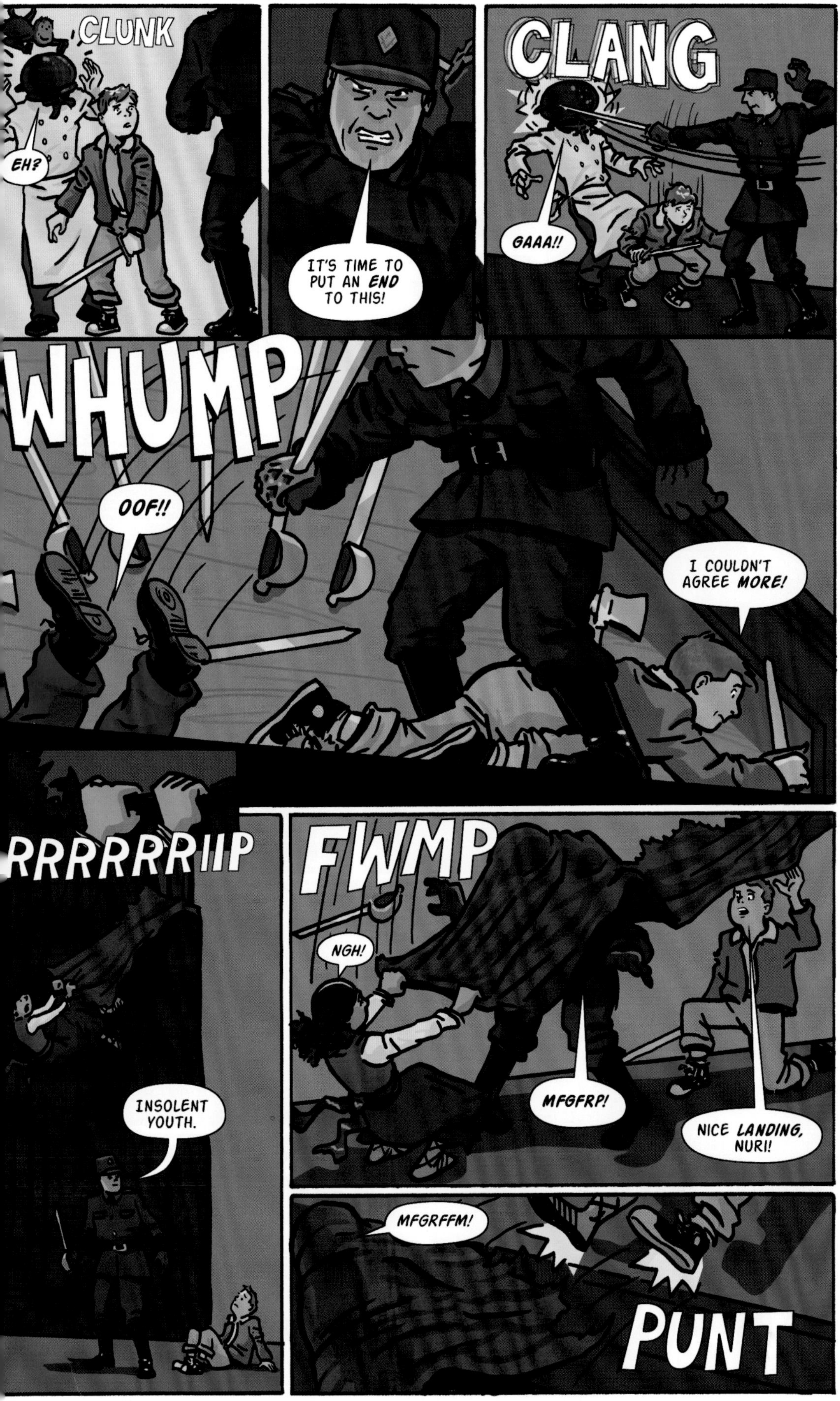
CLUNK
EH?
IT'S TIME TO PUT AN END TO THIS!
CLANG
GAAA!!
WHUMP
OOF!!
I COULDN'T AGREE MORE!
RRRRRRIIP
INSOLENT YOUTH.
FWMP
NGH!
MFGFRP!
NICE LANDING, NURI!
MFGRFFM!
PUNT

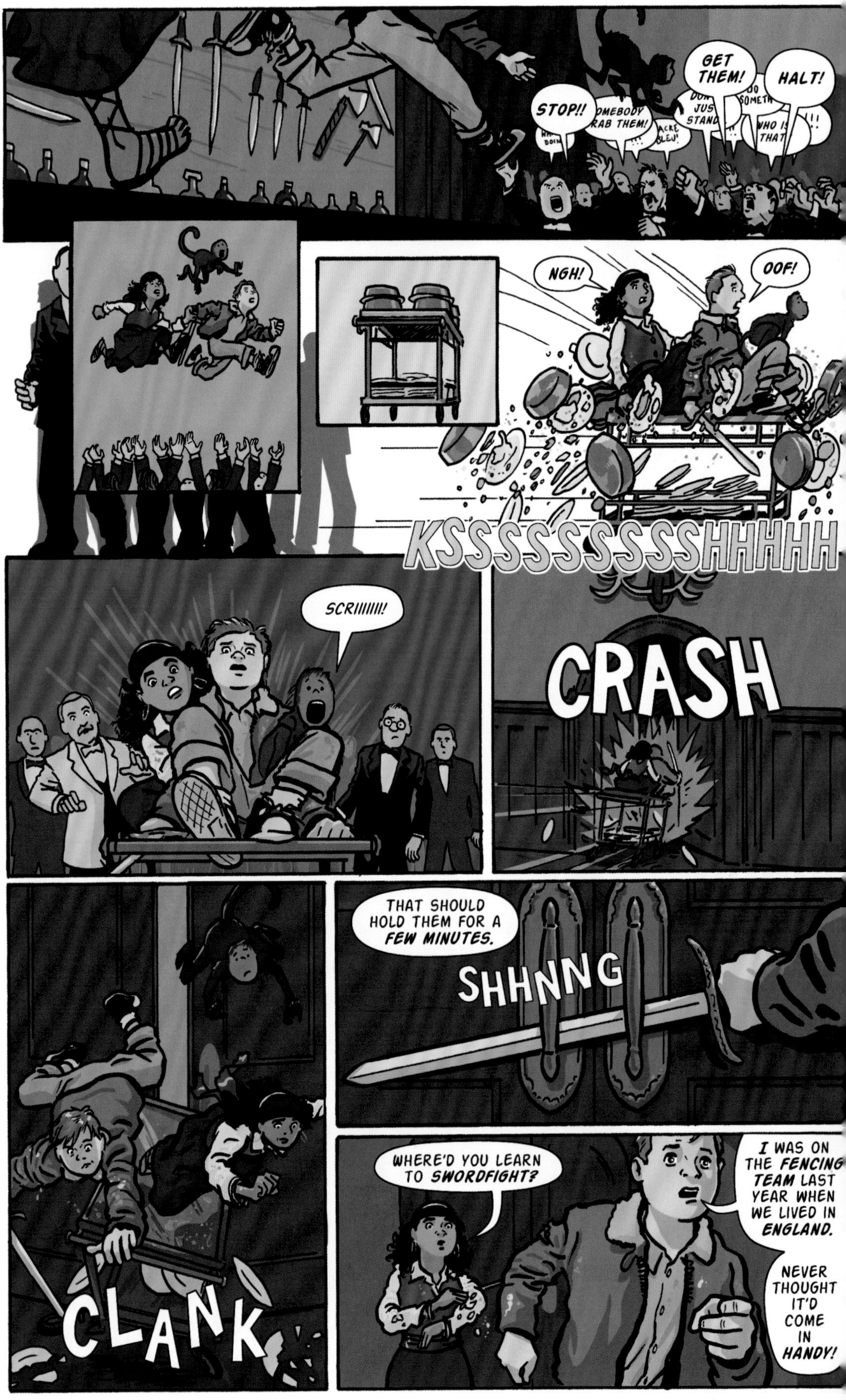
STOP!!
GET THEM!
HALT!
NGH!
OOF!
KSSSSSSSSSSHHHHH
SCRIIIIIII!
CRASH
CLANK
THAT SHOULD HOLD THEM FOR A FEW MINUTES.
SHHNNG
WHERE'D YOU LEARN TO SWORDFIGHT?
I WAS ON THE FENCING TEAM LAST YEAR WHEN WE LIVED IN ENGLAND.
NEVER THOUGHT IT'D COME IN HANDY!

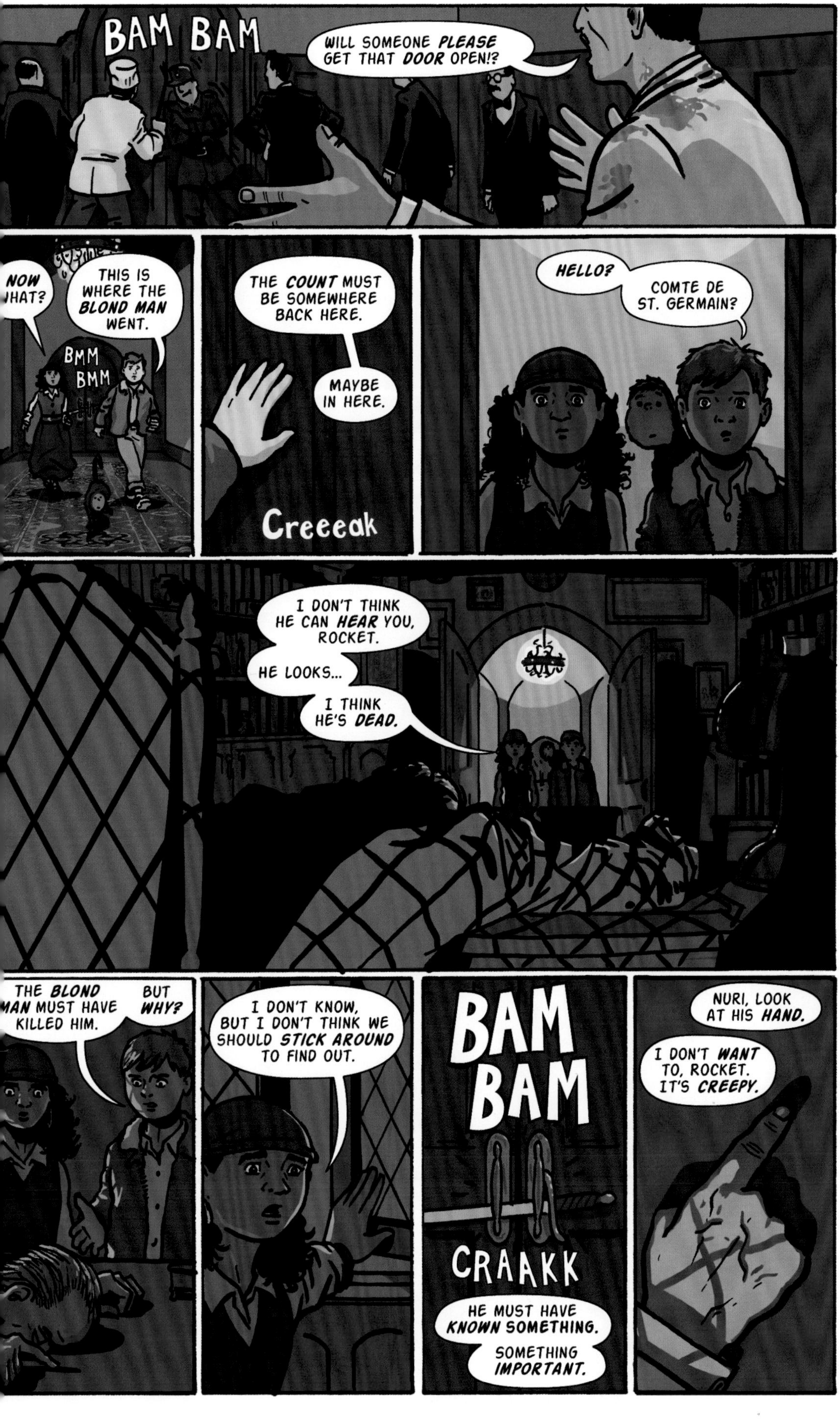
BAM BAM
WILL SOMEONE PLEASE GET THAT DOOR OPEN!?
NOW WHAT?
THIS IS WHERE THE BLOND MAN WENT.
BMM BMM
THE COUNT MUST BE SOMEWHERE BACK HERE.
MAYBE IN HERE.
Creeeak
HELLO?
COMTE DE ST. GERMAIN?
I DON'T THINK HE CAN HEAR YOU, ROCKET.
HE LOOKS...
I THINK HE'S DEAD.
THE BLOND MAN MUST HAVE KILLED HIM.
BUT WHY?
I DON'T KNOW, BUT I DON'T THINK WE SHOULD STICK AROUND TO FIND OUT.
BAM BAM
CRAAKK
HE MUST HAVE KNOWN SOMETHING.
SOMETHING IMPORTANT.
NURI, LOOK AT HIS HAND.
I DON'T WANT TO, ROCKET. IT'S CREEPY.

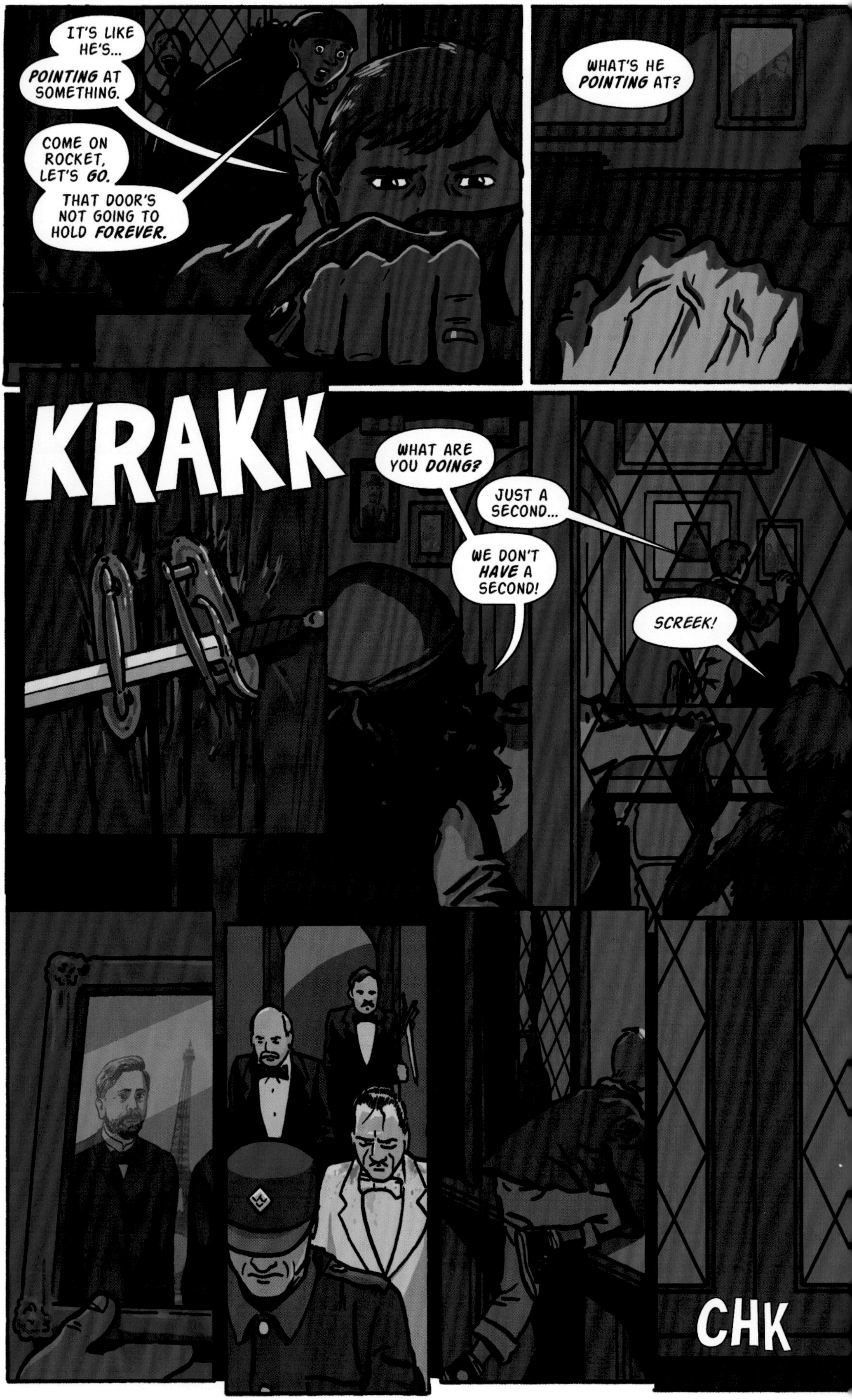

IT'S LIKE HE'S... *POINTING* AT SOMETHING.
COME ON ROCKET, LET'S *GO.*
THAT DOOR'S NOT GOING TO HOLD *FOREVER.*
WHAT'S HE *POINTING* AT?
KRAKK
WHAT ARE YOU *DOING?*
JUST A SECOND...
WE DON'T *HAVE* A SECOND!
SCREEK!
CHK

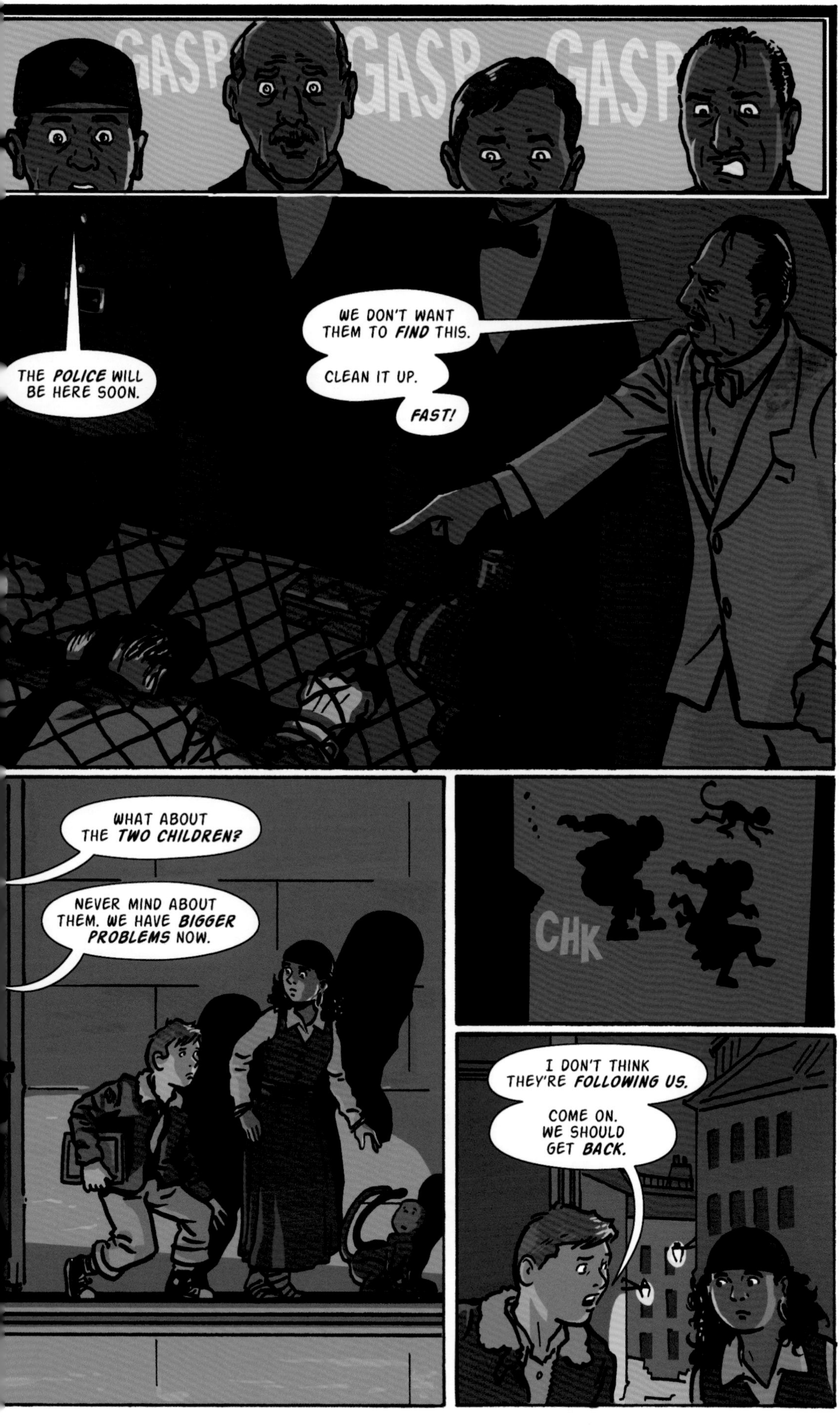
GASP GASP GASP
THE POLICE WILL BE HERE SOON.
WE DON'T WANT THEM TO FIND THIS.
CLEAN IT UP.
FAST!
WHAT ABOUT THE TWO CHILDREN?
NEVER MIND ABOUT THEM. WE HAVE BIGGER PROBLEMS NOW.
CHK
I DON'T THINK THEY'RE FOLLOWING US.
COME ON. WE SHOULD GET BACK.

GUSTAVE... WAIT, REMEMBER THE LIST OF FAMOUS *FREEMASONS*?

GUSTAVE EIFFEL! DESIGNER OF THE *EIFFEL TOWER*!

WHO'S THIS OTHER GUY, *GUGLIELMO*? AND WHAT'S THIS ABOUT A *TRANSMISSION*?

GUGLIELMO...

...MARCONI! IT'S *GOTTA* BE!

WHO?

GUGLIELMO MARCONI WAS AN ITALIAN INVENTOR WHO MADE THE FIRST *WIRELESS RADIO TRANSMITTER*.

THIS LETTER CAME FROM *NEW YORK*. THEY MUST HAVE BEEN TRYING TO MAKE A *TRANSATLANTIC RADIO TRANSMISSION*!

AND WHAT BETTER PLACE TO TRANSMIT FROM THAN THE *TALLEST STRUCTURE* IN *EUROPE*?

BUT WHAT DOES THIS HAVE TO DO WITH THE *PAINTING*?

OBVIOUSLY THE PAINTING IS A *CLUE* TO THE LOCATION OF THE *TREASURE*.

AND YOU'RE SAYING THAT LETTER IS *ALSO* A CLUE?

PROBABLY *NOT*, BUT I BET WHATEVER WAS IN THAT WIRELESS MESSAGE *WAS*.

May, 7, 1900

My Dear Gustave,
You have my congratulat
gratitude for your effo
Guglielmo made an admir
and, despite the fact th
transmission was not re

HOW ARE WE EVER GOING TO FIND *THAT*?

WELL, WE KNOW WHO *SENT* IT...

...AND *WHERE* IT WAS SENT *FROM*.

I THINK IT'S TIME WE PAID A *VISIT* TO PARIS'S *NUMBER ONE ATTRACTION*.

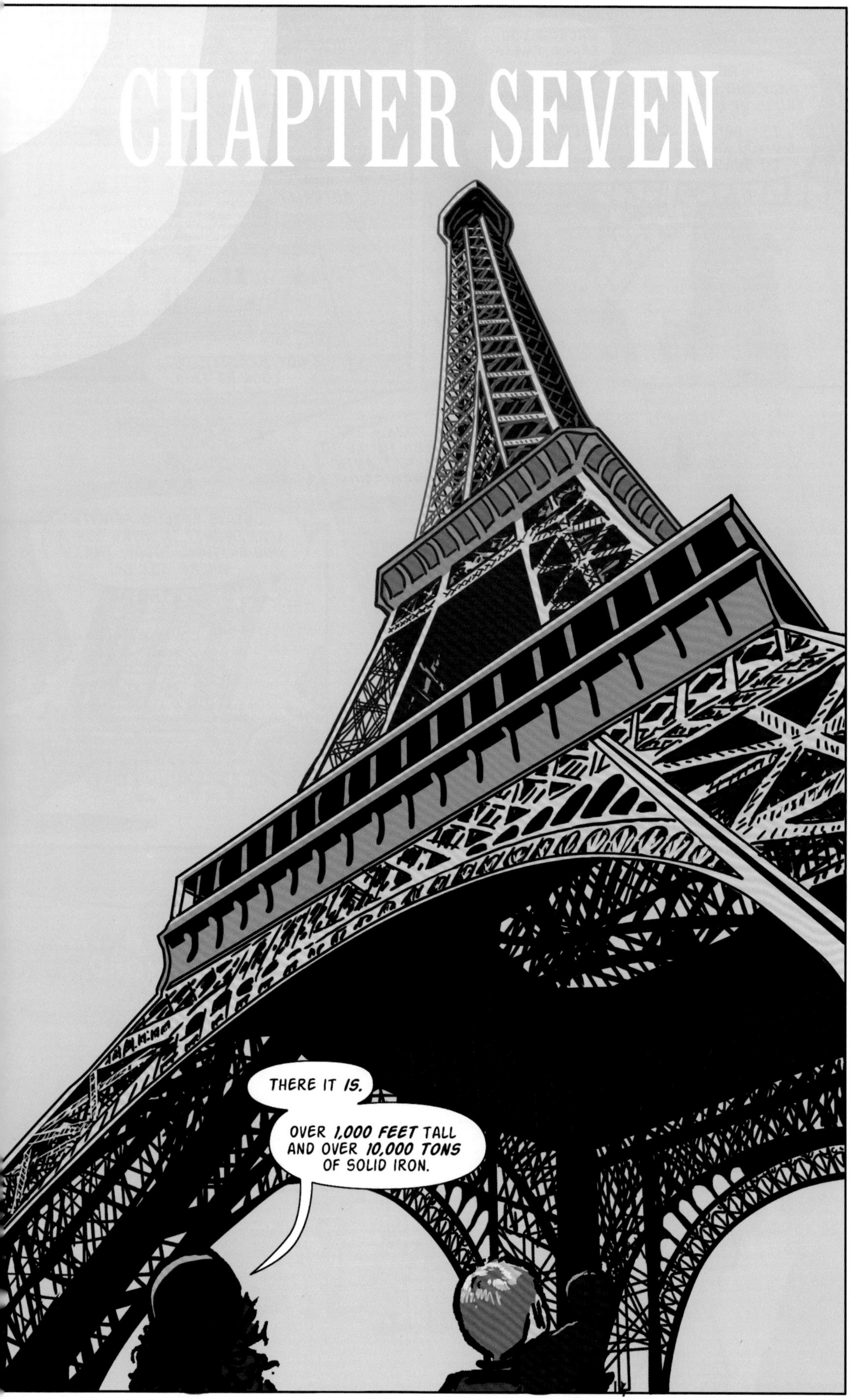
CHAPTER SEVEN
THERE IT *IS.*
OVER ***1,000 FEET*** TALL AND OVER ***10,000 TONS*** OF SOLID IRON.

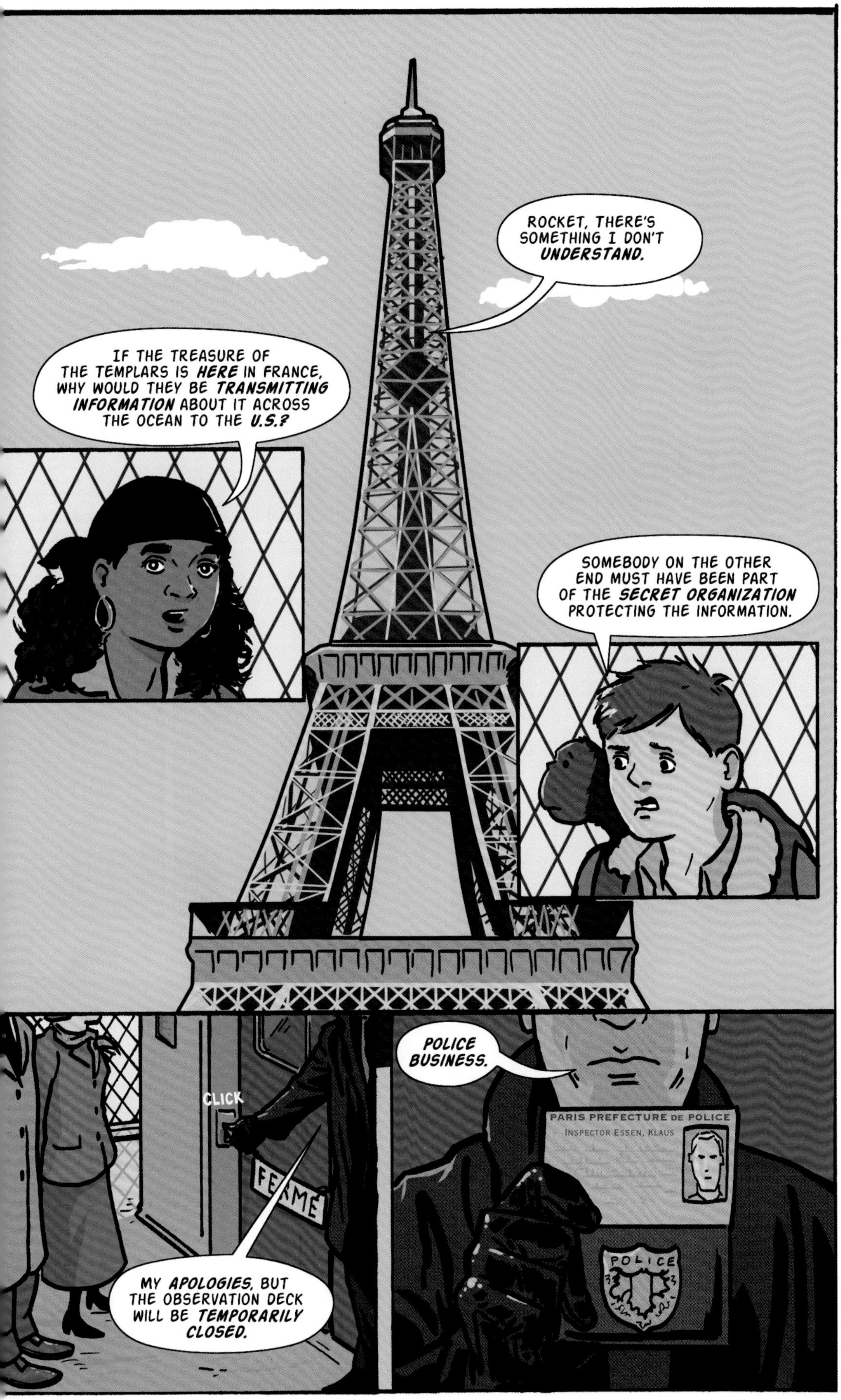
ROCKET, THERE'S SOMETHING I DON'T *UNDERSTAND.*
IF THE TREASURE OF THE TEMPLARS IS *HERE* IN FRANCE, WHY WOULD THEY BE *TRANSMITTING INFORMATION* ABOUT IT ACROSS THE OCEAN TO THE *U.S.?*
SOMEBODY ON THE OTHER END MUST HAVE BEEN PART OF THE *SECRET ORGANIZATION* PROTECTING THE INFORMATION.
CLICK
FERMÉ
MY *APOLOGIES*, BUT THE OBSERVATION DECK WILL BE *TEMPORARILY CLOSED.*
POLICE BUSINESS.
PARIS PREFECTURE DE POLICE
INSPECTOR ESSEN, KLAUS
POLICE

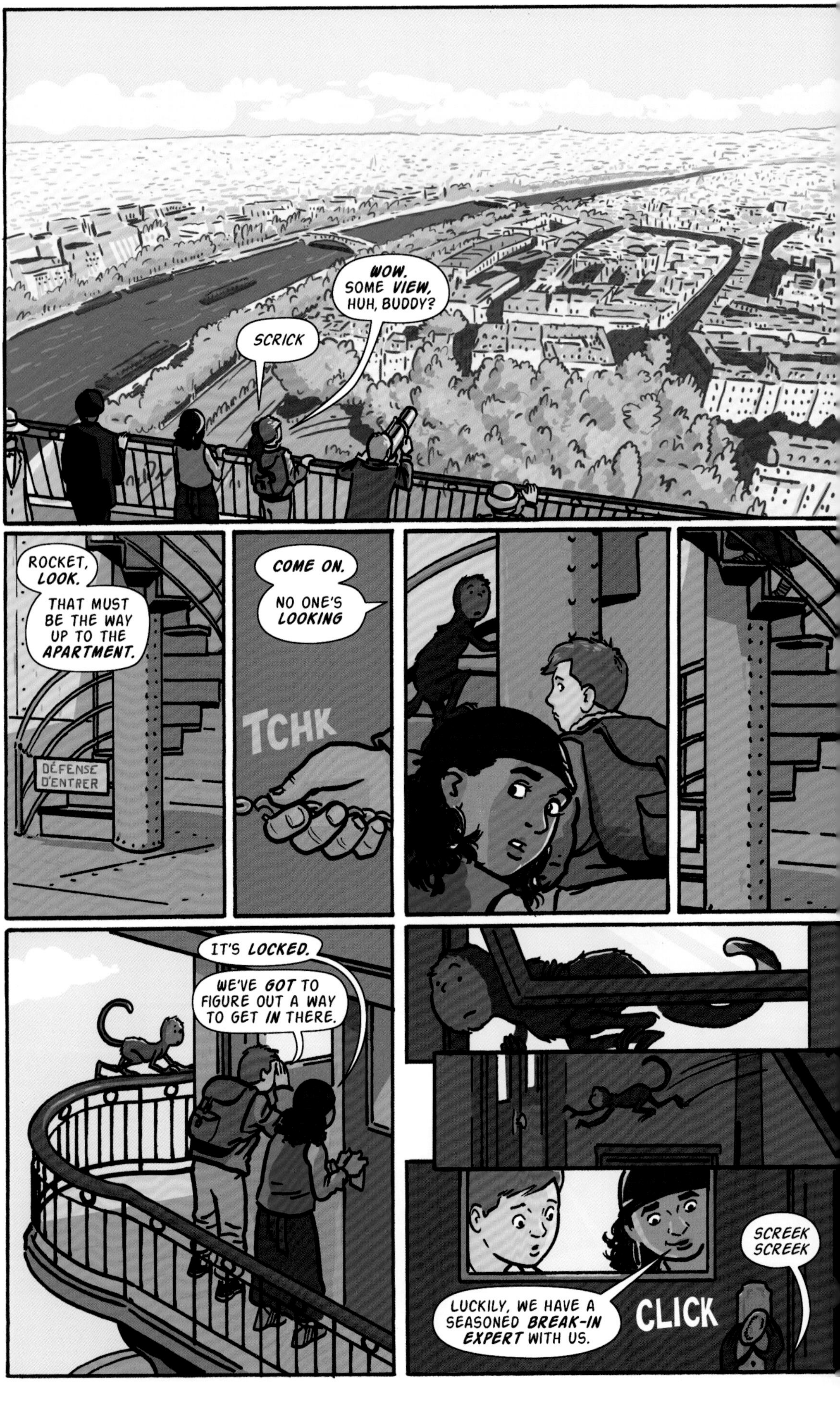
WOW. SOME VIEW, HUH, BUDDY?
SCRICK
ROCKET, LOOK.
THAT MUST BE THE WAY UP TO THE APARTMENT.
DÉFENSE D'ENTRER
COME ON.
NO ONE'S LOOKING
TCHK
IT'S LOCKED.
WE'VE GOT TO FIGURE OUT A WAY TO GET IN THERE.
LUCKILY, WE HAVE A SEASONED BREAK-IN EXPERT WITH US.
CLICK
SCREEK SCREEK

PLUNK
PLUNK

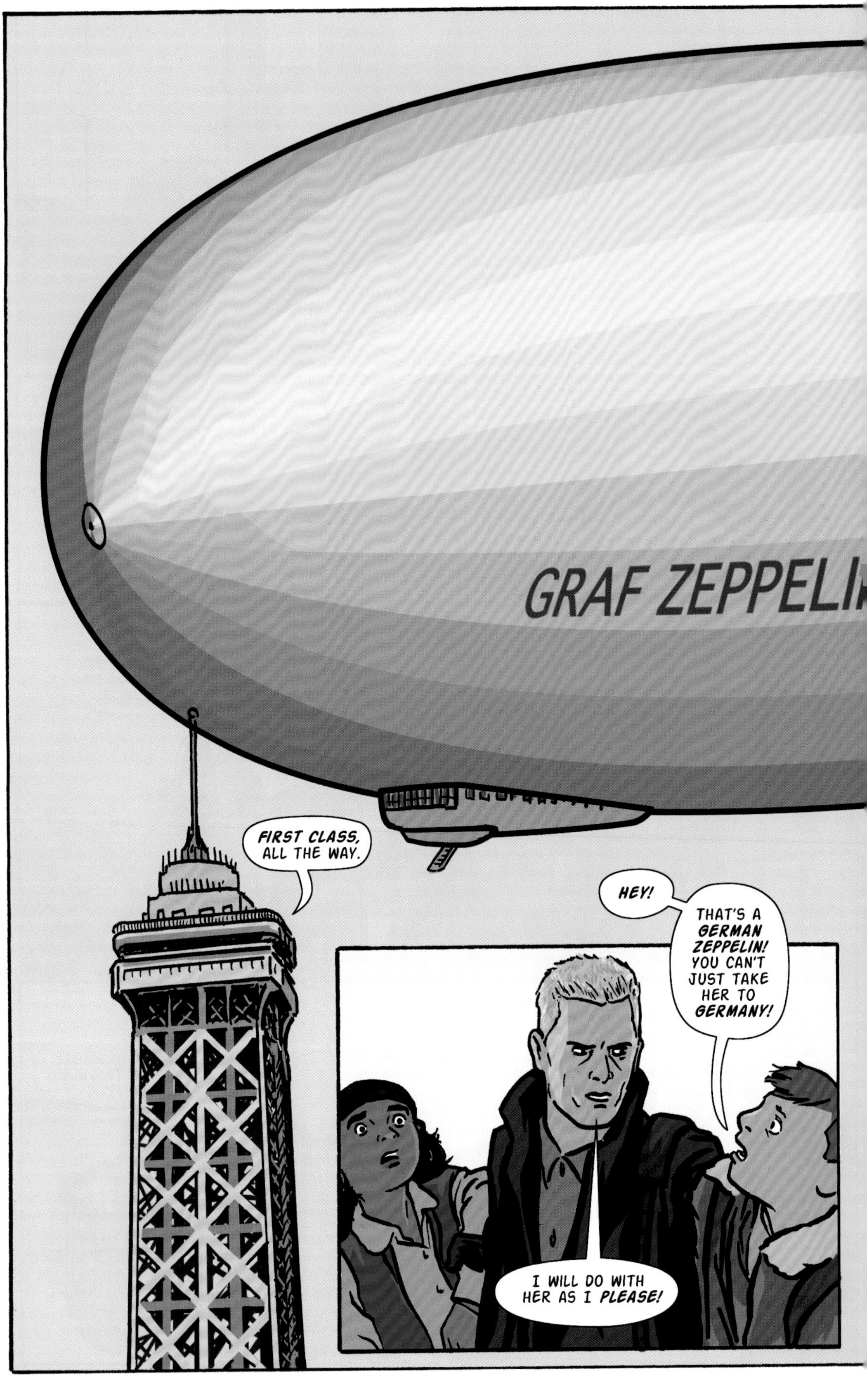
GRAF ZEPPELIN
FIRST CLASS, ALL THE WAY.
HEY!
THAT'S A GERMAN ZEPPELIN! YOU CAN'T JUST TAKE HER TO GERMANY!
I WILL DO WITH HER AS I PLEASE!

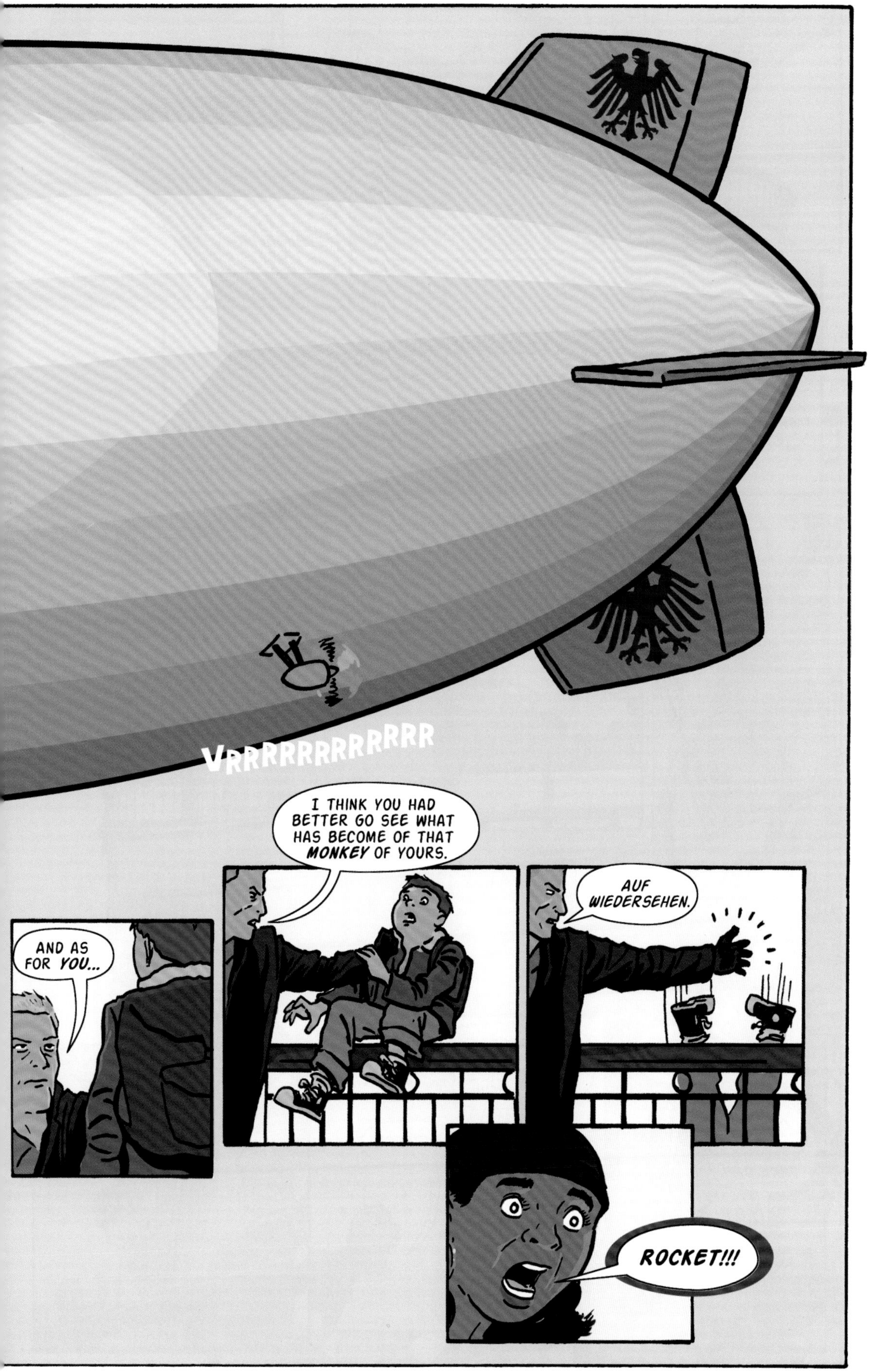

VRRRRRRRRRRRR
AND AS FOR *YOU*...
I THINK YOU HAD BETTER GO SEE WHAT HAS BECOME OF THAT *MONKEY* OF YOURS.
AUF WIEDERSEHEN.
ROCKET!!!

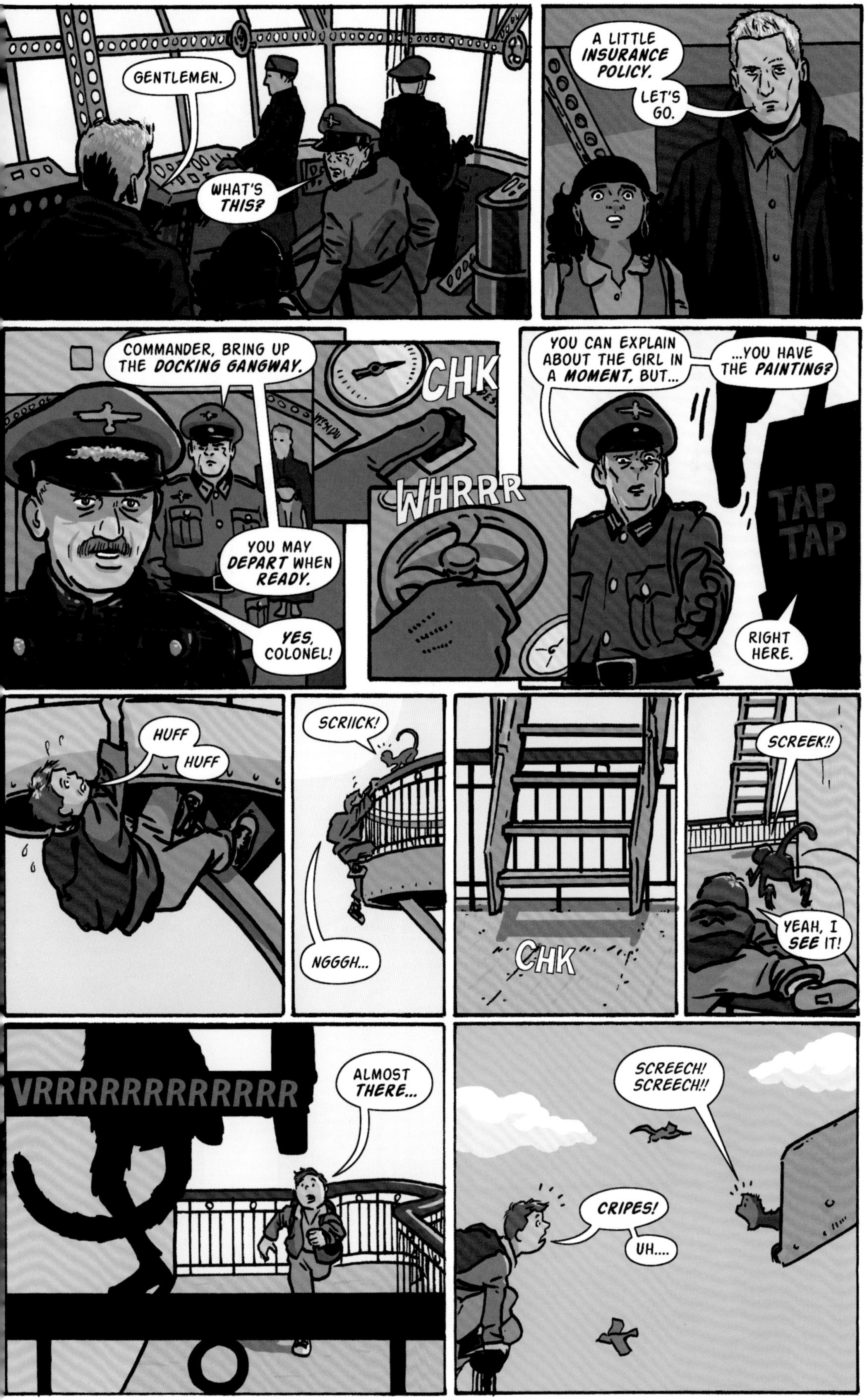
GENTLEMEN.
WHAT'S THIS?
A LITTLE INSURANCE POLICY.
LET'S GO.
COMMANDER, BRING UP THE DOCKING GANGWAY.
YOU MAY DEPART WHEN READY.
YES, COLONEL!
CHK
WHRRR
YOU CAN EXPLAIN ABOUT THE GIRL IN A MOMENT, BUT...
...YOU HAVE THE PAINTING?
TAP TAP
RIGHT HERE.
HUFF
HUFF
SCRIICK!
NGGGH...
CHK
SCREEK!!
YEAH, I SEE IT!
VRRRRRRRRRRRR
ALMOST THERE...
SCREECH! SCREECH!!
CRIPES!
UH....

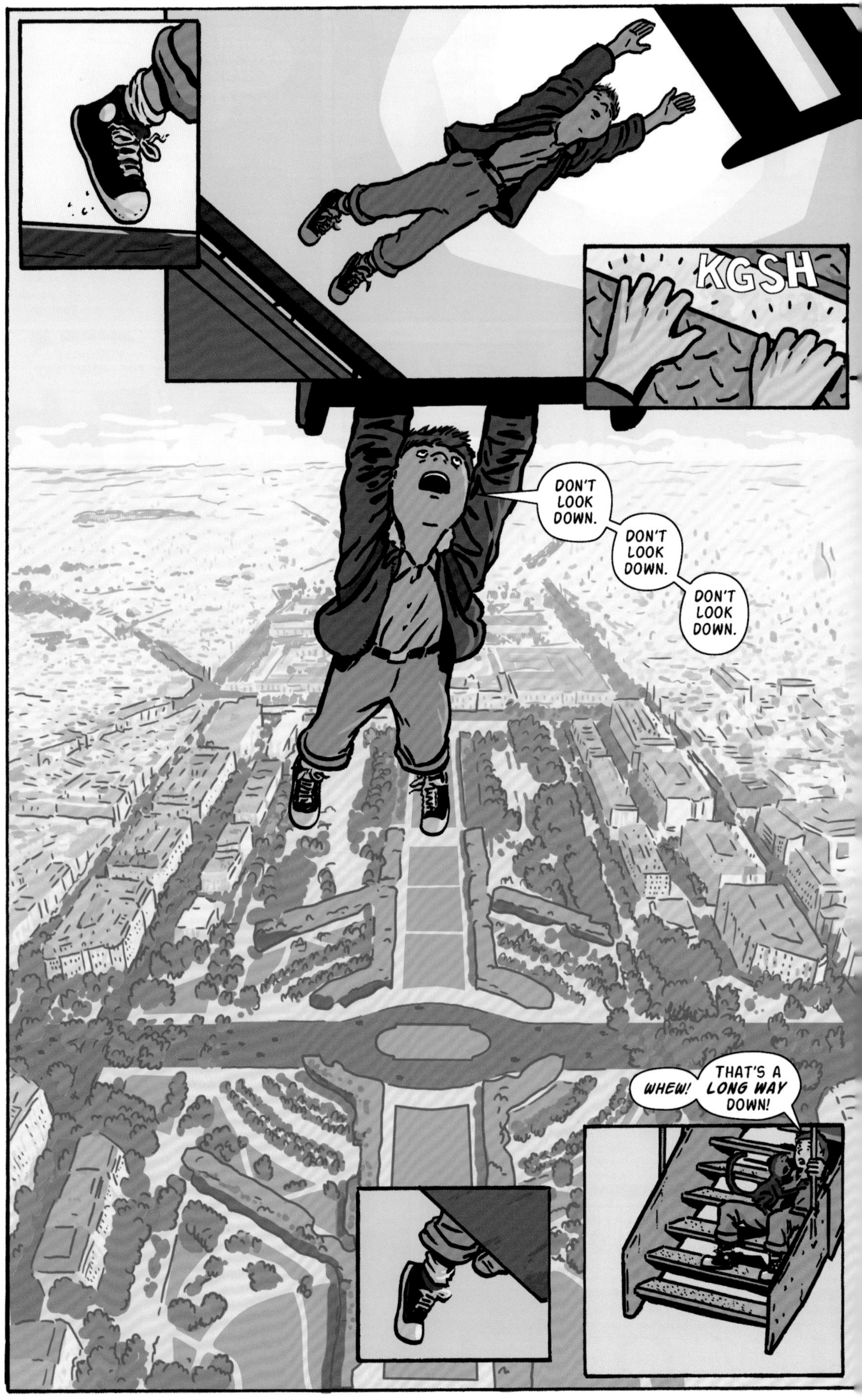
KGSH
DON'T LOOK DOWN.
DON'T LOOK DOWN.
DON'T LOOK DOWN.
WHEW!
THAT'S A LONG WAY DOWN!

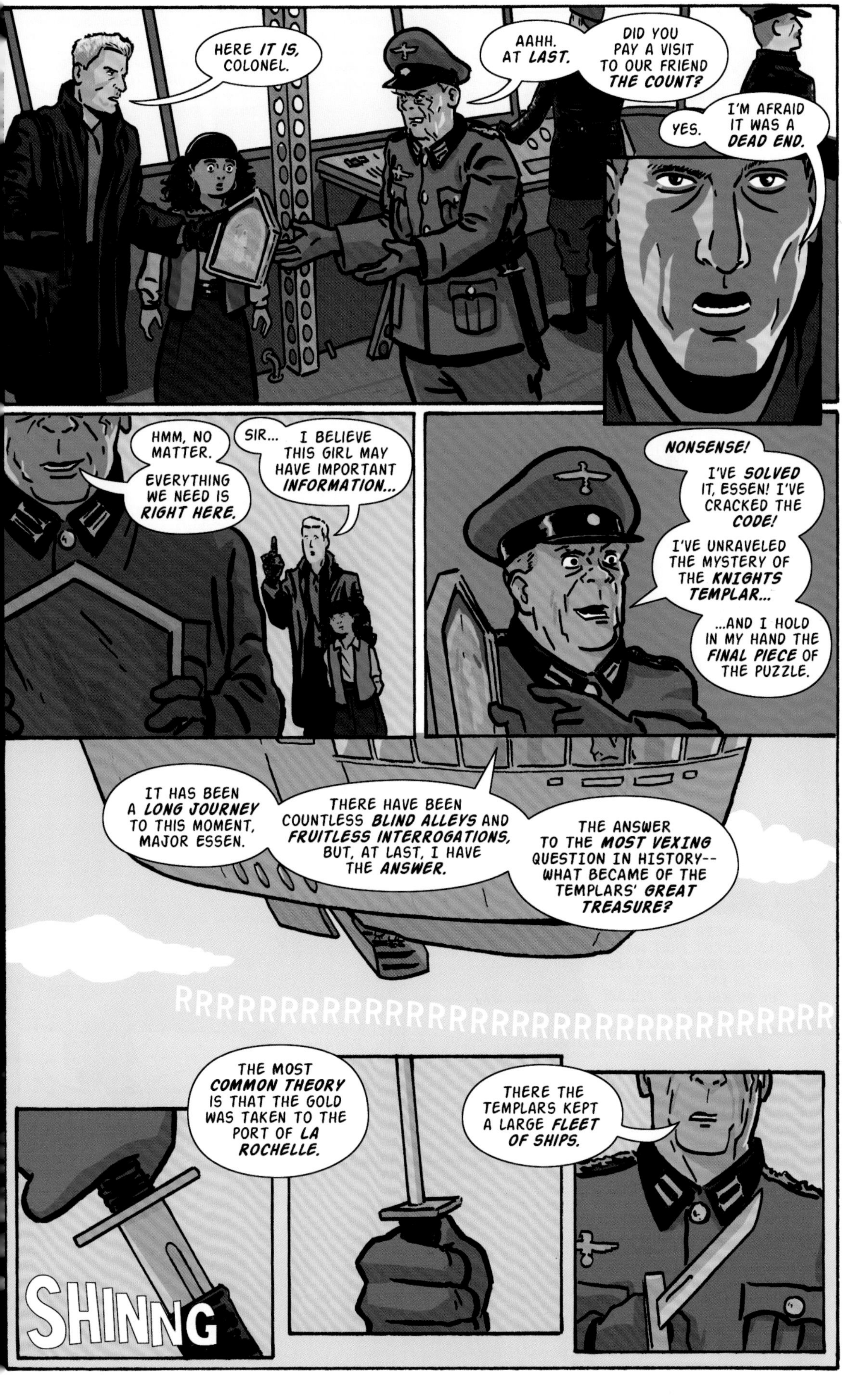
HERE IT IS, COLONEL.
AAHH. AT LAST.
DID YOU PAY A VISIT TO OUR FRIEND THE COUNT?
YES.
I'M AFRAID IT WAS A DEAD END.
HMM, NO MATTER.
EVERYTHING WE NEED IS RIGHT HERE.
SIR...
I BELIEVE THIS GIRL MAY HAVE IMPORTANT INFORMATION...
NONSENSE!
I'VE SOLVED IT, ESSEN! I'VE CRACKED THE CODE!
I'VE UNRAVELED THE MYSTERY OF THE KNIGHTS TEMPLAR...
...AND I HOLD IN MY HAND THE FINAL PIECE OF THE PUZZLE.
IT HAS BEEN A LONG JOURNEY TO THIS MOMENT, MAJOR ESSEN.
THERE HAVE BEEN COUNTLESS BLIND ALLEYS AND FRUITLESS INTERROGATIONS, BUT, AT LAST, I HAVE THE ANSWER.
THE ANSWER TO THE MOST VEXING QUESTION IN HISTORY-- WHAT BECAME OF THE TEMPLARS' GREAT TREASURE?
RRRRRRRRRRRRRRRRRRRRRRRRRRRRRRRR
THE MOST COMMON THEORY IS THAT THE GOLD WAS TAKEN TO THE PORT OF LA ROCHELLE.
SHINNG
THERE THE TEMPLARS KEPT A LARGE FLEET OF SHIPS.

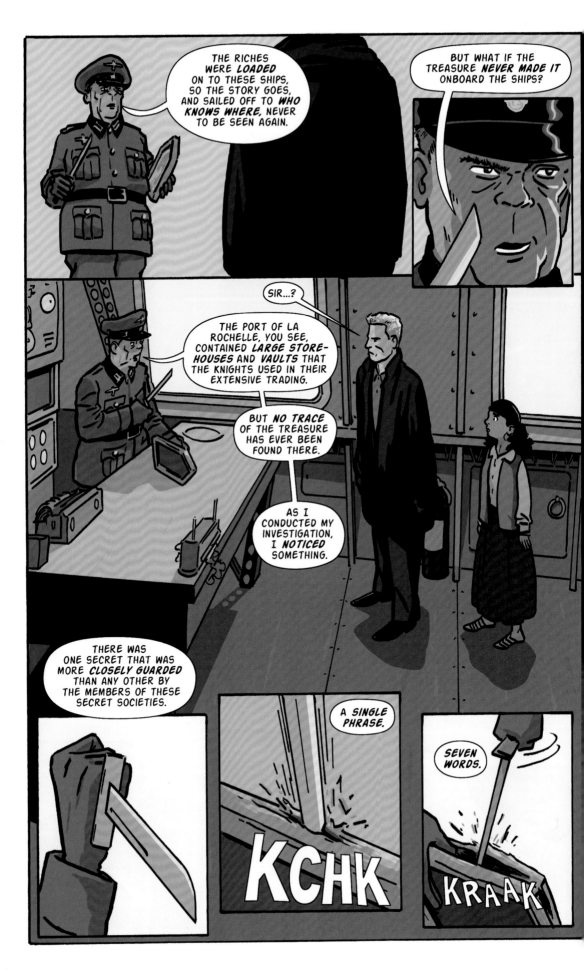

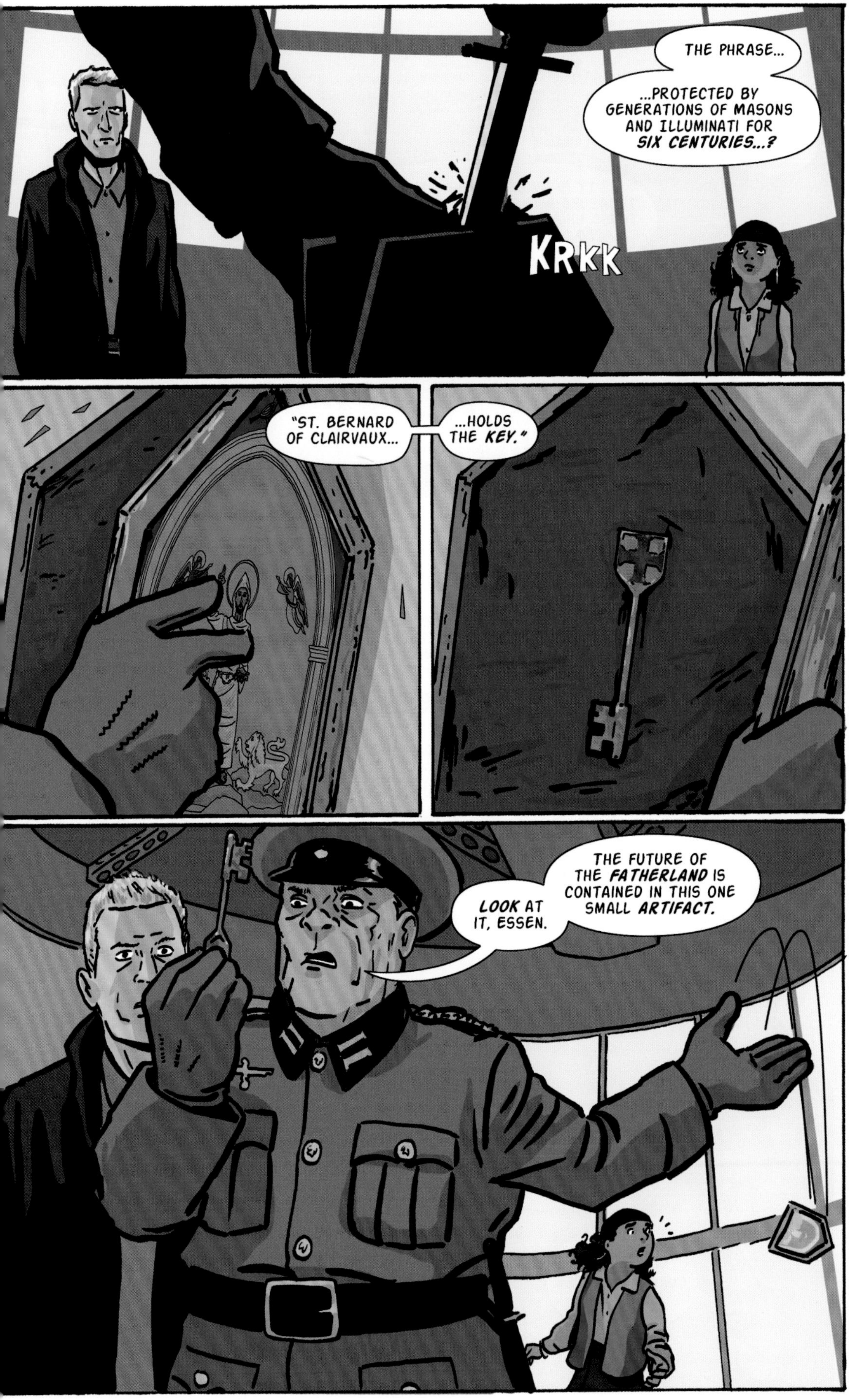
THE PHRASE...
...PROTECTED BY GENERATIONS OF MASONS AND ILLUMINATI FOR SIX CENTURIES...?
KRKK
"ST. BERNARD OF CLAIRVAUX...
...HOLDS THE KEY."
LOOK AT IT, ESSEN.
THE FUTURE OF THE FATHERLAND IS CONTAINED IN THIS ONE SMALL ARTIFACT.

CHAPTER EIGHT

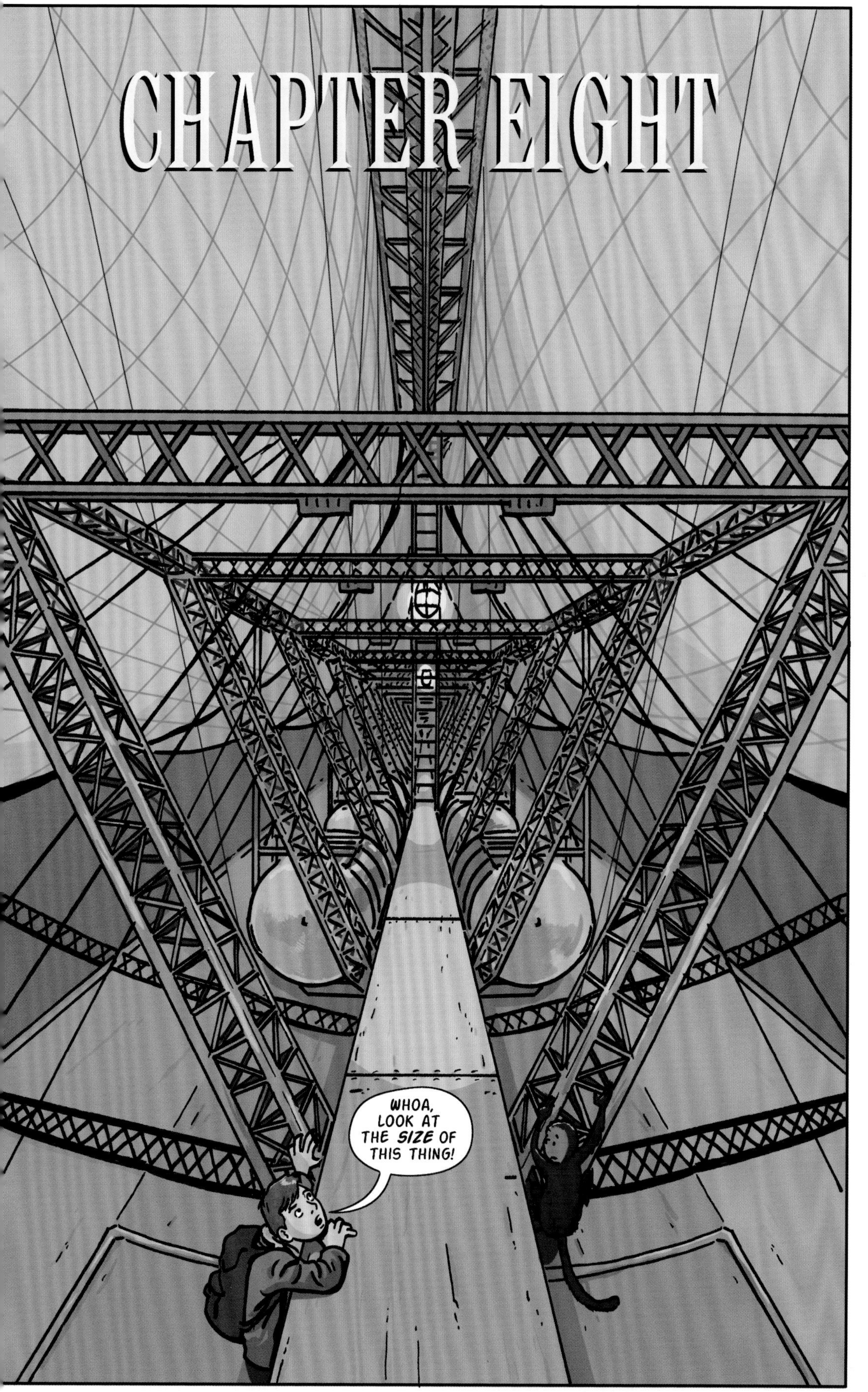
WHOA, LOOK AT THE *SIZE* OF THIS THING!

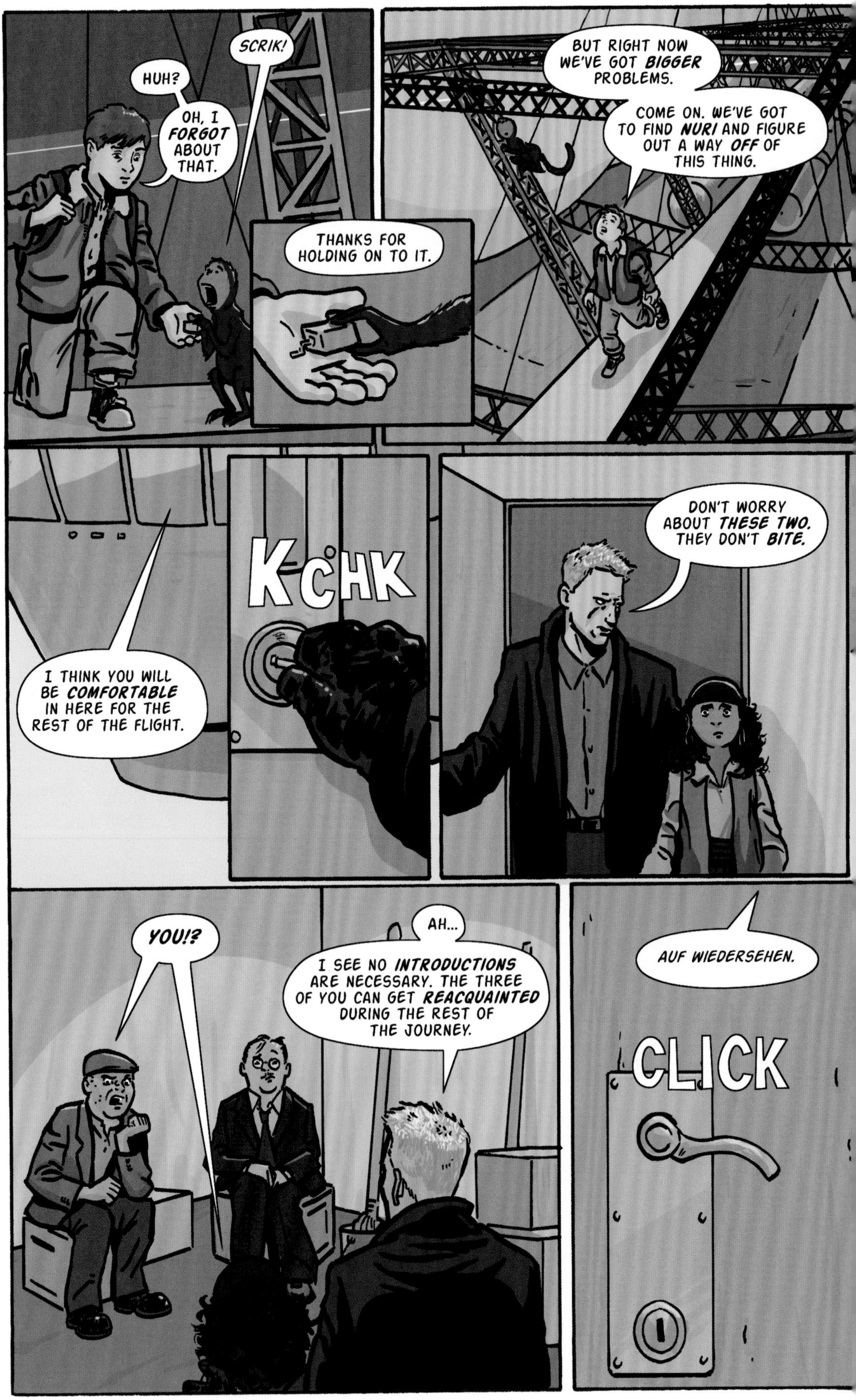
HUH?
SCRIK!
OH, I FORGOT ABOUT THAT.
THANKS FOR HOLDING ON TO IT.
BUT RIGHT NOW WE'VE GOT BIGGER PROBLEMS.
COME ON. WE'VE GOT TO FIND NURI AND FIGURE OUT A WAY OFF OF THIS THING.
I THINK YOU WILL BE COMFORTABLE IN HERE FOR THE REST OF THE FLIGHT.
KCHK
DON'T WORRY ABOUT THESE TWO. THEY DON'T BITE.
YOU!?
AH...
I SEE NO INTRODUCTIONS ARE NECESSARY. THE THREE OF YOU CAN GET REACQUAINTED DURING THE REST OF THE JOURNEY.
AUF WIEDERSEHEN.
CLICK

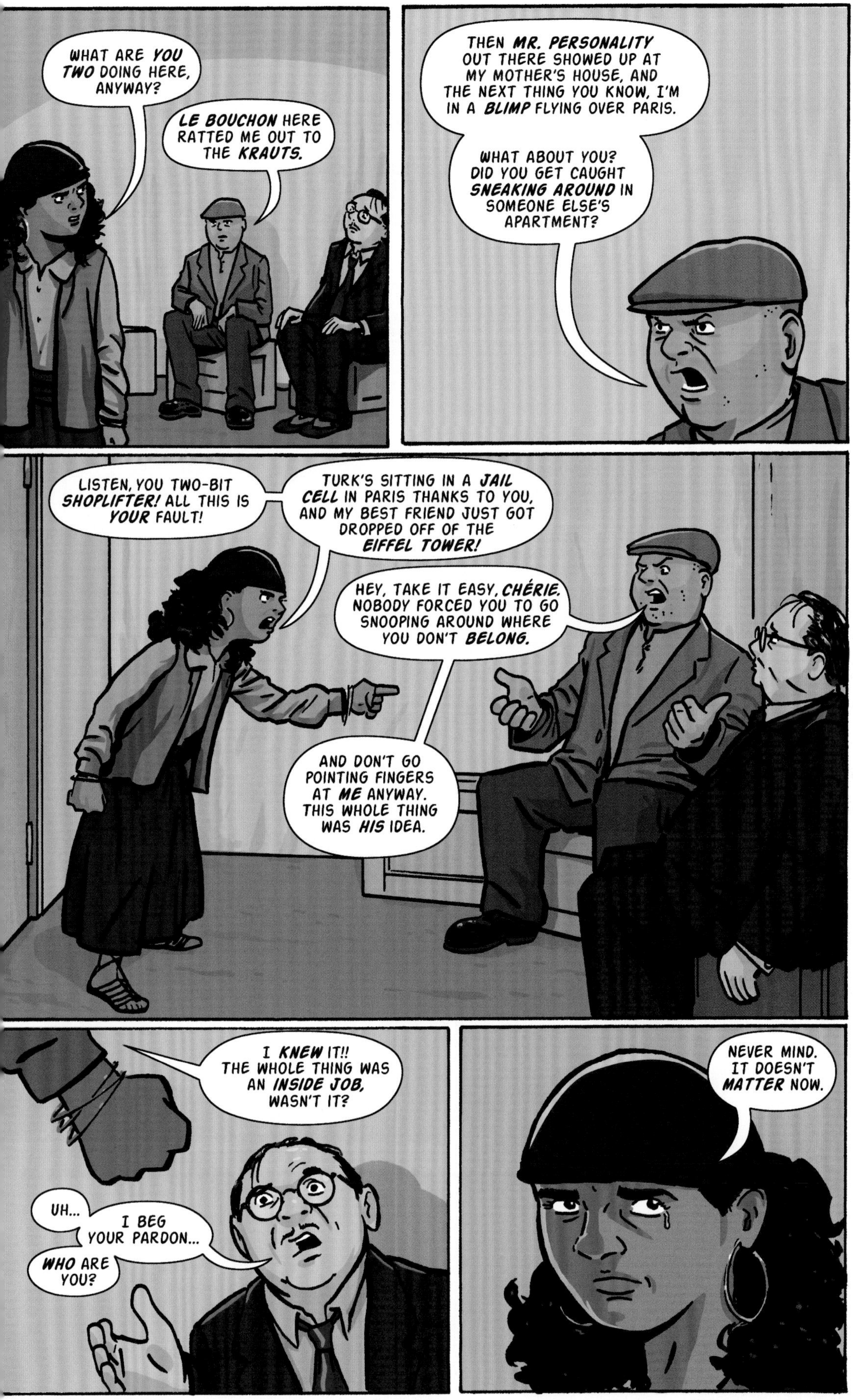
WHAT ARE YOU TWO DOING HERE, ANYWAY?
LE BOUCHON HERE RATTED ME OUT TO THE KRAUTS.
THEN MR. PERSONALITY OUT THERE SHOWED UP AT MY MOTHER'S HOUSE, AND THE NEXT THING YOU KNOW, I'M IN A BLIMP FLYING OVER PARIS.
WHAT ABOUT YOU? DID YOU GET CAUGHT SNEAKING AROUND IN SOMEONE ELSE'S APARTMENT?
LISTEN, YOU TWO-BIT SHOPLIFTER! ALL THIS IS YOUR FAULT!
TURK'S SITTING IN A JAIL CELL IN PARIS THANKS TO YOU, AND MY BEST FRIEND JUST GOT DROPPED OFF OF THE EIFFEL TOWER!
HEY, TAKE IT EASY, CHÉRIE. NOBODY FORCED YOU TO GO SNOOPING AROUND WHERE YOU DON'T BELONG.
AND DON'T GO POINTING FINGERS AT ME ANYWAY. THIS WHOLE THING WAS HIS IDEA.
I KNEW IT!! THE WHOLE THING WAS AN INSIDE JOB, WASN'T IT?
UH...
I BEG YOUR PARDON...
WHO ARE YOU?
NEVER MIND. IT DOESN'T MATTER NOW.

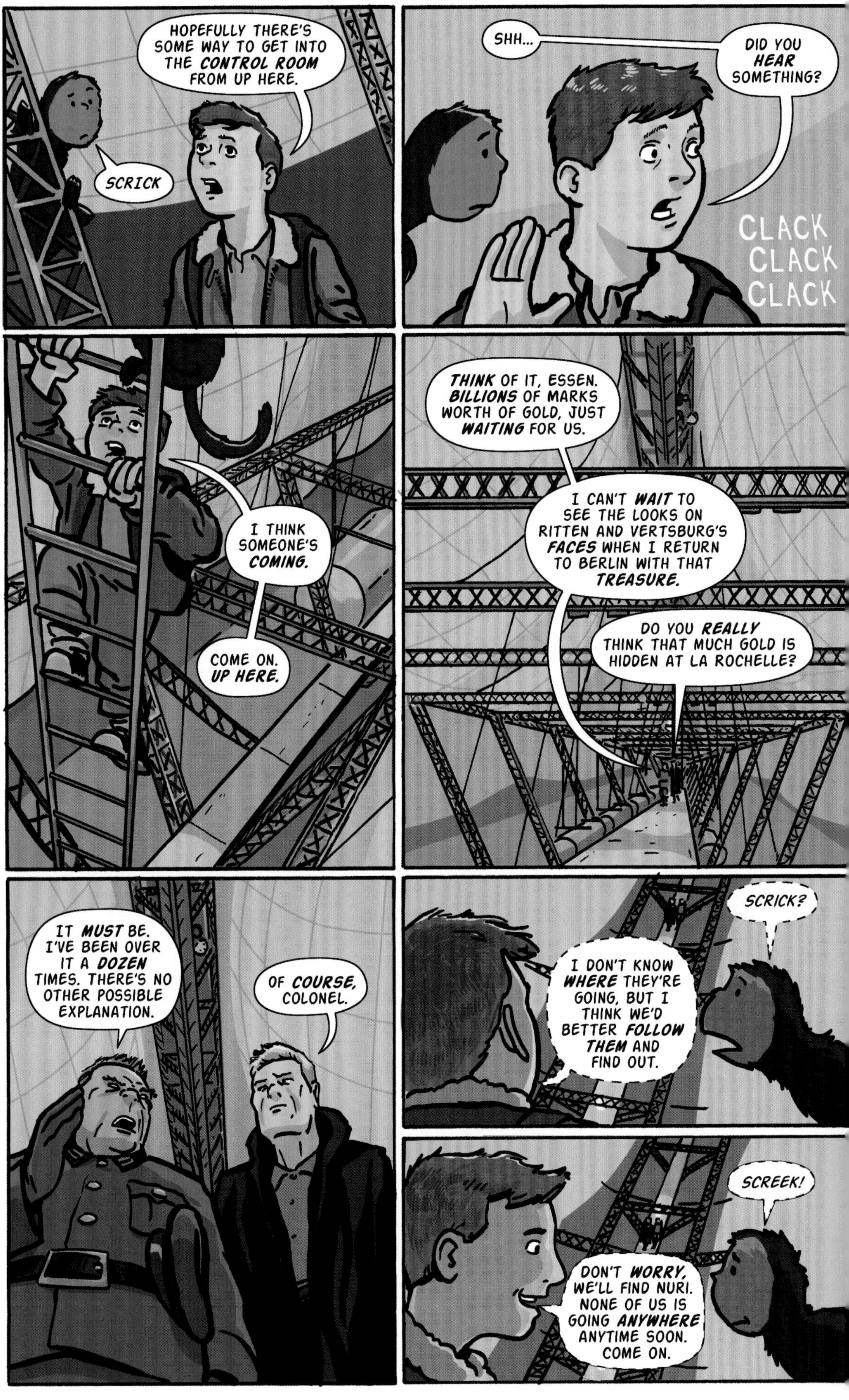
HOPEFULLY THERE'S SOME WAY TO GET INTO THE CONTROL ROOM FROM UP HERE.
SCRICK
SHH...
DID YOU HEAR SOMETHING?
CLACK CLACK CLACK
I THINK SOMEONE'S COMING.
COME ON. UP HERE.
THINK OF IT, ESSEN. BILLIONS OF MARKS WORTH OF GOLD, JUST WAITING FOR US.
I CAN'T WAIT TO SEE THE LOOKS ON RITTEN AND VERTSBURG'S FACES WHEN I RETURN TO BERLIN WITH THAT TREASURE.
DO YOU REALLY THINK THAT MUCH GOLD IS HIDDEN AT LA ROCHELLE?
IT MUST BE. I'VE BEEN OVER IT A DOZEN TIMES. THERE'S NO OTHER POSSIBLE EXPLANATION.
OF COURSE, COLONEL.
SCRICK?
I DON'T KNOW WHERE THEY'RE GOING, BUT I THINK WE'D BETTER FOLLOW THEM AND FIND OUT.
SCREEK!
DON'T WORRY, WE'LL FIND NURI. NONE OF US IS GOING ANYWHERE ANYTIME SOON. COME ON.

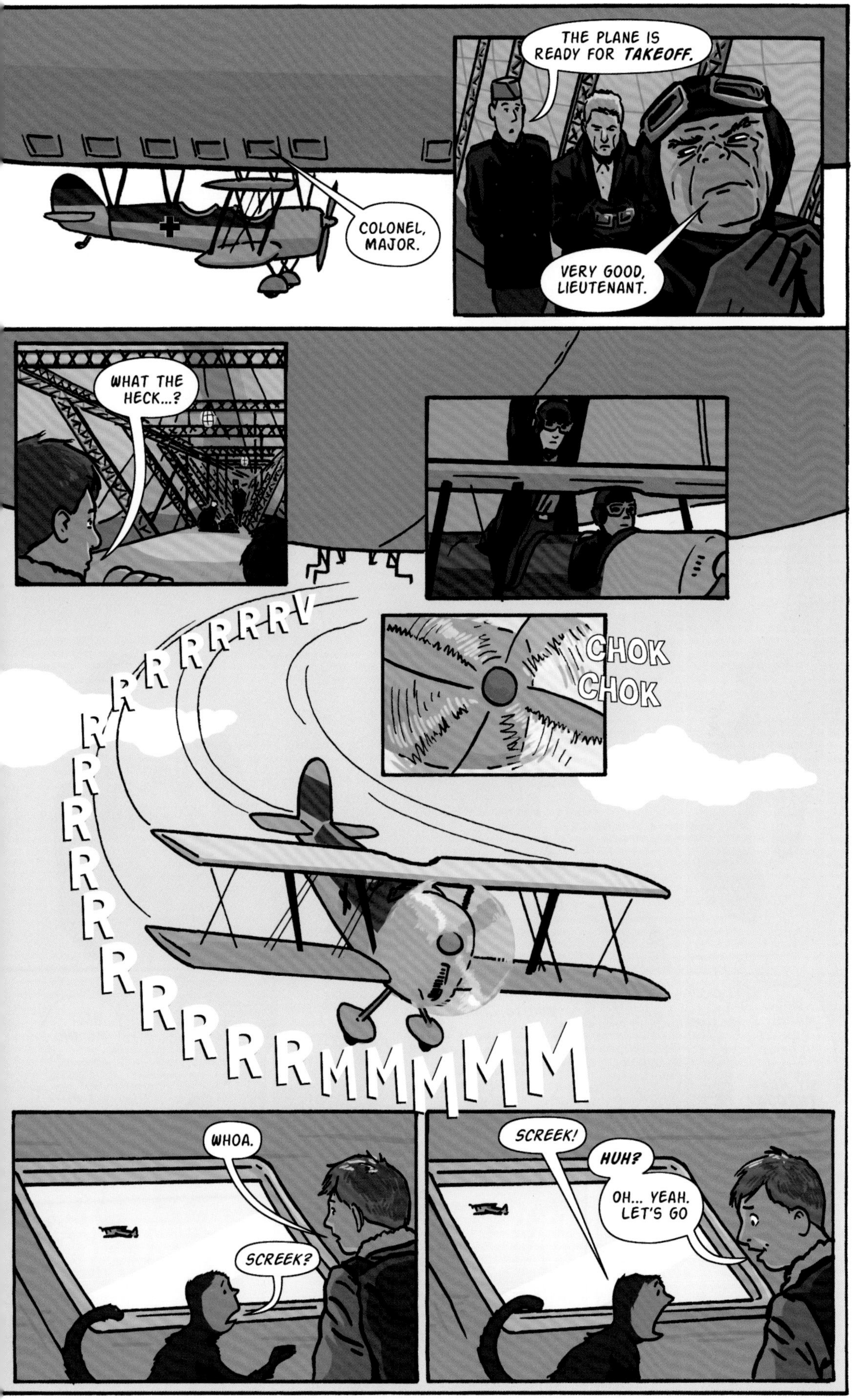
COLONEL, MAJOR.
THE PLANE IS READY FOR TAKEOFF.
VERY GOOD, LIEUTENANT.
WHAT THE HECK...?
RRRRRRRRV
CHOK CHOK
RRRRRRRRRRRRMMMMMM
WHOA.
SCREEK?
SCREEK!
HUH?
OH... YEAH. LET'S GO

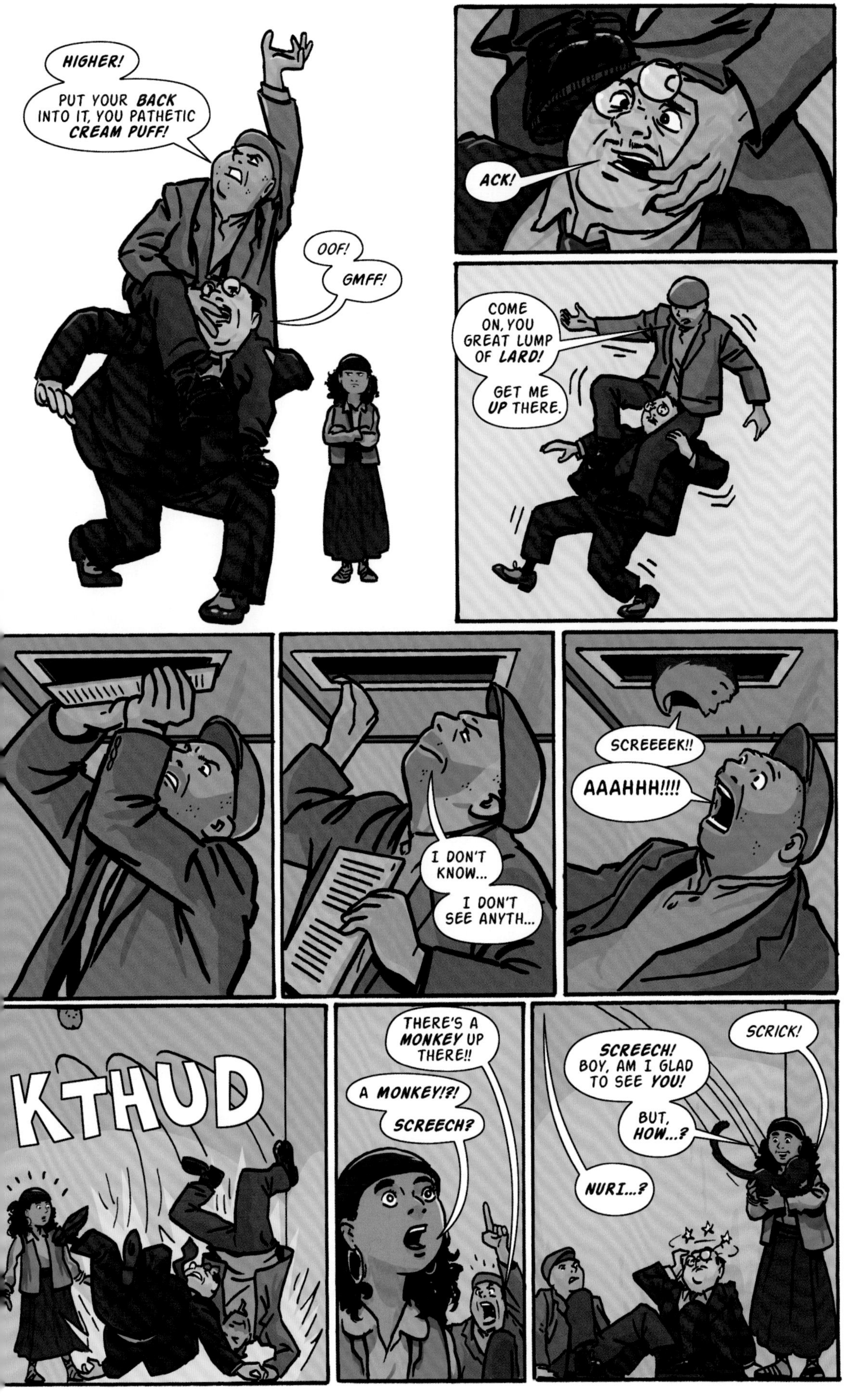
HIGHER!
PUT YOUR BACK INTO IT, YOU PATHETIC CREAM PUFF!
OOF!
GMFF!
ACK!
COME ON, YOU GREAT LUMP OF LARD!
GET ME UP THERE.
I DON'T KNOW...
I DON'T SEE ANYTH...
SCREEEEK!!
AAAHHH!!!!
KTHUD
THERE'S A MONKEY UP THERE!!
A MONKEY!?!
SCREECH?
SCRICK!
SCREECH! BOY, AM I GLAD TO SEE YOU!
BUT, HOW...?
NURI...?

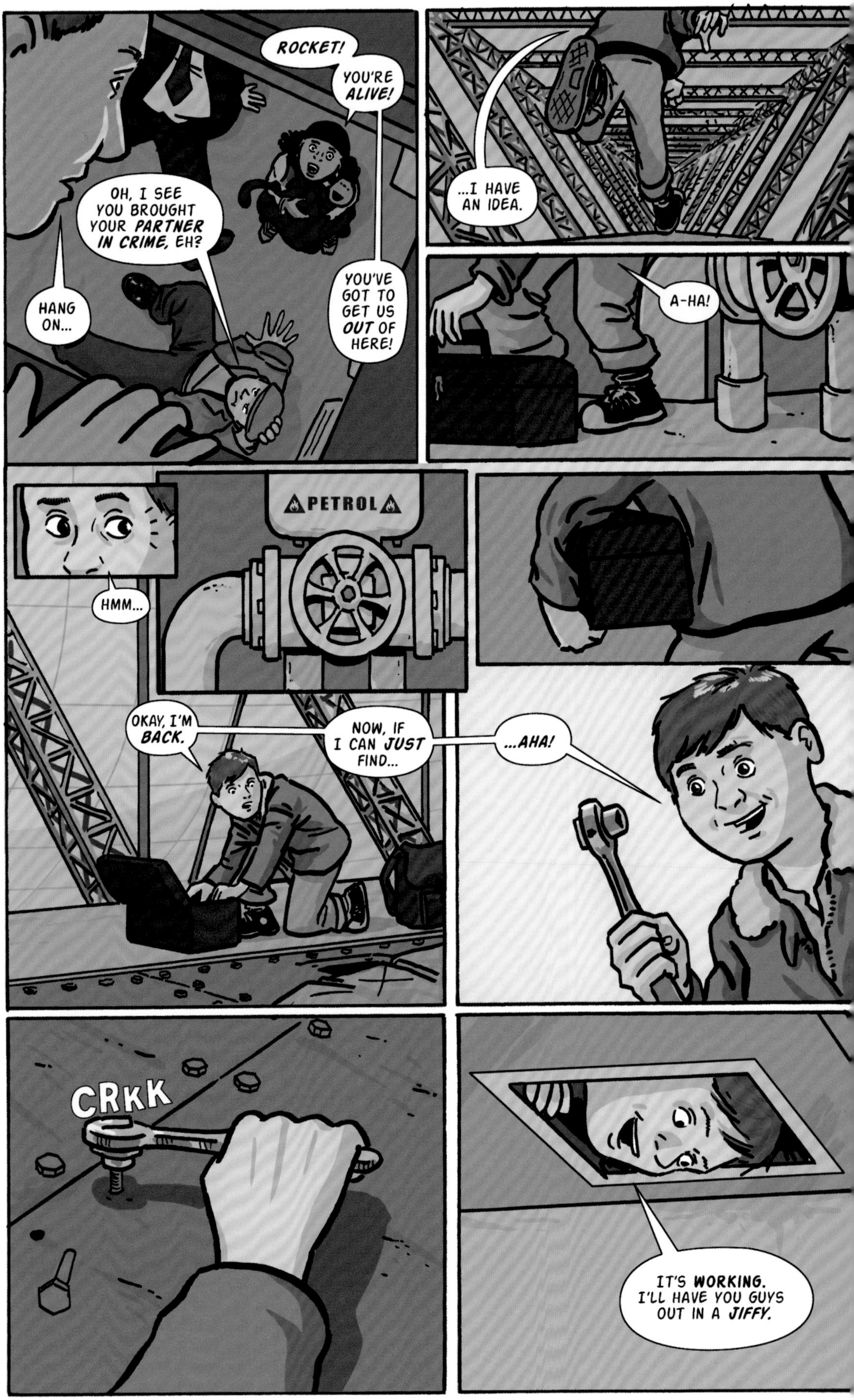
ROCKET!
YOU'RE ALIVE!
OH, I SEE YOU BROUGHT YOUR PARTNER IN CRIME, EH?
HANG ON...
YOU'VE GOT TO GET US OUT OF HERE!
...I HAVE AN IDEA.
A-HA!
HMM...
PETROL
OKAY, I'M BACK.
NOW, IF I CAN JUST FIND...
...AHA!
CRKK
IT'S WORKING. I'LL HAVE YOU GUYS OUT IN A JIFFY.

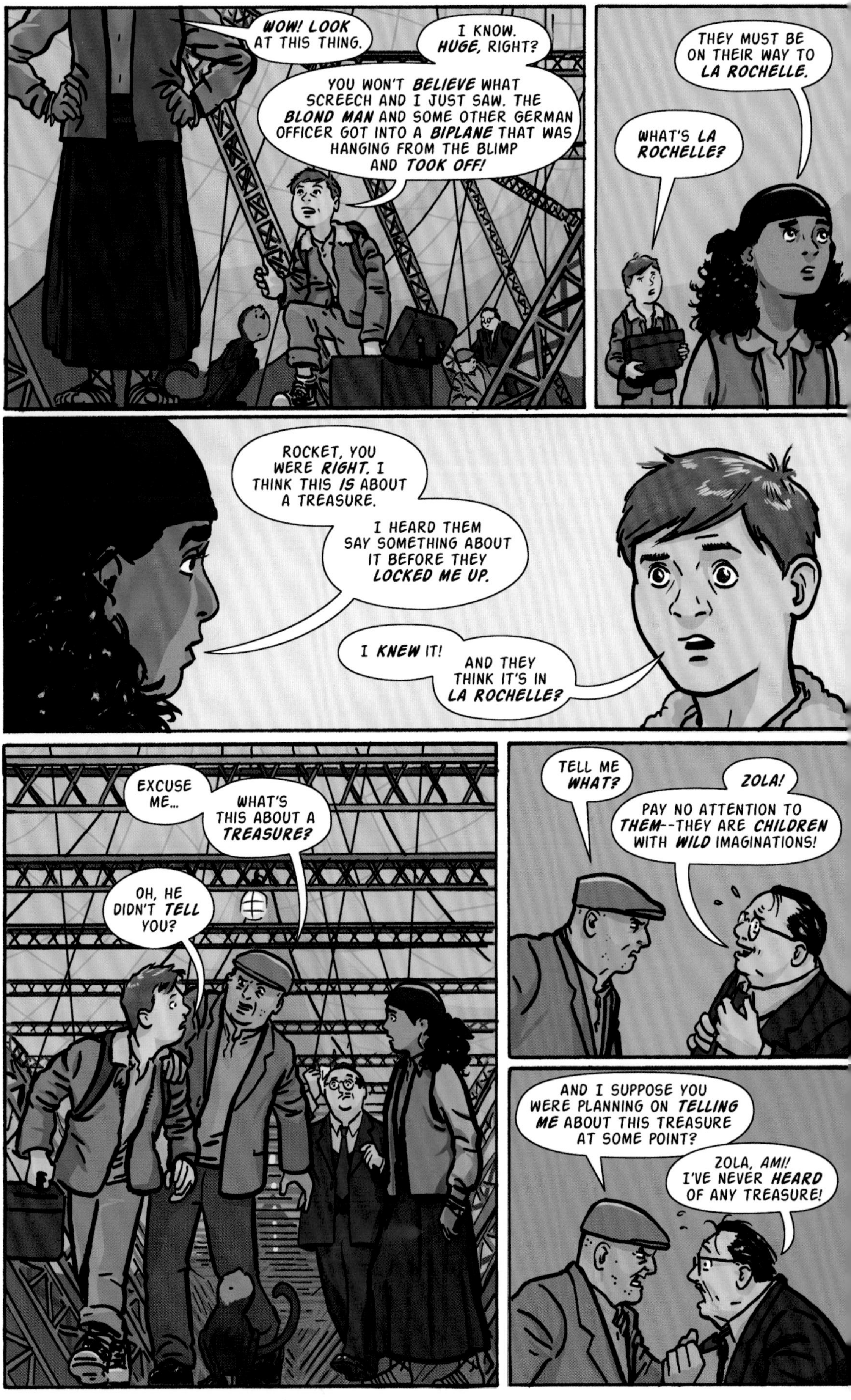
WOW! LOOK AT THIS THING.
I KNOW. HUGE, RIGHT?
YOU WON'T BELIEVE WHAT SCREECH AND I JUST SAW. THE BLOND MAN AND SOME OTHER GERMAN OFFICER GOT INTO A BIPLANE THAT WAS HANGING FROM THE BLIMP AND TOOK OFF!
THEY MUST BE ON THEIR WAY TO LA ROCHELLE.
WHAT'S LA ROCHELLE?
ROCKET, YOU WERE RIGHT. I THINK THIS IS ABOUT A TREASURE.
I HEARD THEM SAY SOMETHING ABOUT IT BEFORE THEY LOCKED ME UP.
I KNEW IT!
AND THEY THINK IT'S IN LA ROCHELLE?
EXCUSE ME...
WHAT'S THIS ABOUT A TREASURE?
OH, HE DIDN'T TELL YOU?
TELL ME WHAT?
ZOLA!
PAY NO ATTENTION TO THEM--THEY ARE CHILDREN WITH WILD IMAGINATIONS!
AND I SUPPOSE YOU WERE PLANNING ON TELLING ME ABOUT THIS TREASURE AT SOME POINT?
ZOLA, AMI! I'VE NEVER HEARD OF ANY TREASURE!

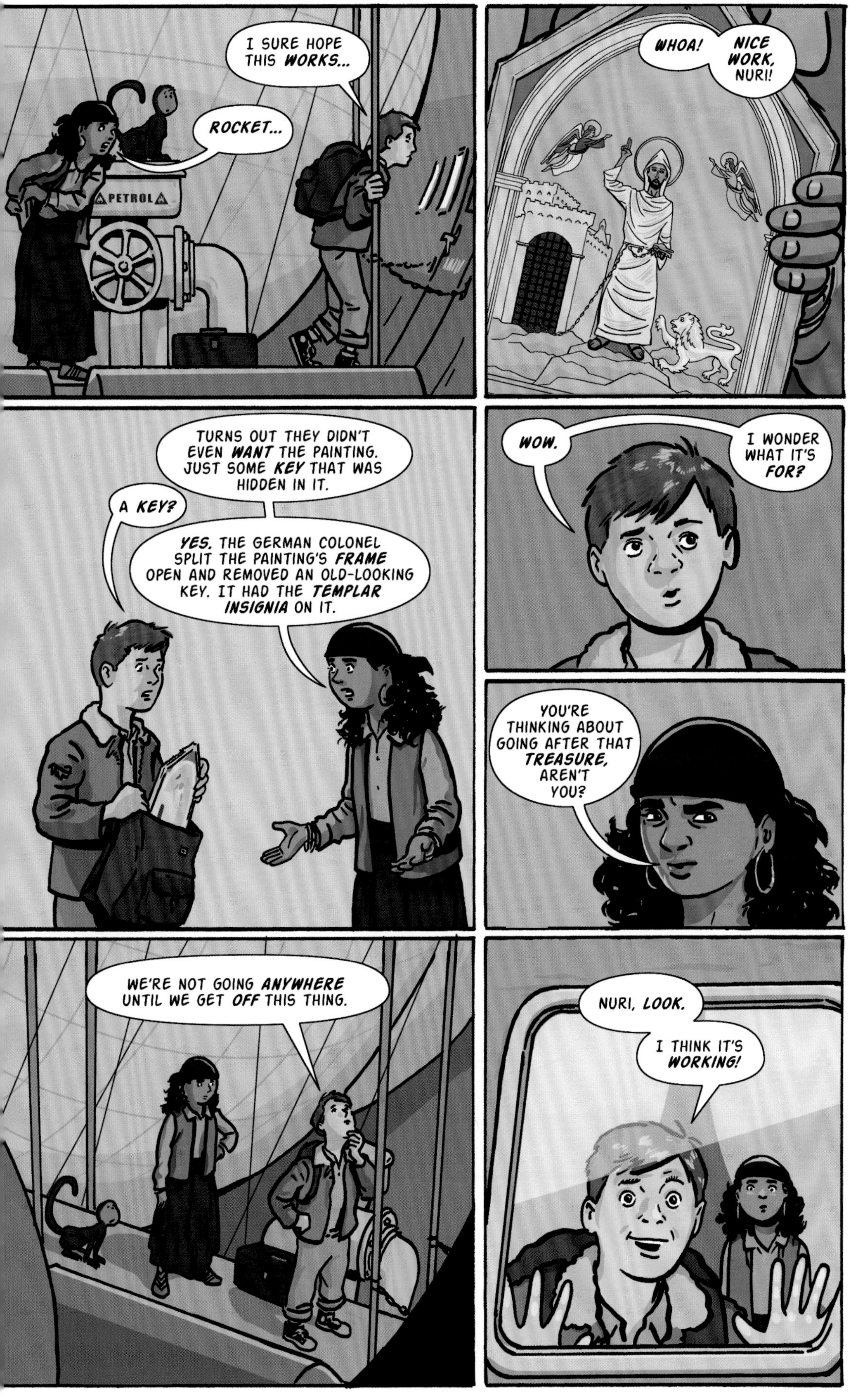
I SURE HOPE THIS WORKS...
ROCKET...
PETROL
WHOA!
NICE WORK, NURI!
TURNS OUT THEY DIDN'T EVEN WANT THE PAINTING. JUST SOME KEY THAT WAS HIDDEN IN IT.
A KEY?
YES. THE GERMAN COLONEL SPLIT THE PAINTING'S FRAME OPEN AND REMOVED AN OLD-LOOKING KEY. IT HAD THE TEMPLAR INSIGNIA ON IT.
WOW.
I WONDER WHAT IT'S FOR?
YOU'RE THINKING ABOUT GOING AFTER THAT TREASURE, AREN'T YOU?
WE'RE NOT GOING ANYWHERE UNTIL WE GET OFF THIS THING.
NURI, LOOK.
I THINK IT'S WORKING!

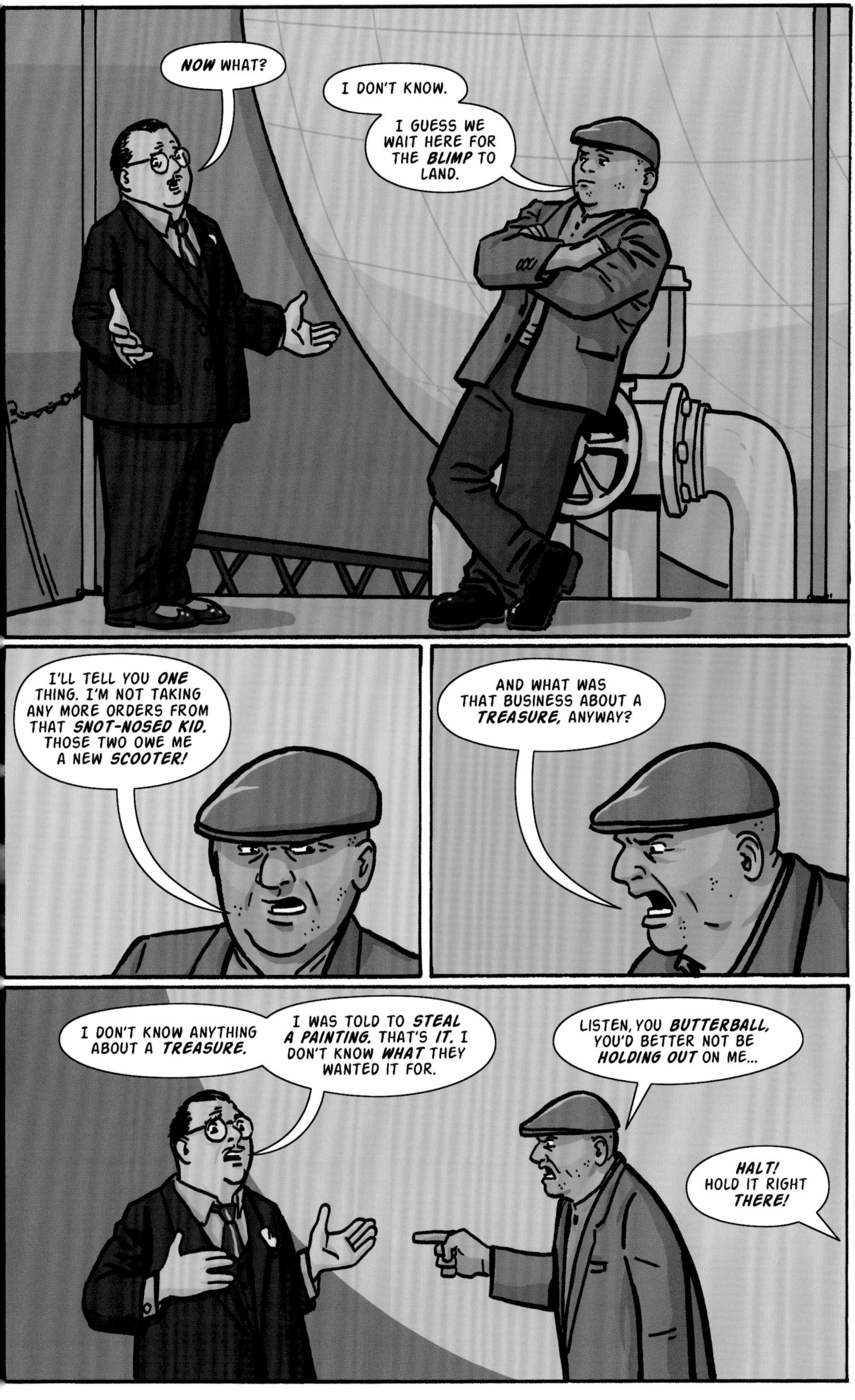
NOW WHAT?
I DON'T KNOW.
I GUESS WE WAIT HERE FOR THE BLIMP TO LAND.
I'LL TELL YOU ONE THING. I'M NOT TAKING ANY MORE ORDERS FROM THAT SNOT-NOSED KID. THOSE TWO OWE ME A NEW SCOOTER!
AND WHAT WAS THAT BUSINESS ABOUT A TREASURE, ANYWAY?
I DON'T KNOW ANYTHING ABOUT A TREASURE.
I WAS TOLD TO STEAL A PAINTING. THAT'S IT. I DON'T KNOW WHAT THEY WANTED IT FOR.
LISTEN, YOU BUTTERBALL, YOU'D BETTER NOT BE HOLDING OUT ON ME...
HALT! HOLD IT RIGHT THERE!

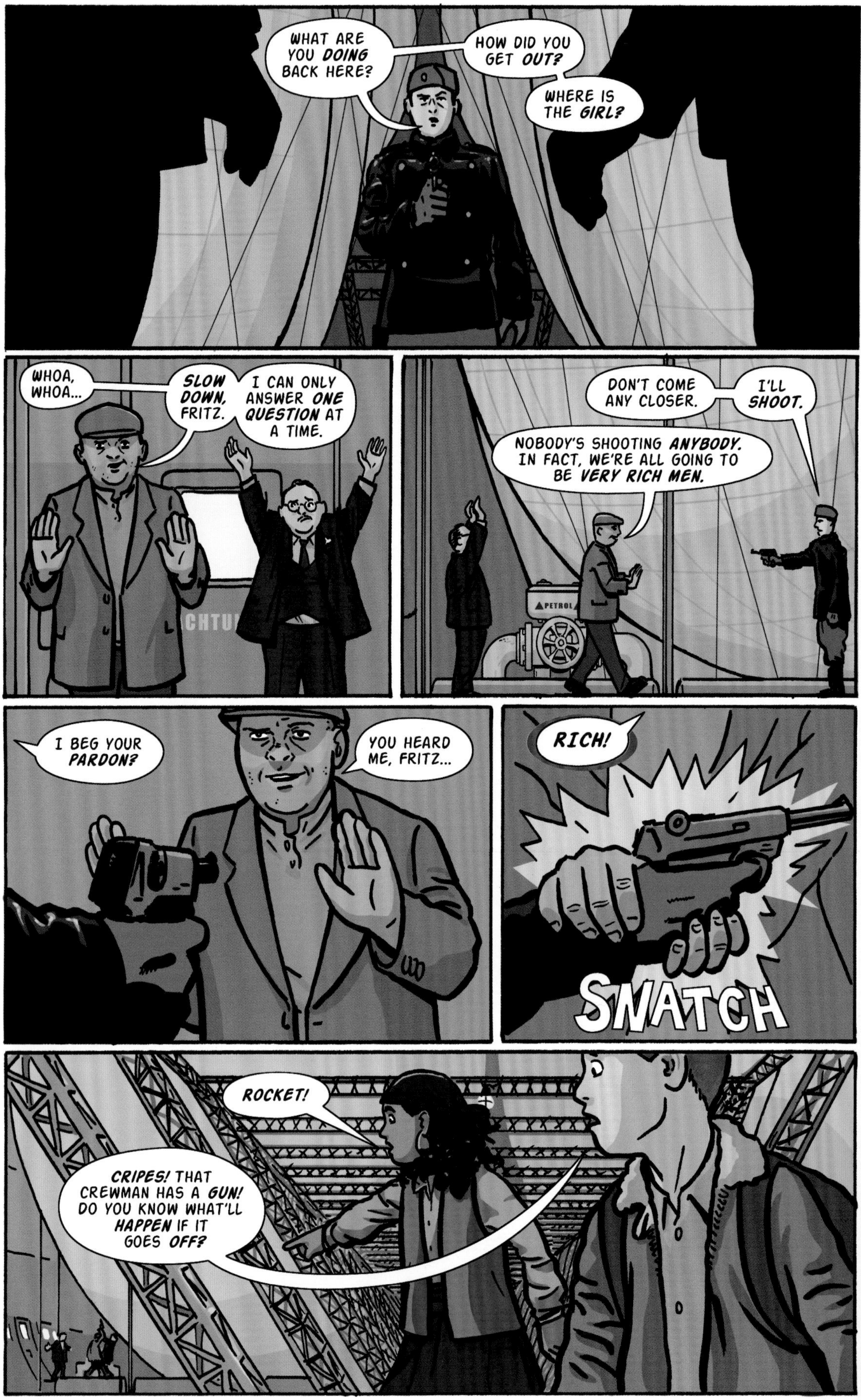

WHAT ARE YOU DOING BACK HERE?
HOW DID YOU GET OUT?
WHERE IS THE GIRL?
WHOA, WHOA...
SLOW DOWN, FRITZ.
I CAN ONLY ANSWER ONE QUESTION AT A TIME.
DON'T COME ANY CLOSER.
I'LL SHOOT.
NOBODY'S SHOOTING ANYBODY. IN FACT, WE'RE ALL GOING TO BE VERY RICH MEN.
PETROL
I BEG YOUR PARDON?
YOU HEARD ME, FRITZ...
RICH!
SNATCH
ROCKET!
CRIPES! THAT CREWMAN HAS A GUN! DO YOU KNOW WHAT'LL HAPPEN IF IT GOES OFF?

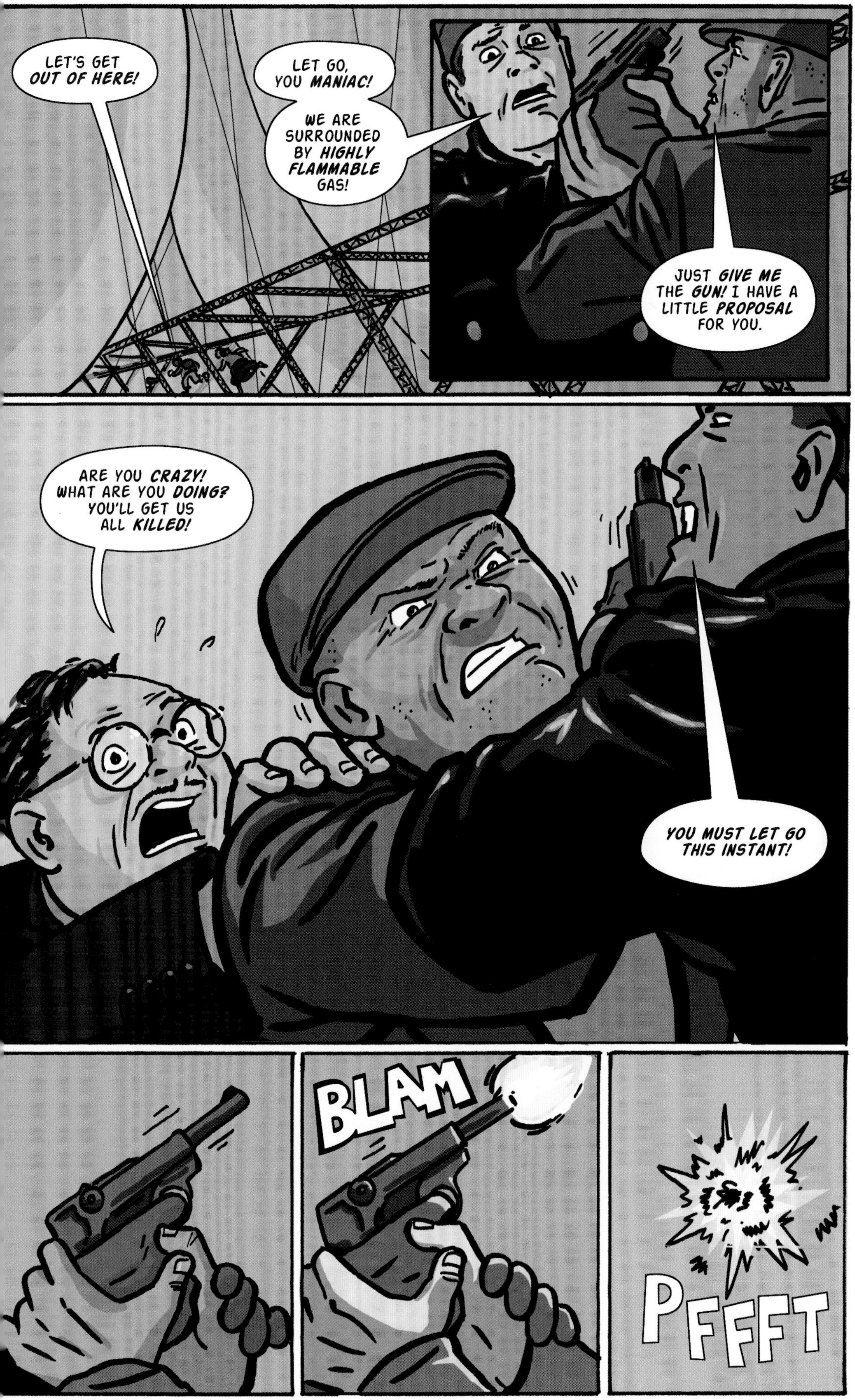
LET'S GET OUT OF HERE!
LET GO, YOU MANIAC!
WE ARE SURROUNDED BY HIGHLY FLAMMABLE GAS!
JUST GIVE ME THE GUN! I HAVE A LITTLE PROPOSAL FOR YOU.
ARE YOU CRAZY! WHAT ARE YOU DOING? YOU'LL GET US ALL KILLED!
YOU MUST LET GO THIS INSTANT!
BLAM
PFFFT

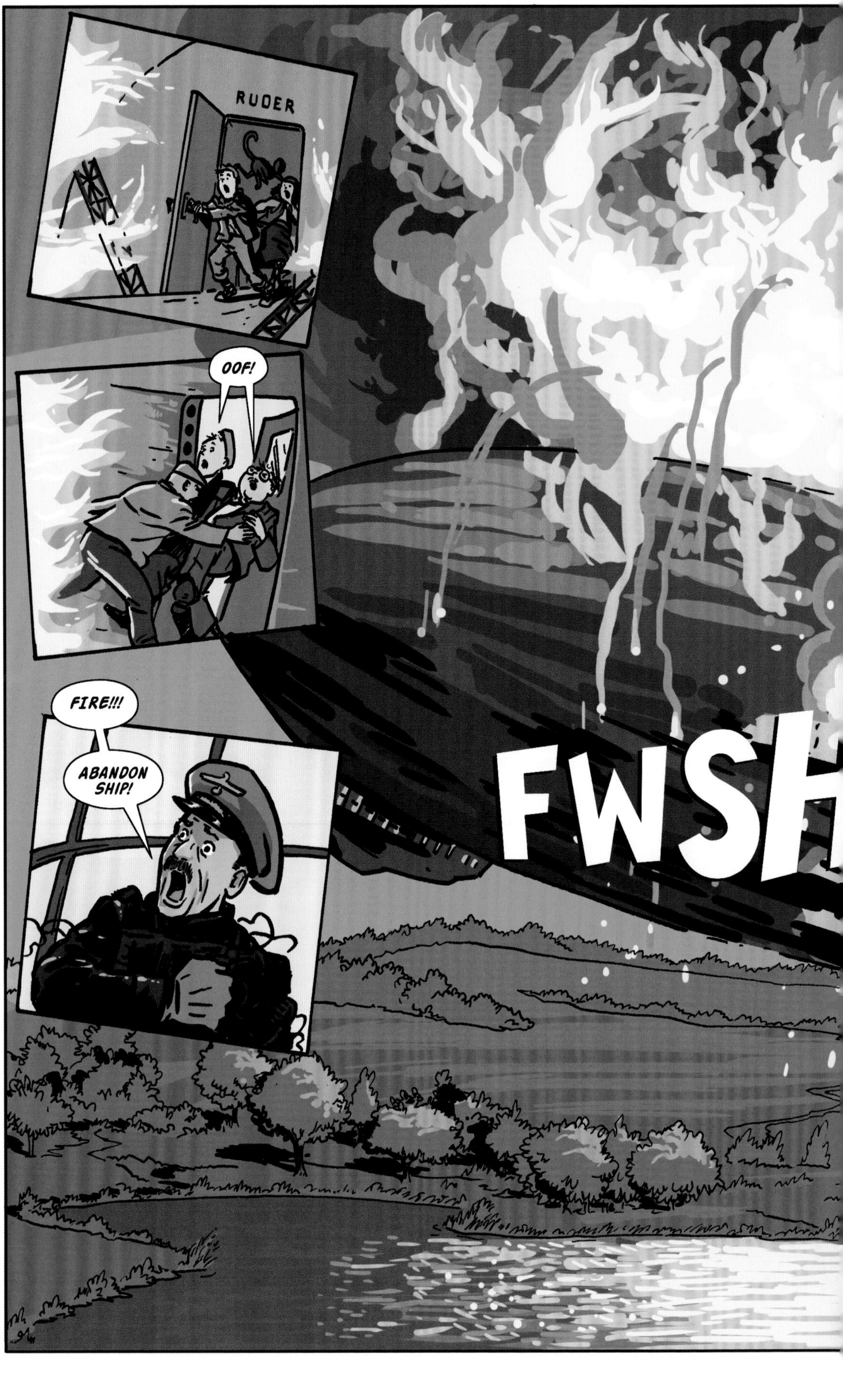
RUDER
OOF!
FIRE!!!
ABANDON SHIP!
FWSH

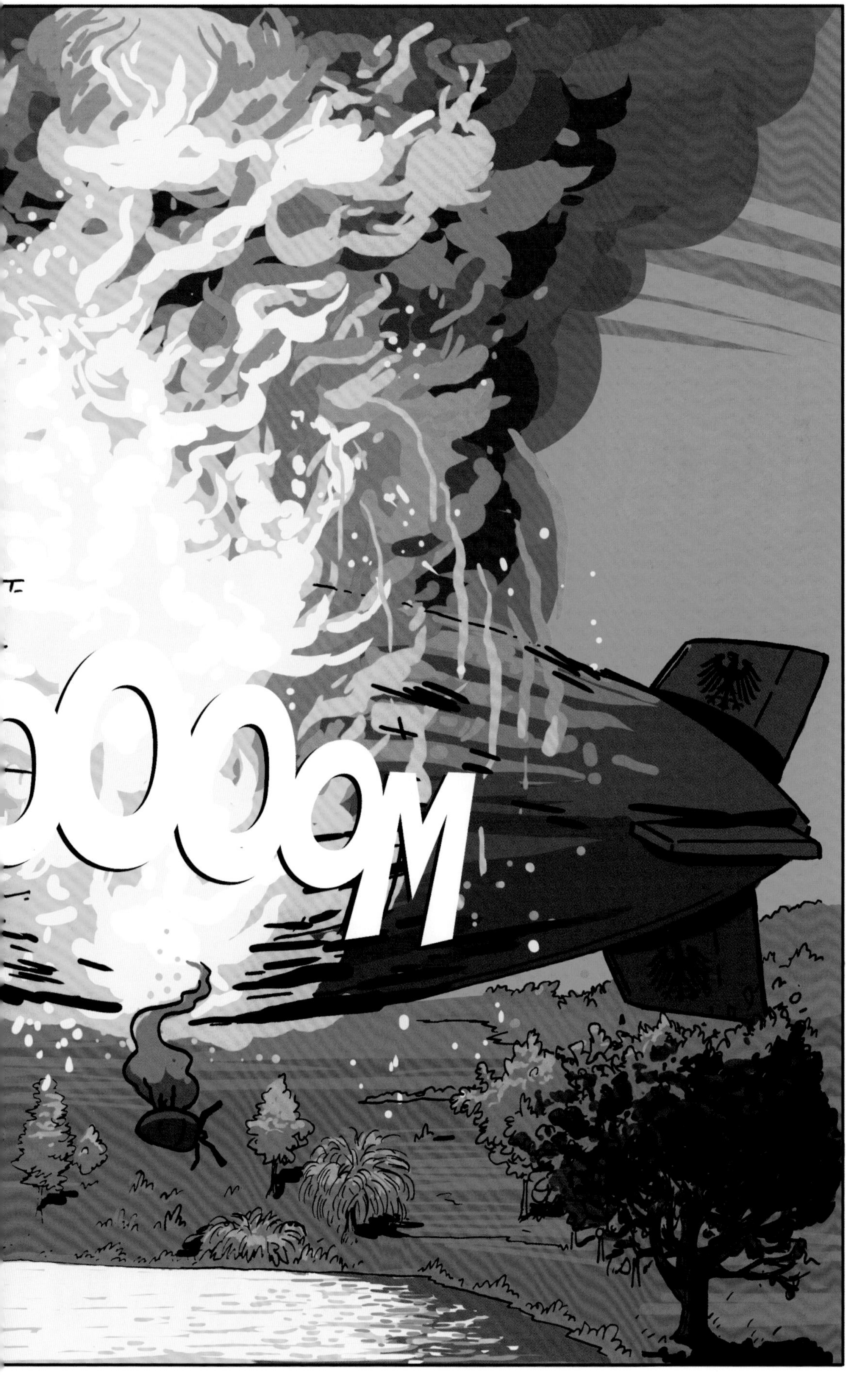
OOOOOM

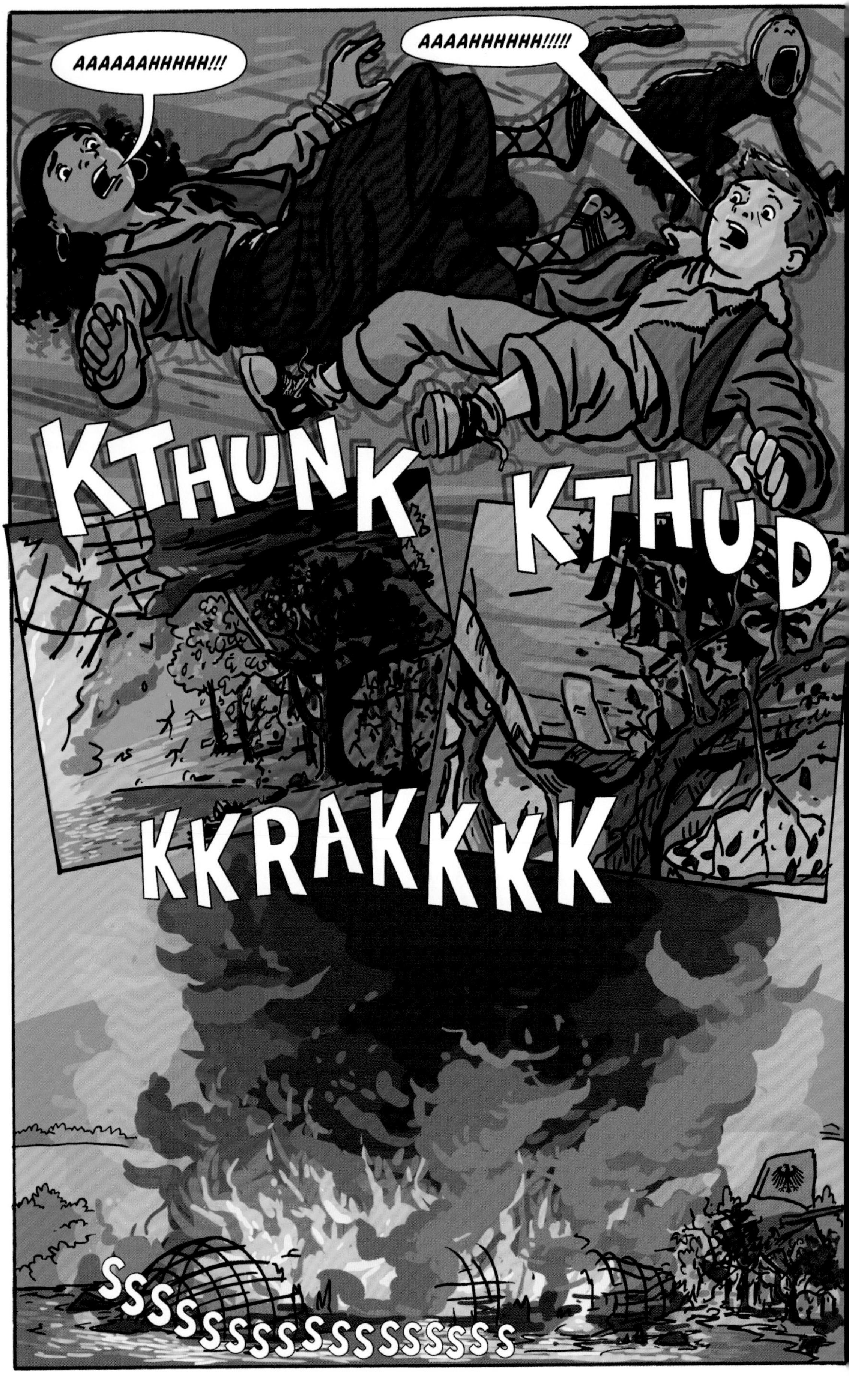
AAAAAAHHHHH!!!
AAAAHHHHHH!!!!!
KTHUNK
KTHUD
KKRAKKKK
SSSSSSSSSSSSSSSSSS

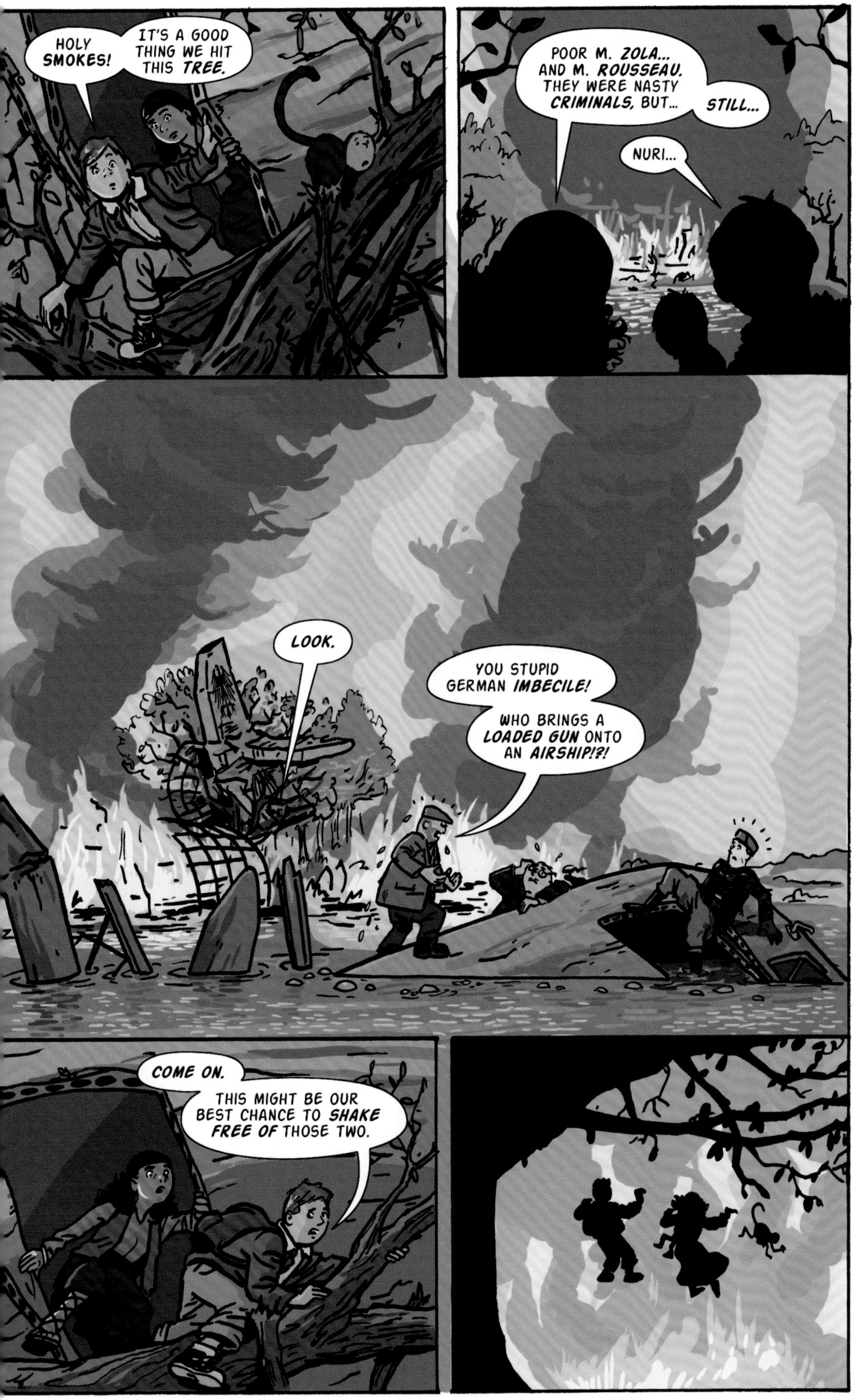
HOLY SMOKES!
IT'S A GOOD THING WE HIT THIS TREE.
POOR M. ZOLA... AND M. ROUSSEAU. THEY WERE NASTY CRIMINALS, BUT...
STILL...
NURI...
LOOK.
YOU STUPID GERMAN IMBECILE!
WHO BRINGS A LOADED GUN ONTO AN AIRSHIP!?!
COME ON.
THIS MIGHT BE OUR BEST CHANCE TO SHAKE FREE OF THOSE TWO.

BUT, INSPECTOR, THIS IS *URGENT!*

I'M AFRAID WE HAVE *NO RECORD* OF A TRANSFER OR AN *INSPECTOR ESSEN.*

BUT THAT'S *IMPOSSIBLE.* I HAVE HIS PAPERWORK *RIGHT HERE.* THERE MUST BE SOME *MISTAKE.*

THERE IS *NO MISTAKE.* WE CHECKED THREE TIMES. THERE'S *NO MEMBER* OF THE PARIS POLICE FORCE WITH THAT NAME.

HM... *VERY WELL.* MERCI...

INSPECTOR!

MME. VERANT. IF YOU DON'T *MIND,* I AM A LITTLE *BUSY* TODAY!

PLEASE, JUST *LISTEN* TO ME. DO YOU REMEMBER THE *TWO CHILDREN* THAT CAME TO SEE ME? *ROCKET* AND *NURI?*

YES. THE *GIRL* IS RELATED TO THE *THIEF.*

YES, WELL, THEY WERE *VERY CURIOUS* ABOUT THE HISTORY OF THE MISSING PAINTING. THEY ALSO INSISTED THAT *MARCEL ROUSSEAU,* THE DIRECTOR OF MEDIEVAL ART, WAS *INVOLVED* IN THE ROBBERY.

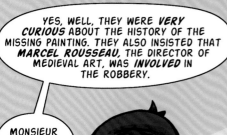

MONSIEUR ROUSSEAU *DIDN'T SHOW UP* FOR WORK TODAY.

NOBODY'S HEARD FROM HIM.

WONDERFUL. A MISSING DETECTIVE *AND* A MISSING WITNESS.

...SO, SINCE I COULDN'T *INTERVIEW* HIM, I DECIDED TO TAKE A LITTLE LOOK AROUND HIS *OFFICE...*

...WHERE I FOUND *THIS!*

DATE: MAI 16, 1933
TIME FILED: 08.15
SENDING STATION: BERLIN, GER

TELEGRAMME
La Poste Mondiale Service Telegraphique

M. ROUSSEAU CONGRATULATIONS ON YOUR RECENT SUCCESS —STOP— I AM EAGER TO COLLECT THE ITEM AT THE EARLIEST CONVENIENCE —STOP— PLEASE REMEMBER THAT OUR FÜHRER REWARDS LOYALTY BUT HAS LITTLE PATIENCE FOR FAILURE.

COL KREUTZ —END

I ADMIT IT'S A BIT *SUSPICIOUS.* BUT THIS DOESN'T PROVE...

CHAPTER NINE

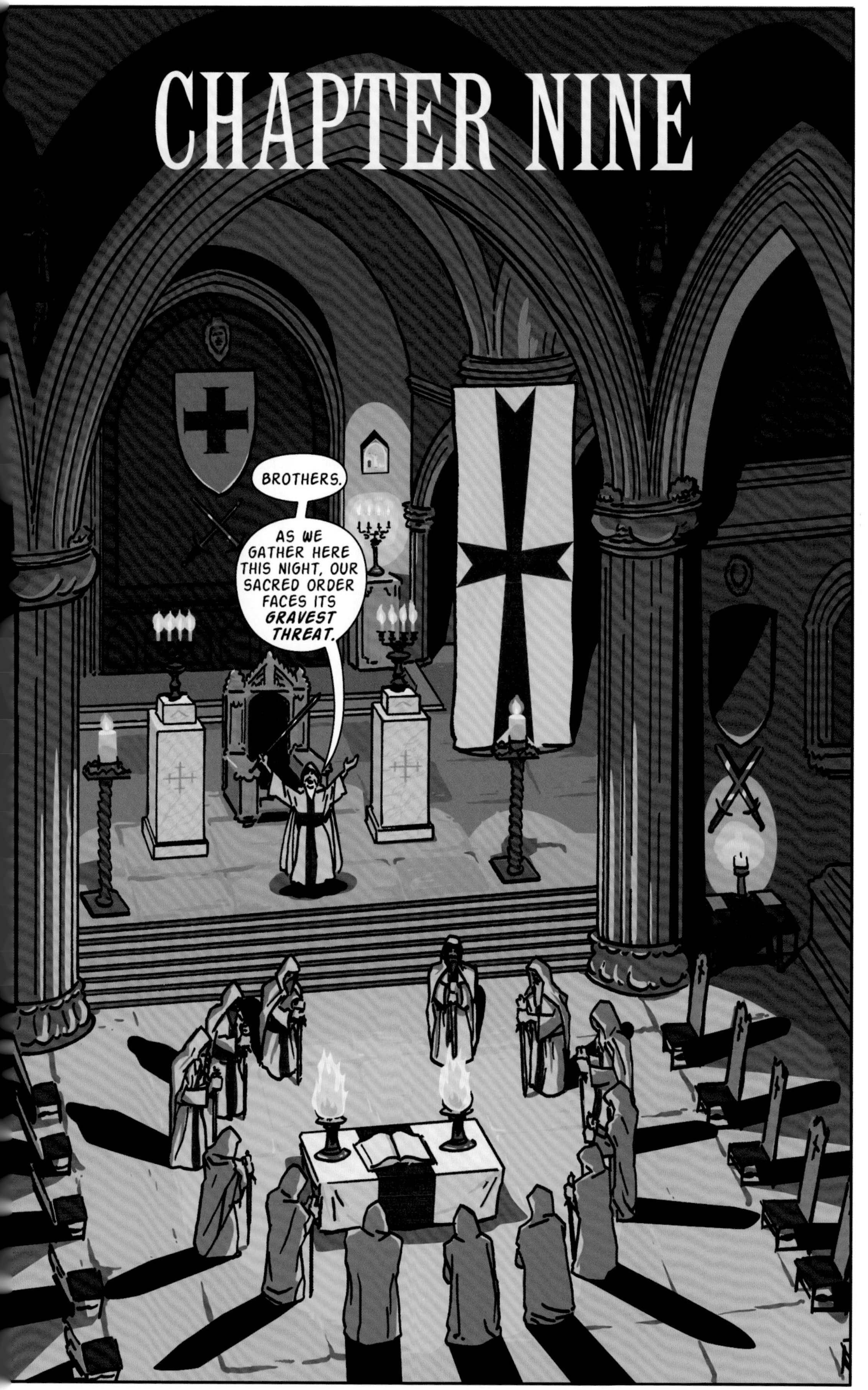
BROTHERS.
AS WE GATHER HERE THIS NIGHT, OUR SACRED ORDER FACES ITS *GRAVEST THREAT.*

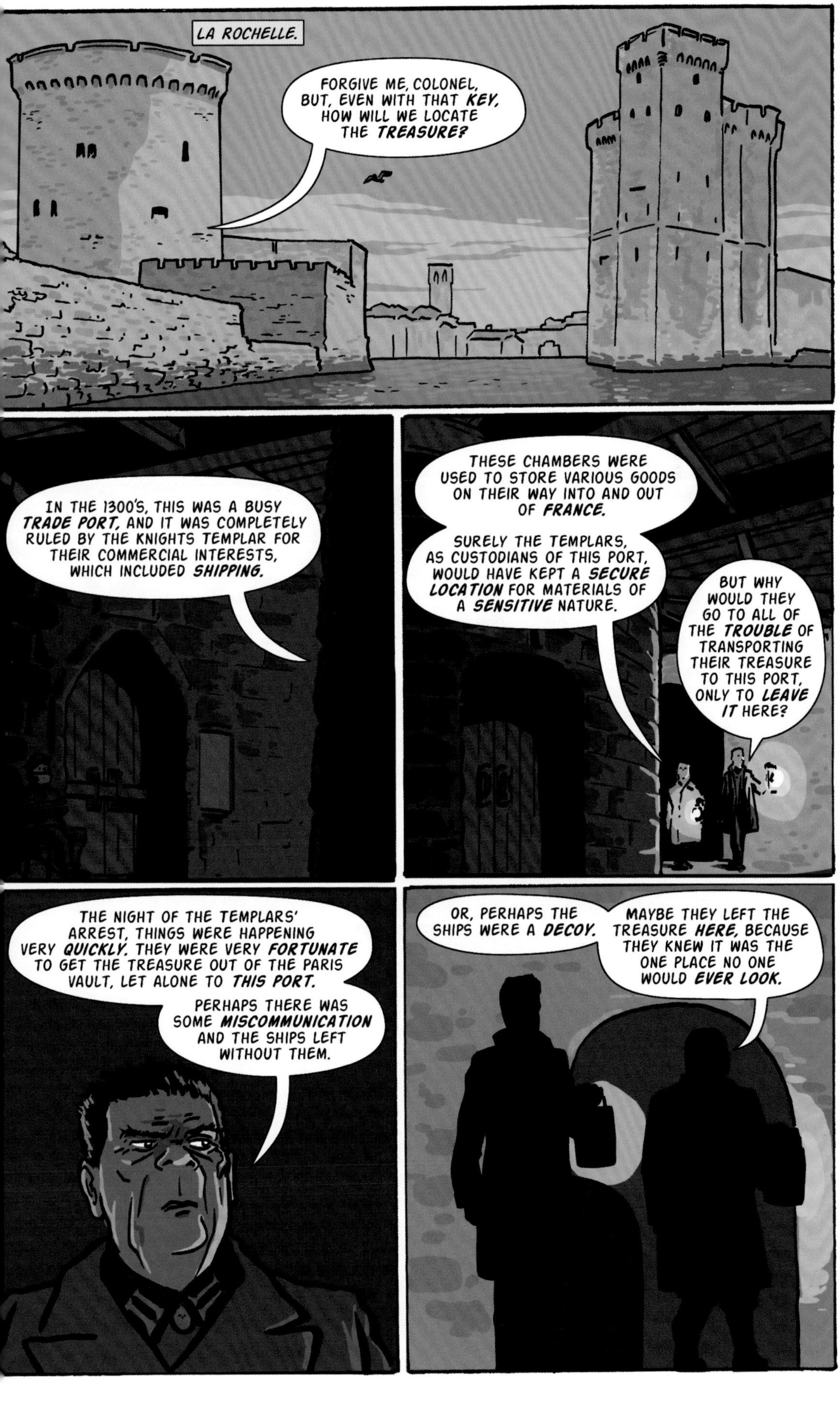
LA ROCHELLE.
FORGIVE ME, COLONEL, BUT, EVEN WITH THAT KEY, HOW WILL WE LOCATE THE TREASURE?
IN THE 1300'S, THIS WAS A BUSY TRADE PORT, AND IT WAS COMPLETELY RULED BY THE KNIGHTS TEMPLAR FOR THEIR COMMERCIAL INTERESTS, WHICH INCLUDED SHIPPING.
THESE CHAMBERS WERE USED TO STORE VARIOUS GOODS ON THEIR WAY INTO AND OUT OF FRANCE.
SURELY THE TEMPLARS, AS CUSTODIANS OF THIS PORT, WOULD HAVE KEPT A SECURE LOCATION FOR MATERIALS OF A SENSITIVE NATURE.
BUT WHY WOULD THEY GO TO ALL OF THE TROUBLE OF TRANSPORTING THEIR TREASURE TO THIS PORT, ONLY TO LEAVE IT HERE?
THE NIGHT OF THE TEMPLARS' ARREST, THINGS WERE HAPPENING VERY QUICKLY. THEY WERE VERY FORTUNATE TO GET THE TREASURE OUT OF THE PARIS VAULT, LET ALONE TO THIS PORT.
PERHAPS THERE WAS SOME MISCOMMUNICATION AND THE SHIPS LEFT WITHOUT THEM.
OR, PERHAPS THE SHIPS WERE A DECOY.
MAYBE THEY LEFT THE TREASURE HERE, BECAUSE THEY KNEW IT WAS THE ONE PLACE NO ONE WOULD EVER LOOK.

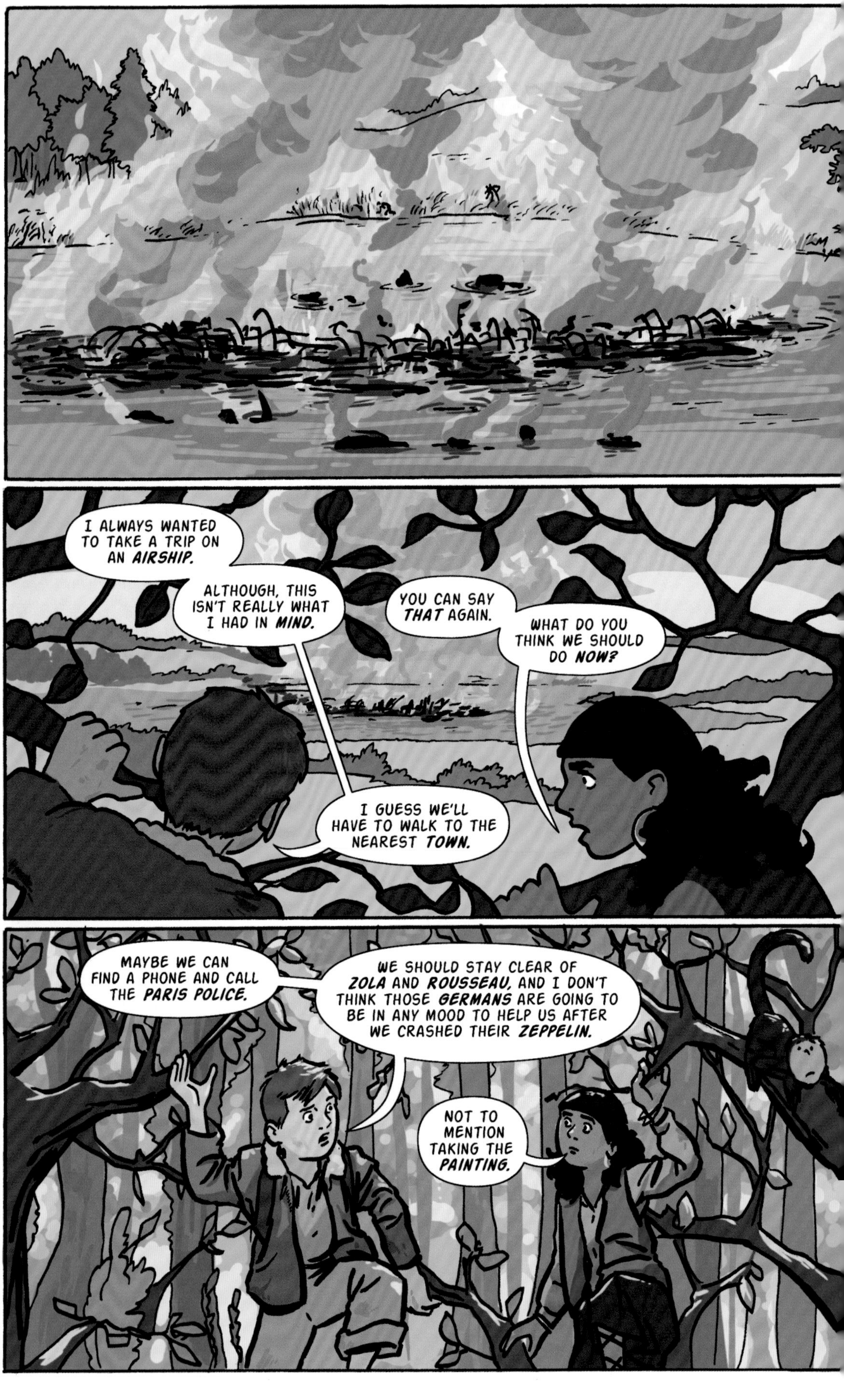

I ALWAYS WANTED TO TAKE A TRIP ON AN *AIRSHIP.*
ALTHOUGH, THIS ISN'T REALLY WHAT I HAD IN *MIND.*
YOU CAN SAY *THAT* AGAIN.
WHAT DO YOU THINK WE SHOULD DO *NOW?*
I GUESS WE'LL HAVE TO WALK TO THE NEAREST *TOWN.*
MAYBE WE CAN FIND A PHONE AND CALL THE *PARIS POLICE.*
WE SHOULD STAY CLEAR OF *ZOLA* AND *ROUSSEAU,* AND I DON'T THINK THOSE *GERMANS* ARE GOING TO BE IN ANY MOOD TO HELP US AFTER WE CRASHED THEIR *ZEPPELIN.*
NOT TO MENTION TAKING THE *PAINTING.*

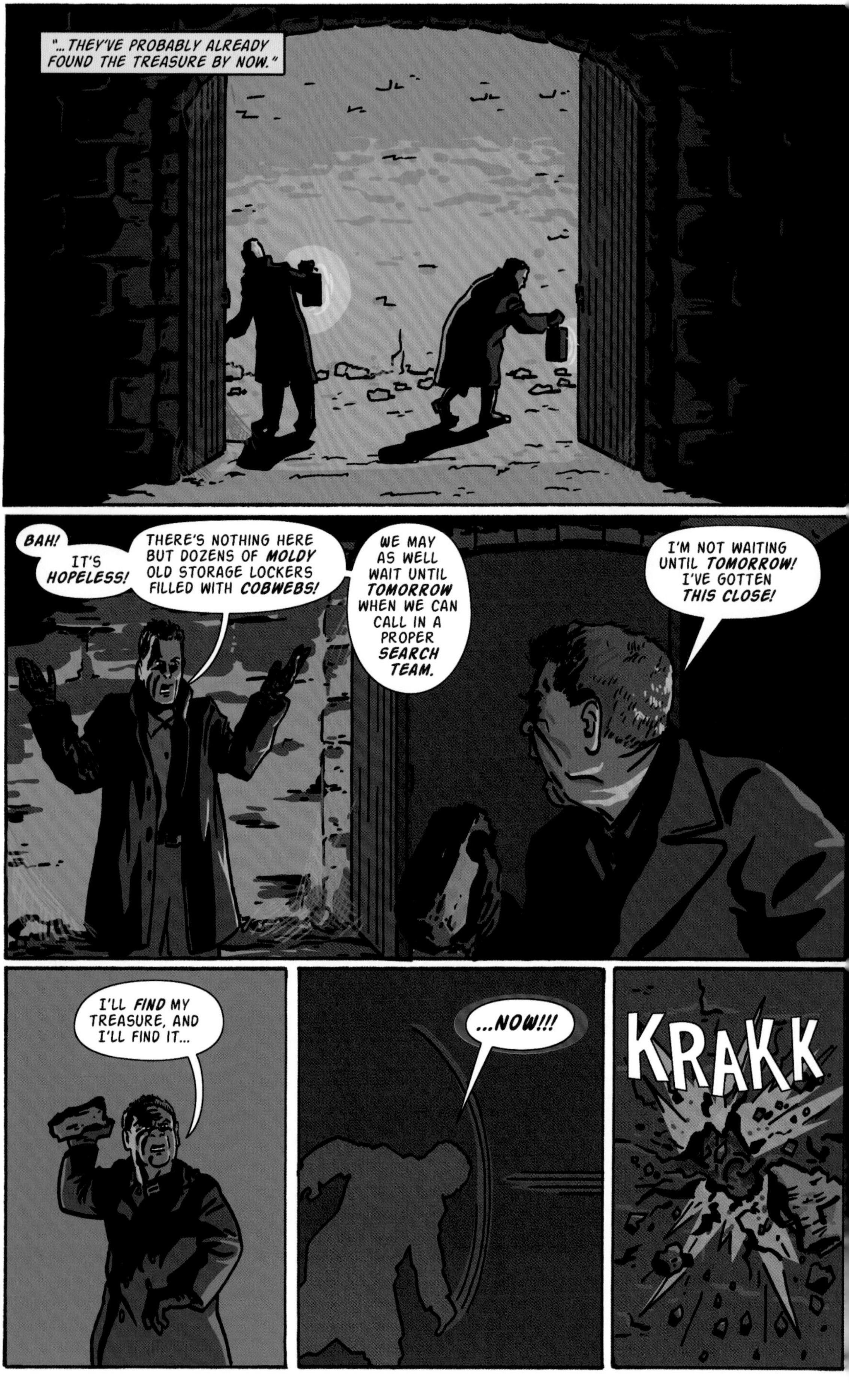

"...THEY'VE PROBABLY ALREADY FOUND THE TREASURE BY NOW."
BAH! IT'S HOPELESS!
THERE'S NOTHING HERE BUT DOZENS OF MOLDY OLD STORAGE LOCKERS FILLED WITH COBWEBS!
WE MAY AS WELL WAIT UNTIL TOMORROW WHEN WE CAN CALL IN A PROPER SEARCH TEAM.
I'M NOT WAITING UNTIL TOMORROW! I'VE GOTTEN THIS CLOSE!
I'LL FIND MY TREASURE, AND I'LL FIND IT...
...NOW!!!
KRAKK

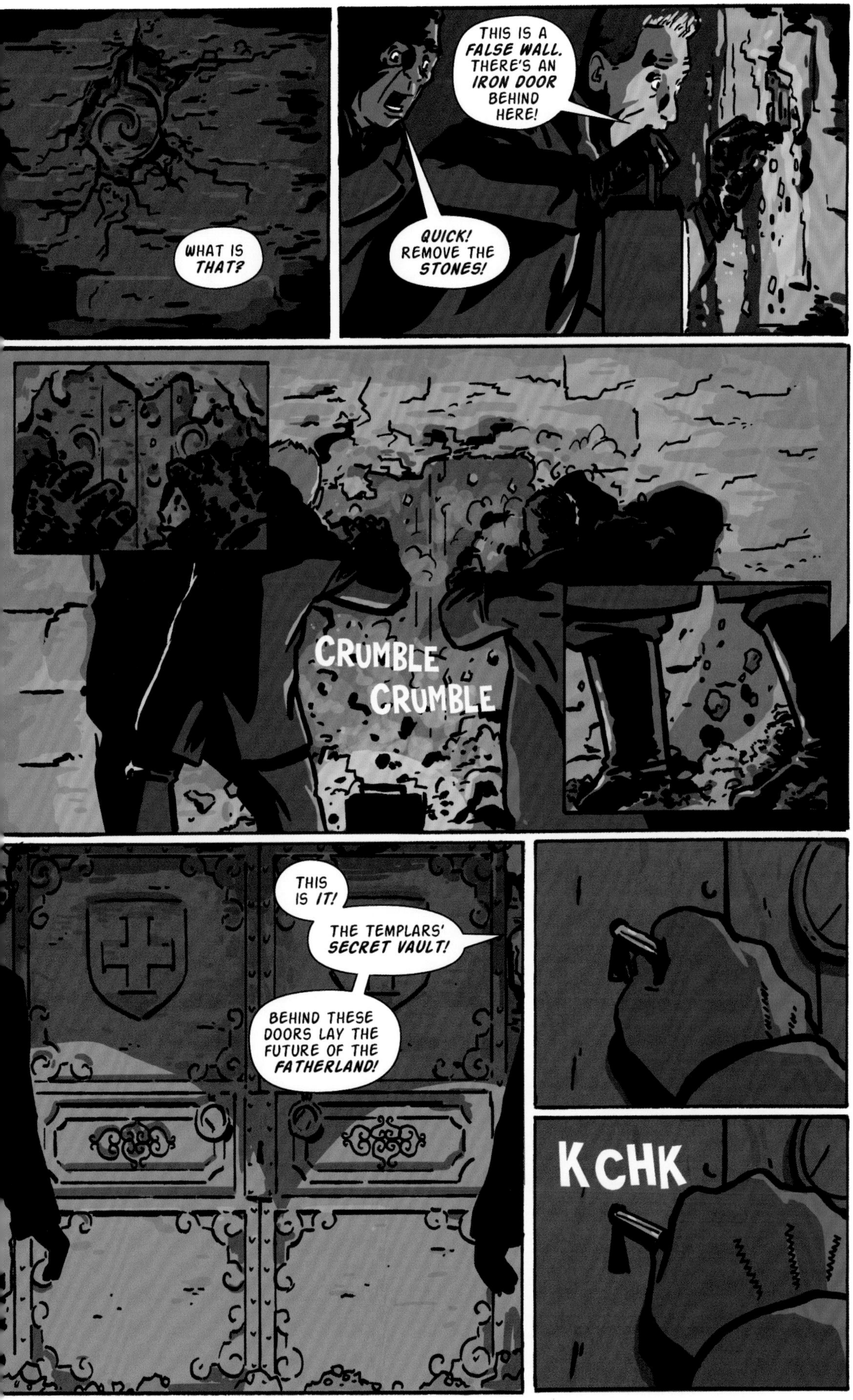
WHAT IS THAT?
THIS IS A FALSE WALL. THERE'S AN IRON DOOR BEHIND HERE!
QUICK! REMOVE THE STONES!
CRUMBLE CRUMBLE
THIS IS IT!
THE TEMPLARS' SECRET VAULT!
BEHIND THESE DOORS LAY THE FUTURE OF THE FATHERLAND!
KCHK

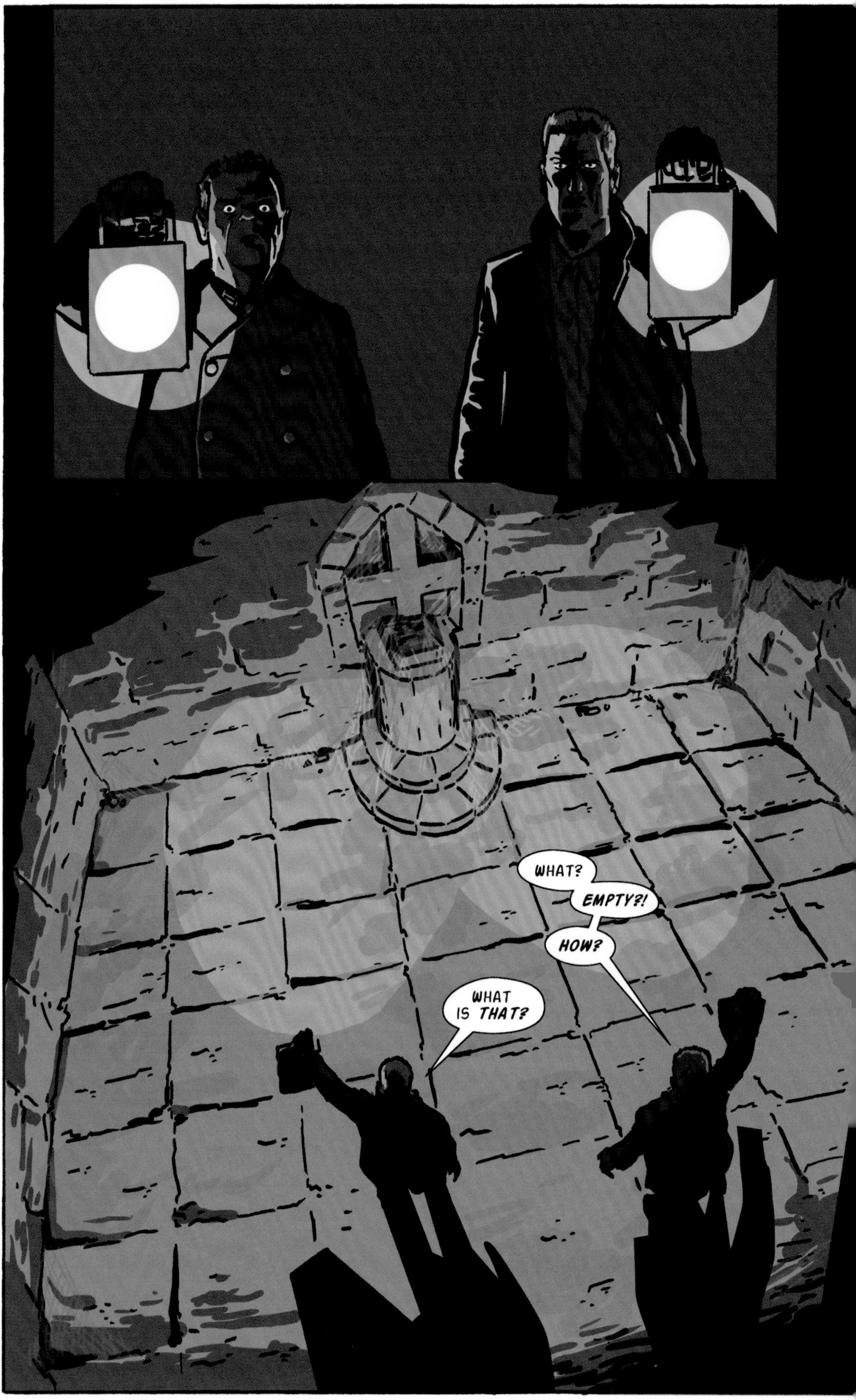
WHAT?
EMPTY?!
HOW?
WHAT IS THAT?

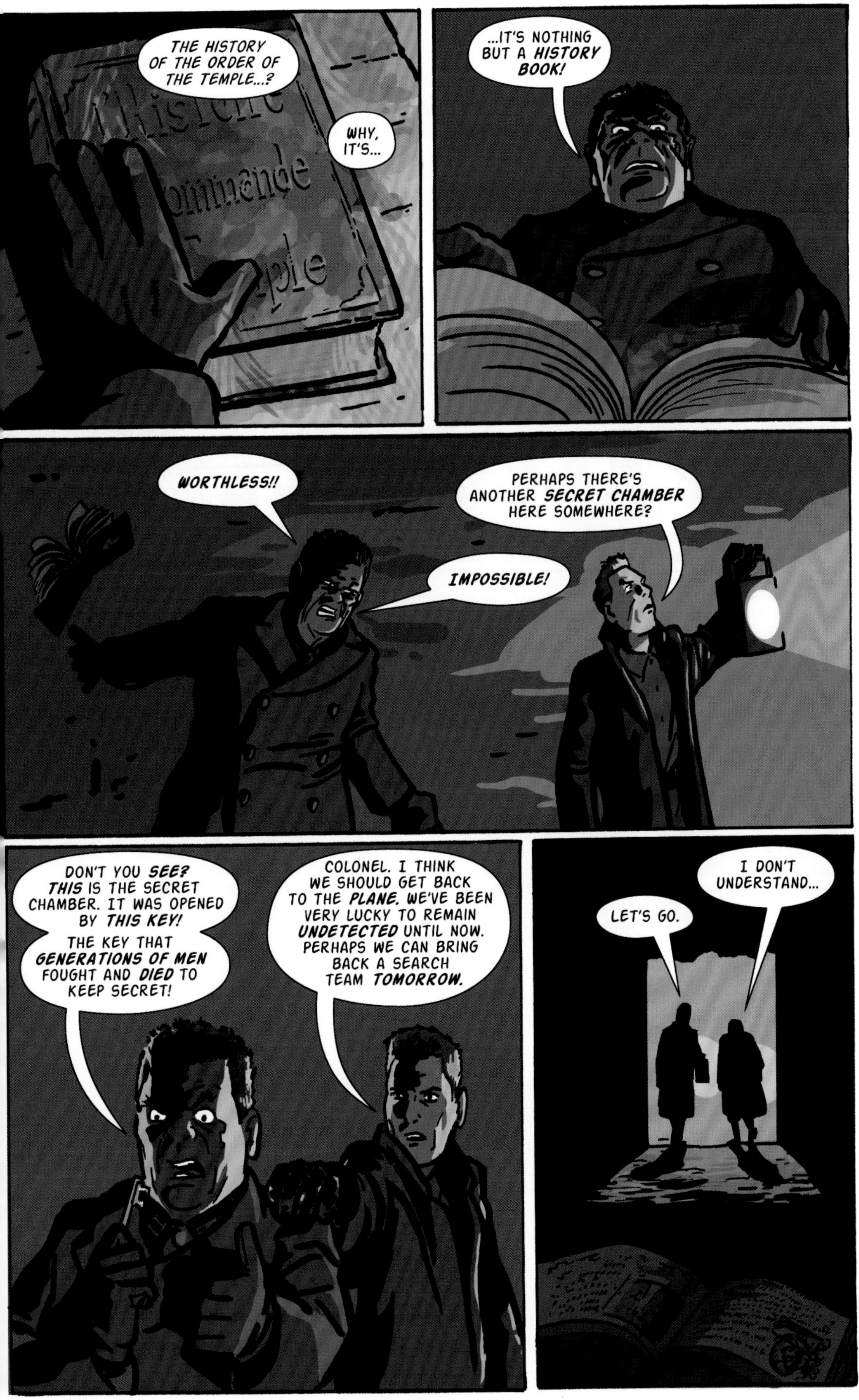
THE HISTORY OF THE ORDER OF THE TEMPLE...?
WHY, IT'S...
...IT'S NOTHING BUT A *HISTORY BOOK!*
WORTHLESS!!
PERHAPS THERE'S ANOTHER *SECRET CHAMBER* HERE SOMEWHERE?
IMPOSSIBLE!
DON'T YOU *SEE? THIS* IS THE SECRET CHAMBER. IT WAS OPENED BY *THIS KEY!*
THE KEY THAT *GENERATIONS OF MEN* FOUGHT AND *DIED* TO KEEP SECRET!
COLONEL. I THINK WE SHOULD GET BACK TO THE *PLANE.* WE'VE BEEN VERY LUCKY TO REMAIN *UNDETECTED* UNTIL NOW. PERHAPS WE CAN BRING BACK A SEARCH TEAM *TOMORROW.*
LET'S GO.
I DON'T UNDERSTAND...

DOESN'T LOOK LIKE WE'RE REAL CLOSE TO *ANYTHING*.

ROCKET, LOOK AT *THAT*.

THE *LION* ON THAT SIGN...

RÉGION AQUITAINE

LIBOURNE 30 KM

ORE 25 KM

IT'S JUST LIKE THE ONE ON THE *PAINTING*.

WHAT WAS THAT IN YOUR *ROBIN HOOD* BOOK?

SOMETHING ABOUT *AQUITAINE?*

UH...

IT'S...

...IT'S RIGHT *HERE*.

LET'S SEE...

HERE IT IS.

"IN HIS LATER YEARS, RICHARD SPENT MUCH TIME IN HIS CASTLES IN FRANCE, INCLUDING **CHÂTEAU DE BEYNAC** IN **AQUITAINE**, THE ANCESTRAL HOME OF RICHARD'S MOTHER, *ELEANOR OF AQUITAINE*."

ROCKET...

LIBOURNE 30 KM

SORE 25 KM

BEYNAC 20 KM

LOOK.

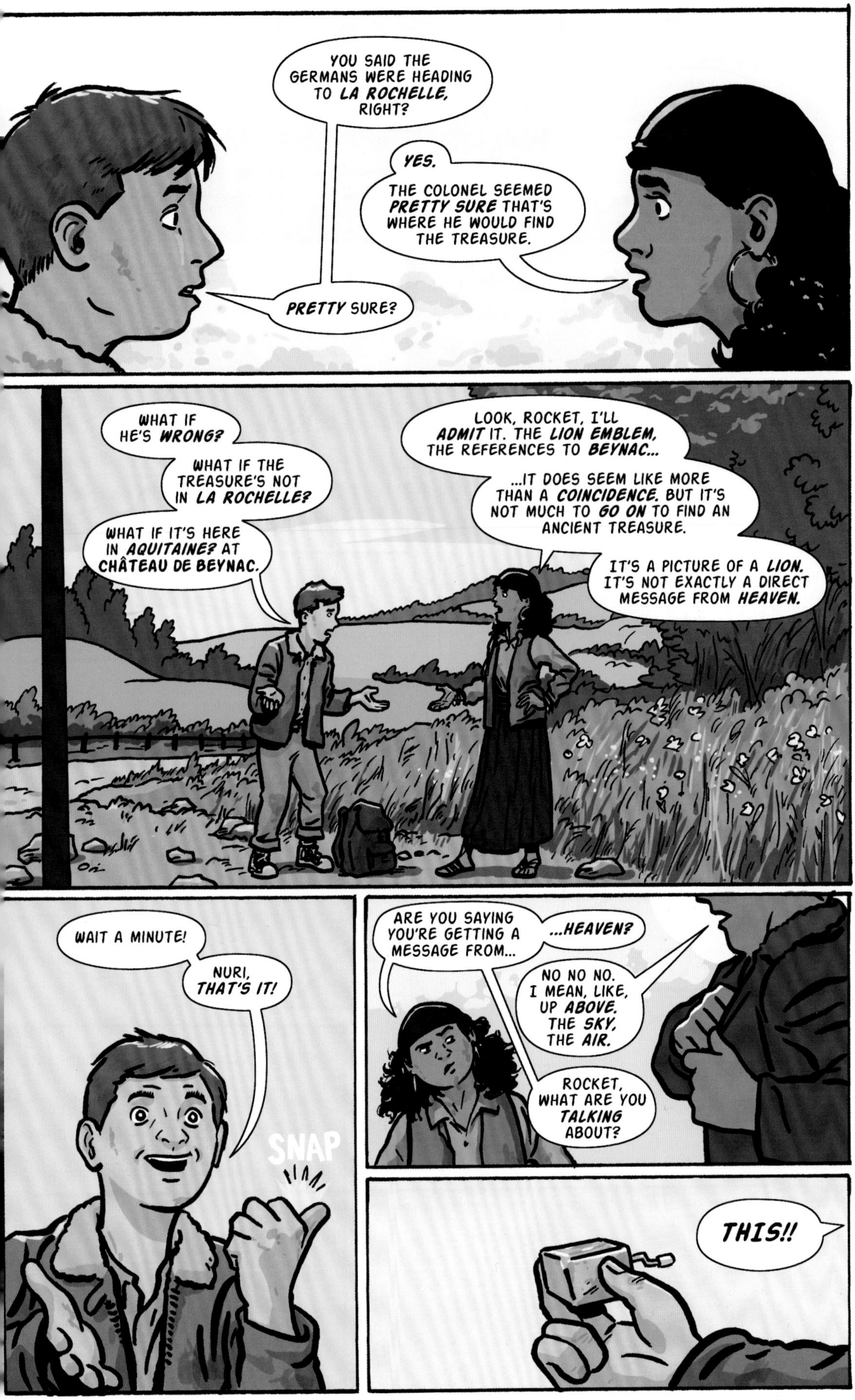
YOU SAID THE GERMANS WERE HEADING TO LA ROCHELLE, RIGHT?
PRETTY SURE?
YES.
THE COLONEL SEEMED PRETTY SURE THAT'S WHERE HE WOULD FIND THE TREASURE.
WHAT IF HE'S WRONG?
WHAT IF THE TREASURE'S NOT IN LA ROCHELLE?
WHAT IF IT'S HERE IN AQUITAINE? AT CHÂTEAU DE BEYNAC.
LOOK, ROCKET, I'LL ADMIT IT. THE LION EMBLEM, THE REFERENCES TO BEYNAC...
...IT DOES SEEM LIKE MORE THAN A COINCIDENCE. BUT IT'S NOT MUCH TO GO ON TO FIND AN ANCIENT TREASURE.
IT'S A PICTURE OF A LION. IT'S NOT EXACTLY A DIRECT MESSAGE FROM HEAVEN.
WAIT A MINUTE!
NURI, THAT'S IT!
SNAP
ARE YOU SAYING YOU'RE GETTING A MESSAGE FROM...
...HEAVEN?
NO NO NO. I MEAN, LIKE, UP ABOVE. THE SKY, THE AIR.
ROCKET, WHAT ARE YOU TALKING ABOUT?
THIS!!

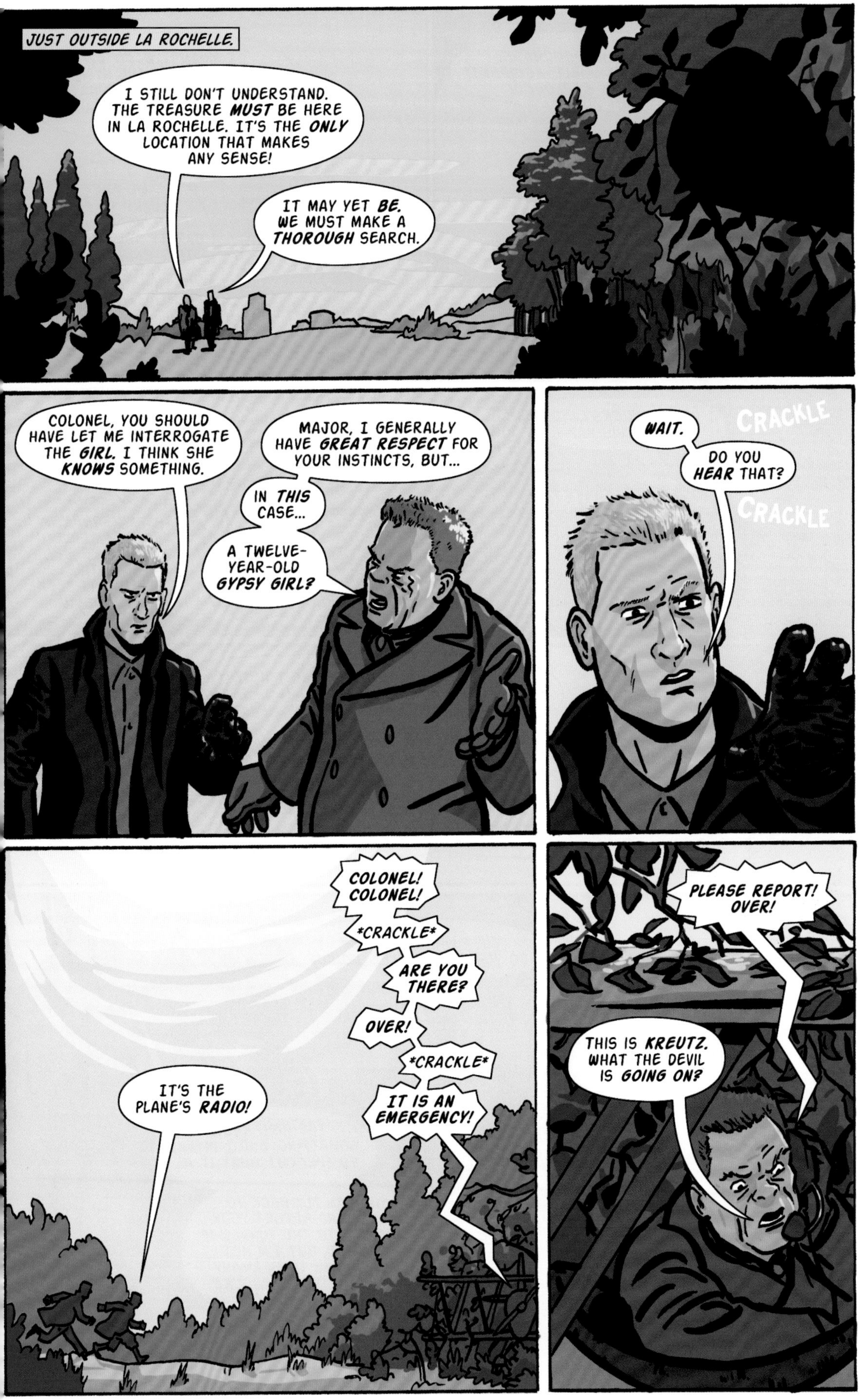
JUST OUTSIDE LA ROCHELLE.
I STILL DON'T UNDERSTAND. THE TREASURE MUST BE HERE IN LA ROCHELLE. IT'S THE ONLY LOCATION THAT MAKES ANY SENSE!
IT MAY YET BE. WE MUST MAKE A THOROUGH SEARCH.
COLONEL, YOU SHOULD HAVE LET ME INTERROGATE THE GIRL. I THINK SHE KNOWS SOMETHING.
MAJOR, I GENERALLY HAVE GREAT RESPECT FOR YOUR INSTINCTS, BUT...
IN THIS CASE...
A TWELVE-YEAR-OLD GYPSY GIRL?
CRACKLE
WAIT.
DO YOU HEAR THAT?
CRACKLE
COLONEL! COLONEL!
CRACKLE
ARE YOU THERE?
OVER!
CRACKLE
IT IS AN EMERGENCY!
IT'S THE PLANE'S RADIO!
PLEASE REPORT! OVER!
THIS IS KREUTZ. WHAT THE DEVIL IS GOING ON?

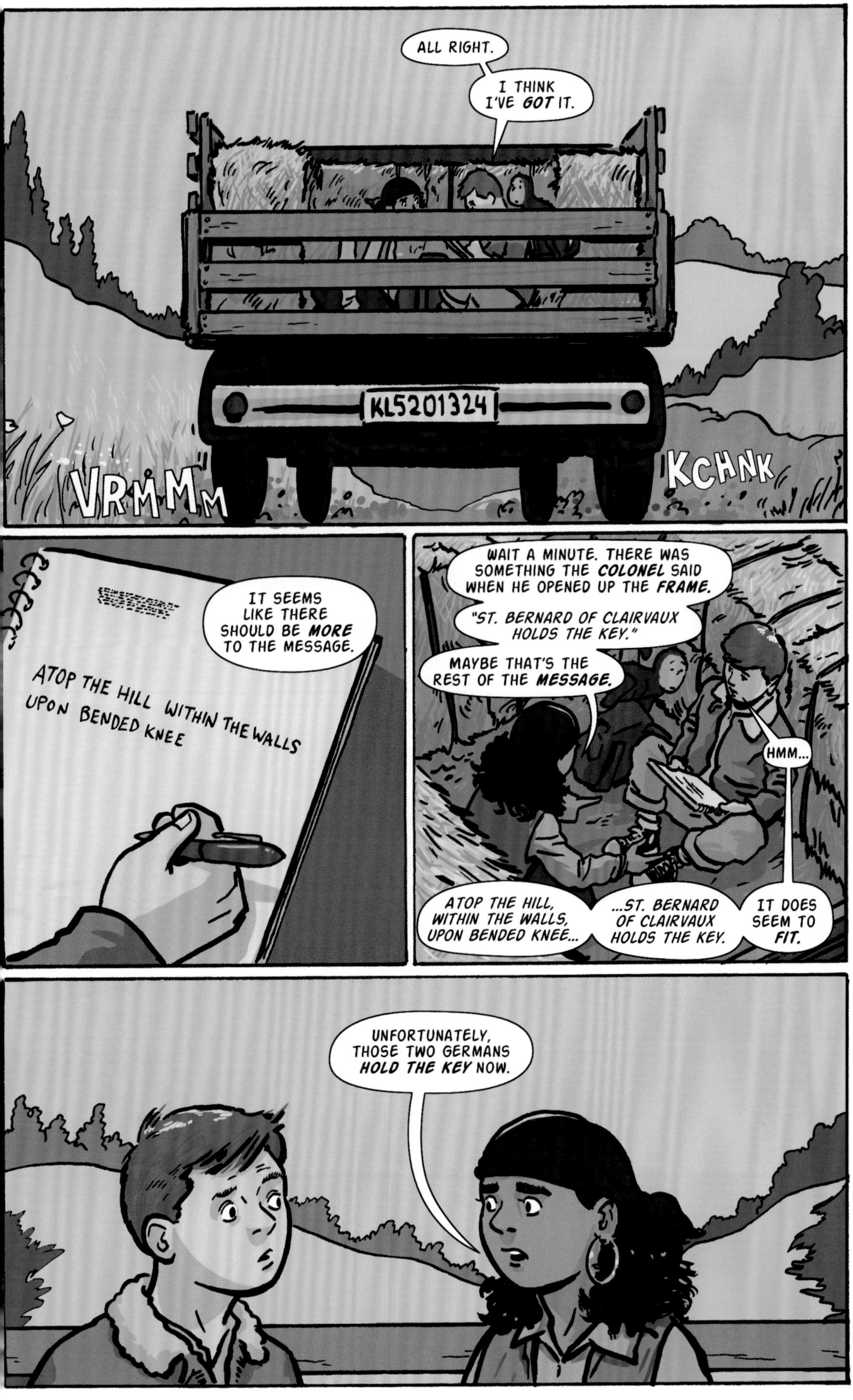
ALL RIGHT.
I THINK I'VE *GOT* IT.
KL5201324
VRMMM
KCHNK
IT SEEMS LIKE THERE SHOULD BE *MORE* TO THE MESSAGE.
ATOP THE HILL WITHIN THE WALLS
UPON BENDED KNEE
WAIT A MINUTE. THERE WAS SOMETHING THE *COLONEL* SAID WHEN HE OPENED UP THE *FRAME*.
"ST. BERNARD OF CLAIRVAUX HOLDS THE KEY."
MAYBE THAT'S THE REST OF THE *MESSAGE*.
HMM...
ATOP THE HILL, WITHIN THE WALLS, UPON BENDED KNEE...
...ST. BERNARD OF CLAIRVAUX HOLDS THE KEY.
IT DOES SEEM TO *FIT*.
UNFORTUNATELY, THOSE TWO GERMANS *HOLD THE KEY* NOW.

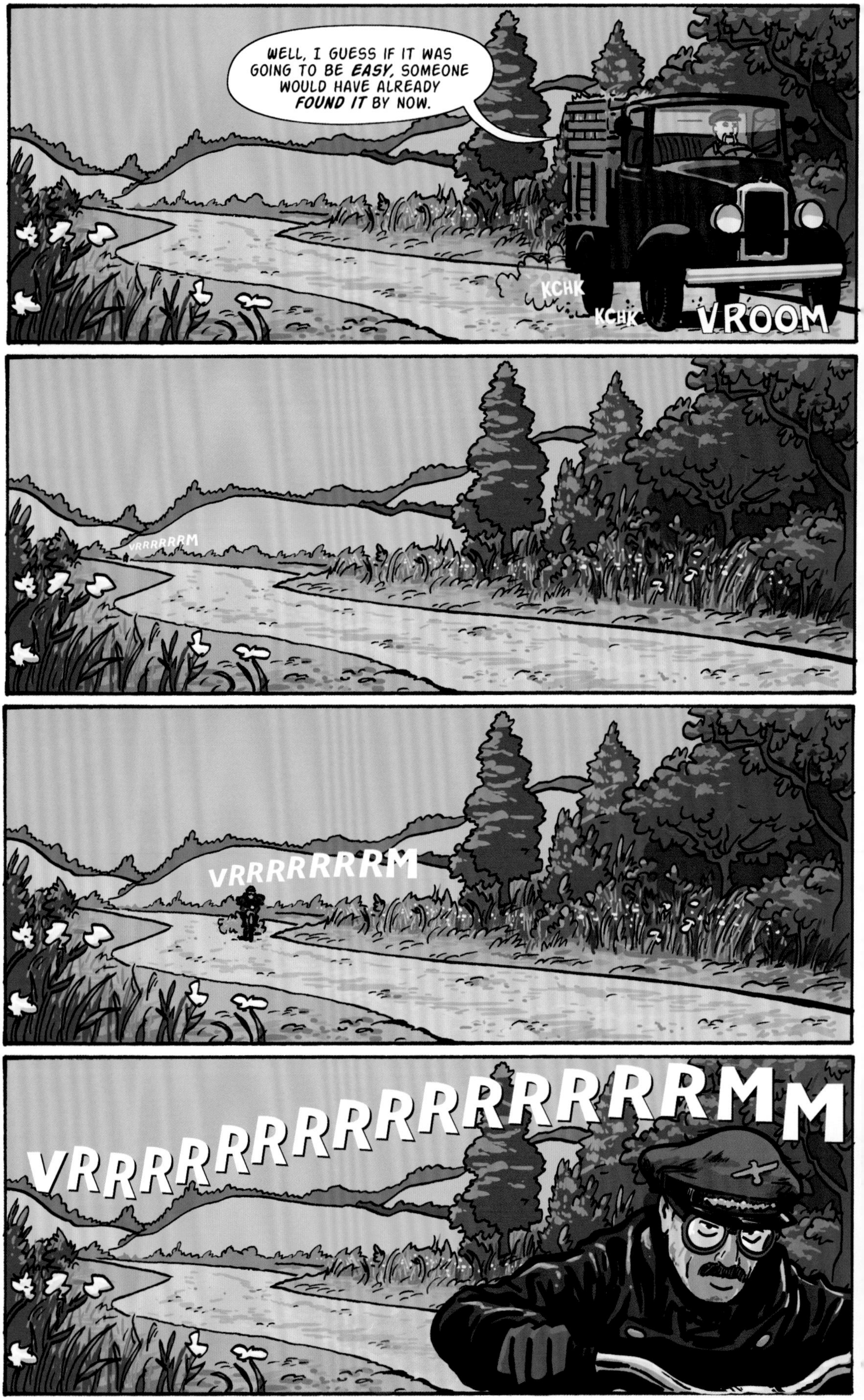
WELL, I GUESS IF IT WAS GOING TO BE EASY, SOMEONE WOULD HAVE ALREADY FOUND IT BY NOW.
KCHK
KCHK
VROOM
VRRRRRRM
VRRRRRRRM
VRRRRRRRRRRRRRRRMM

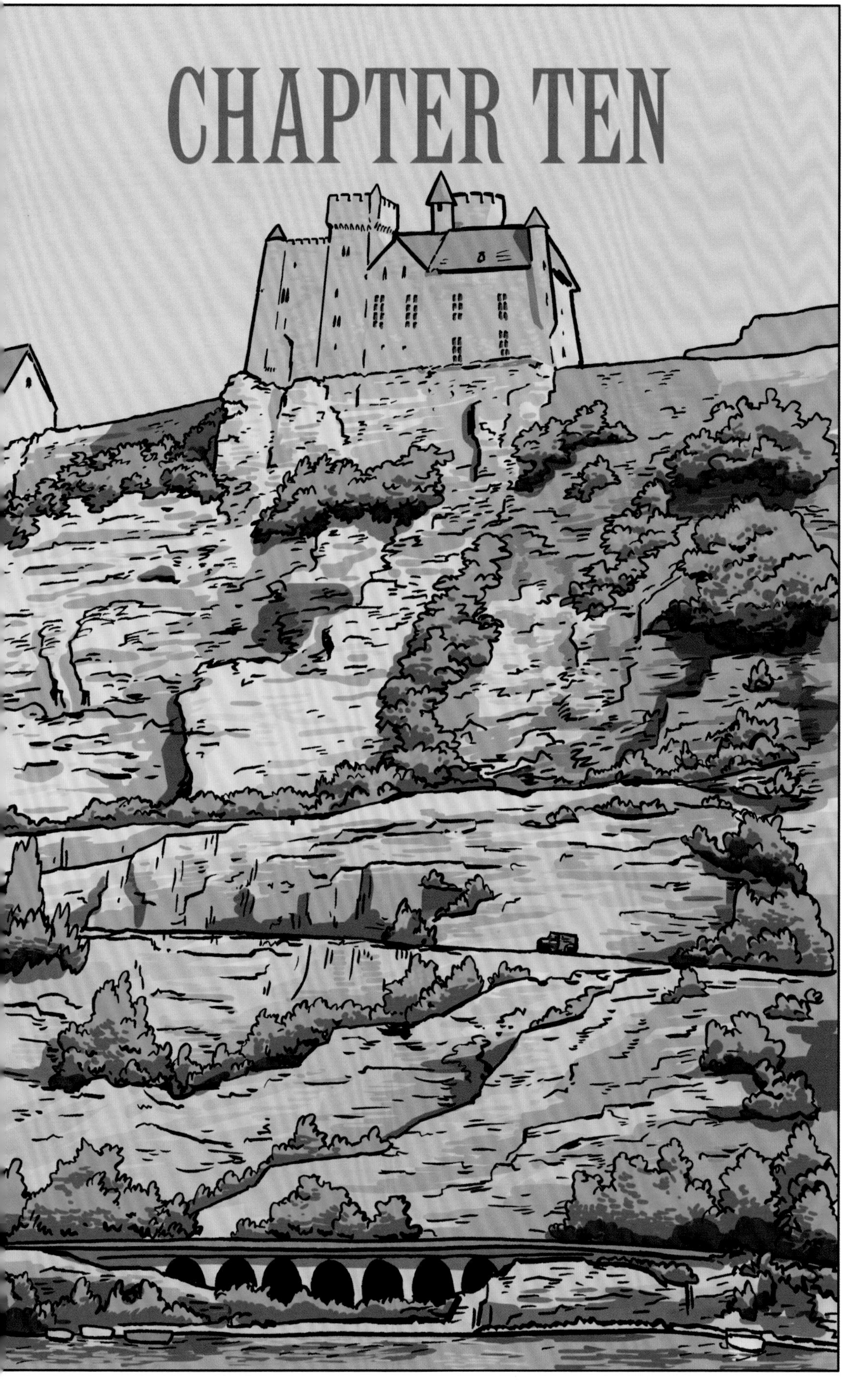
CHAPTER TEN

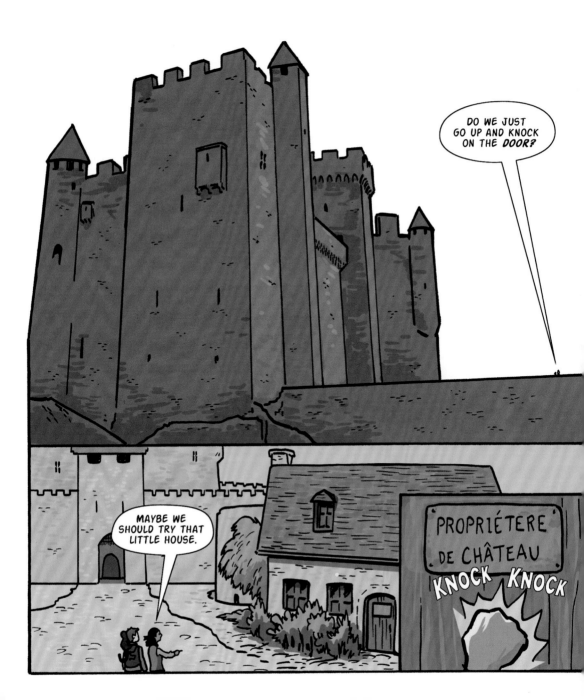

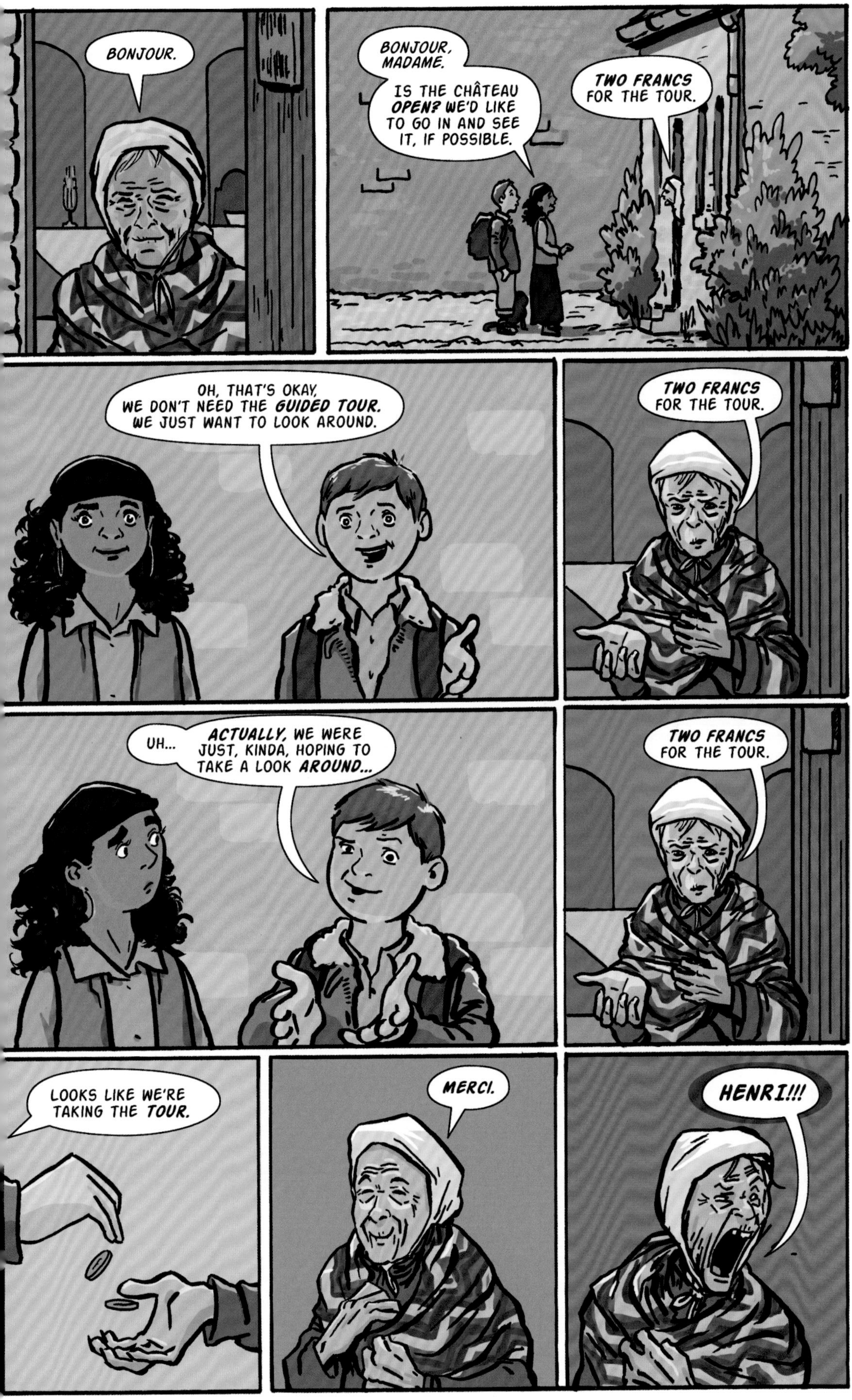
BONJOUR.
BONJOUR, MADAME.
IS THE CHÂTEAU OPEN? WE'D LIKE TO GO IN AND SEE IT, IF POSSIBLE.
TWO FRANCS FOR THE TOUR.
OH, THAT'S OKAY, WE DON'T NEED THE GUIDED TOUR. WE JUST WANT TO LOOK AROUND.
TWO FRANCS FOR THE TOUR.
UH...
ACTUALLY, WE WERE JUST, KINDA, HOPING TO TAKE A LOOK AROUND...
TWO FRANCS FOR THE TOUR.
LOOKS LIKE WE'RE TAKING THE TOUR.
MERCI.
HENRI!!!

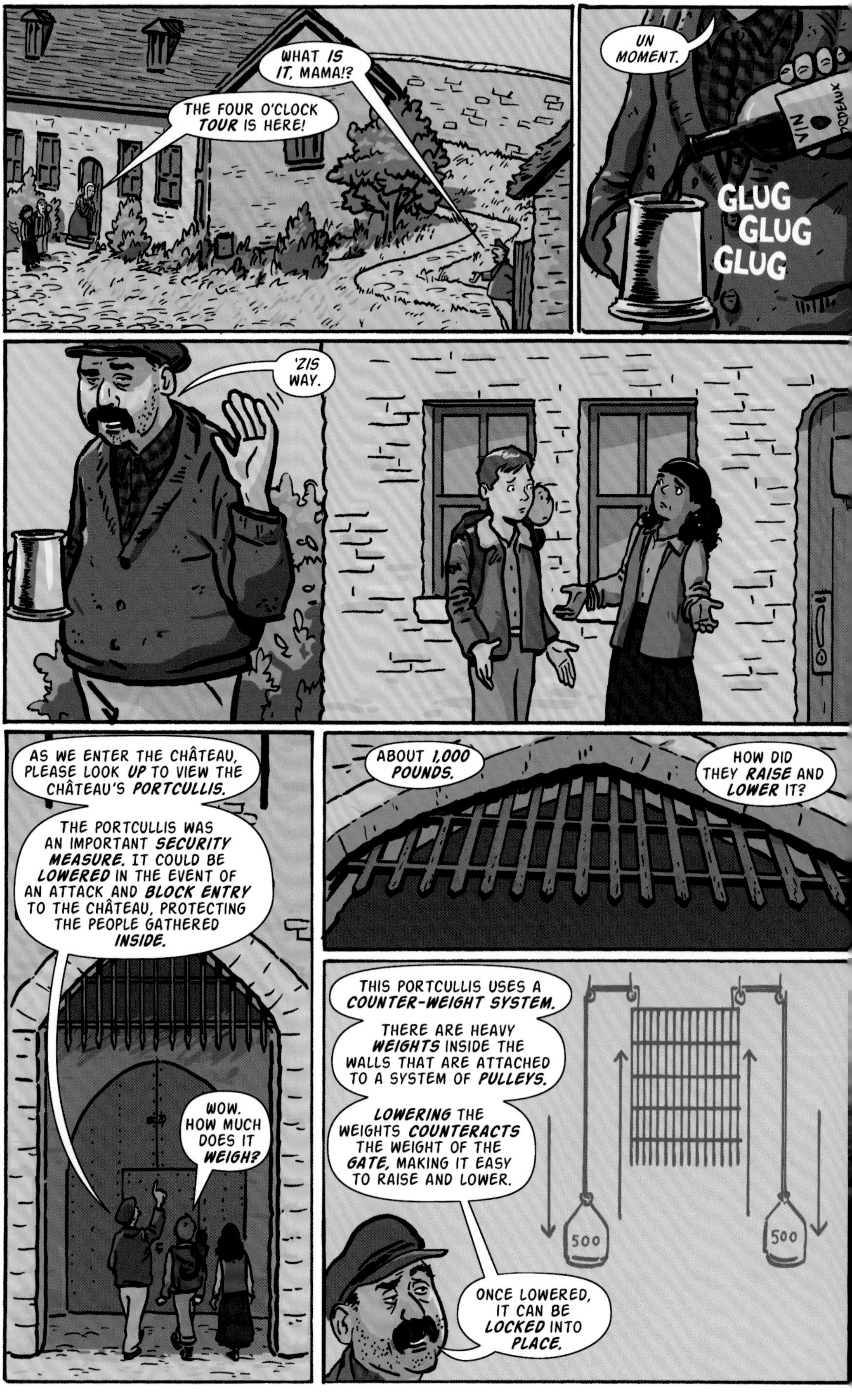

THE FOUR O'CLOCK TOUR IS HERE!
WHAT IS IT, MAMA!?
UN MOMENT.
VIN BORDEAUX
GLUG GLUG GLUG
'ZIS WAY.
AS WE ENTER THE CHÂTEAU, PLEASE LOOK UP TO VIEW THE CHÂTEAU'S PORTCULLIS.
THE PORTCULLIS WAS AN IMPORTANT SECURITY MEASURE. IT COULD BE LOWERED IN THE EVENT OF AN ATTACK AND BLOCK ENTRY TO THE CHÂTEAU, PROTECTING THE PEOPLE GATHERED INSIDE.
WOW. HOW MUCH DOES IT WEIGH?
ABOUT 1,000 POUNDS.
HOW DID THEY RAISE AND LOWER IT?
THIS PORTCULLIS USES A COUNTER-WEIGHT SYSTEM.
THERE ARE HEAVY WEIGHTS INSIDE THE WALLS THAT ARE ATTACHED TO A SYSTEM OF PULLEYS.
LOWERING THE WEIGHTS COUNTERACTS THE WEIGHT OF THE GATE, MAKING IT EASY TO RAISE AND LOWER.
500
500
ONCE LOWERED, IT CAN BE LOCKED INTO PLACE.

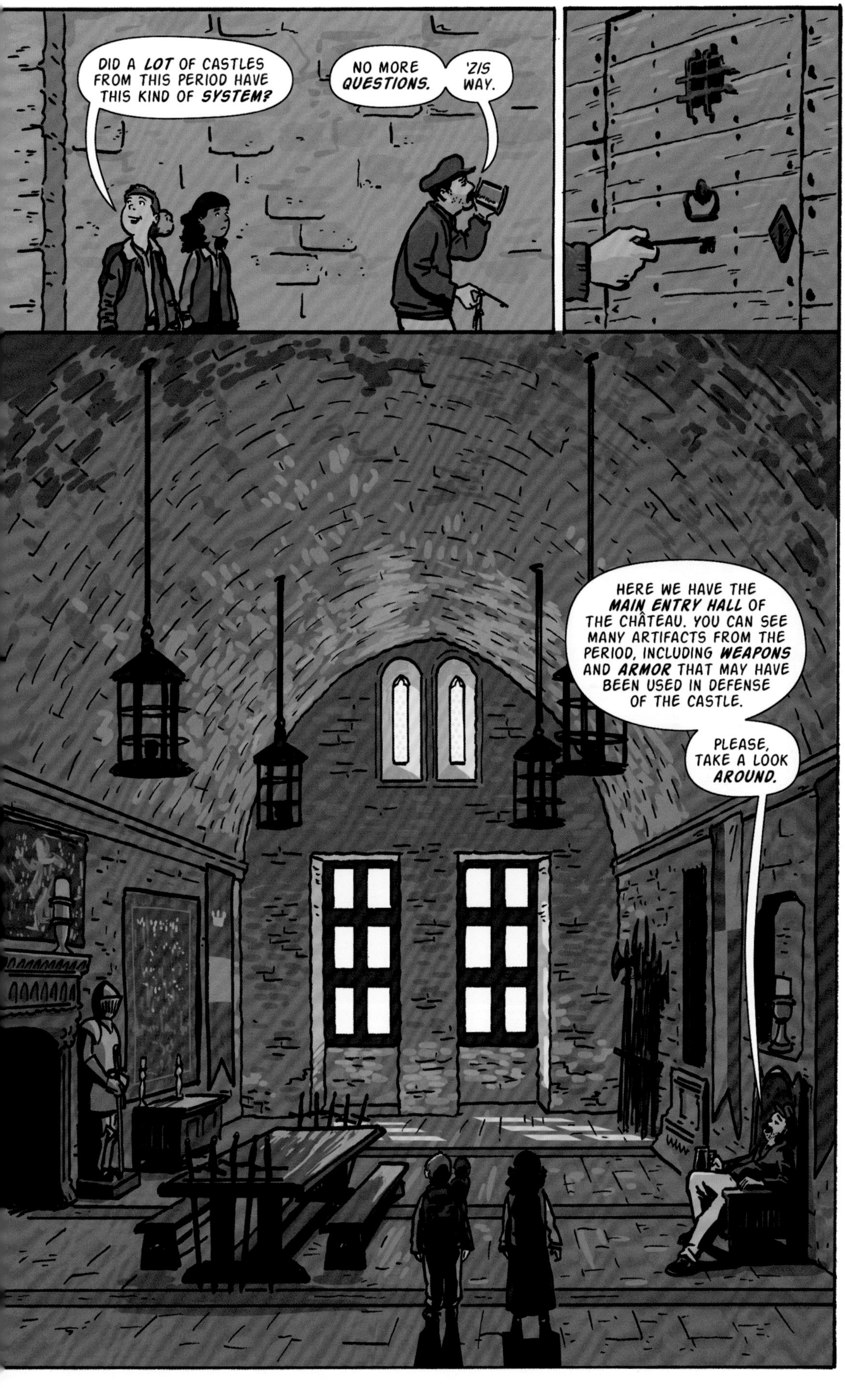
DID A *LOT* OF CASTLES FROM THIS PERIOD HAVE THIS KIND OF *SYSTEM?*
NO MORE *QUESTIONS.*
'ZIS WAY.
HERE WE HAVE THE *MAIN ENTRY HALL* OF THE CHÂTEAU. YOU CAN SEE MANY ARTIFACTS FROM THE PERIOD, INCLUDING *WEAPONS* AND *ARMOR* THAT MAY HAVE BEEN USED IN DEFENSE OF THE CASTLE.
PLEASE, TAKE A LOOK *AROUND.*

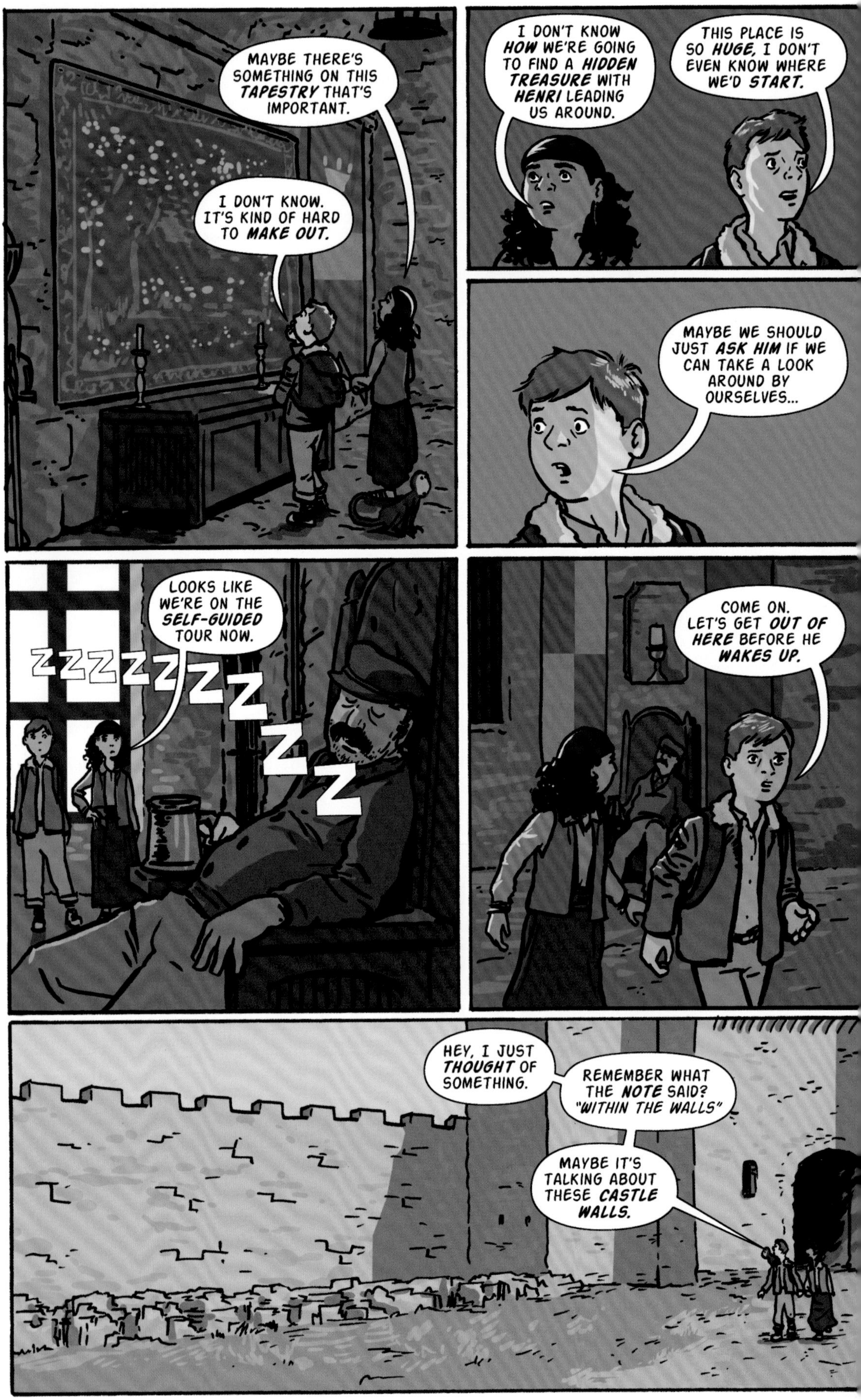
MAYBE THERE'S SOMETHING ON THIS *TAPESTRY* THAT'S IMPORTANT.
I DON'T KNOW. IT'S KIND OF HARD TO *MAKE OUT.*
I DON'T KNOW *HOW* WE'RE GOING TO FIND A *HIDDEN TREASURE* WITH *HENRI* LEADING US AROUND.
THIS PLACE IS SO *HUGE,* I DON'T EVEN KNOW WHERE WE'D *START.*
MAYBE WE SHOULD JUST *ASK HIM* IF WE CAN TAKE A LOOK AROUND BY OURSELVES...
LOOKS LIKE WE'RE ON THE *SELF-GUIDED* TOUR NOW.
ZZZZZZZZZ
COME ON. LET'S GET *OUT OF HERE* BEFORE HE *WAKES UP.*
HEY, I JUST *THOUGHT* OF SOMETHING.
REMEMBER WHAT THE *NOTE* SAID? *"WITHIN THE WALLS"*
MAYBE IT'S TALKING ABOUT THESE *CASTLE WALLS.*

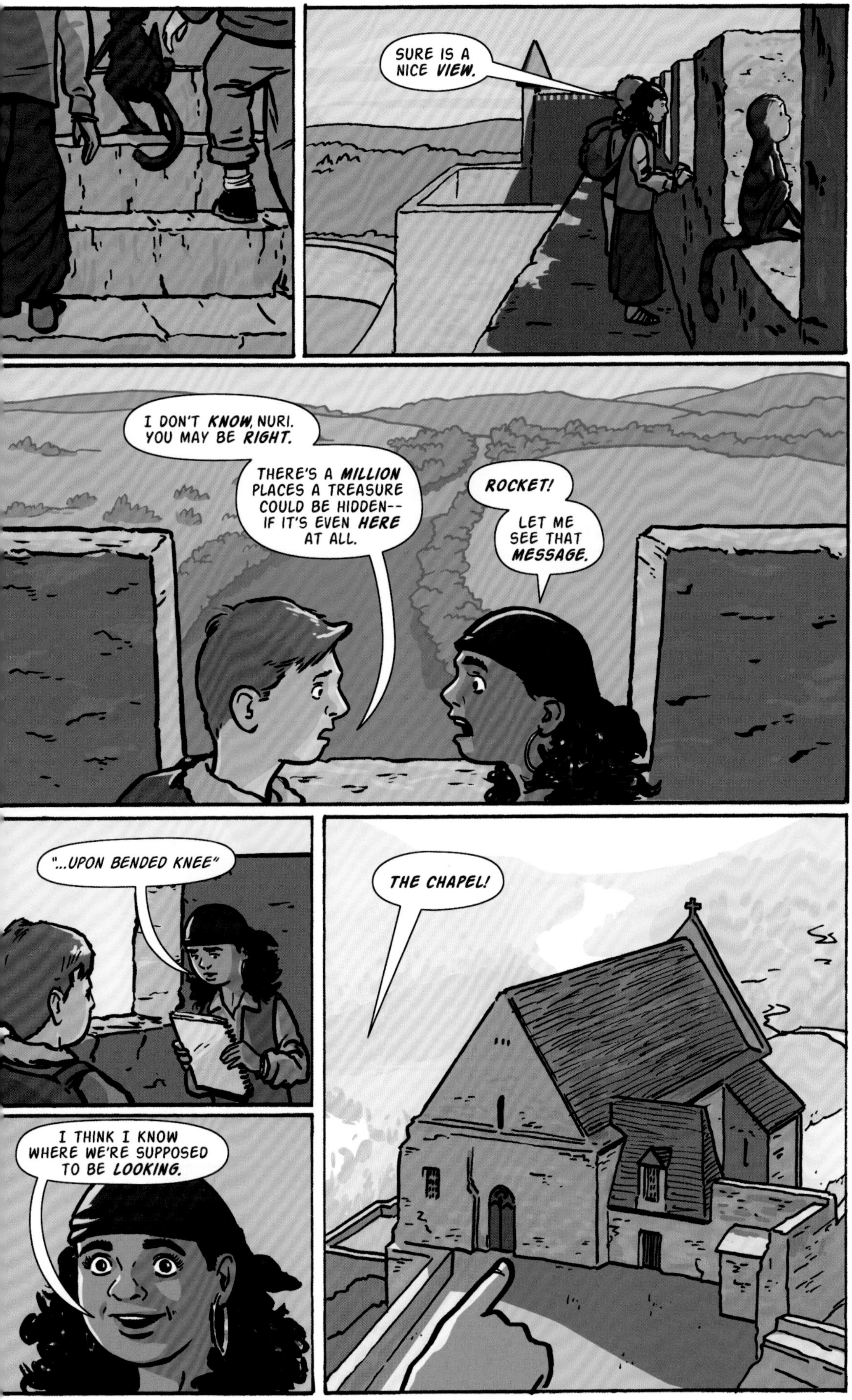
SURE IS A NICE VIEW.
I DON'T KNOW, NURI. YOU MAY BE RIGHT.
THERE'S A MILLION PLACES A TREASURE COULD BE HIDDEN-- IF IT'S EVEN HERE AT ALL.
ROCKET!
LET ME SEE THAT MESSAGE.
"...UPON BENDED KNEE"
I THINK I KNOW WHERE WE'RE SUPPOSED TO BE LOOKING.
THE CHAPEL!

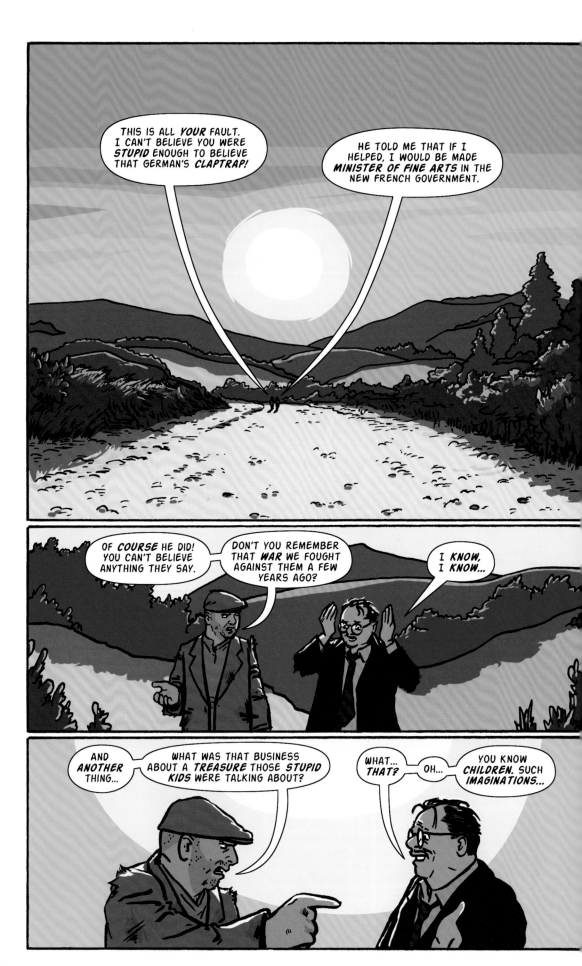

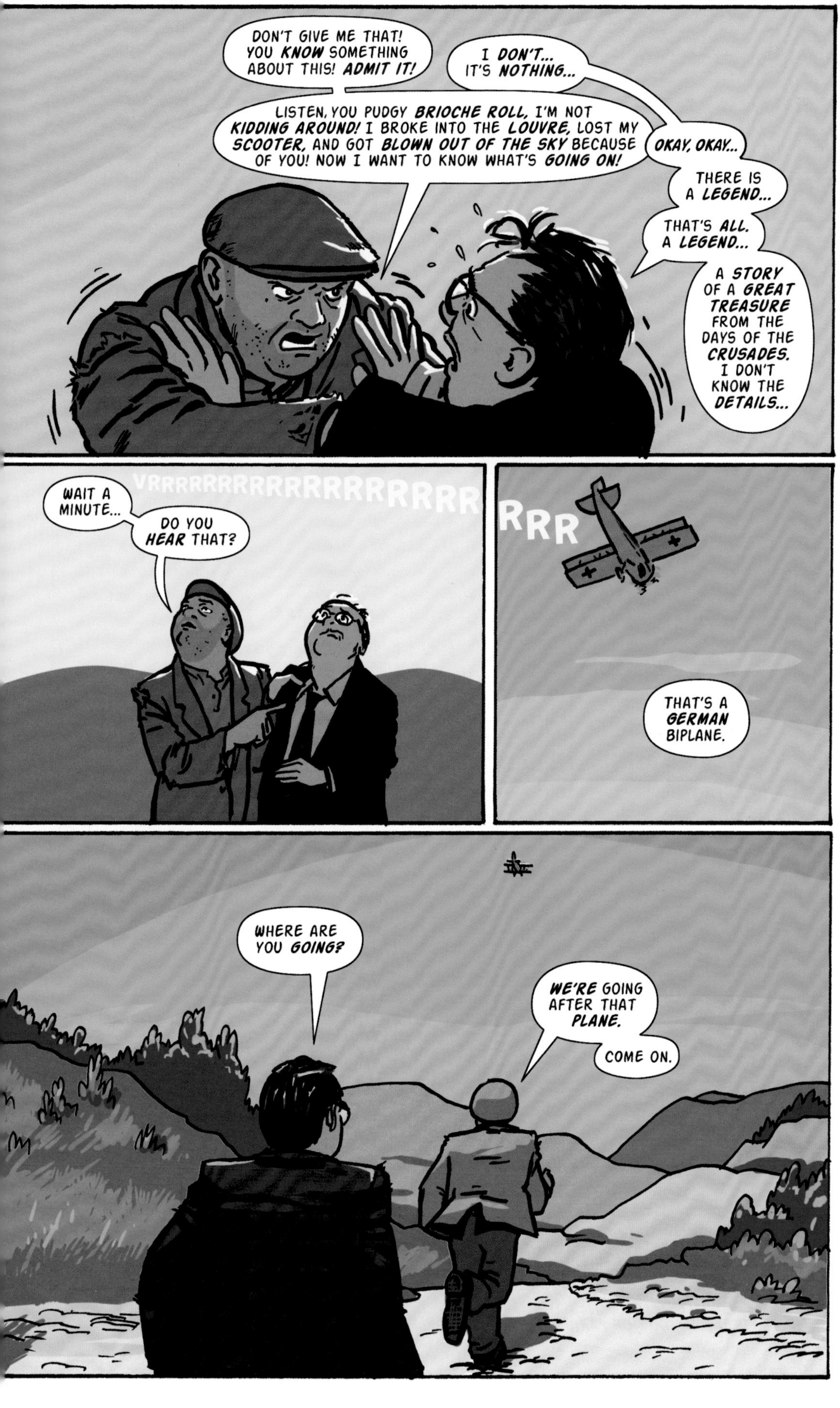
DON'T GIVE ME THAT! YOU KNOW SOMETHING ABOUT THIS! ADMIT IT!
I DON'T... IT'S NOTHING...
LISTEN, YOU PUDGY BRIOCHE ROLL, I'M NOT KIDDING AROUND! I BROKE INTO THE LOUVRE, LOST MY SCOOTER, AND GOT BLOWN OUT OF THE SKY BECAUSE OF YOU! NOW I WANT TO KNOW WHAT'S GOING ON!
OKAY, OKAY...
THERE IS A LEGEND...
THAT'S ALL. A LEGEND...
A STORY OF A GREAT TREASURE FROM THE DAYS OF THE CRUSADES. I DON'T KNOW THE DETAILS...
WAIT A MINUTE...
DO YOU HEAR THAT?
VRRRRRRRRRRRRRRRRRRRRR
THAT'S A GERMAN BIPLANE.
WHERE ARE YOU GOING?
WE'RE GOING AFTER THAT PLANE.
COME ON.

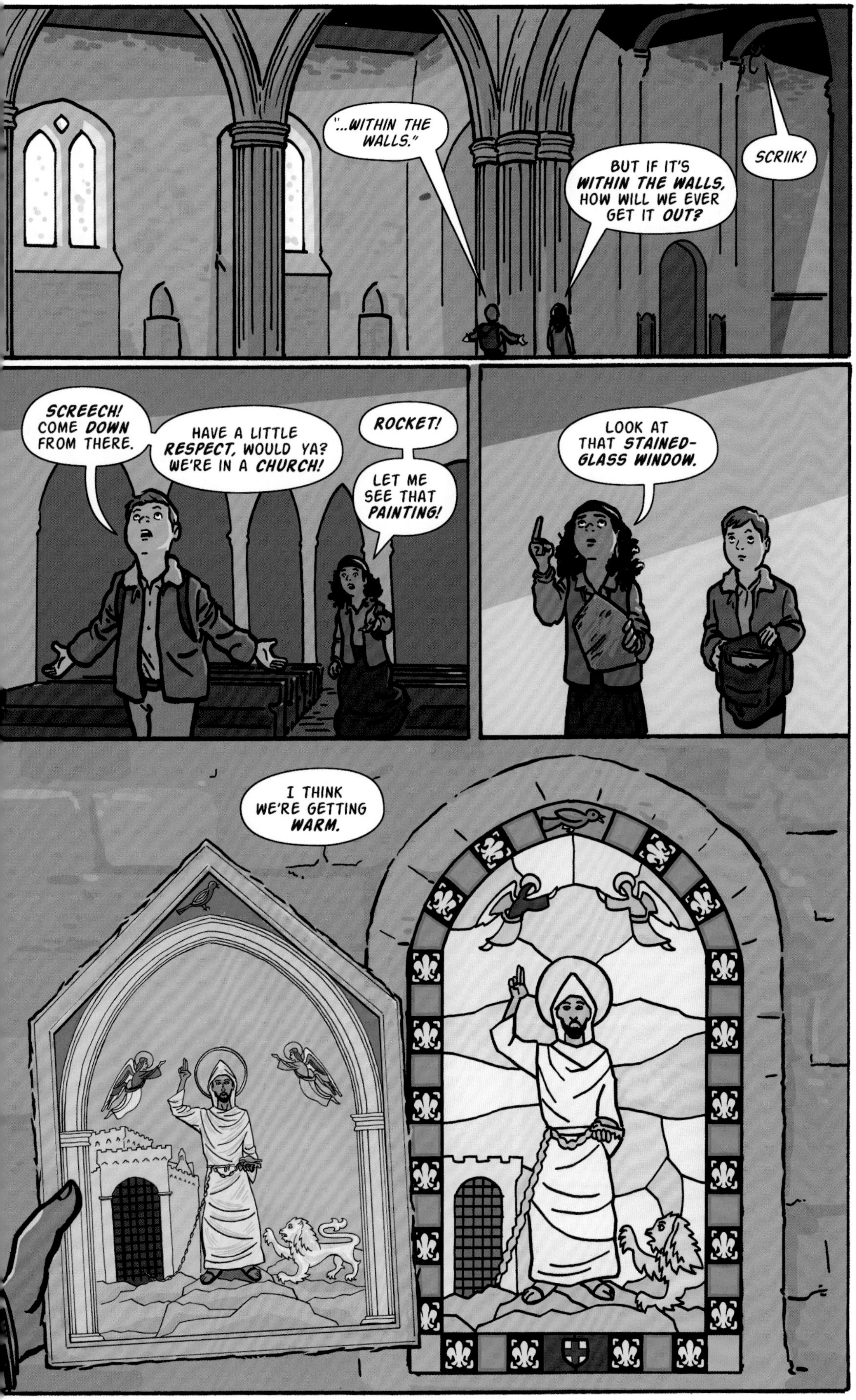
"...WITHIN THE WALLS."
BUT IF IT'S WITHIN THE WALLS, HOW WILL WE EVER GET IT OUT?
SCRIIK!
SCREECH! COME DOWN FROM THERE.
HAVE A LITTLE RESPECT, WOULD YA? WE'RE IN A CHURCH!
ROCKET!
LET ME SEE THAT PAINTING!
LOOK AT THAT STAINED-GLASS WINDOW.
I THINK WE'RE GETTING WARM.

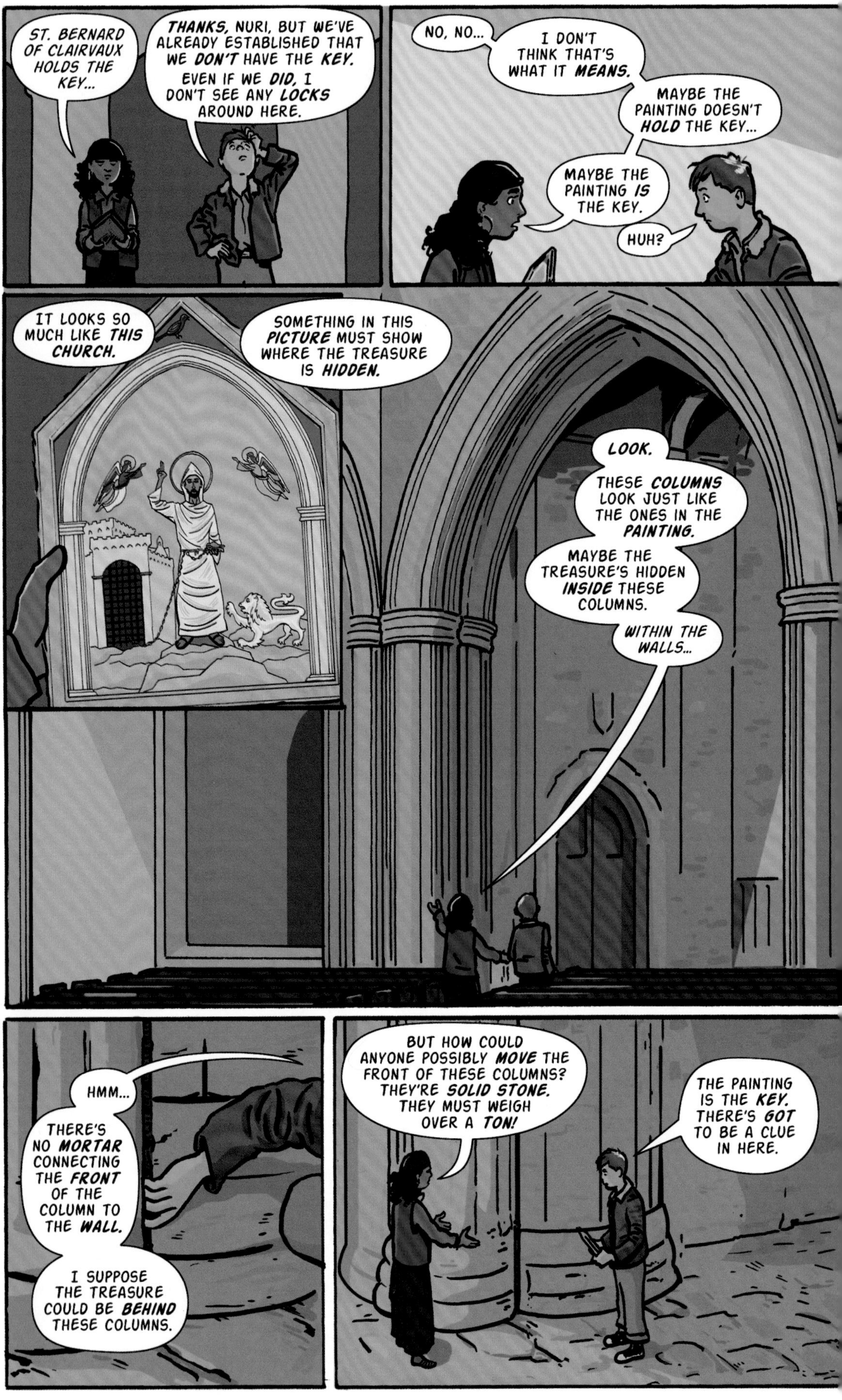
ST. BERNARD OF CLAIRVAUX HOLDS THE KEY...
THANKS, NURI, BUT WE'VE ALREADY ESTABLISHED THAT WE DON'T HAVE THE KEY.
EVEN IF WE DID, I DON'T SEE ANY LOCKS AROUND HERE.
NO, NO...
I DON'T THINK THAT'S WHAT IT MEANS.
MAYBE THE PAINTING DOESN'T HOLD THE KEY...
MAYBE THE PAINTING IS THE KEY.
HUH?
IT LOOKS SO MUCH LIKE THIS CHURCH.
SOMETHING IN THIS PICTURE MUST SHOW WHERE THE TREASURE IS HIDDEN.
LOOK.
THESE COLUMNS LOOK JUST LIKE THE ONES IN THE PAINTING.
MAYBE THE TREASURE'S HIDDEN INSIDE THESE COLUMNS.
WITHIN THE WALLS...
HMM...
THERE'S NO MORTAR CONNECTING THE FRONT OF THE COLUMN TO THE WALL.
I SUPPOSE THE TREASURE COULD BE BEHIND THESE COLUMNS.
BUT HOW COULD ANYONE POSSIBLY MOVE THE FRONT OF THESE COLUMNS? THEY'RE SOLID STONE. THEY MUST WEIGH OVER A TON!
THE PAINTING IS THE KEY. THERE'S GOT TO BE A CLUE IN HERE.

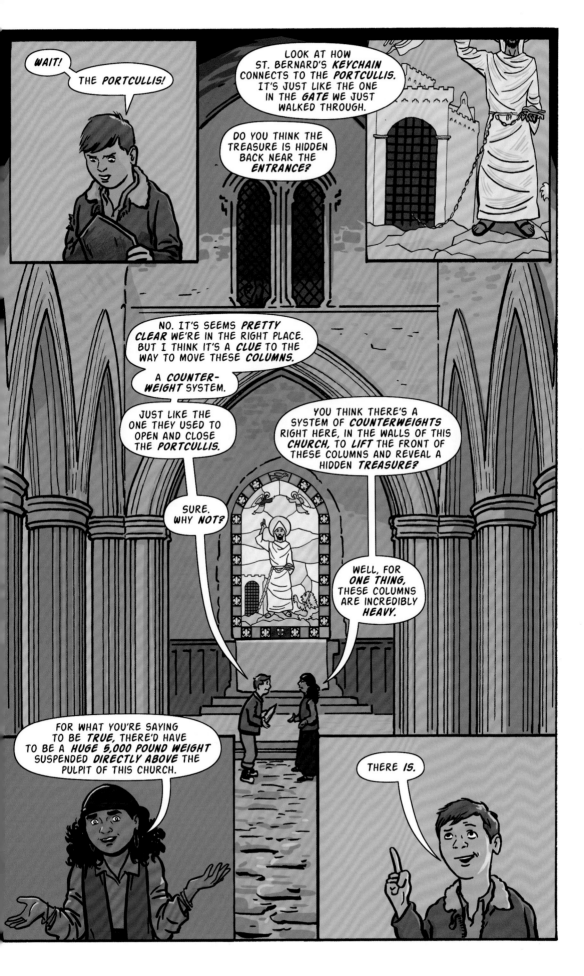

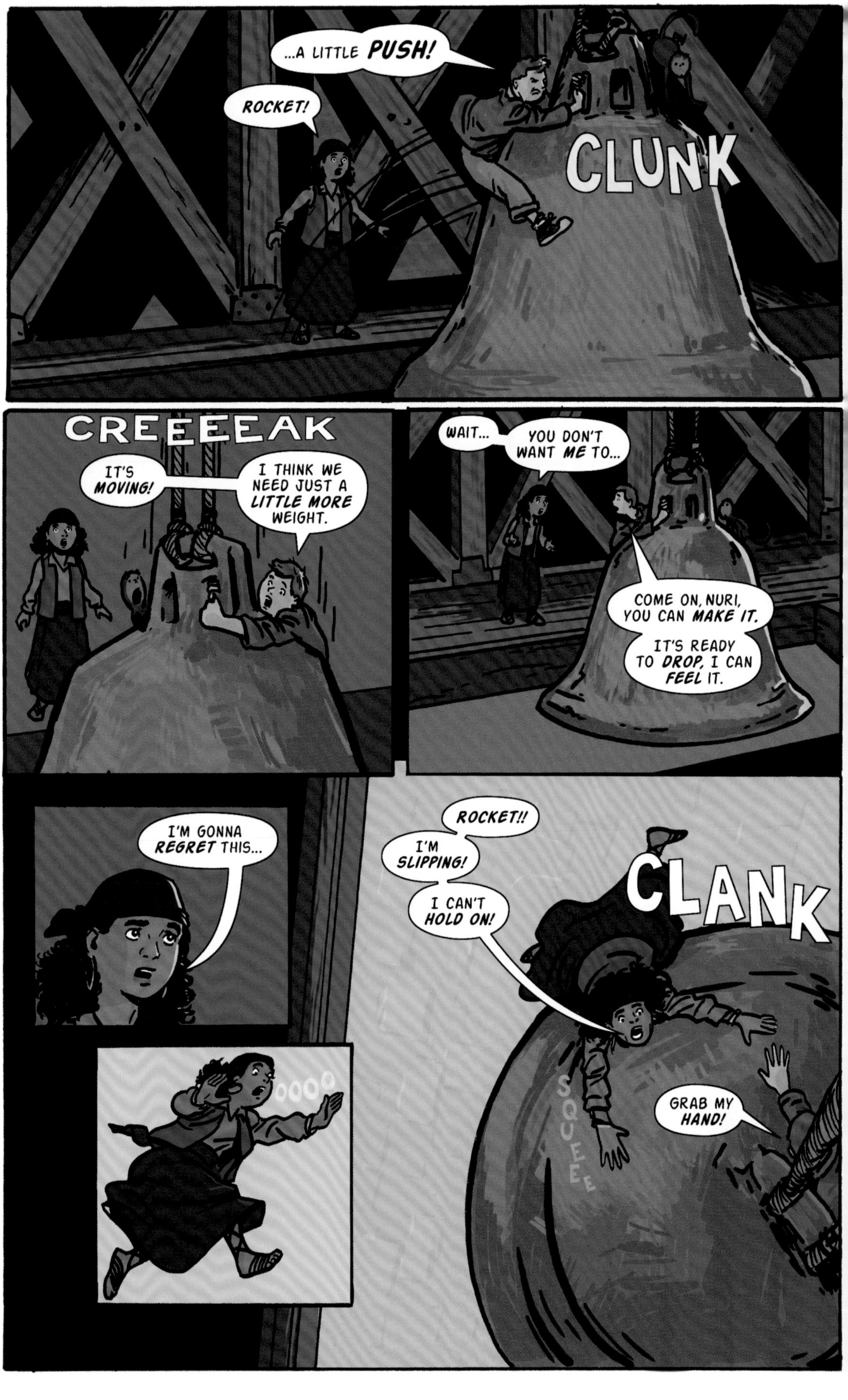
...A LITTLE PUSH!
ROCKET!
CLUNK
CREEEEAK
IT'S MOVING!
I THINK WE NEED JUST A LITTLE MORE WEIGHT.
WAIT...
YOU DON'T WANT ME TO...
COME ON, NURI, YOU CAN MAKE IT.
IT'S READY TO DROP, I CAN FEEL IT.
I'M GONNA REGRET THIS...
OOOO
ROCKET!!
I'M SLIPPING!
I CAN'T HOLD ON!
CLANK
SQUEEE
GRAB MY HAND!

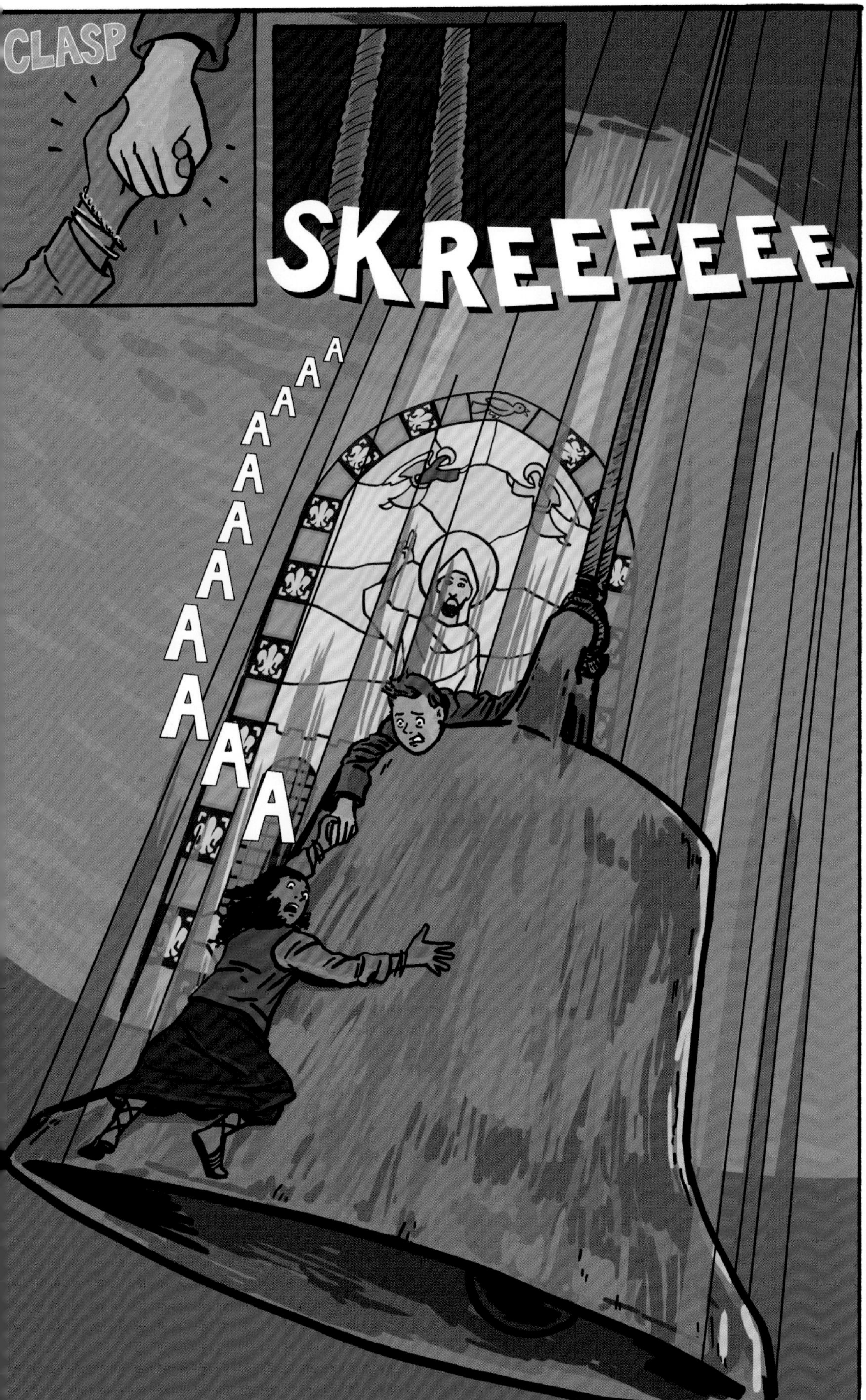
CLASP
SKREEEEEEE
AAAAAAAAAAAAA

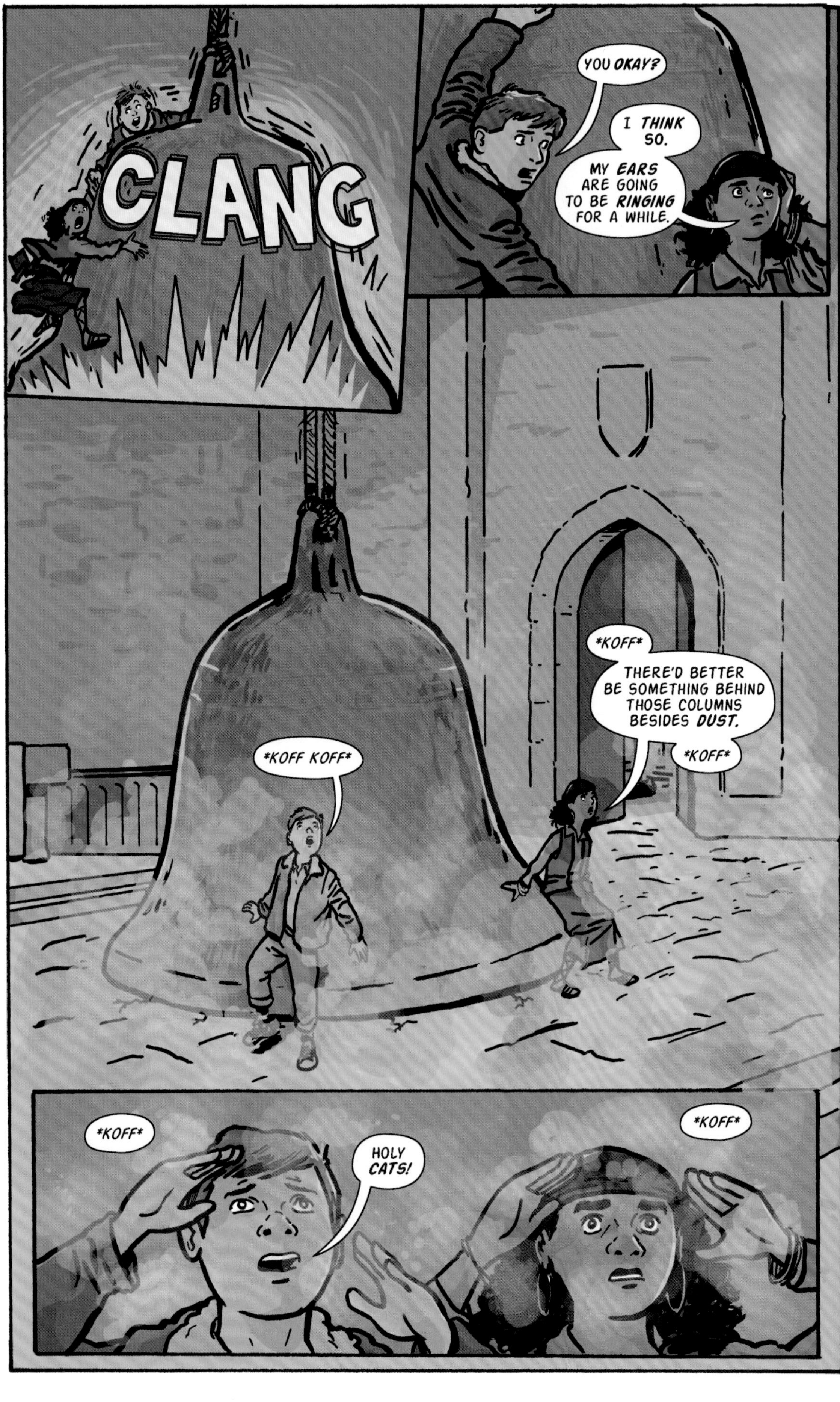
CLANG
YOU OKAY?
I THINK SO.
MY EARS ARE GOING TO BE RINGING FOR A WHILE.
KOFF KOFF
KOFF
THERE'D BETTER BE SOMETHING BEHIND THOSE COLUMNS BESIDES DUST.
KOFF
KOFF
HOLY CATS!
KOFF

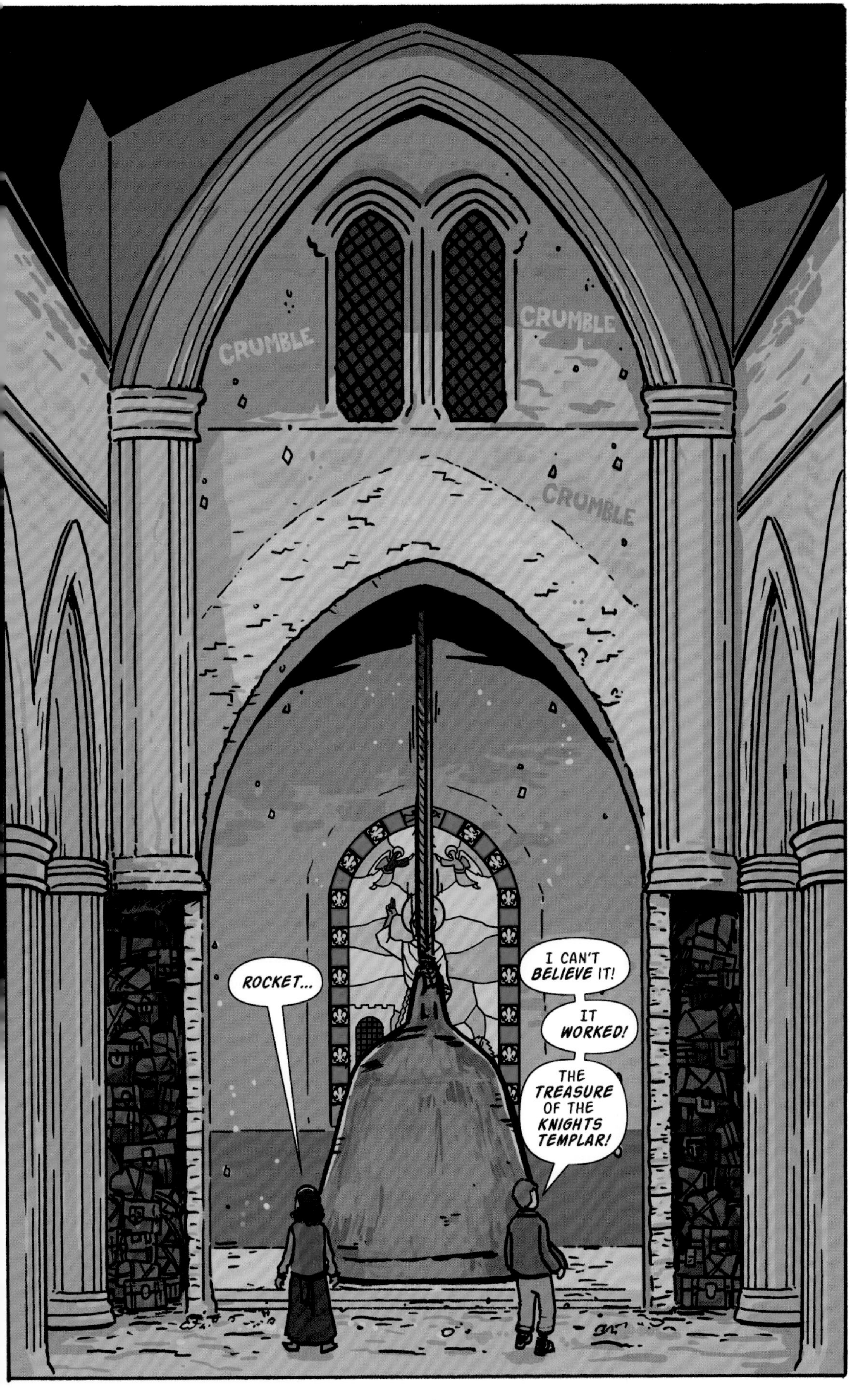
CRUMBLE
CRUMBLE
CRUMBLE
ROCKET...
I CAN'T BELIEVE IT!
IT WORKED!
THE TREASURE OF THE KNIGHTS TEMPLAR!

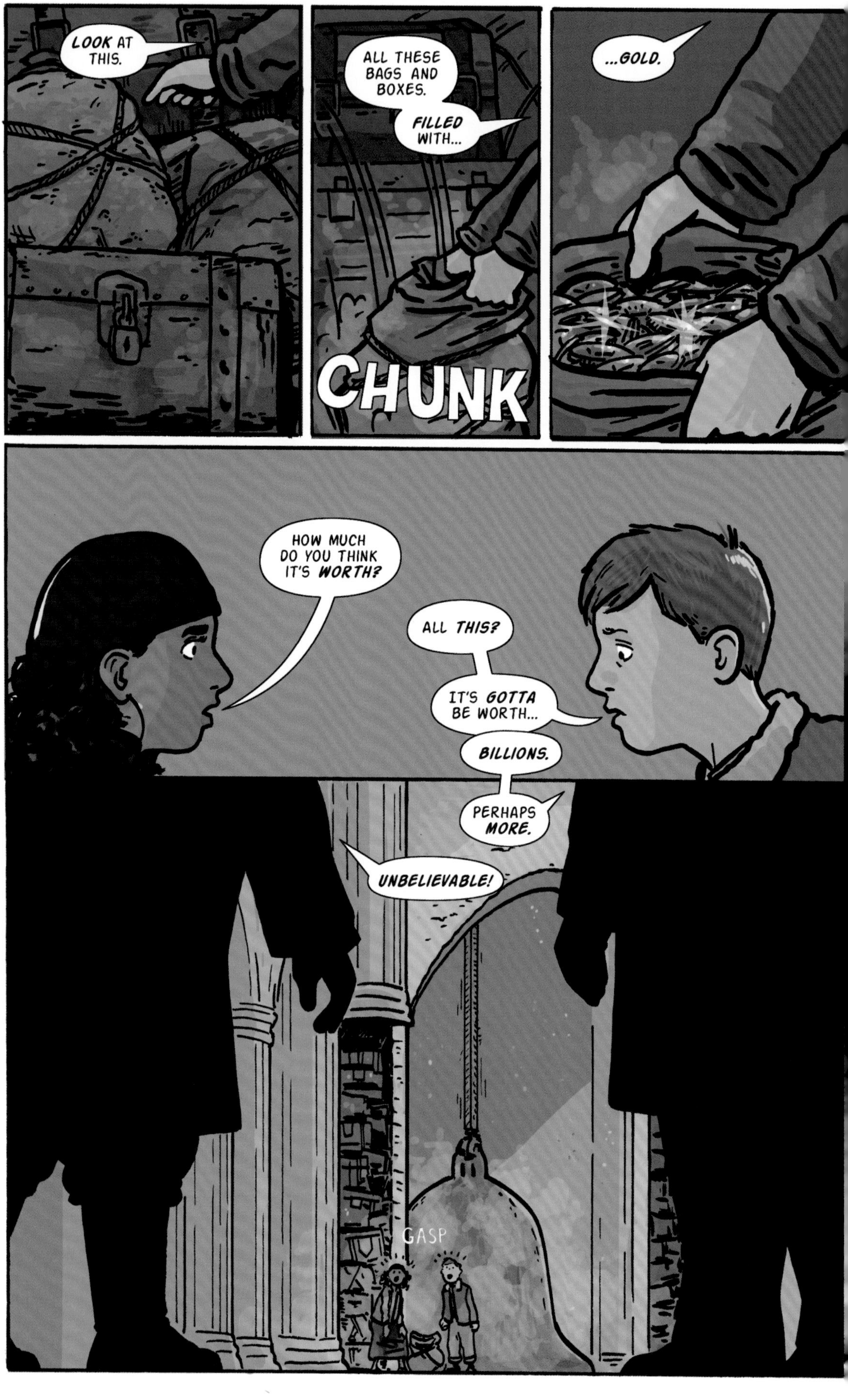

LOOK AT THIS.
ALL THESE BAGS AND BOXES.
FILLED WITH...
CHUNK
...GOLD.
HOW MUCH DO YOU THINK IT'S WORTH?
ALL THIS?
IT'S GOTTA BE WORTH...
BILLIONS.
PERHAPS MORE.
UNBELIEVABLE!
GASP

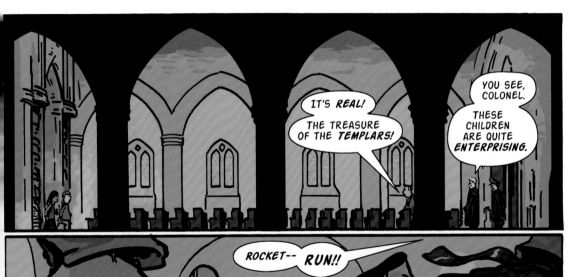

IT'S *REAL!* THE TREASURE OF THE *TEMPLARS!*

YOU SEE, COLONEL. THESE CHILDREN ARE QUITE *ENTERPRISING.*

ROCKET-- *RUN!!*

STOP THEM.

AH AH. NOT SO *FAST.*

SNATCH

YOU MUST BE THE ONE THAT BLEW UP MY *ZEPPELIN!*

UH...

I CAN *EXPLAIN* THAT...

IT IS GREATER THAN I EVER DARED *IMAGINE.* DO YOU REALIZE WHAT THIS *MEANS,* ESSEN?

OUR ROLE IN THE HISTORY OF THE *THIRD REICH* IS *ASSURED!*

THEY WILL MARCH US THROUGH THE STREETS OF *BERLIN* AS HEROES!

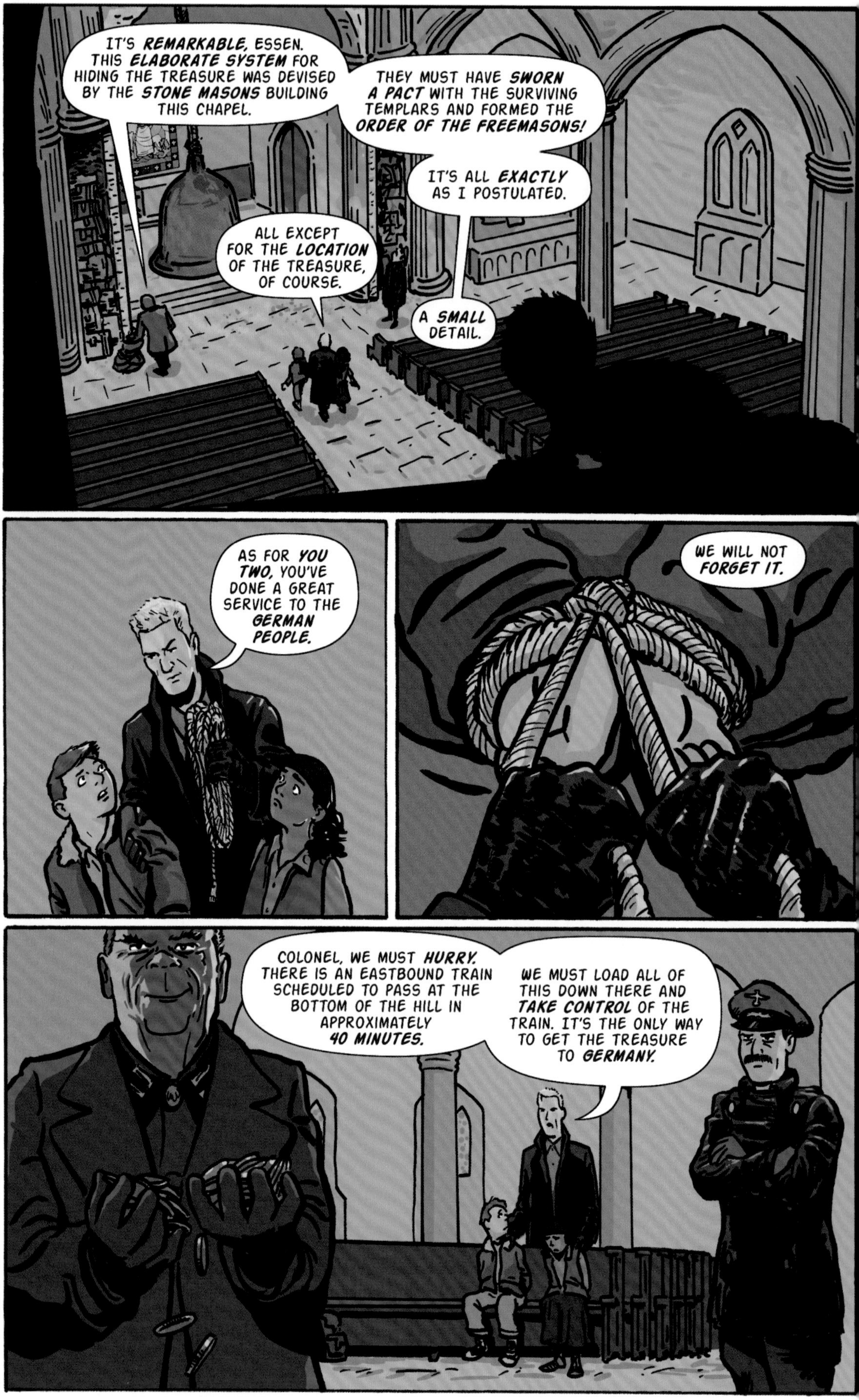
IT'S REMARKABLE, ESSEN. THIS ELABORATE SYSTEM FOR HIDING THE TREASURE WAS DEVISED BY THE STONE MASONS BUILDING THIS CHAPEL.
THEY MUST HAVE SWORN A PACT WITH THE SURVIVING TEMPLARS AND FORMED THE ORDER OF THE FREEMASONS!
IT'S ALL EXACTLY AS I POSTULATED.
ALL EXCEPT FOR THE LOCATION OF THE TREASURE, OF COURSE.
A SMALL DETAIL.
AS FOR YOU TWO, YOU'VE DONE A GREAT SERVICE TO THE GERMAN PEOPLE.
WE WILL NOT FORGET IT.
COLONEL, WE MUST HURRY. THERE IS AN EASTBOUND TRAIN SCHEDULED TO PASS AT THE BOTTOM OF THE HILL IN APPROXIMATELY 40 MINUTES.
WE MUST LOAD ALL OF THIS DOWN THERE AND TAKE CONTROL OF THE TRAIN. IT'S THE ONLY WAY TO GET THE TREASURE TO GERMANY.

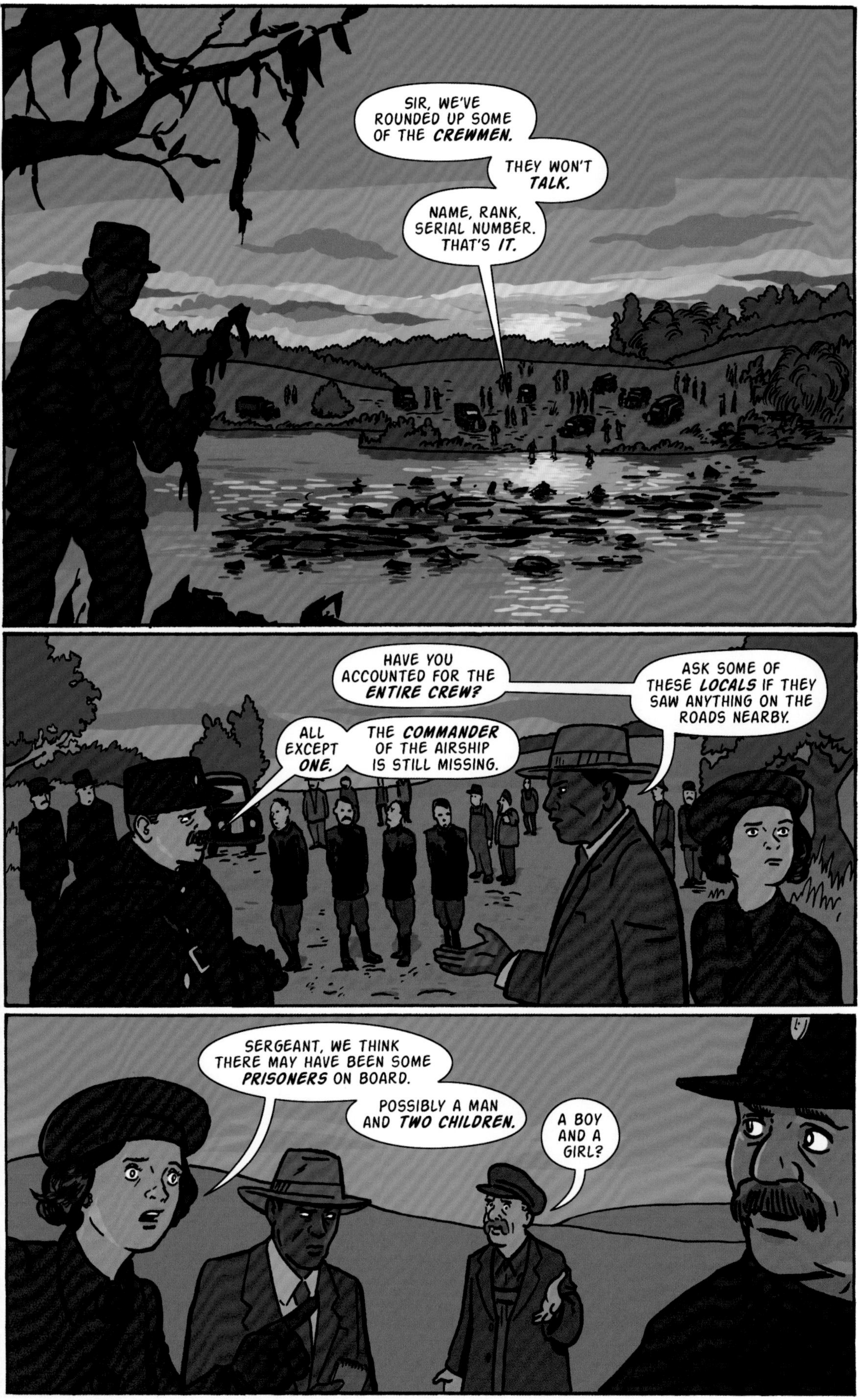
SIR, WE'VE ROUNDED UP SOME OF THE *CREWMEN.*
THEY WON'T *TALK.*
NAME, RANK, SERIAL NUMBER. THAT'S *IT.*
HAVE YOU ACCOUNTED FOR THE *ENTIRE CREW?*
ALL EXCEPT *ONE.*
THE *COMMANDER* OF THE AIRSHIP IS STILL MISSING.
ASK SOME OF THESE *LOCALS* IF THEY SAW ANYTHING ON THE ROADS NEARBY.
SERGEANT, WE THINK THERE MAY HAVE BEEN SOME *PRISONERS* ON BOARD.
POSSIBLY A MAN AND *TWO CHILDREN.*
A BOY AND A GIRL?

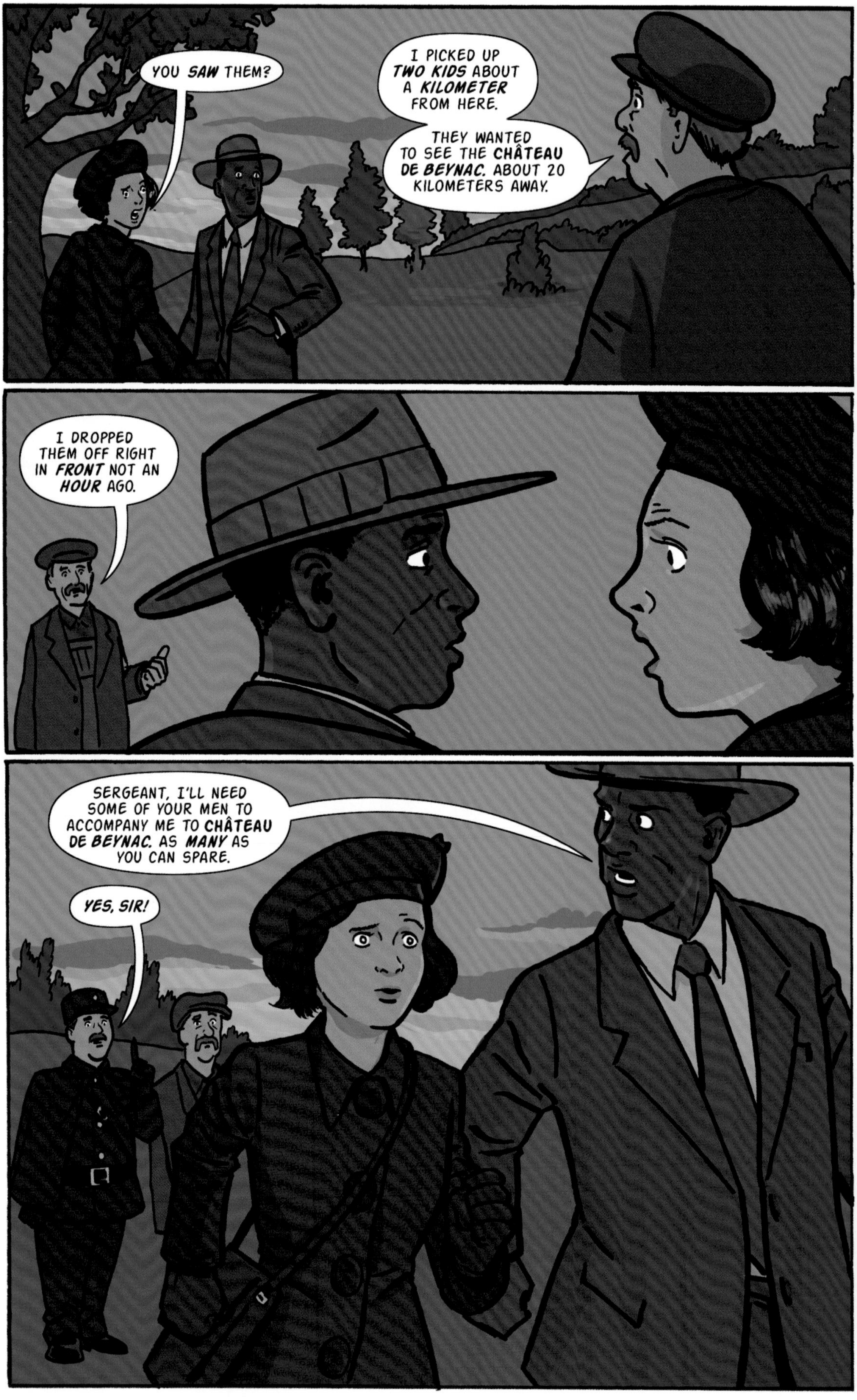
YOU SAW THEM?
I PICKED UP TWO KIDS ABOUT A KILOMETER FROM HERE.
THEY WANTED TO SEE THE CHÂTEAU DE BEYNAC. ABOUT 20 KILOMETERS AWAY.
I DROPPED THEM OFF RIGHT IN FRONT NOT AN HOUR AGO.
SERGEANT, I'LL NEED SOME OF YOUR MEN TO ACCOMPANY ME TO CHÂTEAU DE BEYNAC. AS MANY AS YOU CAN SPARE.
YES, SIR!

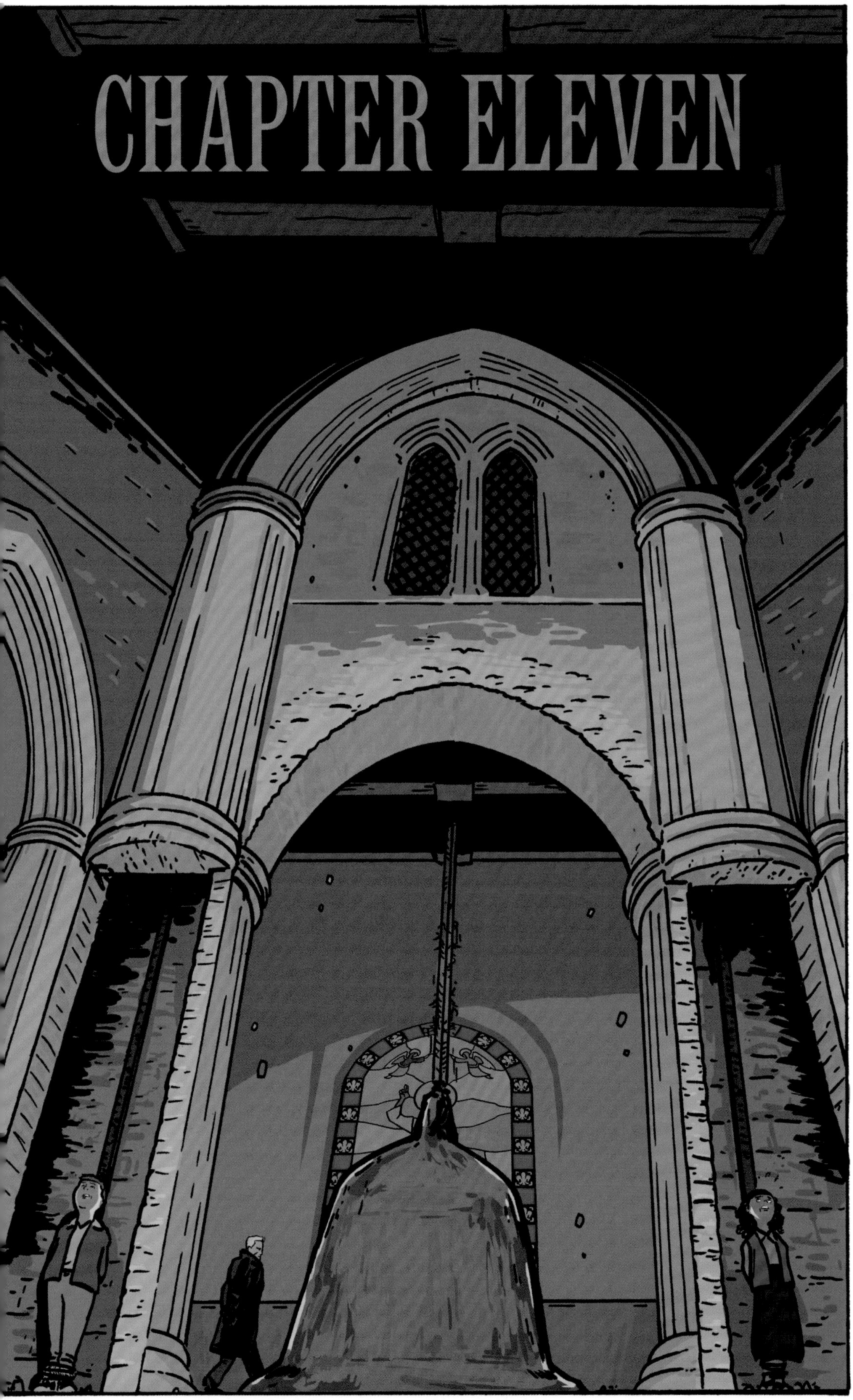
CHAPTER ELEVEN

REMARKABLE.

THESE ROPES MUST HAVE BEEN MADE FROM THE *STRONGEST HEMP* AVAILABLE.

STILL, THEY ARE SHOWING THEIR *AGE*.

I CAN'T IMAGINE THAT THEY'LL BE ABLE TO HOLD THE *WEIGHT* OF THESE *STONE COLUMNS* FOR MUCH LONGER.

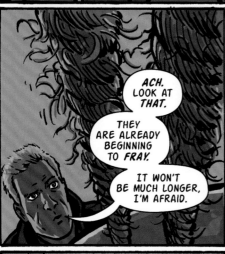

ACH. LOOK AT *THAT.*

THEY ARE ALREADY BEGINNING TO *FRAY.*

IT WON'T BE MUCH LONGER, I'M AFRAID.

Y-YOU DON'T HAVE TO *DO* THIS! YOU *HAVE* THE TREASURE.

WHY NOT JUST LET US *GO?* WE WON'T TELL *ANYONE!*

I APPRECIATE YOUR *DISCRETION*, BUT I'M *AFRAID* I CAN'T TAKE THAT CHANCE.

I DON'T KNOW WHERE YOU TWO *CAME FROM*, BUT YOU ARE CERTAINLY *RESOURCEFUL.*

AND YOU HAVE A REMARKABLE *SKILL* FOR STAYING ALIVE.

WE WILL SEE HOW LONG THAT *LASTS.*

AUF WIEDERSEHEN.

CREAK

CREAK

CLACK CLACK CLACK

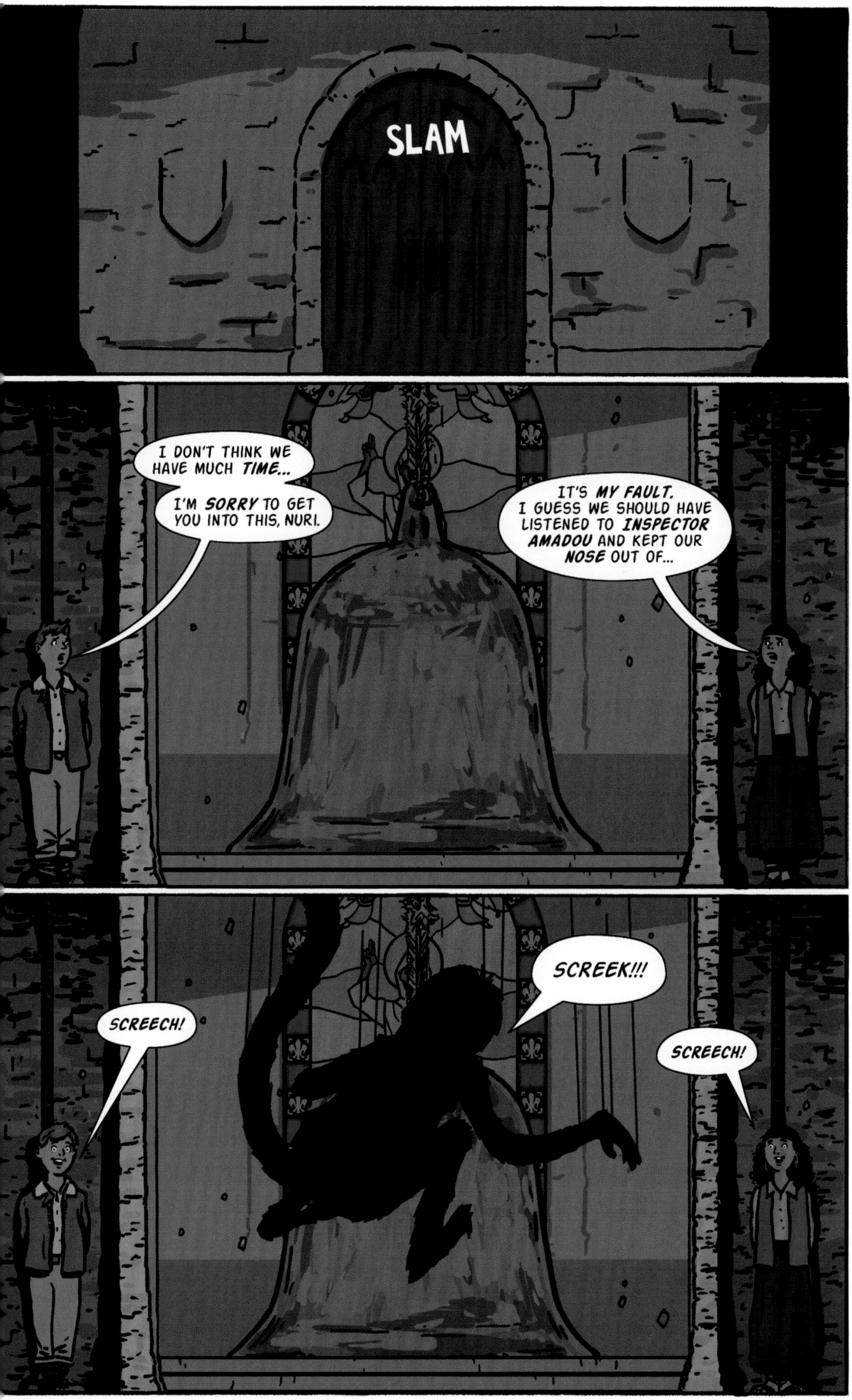
SLAM
I DON'T THINK WE HAVE MUCH *TIME...*
I'M *SORRY* TO GET YOU INTO THIS, NURI.
IT'S *MY FAULT.* I GUESS WE SHOULD HAVE LISTENED TO *INSPECTOR AMADOU* AND KEPT OUR *NOSE* OUT OF...
SCREECH!
SCREEK!!!
SCREECH!

IT WILL CERTAINLY AROUSE *SUSPICION* AS IT *IS*.

CHK

SHCHHHK

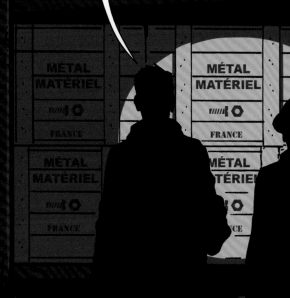

BUT *PERHAPS*...

MÉTAL MATÉRIEL
FRANCE

MÉTAL MATÉRIEL
FRANCE

MÉTAL MATÉRIEL

MÉTAL MATÉRIEL
FRANCE

MÉTAL TÉRIEL

MÉTAL TÉRIEL

COMMANDER!

COME OVER HERE, AND BRING THE TWO *PRISONERS* WITH YOU.

WE HAVE SOME *PACKING* TO DO!

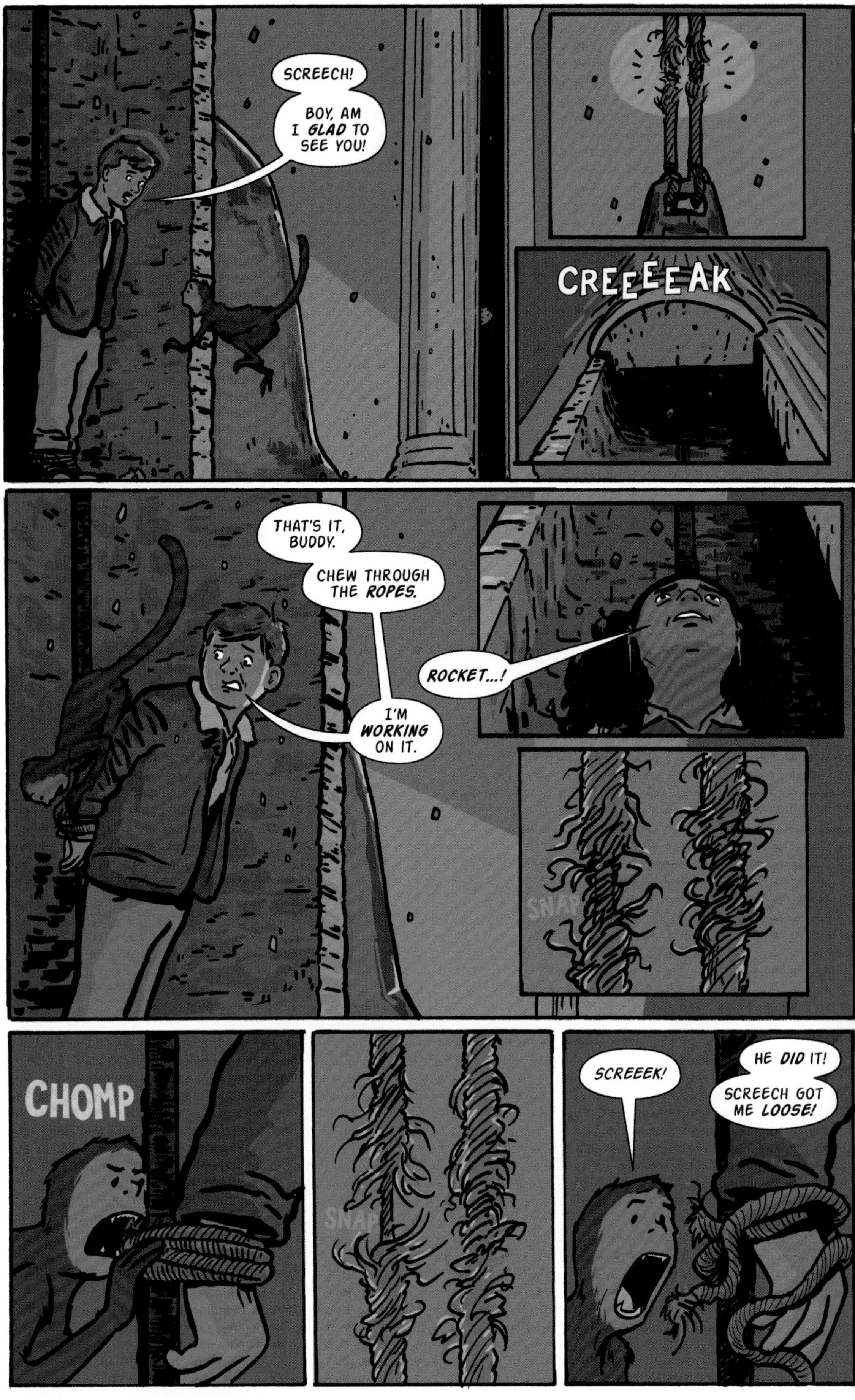
SCREECH!
BOY, AM I GLAD TO SEE YOU!
CREEEEAK
THAT'S IT, BUDDY.
CHEW THROUGH THE ROPES.
I'M WORKING ON IT.
ROCKET...!
SNAP
CHOMP
SNAP
SCREEEK!
HE DID IT!
SCREECH GOT ME LOOSE!

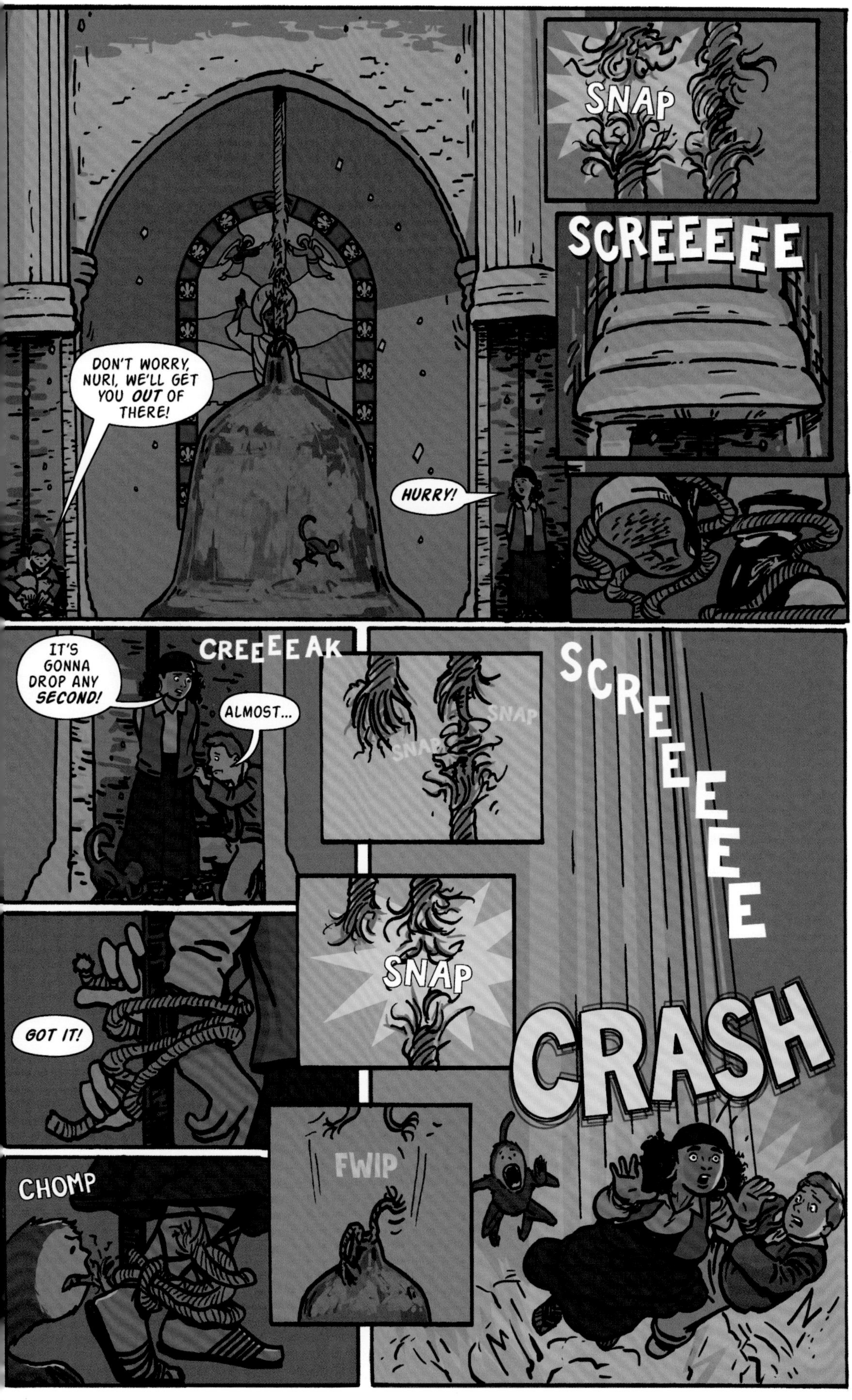
DON'T WORRY, NURI, WE'LL GET YOU OUT OF THERE!
HURRY!
SNAP
SCREEEEEE
IT'S GONNA DROP ANY SECOND!
CREEEEEAK
ALMOST...
SNAP
SNAP
SCREEEEEE
GOT IT!
SNAP
CRASH
CHOMP
FWIP

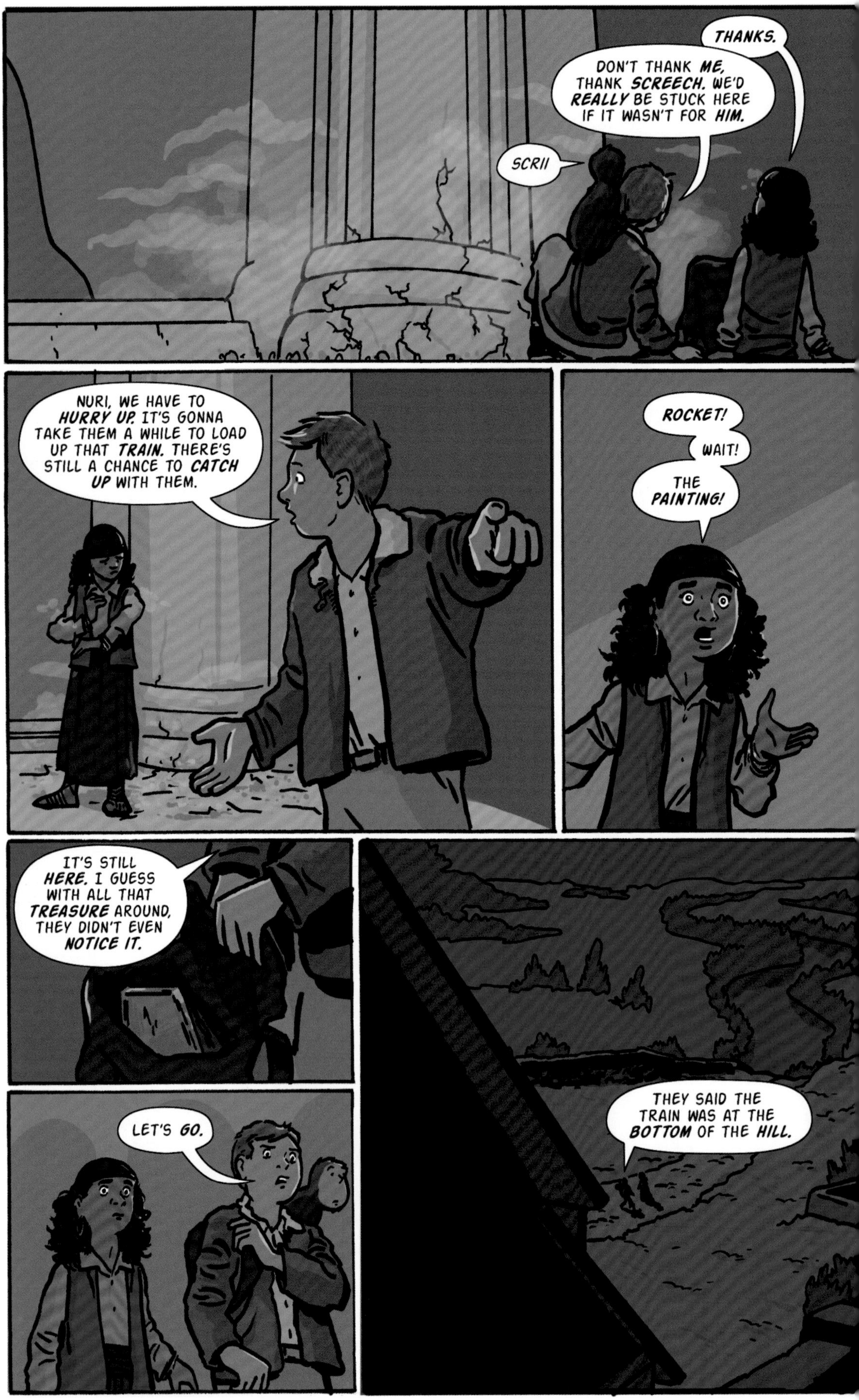
THANKS.
DON'T THANK ME, THANK SCREECH. WE'D REALLY BE STUCK HERE IF IT WASN'T FOR HIM.
SCRII
NURI, WE HAVE TO HURRY UP. IT'S GONNA TAKE THEM A WHILE TO LOAD UP THAT TRAIN. THERE'S STILL A CHANCE TO CATCH UP WITH THEM.
ROCKET!
WAIT!
THE PAINTING!
IT'S STILL HERE. I GUESS WITH ALL THAT TREASURE AROUND, THEY DIDN'T EVEN NOTICE IT.
LET'S GO.
THEY SAID THE TRAIN WAS AT THE BOTTOM OF THE HILL.

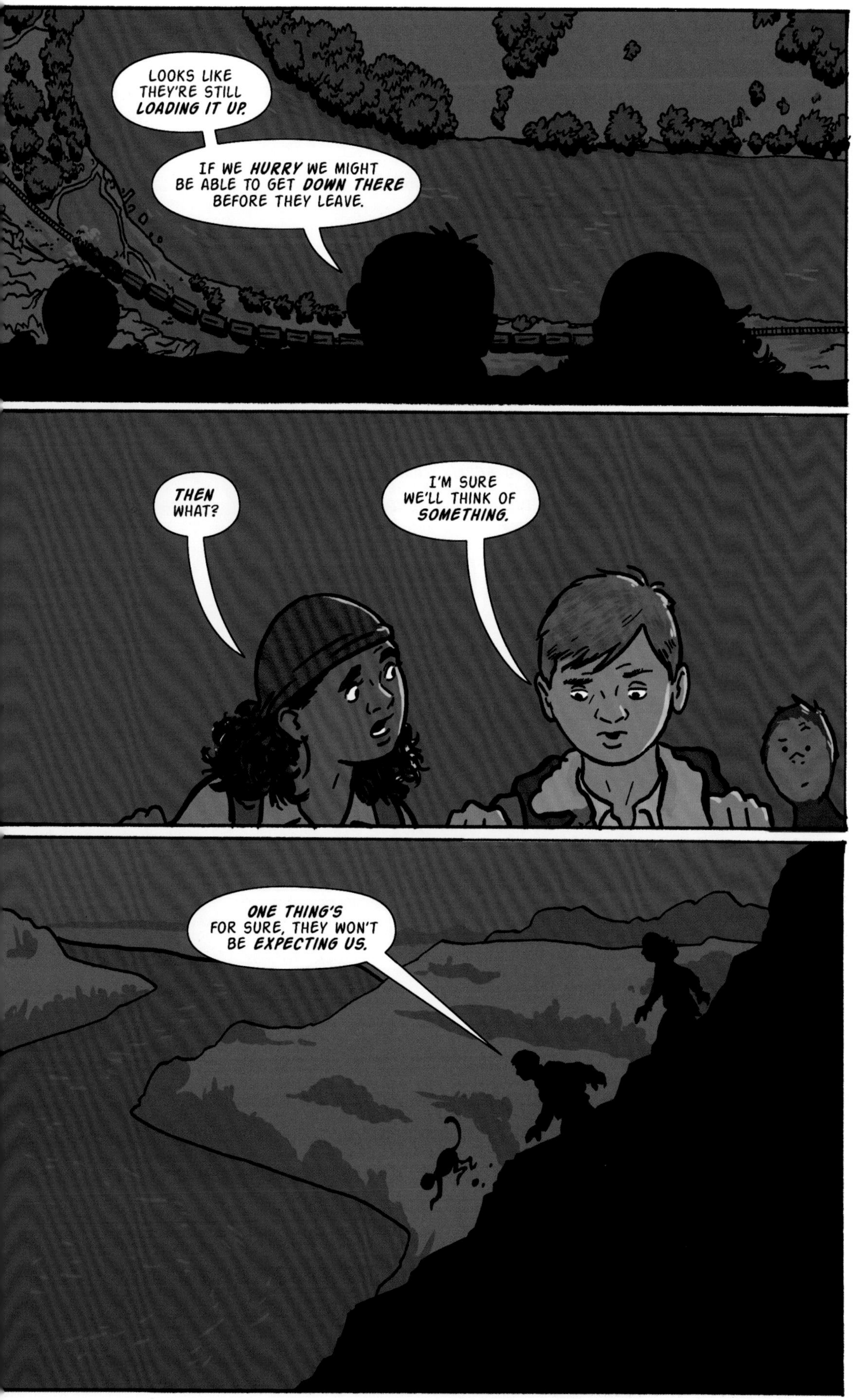
LOOKS LIKE THEY'RE STILL LOADING IT UP.
IF WE HURRY WE MIGHT BE ABLE TO GET DOWN THERE BEFORE THEY LEAVE.
THEN WHAT?
I'M SURE WE'LL THINK OF SOMETHING.
ONE THING'S FOR SURE, THEY WON'T BE EXPECTING US.

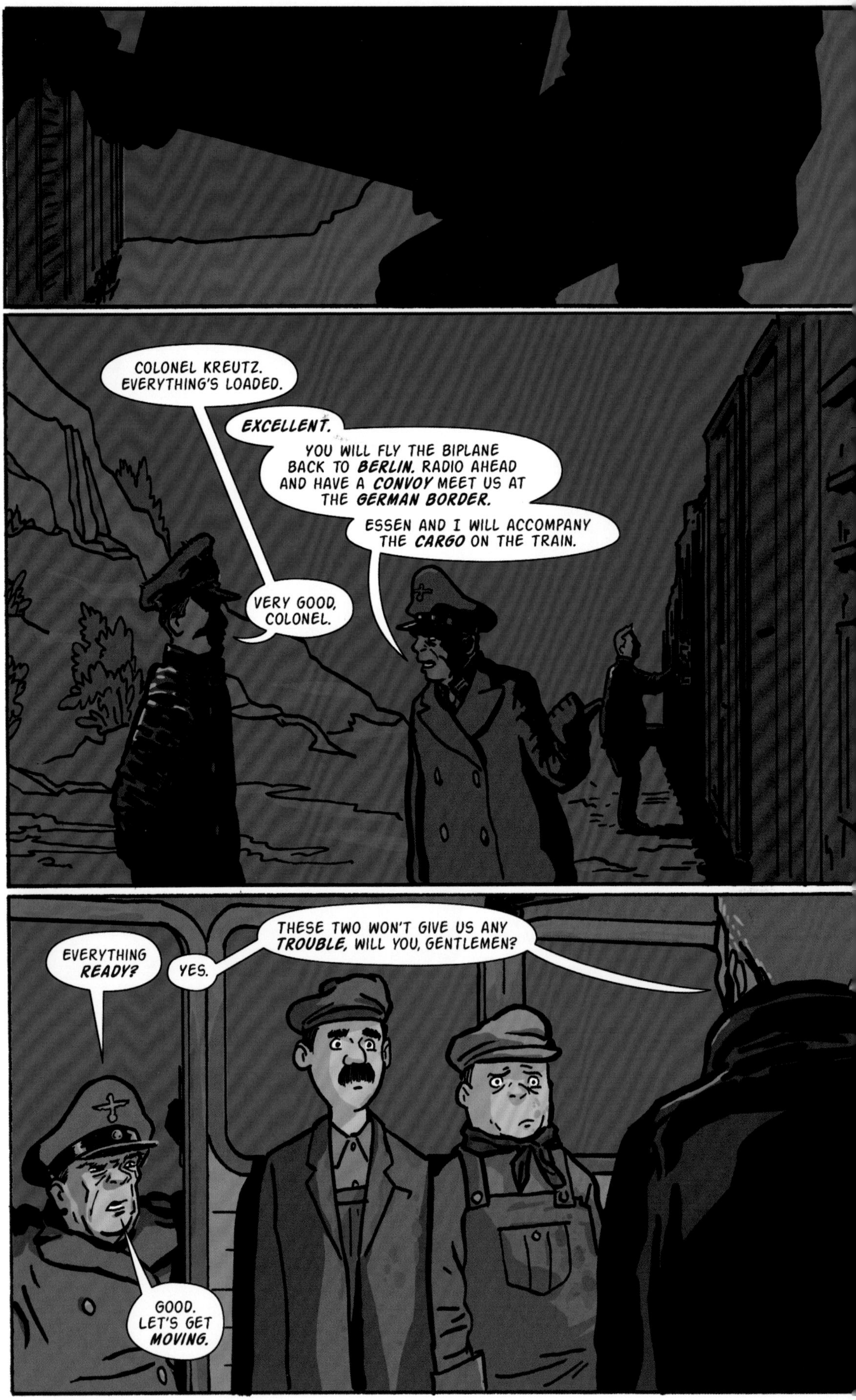
COLONEL KREUTZ. EVERYTHING'S LOADED.
EXCELLENT.
YOU WILL FLY THE BIPLANE BACK TO BERLIN. RADIO AHEAD AND HAVE A CONVOY MEET US AT THE GERMAN BORDER.
ESSEN AND I WILL ACCOMPANY THE CARGO ON THE TRAIN.
VERY GOOD, COLONEL.
EVERYTHING READY?
YES.
THESE TWO WON'T GIVE US ANY TROUBLE, WILL YOU, GENTLEMEN?
GOOD. LET'S GET MOVING.

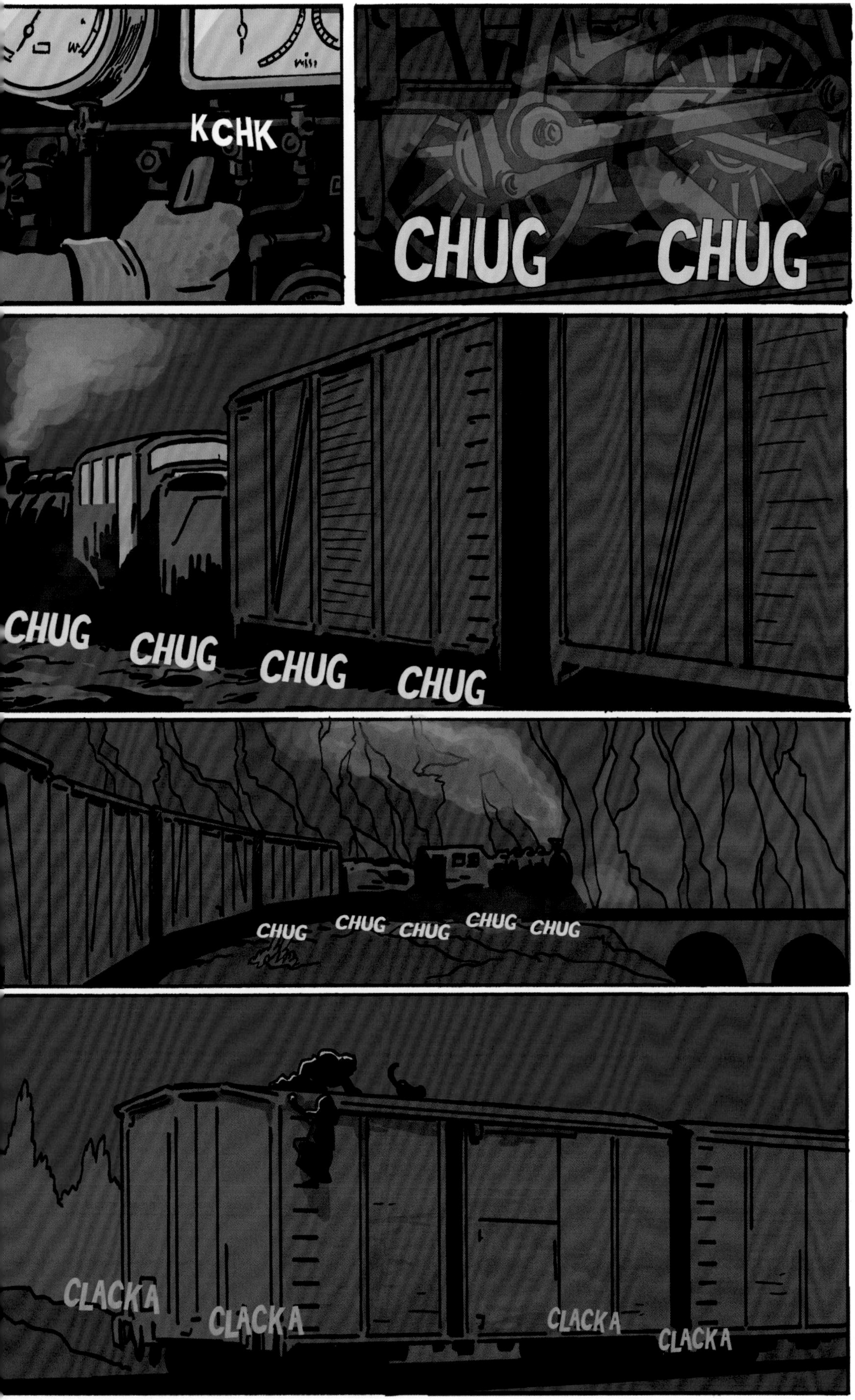
KCHK
CHUG CHUG
CHUG CHUG CHUG CHUG
CHUG CHUG CHUG CHUG CHUG
CLACKA CLACKA CLACKA CLACKA

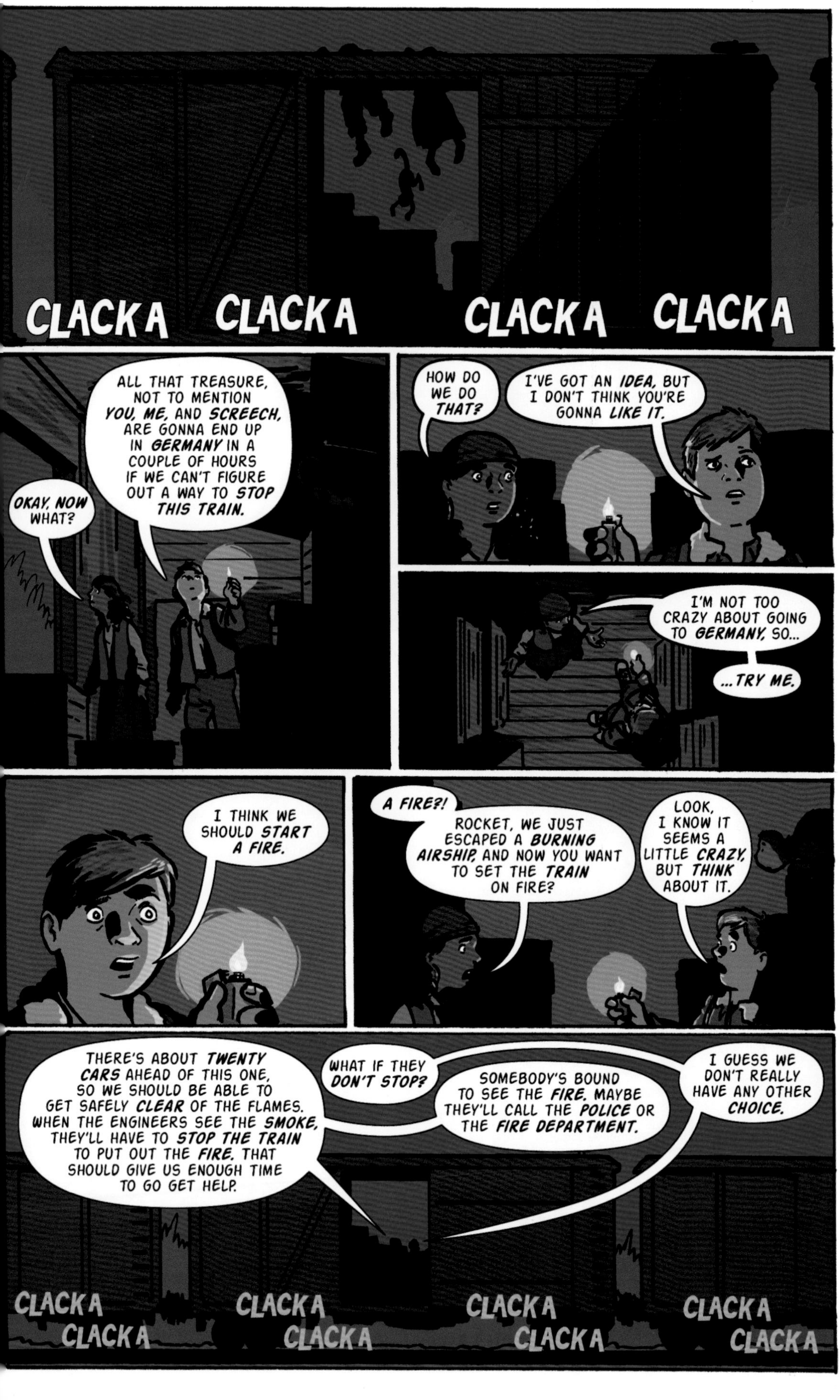
CLACKA CLACKA CLACKA CLACKA
OKAY, NOW WHAT?
ALL THAT TREASURE, NOT TO MENTION YOU, ME, AND SCREECH, ARE GONNA END UP IN GERMANY IN A COUPLE OF HOURS IF WE CAN'T FIGURE OUT A WAY TO STOP THIS TRAIN.
HOW DO WE DO THAT?
I'VE GOT AN IDEA, BUT I DON'T THINK YOU'RE GONNA LIKE IT.
I'M NOT TOO CRAZY ABOUT GOING TO GERMANY, SO...
...TRY ME.
I THINK WE SHOULD START A FIRE.
A FIRE?!
ROCKET, WE JUST ESCAPED A BURNING AIRSHIP, AND NOW YOU WANT TO SET THE TRAIN ON FIRE?
LOOK, I KNOW IT SEEMS A LITTLE CRAZY, BUT THINK ABOUT IT.
THERE'S ABOUT TWENTY CARS AHEAD OF THIS ONE, SO WE SHOULD BE ABLE TO GET SAFELY CLEAR OF THE FLAMES. WHEN THE ENGINEERS SEE THE SMOKE, THEY'LL HAVE TO STOP THE TRAIN TO PUT OUT THE FIRE. THAT SHOULD GIVE US ENOUGH TIME TO GO GET HELP.
WHAT IF THEY DON'T STOP?
SOMEBODY'S BOUND TO SEE THE FIRE. MAYBE THEY'LL CALL THE POLICE OR THE FIRE DEPARTMENT.
I GUESS WE DON'T REALLY HAVE ANY OTHER CHOICE.
CLACKA CLACKA CLACKA CLACKA CLACKA CLACKA CLACKA CLACKA

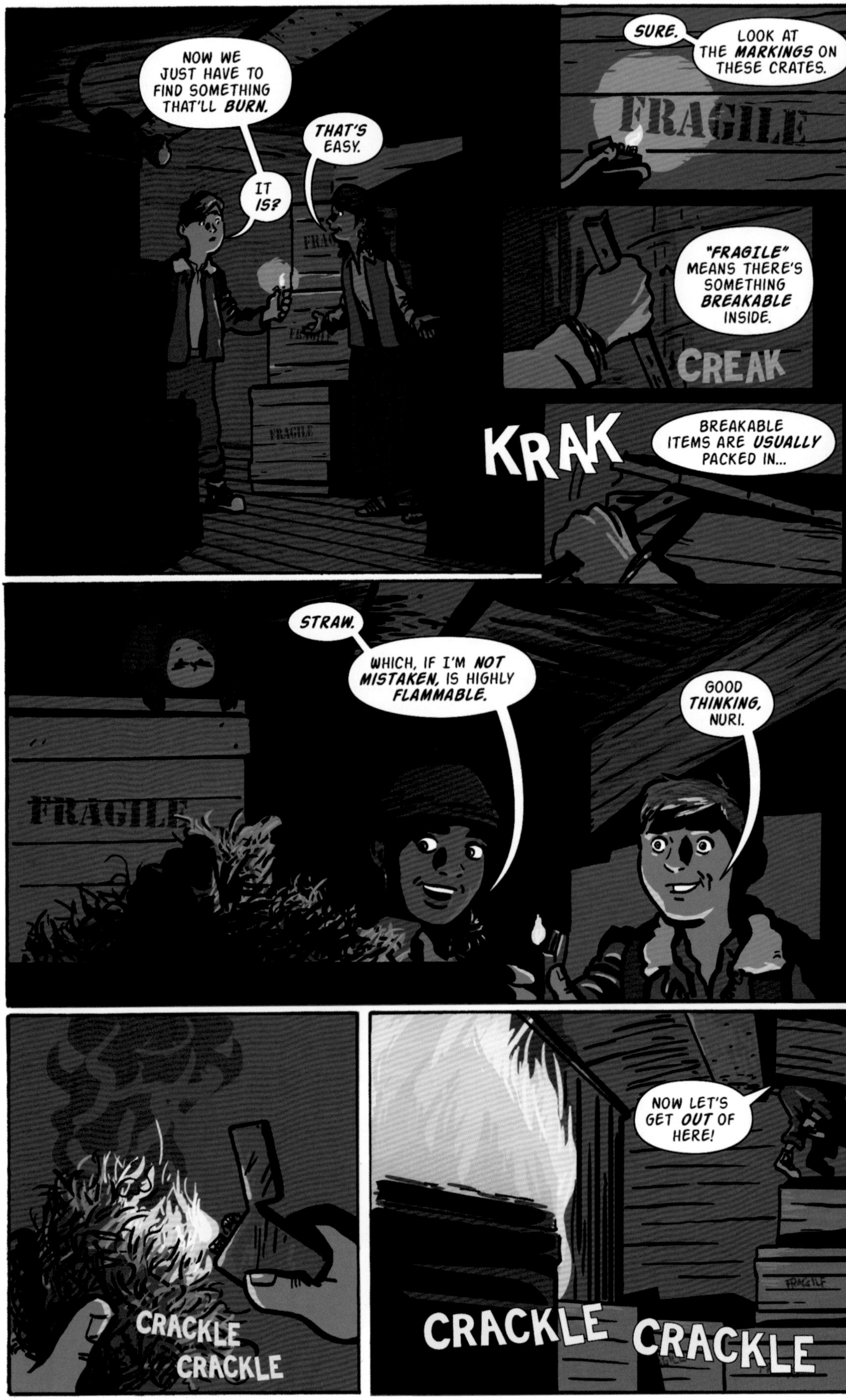
NOW WE JUST HAVE TO FIND SOMETHING THAT'LL BURN.
IT IS?
THAT'S EASY.
FRAGILE
FRAGILE
FRAGILE
SURE.
LOOK AT THE MARKINGS ON THESE CRATES.
FRAGILE
"FRAGILE" MEANS THERE'S SOMETHING BREAKABLE INSIDE.
CREAK
KRAK
BREAKABLE ITEMS ARE USUALLY PACKED IN...
STRAW.
WHICH, IF I'M NOT MISTAKEN, IS HIGHLY FLAMMABLE.
GOOD THINKING, NURI.
FRAGILE
CRACKLE
CRACKLE
NOW LET'S GET OUT OF HERE!
FRAGILE
CRACKLE
CRACKLE

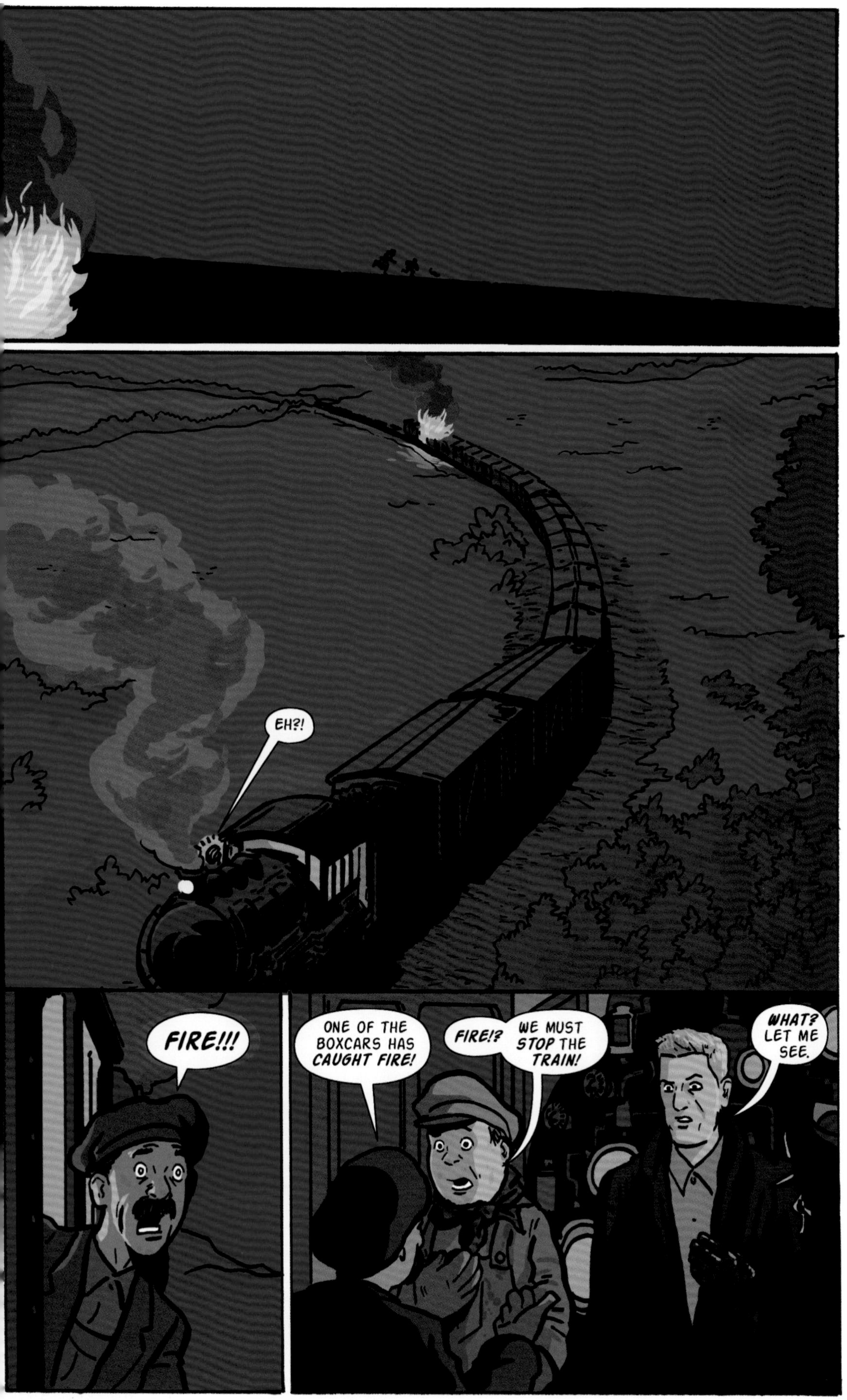
EH?!
FIRE!!!
ONE OF THE BOXCARS HAS CAUGHT FIRE!
FIRE!?
WE MUST STOP THE TRAIN!
WHAT? LET ME SEE.

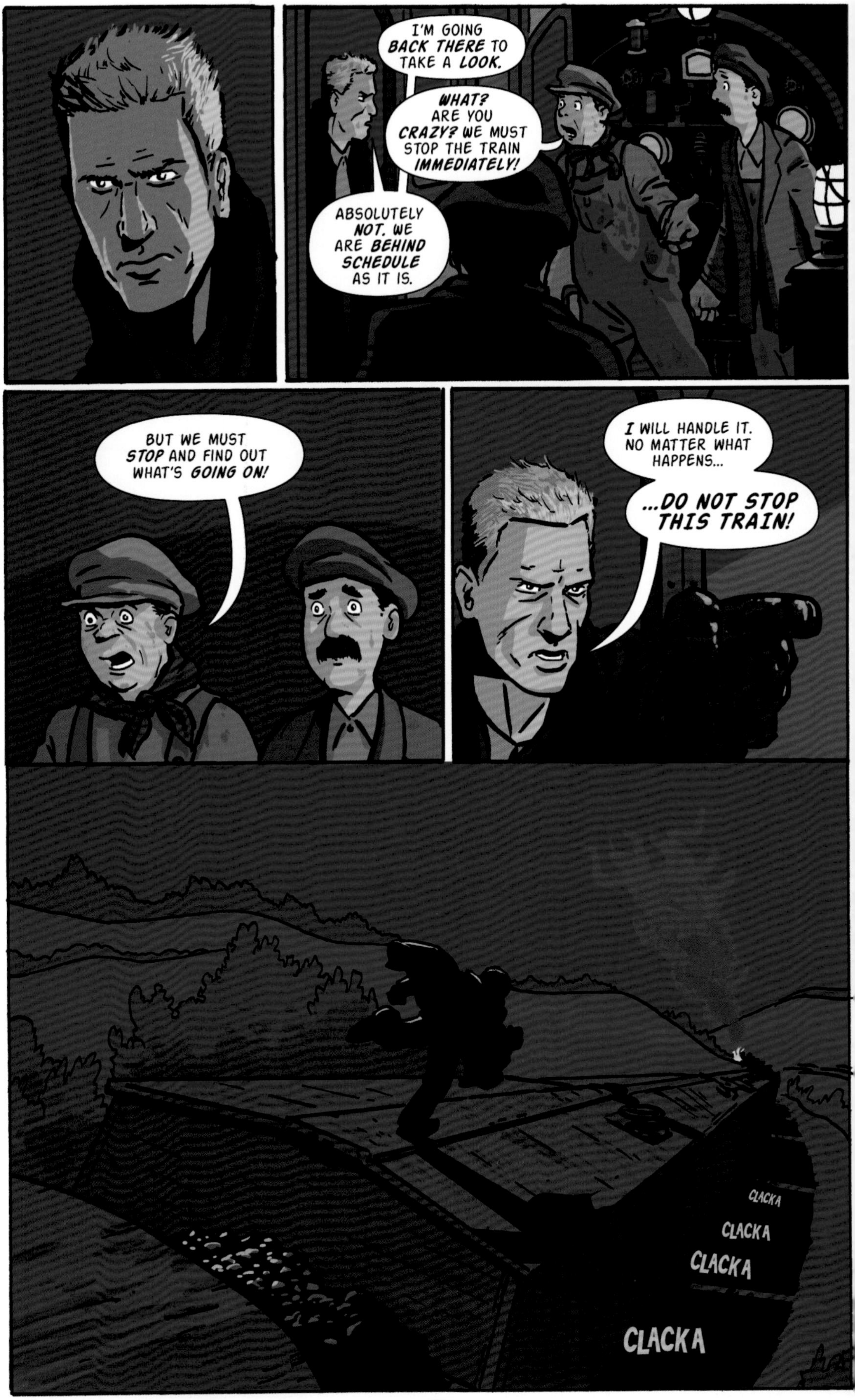
I'M GOING BACK THERE TO TAKE A LOOK.
WHAT? ARE YOU CRAZY? WE MUST STOP THE TRAIN IMMEDIATELY!
ABSOLUTELY NOT. WE ARE BEHIND SCHEDULE AS IT IS.
BUT WE MUST STOP AND FIND OUT WHAT'S GOING ON!
I WILL HANDLE IT. NO MATTER WHAT HAPPENS...
...DO NOT STOP THIS TRAIN!
CLACKA
CLACKA
CLACKA
CLACKA

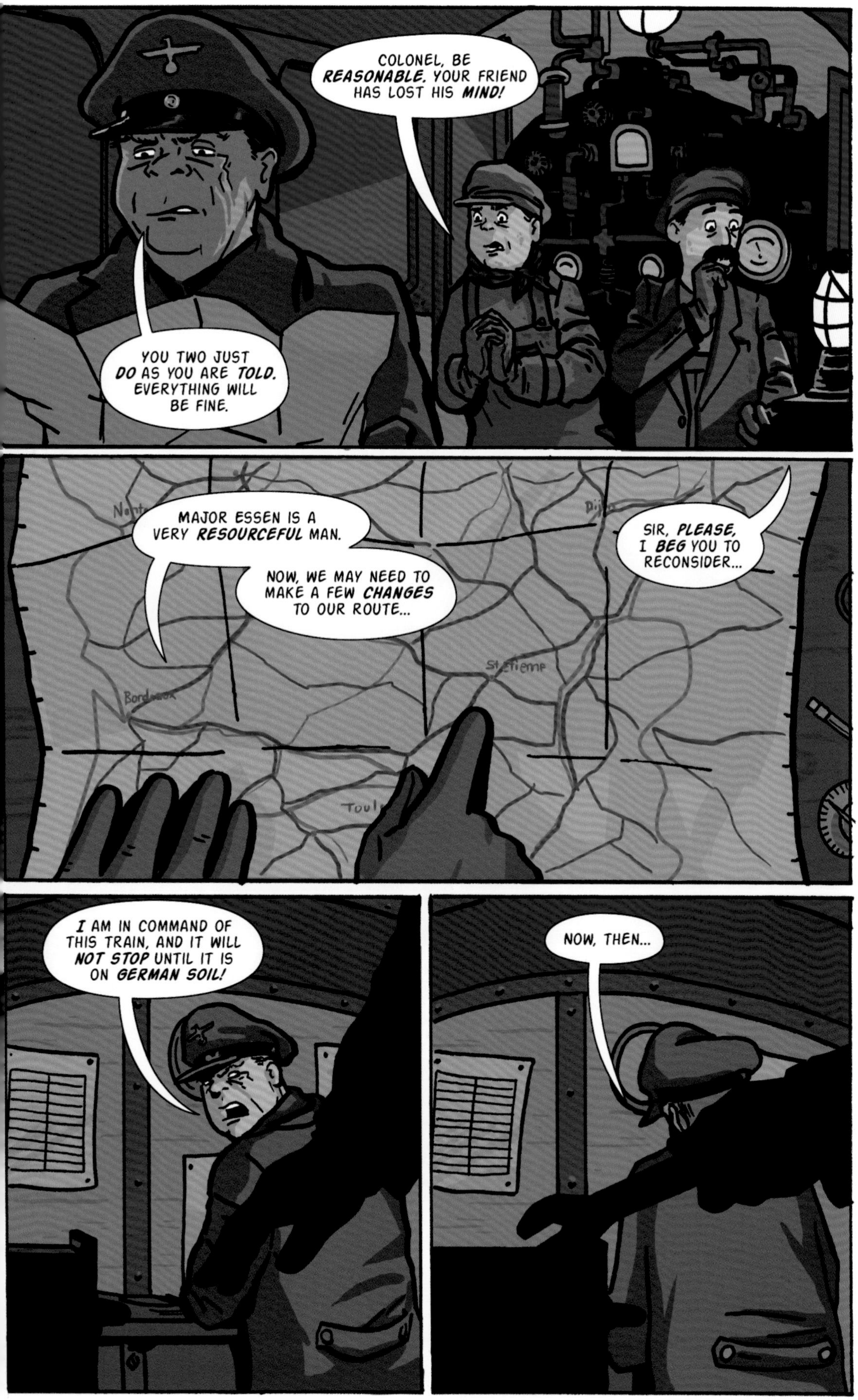

COLONEL, BE REASONABLE. YOUR FRIEND HAS LOST HIS MIND!
YOU TWO JUST DO AS YOU ARE TOLD. EVERYTHING WILL BE FINE.
MAJOR ESSEN IS A VERY RESOURCEFUL MAN.
NOW, WE MAY NEED TO MAKE A FEW CHANGES TO OUR ROUTE...
SIR, PLEASE, I BEG YOU TO RECONSIDER...
I AM IN COMMAND OF THIS TRAIN, AND IT WILL NOT STOP UNTIL IT IS ON GERMAN SOIL!
NOW, THEN...

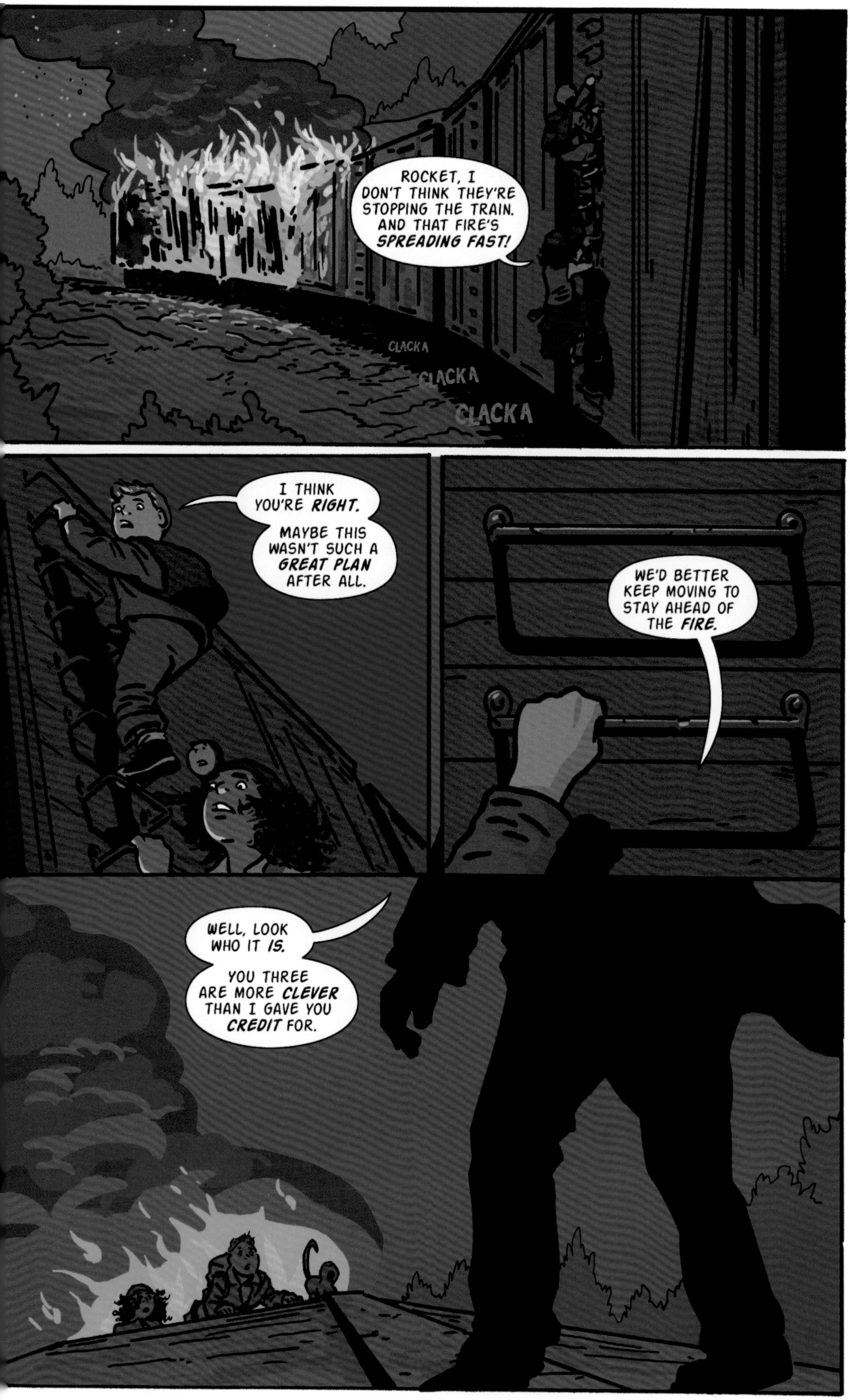
ROCKET, I DON'T THINK THEY'RE STOPPING THE TRAIN. AND THAT FIRE'S SPREADING FAST!
CLACKA
CLACKA
CLACKA
I THINK YOU'RE RIGHT.
MAYBE THIS WASN'T SUCH A GREAT PLAN AFTER ALL.
WE'D BETTER KEEP MOVING TO STAY AHEAD OF THE FIRE.
WELL, LOOK WHO IT IS.
YOU THREE ARE MORE CLEVER THAN I GAVE YOU CREDIT FOR.

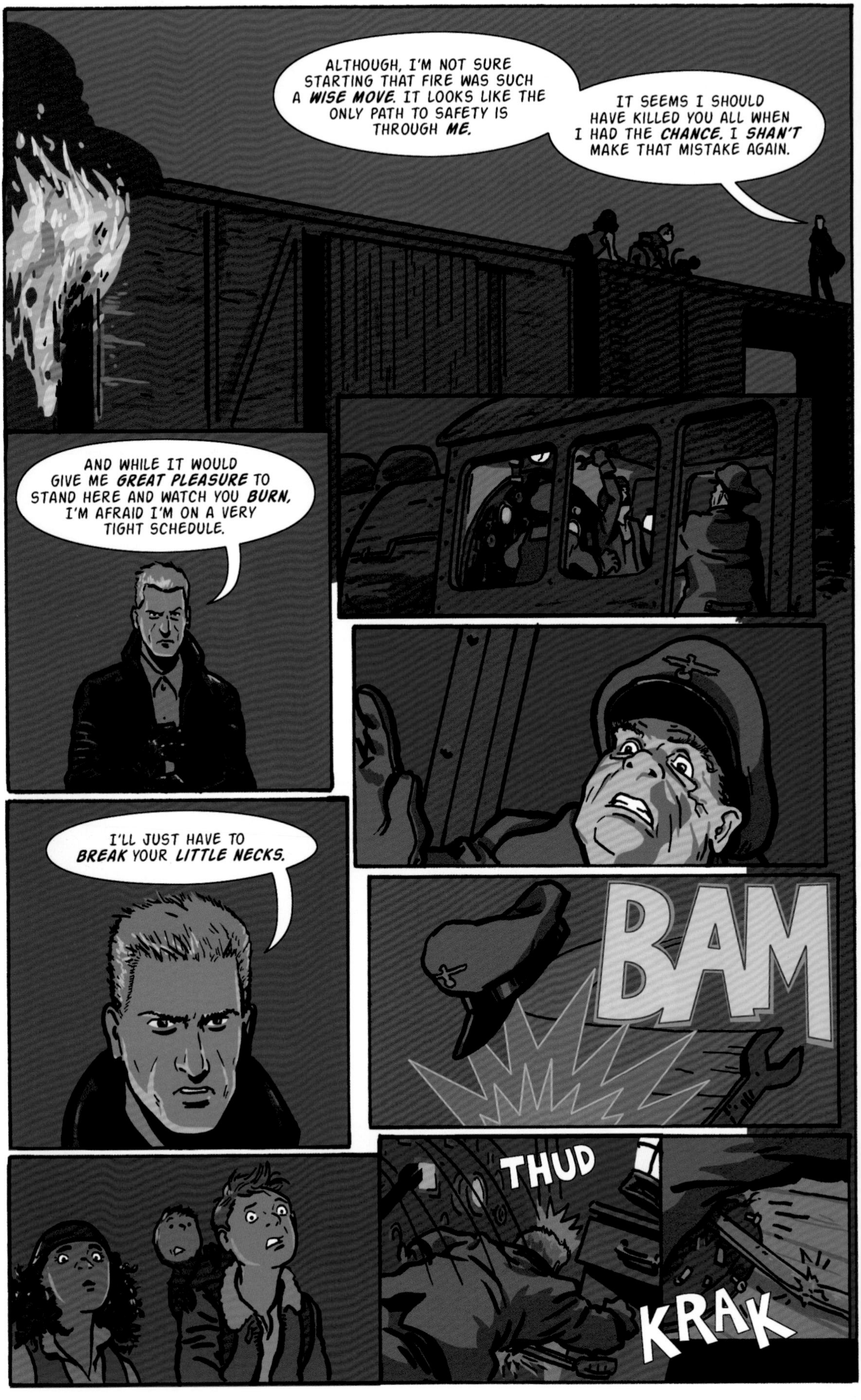
ALTHOUGH, I'M NOT SURE STARTING THAT FIRE WAS SUCH A WISE MOVE. IT LOOKS LIKE THE ONLY PATH TO SAFETY IS THROUGH ME.
IT SEEMS I SHOULD HAVE KILLED YOU ALL WHEN I HAD THE CHANCE. I SHAN'T MAKE THAT MISTAKE AGAIN.
AND WHILE IT WOULD GIVE ME GREAT PLEASURE TO STAND HERE AND WATCH YOU BURN, I'M AFRAID I'M ON A VERY TIGHT SCHEDULE.
I'LL JUST HAVE TO BREAK YOUR LITTLE NECKS.
BAM
THUD
KRAK

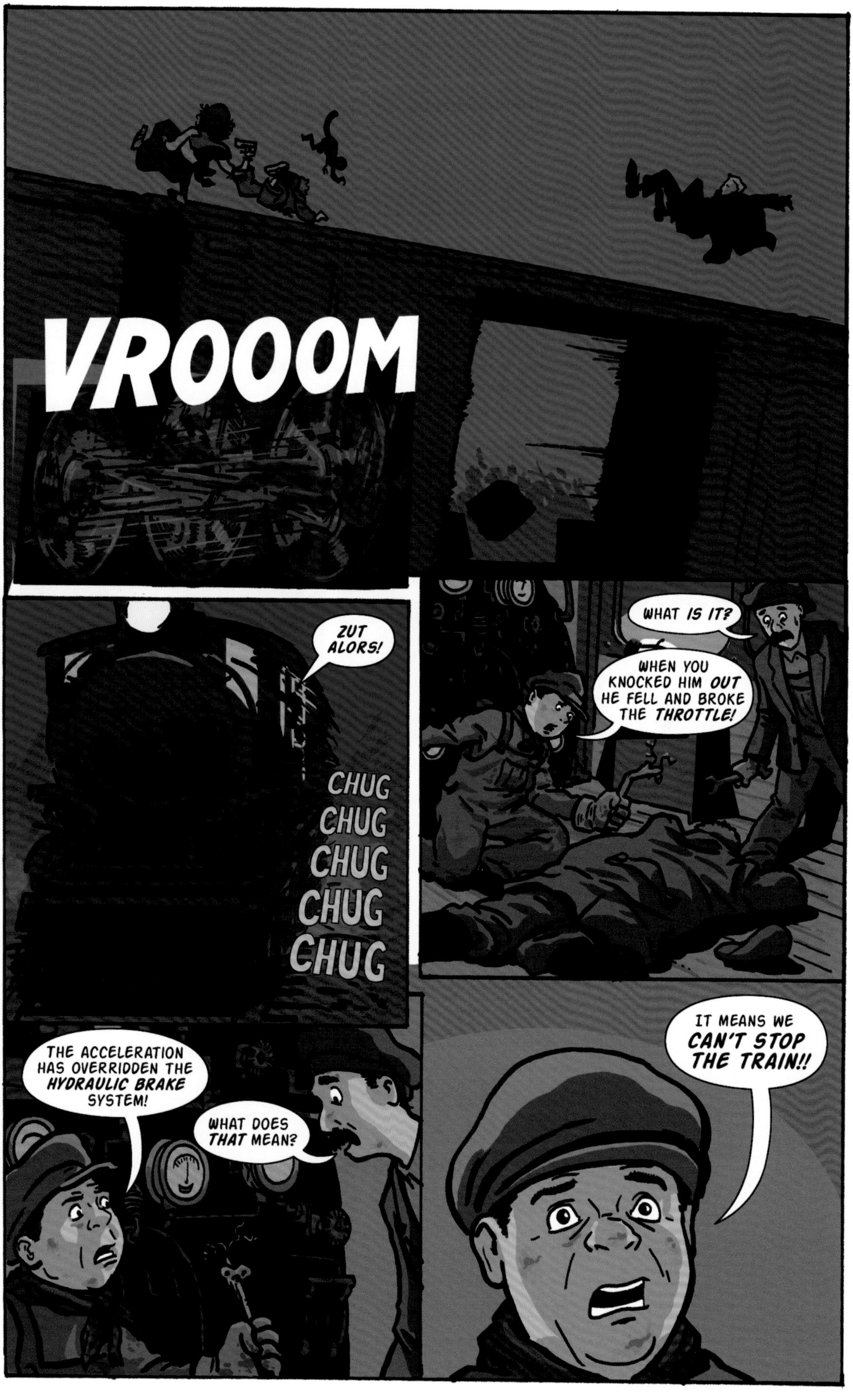
VROOOM
ZUT ALORS!
CHUG
CHUG
CHUG
CHUG
CHUG
WHAT IS IT?
WHEN YOU KNOCKED HIM OUT HE FELL AND BROKE THE THROTTLE!
THE ACCELERATION HAS OVERRIDDEN THE HYDRAULIC BRAKE SYSTEM!
WHAT DOES THAT MEAN?
IT MEANS WE CAN'T STOP THE TRAIN!!

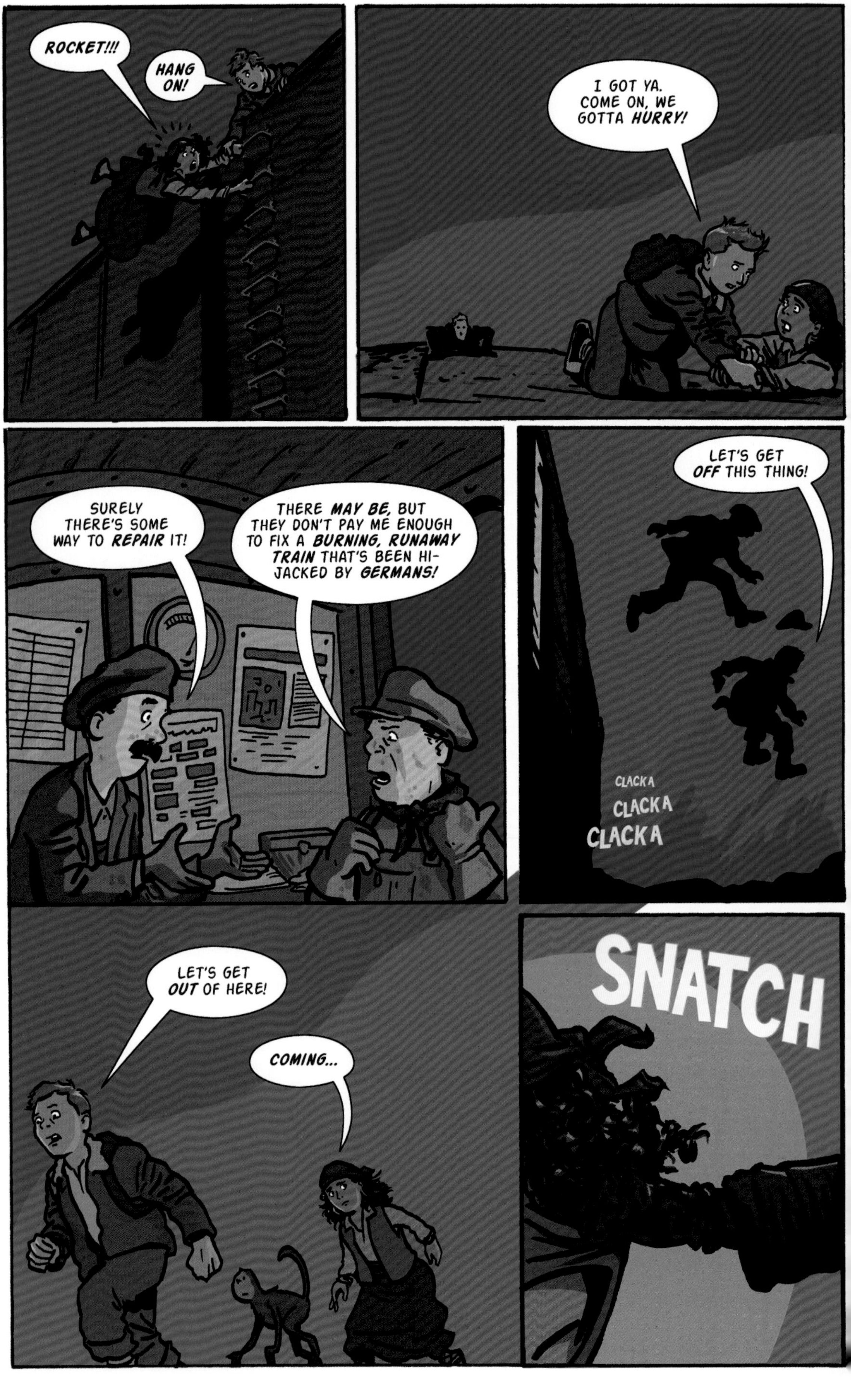
ROCKET!!!
HANG ON!
I GOT YA. COME ON, WE GOTTA HURRY!
SURELY THERE'S SOME WAY TO REPAIR IT!
THERE MAY BE, BUT THEY DON'T PAY ME ENOUGH TO FIX A BURNING, RUNAWAY TRAIN THAT'S BEEN HI-JACKED BY GERMANS!
LET'S GET OFF THIS THING!
CLACKA
CLACKA
CLACKA
LET'S GET OUT OF HERE!
COMING...
SNATCH

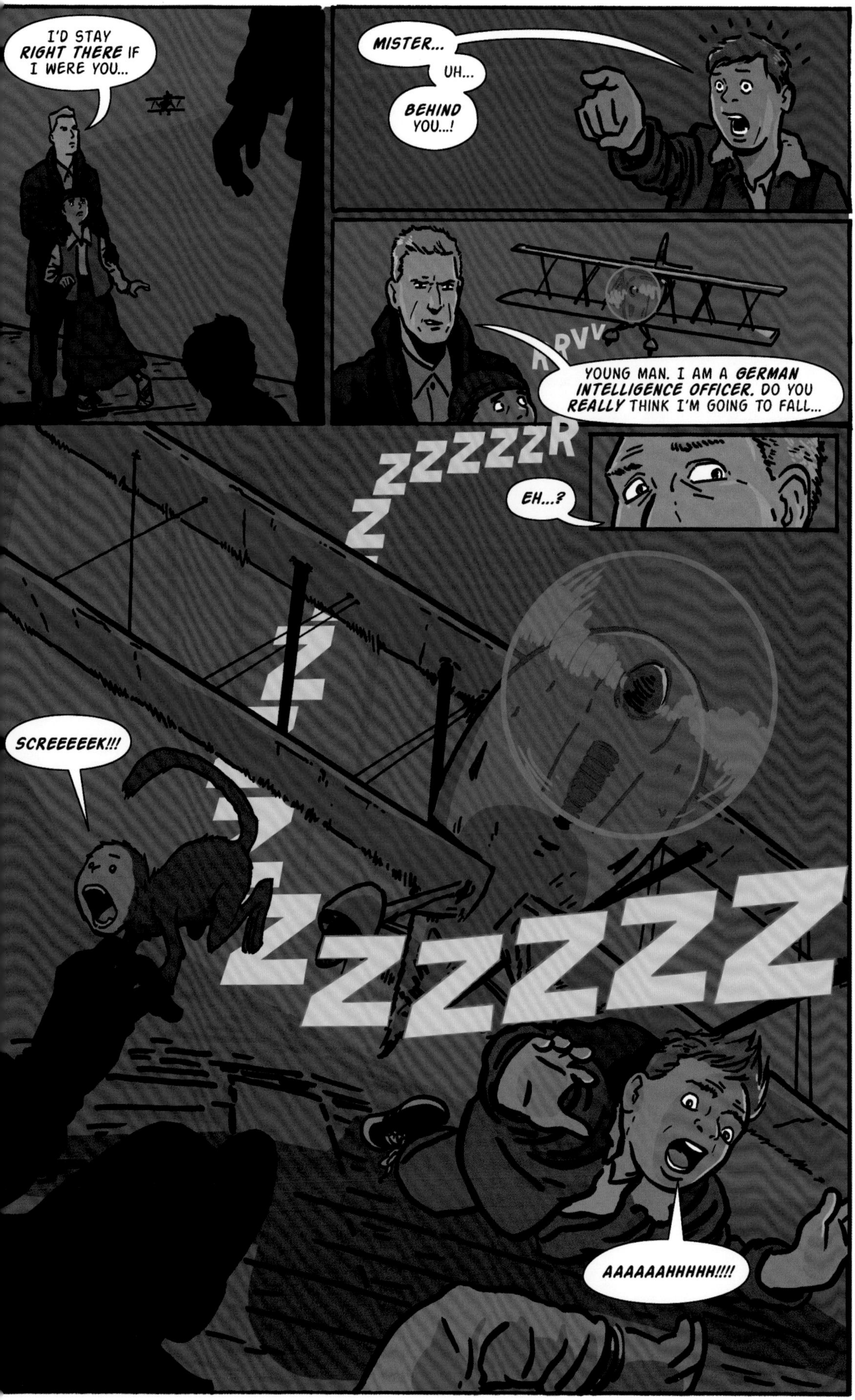
I'D STAY RIGHT THERE IF I WERE YOU...
MISTER...
UH...
BEHIND YOU...!
YOUNG MAN. I AM A GERMAN INTELLIGENCE OFFICER. DO YOU REALLY THINK I'M GOING TO FALL...
ZZZZZZZR
EH...?
SCREEEEEK!!!
ZZZZZZ
AAAAAAHHHHH!!!!

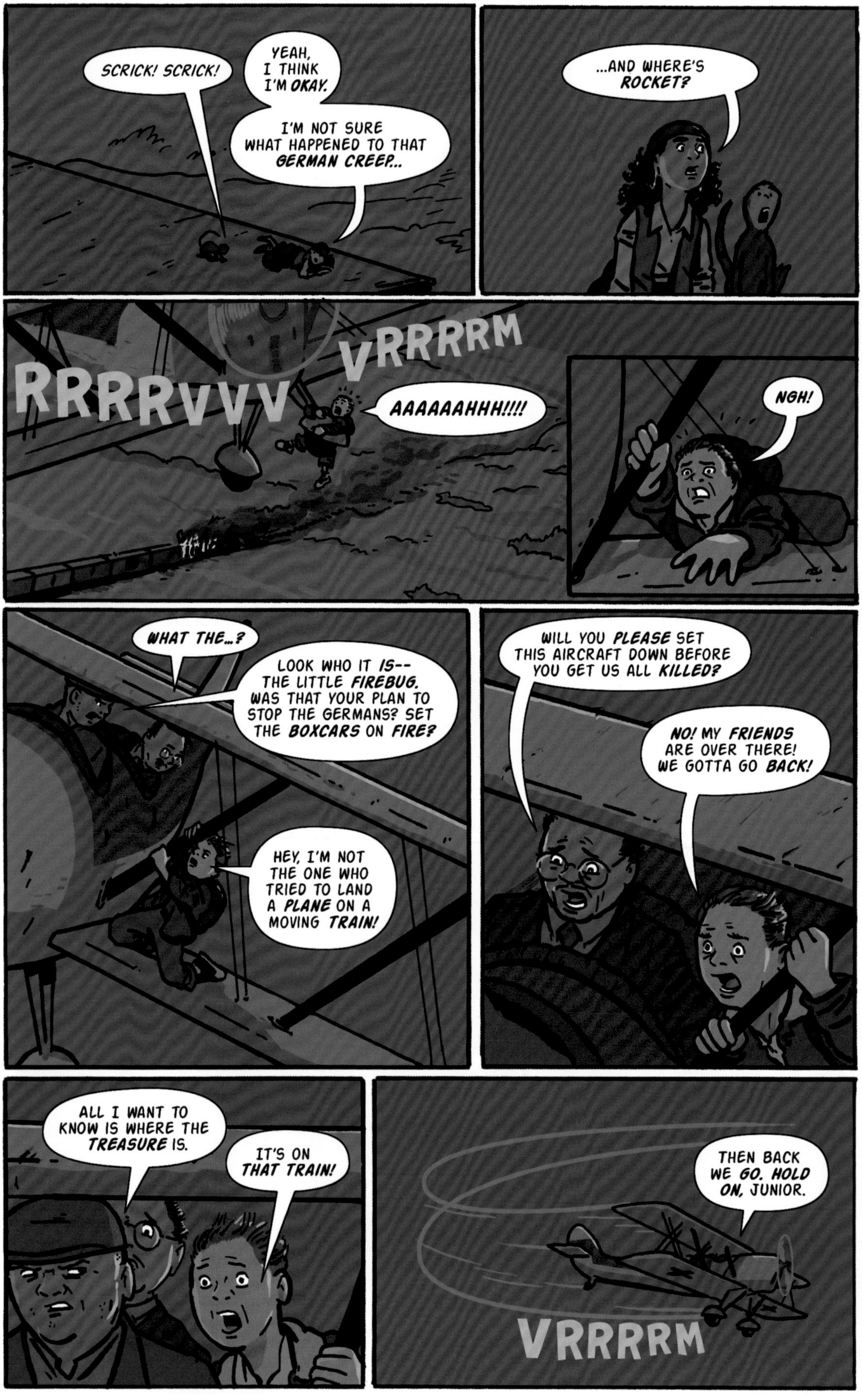
SCRICK! SCRICK!
YEAH, I THINK I'M OKAY.
I'M NOT SURE WHAT HAPPENED TO THAT GERMAN CREEP...
...AND WHERE'S ROCKET?
RRRRVVVV
VRRRRM
AAAAAAHHH!!!!
NGH!
WHAT THE...?
LOOK WHO IT IS-- THE LITTLE FIREBUG. WAS THAT YOUR PLAN TO STOP THE GERMANS? SET THE BOXCARS ON FIRE?
HEY, I'M NOT THE ONE WHO TRIED TO LAND A PLANE ON A MOVING TRAIN!
WILL YOU PLEASE SET THIS AIRCRAFT DOWN BEFORE YOU GET US ALL KILLED?
NO! MY FRIENDS ARE OVER THERE! WE GOTTA GO BACK!
ALL I WANT TO KNOW IS WHERE THE TREASURE IS.
IT'S ON THAT TRAIN!
THEN BACK WE GO. HOLD ON, JUNIOR.
VRRRRM

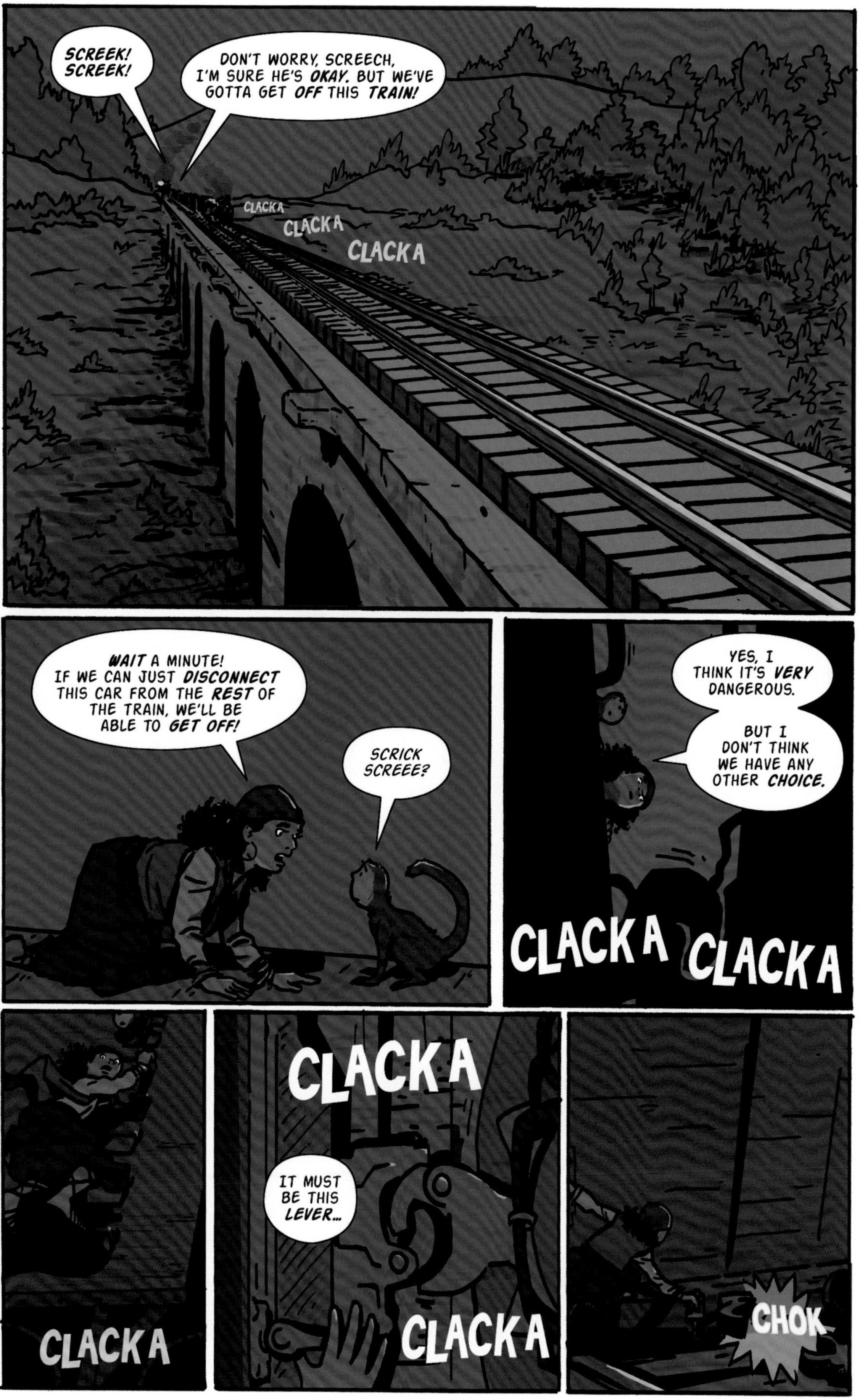
SCREEK! SCREEK!
DON'T WORRY, SCREECH, I'M SURE HE'S OKAY. BUT WE'VE GOTTA GET OFF THIS TRAIN!
CLACKA
CLACKA
CLACKA
WAIT A MINUTE! IF WE CAN JUST DISCONNECT THIS CAR FROM THE REST OF THE TRAIN, WE'LL BE ABLE TO GET OFF!
SCRICK SCREEE?
YES, I THINK IT'S VERY DANGEROUS.
BUT I DON'T THINK WE HAVE ANY OTHER CHOICE.
CLACKA
CLACKA
CLACKA
CLACKA
IT MUST BE THIS LEVER...
CLACKA
CHOK

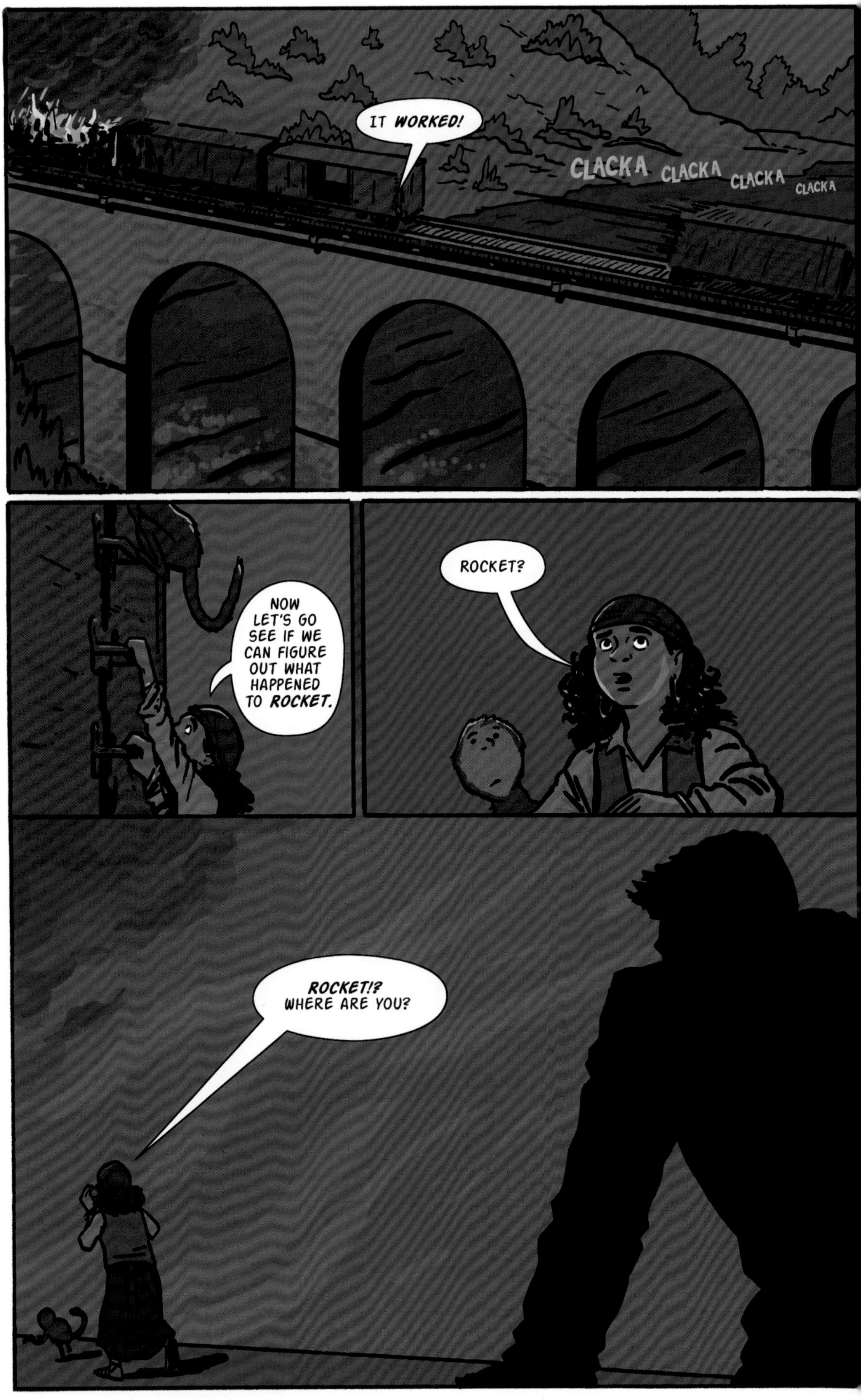
IT WORKED!
CLACKA CLACKA CLACKA CLACKA
NOW LET'S GO SEE IF WE CAN FIGURE OUT WHAT HAPPENED TO ROCKET.
ROCKET?
ROCKET!? WHERE ARE YOU?

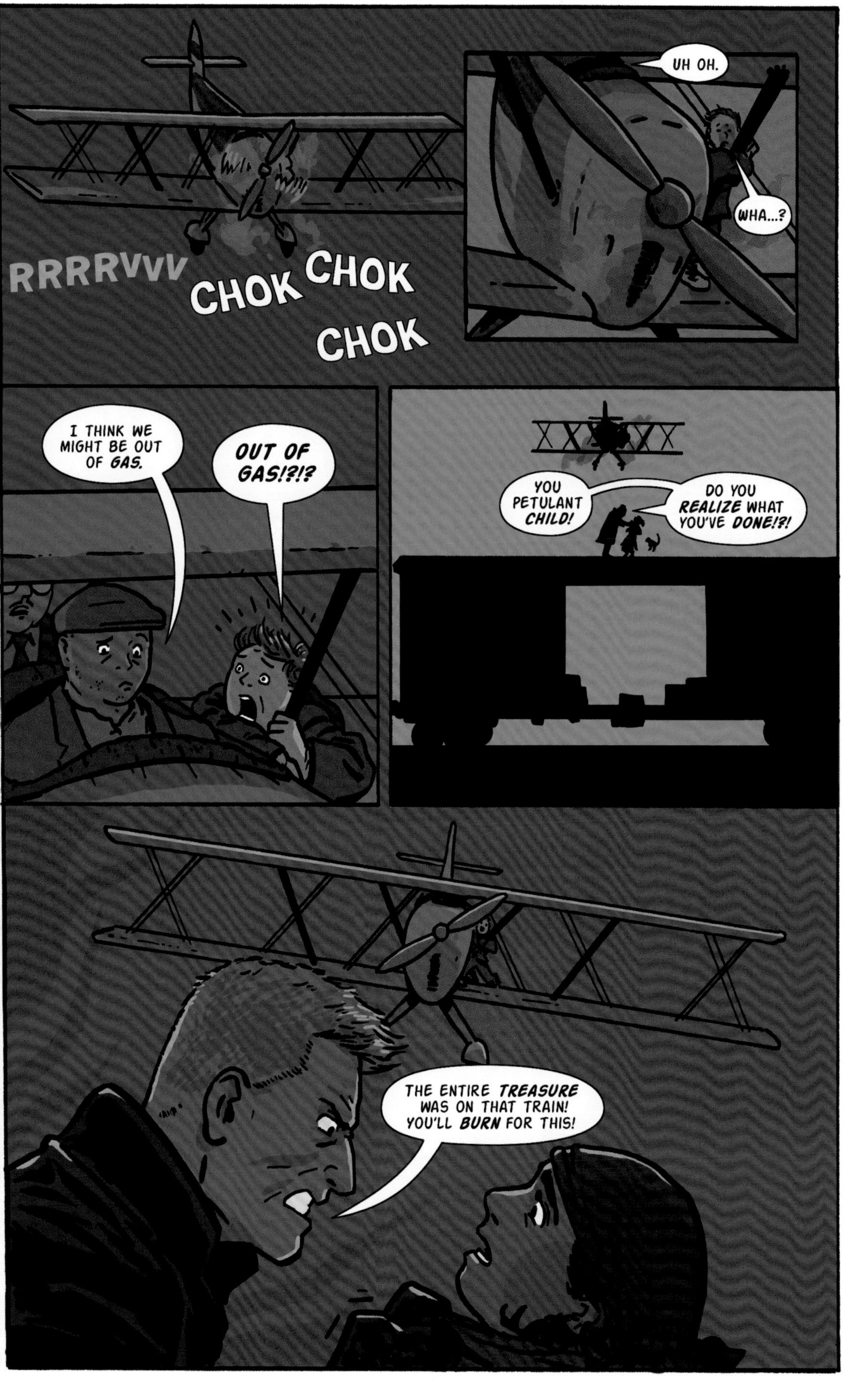
RRRRVVV
CHOK CHOK
CHOK
UH OH.
WHA...?
I THINK WE MIGHT BE OUT OF GAS.
OUT OF GAS!?!?
YOU PETULANT CHILD!
DO YOU REALIZE WHAT YOU'VE DONE!?!
THE ENTIRE TREASURE WAS ON THAT TRAIN! YOU'LL BURN FOR THIS!

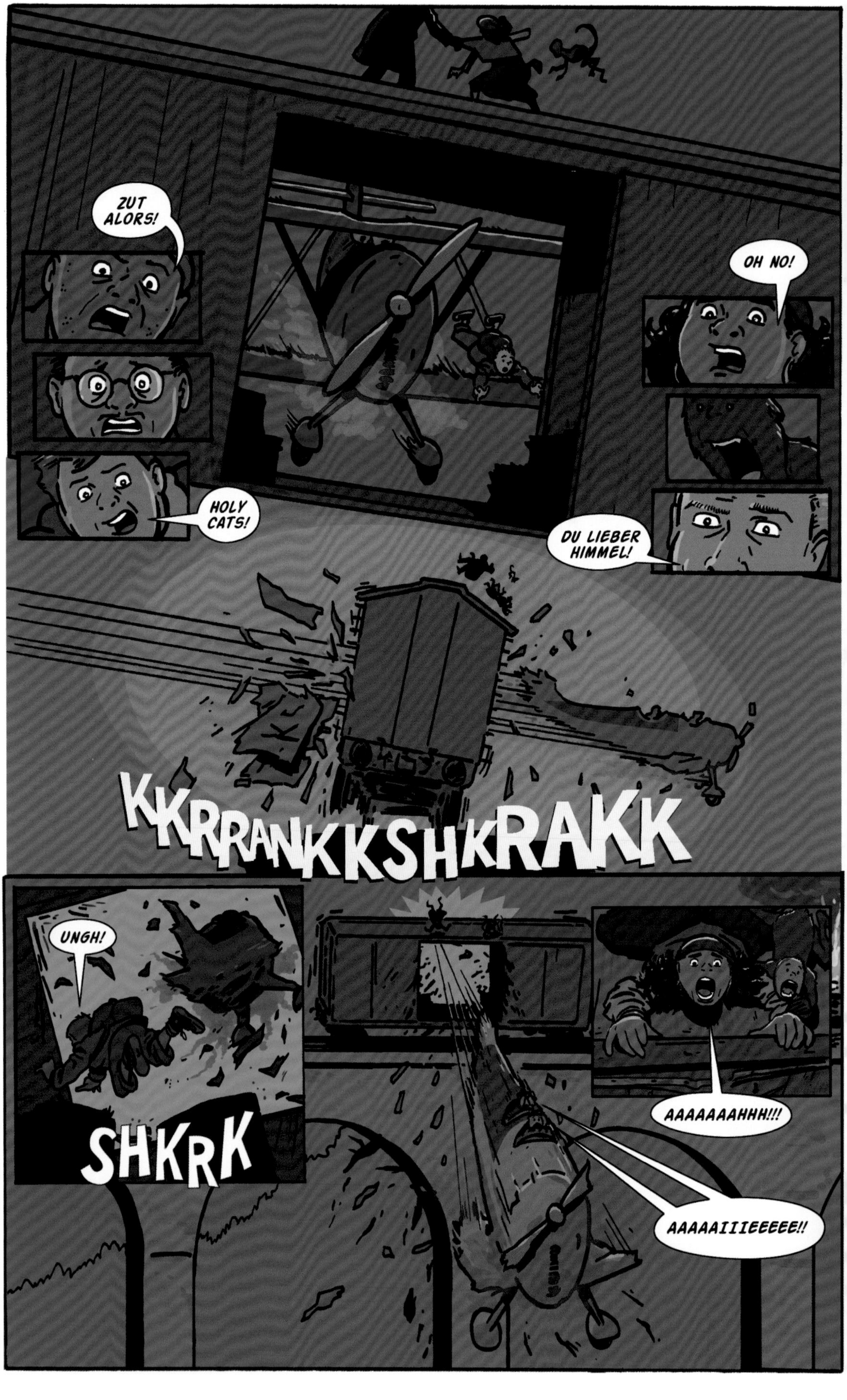
ZUT ALORS!
OH NO!
HOLY CATS!
DU LIEBER HIMMEL!
KKRRANKKSHKRAKK
UNGH!
SHKRK
AAAAAAAHHH!!!
AAAAAIIIEEEEE!!

FWOOSH

OOOF!!

FWSHKCH

CREEEEEEEEAK

KATHUNK

NGHH!!

SCREE!

I'M OKAY. THANK GOODNESS I WAS ABLE TO *HANG ON.*

SCRICK SCRICK!

I DON'T THINK *HERR ESSEN* WAS AS *LUCKY...*

WE'D BETTER GET OFF THIS THING. THAT *FIRE'S* GETTING *CLOSER.*

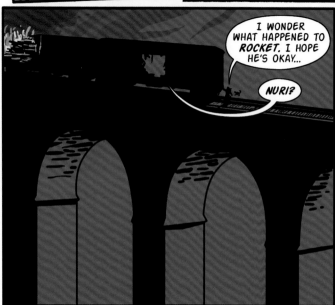

I WONDER WHAT HAPPENED TO *ROCKET.* I HOPE HE'S OKAY...

NURI?

SCREEEK!!

ROCKET!

HI, GUYS.

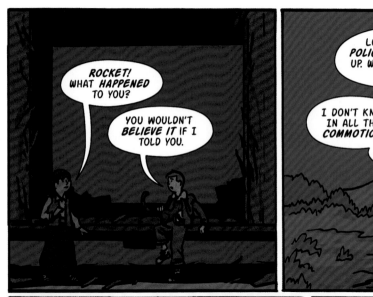

ROCKET! WHAT *HAPPENED* TO YOU?

YOU WOULDN'T *BELIEVE IT* IF I TOLD YOU.

LOOKS LIKE THE *POLICE* FINALLY SHOWED UP. WHAT HAPPENED TO *MR. ESSEN?*

I DON'T KNOW. IN ALL THE *COMMOTION...*

ROCKET...

...LOOK.

WHAT SHOULD WE *DO?*

UH... WAIT FOR THE *POLICE,* I GUESS...

DON'T *BOTHER.* I WILL *NOT* BE CAPTURED.

BUT, I *PROMISE* YOU, WE WILL SEE EACH OTHER *AGAIN.*

UNTIL THEN, *AUF WIEDERSEHEN.*

GASP

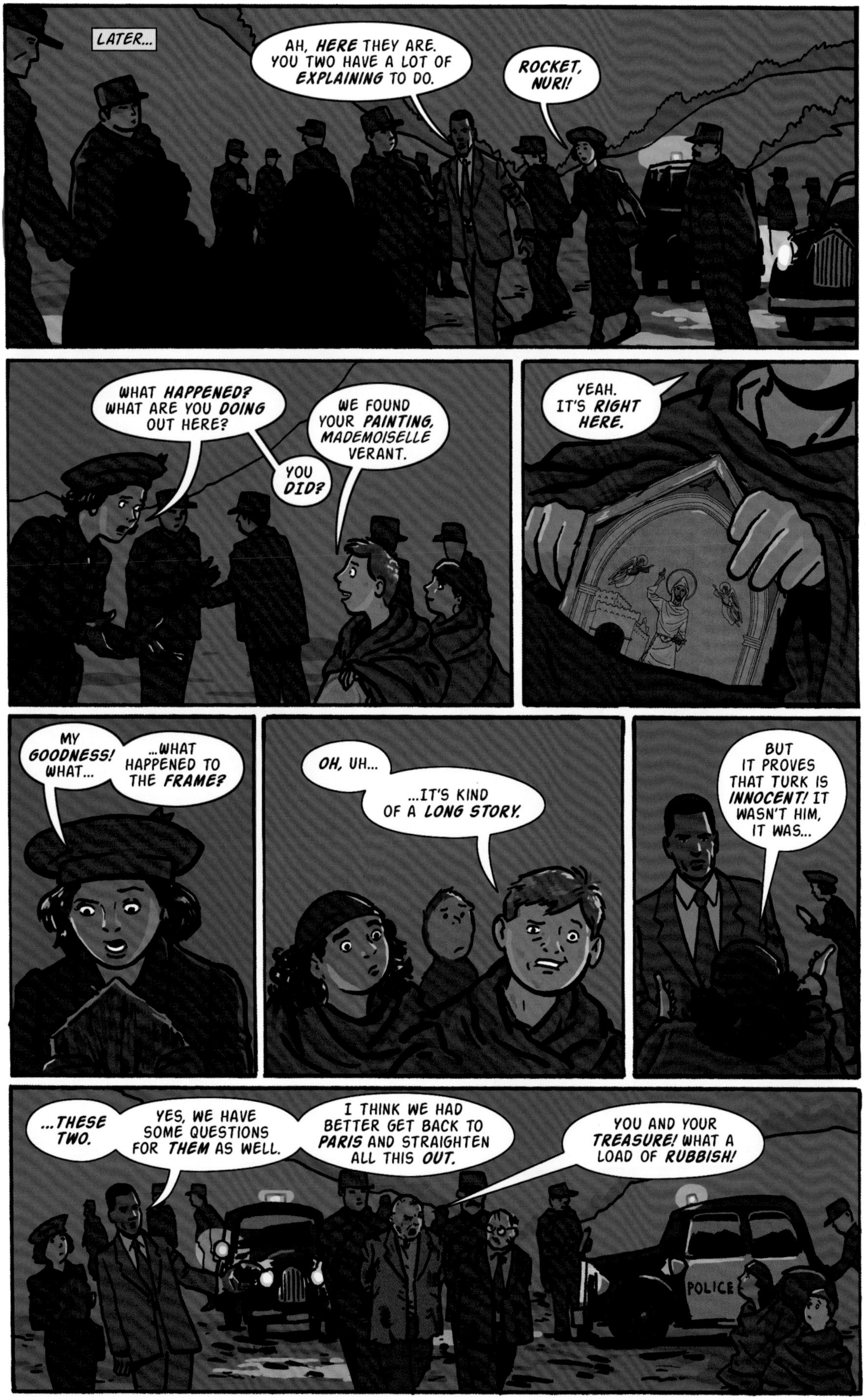
LATER...
AH, HERE THEY ARE. YOU TWO HAVE A LOT OF EXPLAINING TO DO.
ROCKET, NURI!
WHAT HAPPENED? WHAT ARE YOU DOING OUT HERE?
WE FOUND YOUR PAINTING, MADEMOISELLE VERANT.
YOU DID?
YEAH. IT'S RIGHT HERE.
MY GOODNESS! WHAT...
...WHAT HAPPENED TO THE FRAME?
OH, UH...
...IT'S KIND OF A LONG STORY.
BUT IT PROVES THAT TURK IS INNOCENT! IT WASN'T HIM, IT WAS...
...THESE TWO.
YES, WE HAVE SOME QUESTIONS FOR THEM AS WELL.
I THINK WE HAD BETTER GET BACK TO PARIS AND STRAIGHTEN ALL THIS OUT.
YOU AND YOUR TREASURE! WHAT A LOAD OF RUBBISH!
POLICE

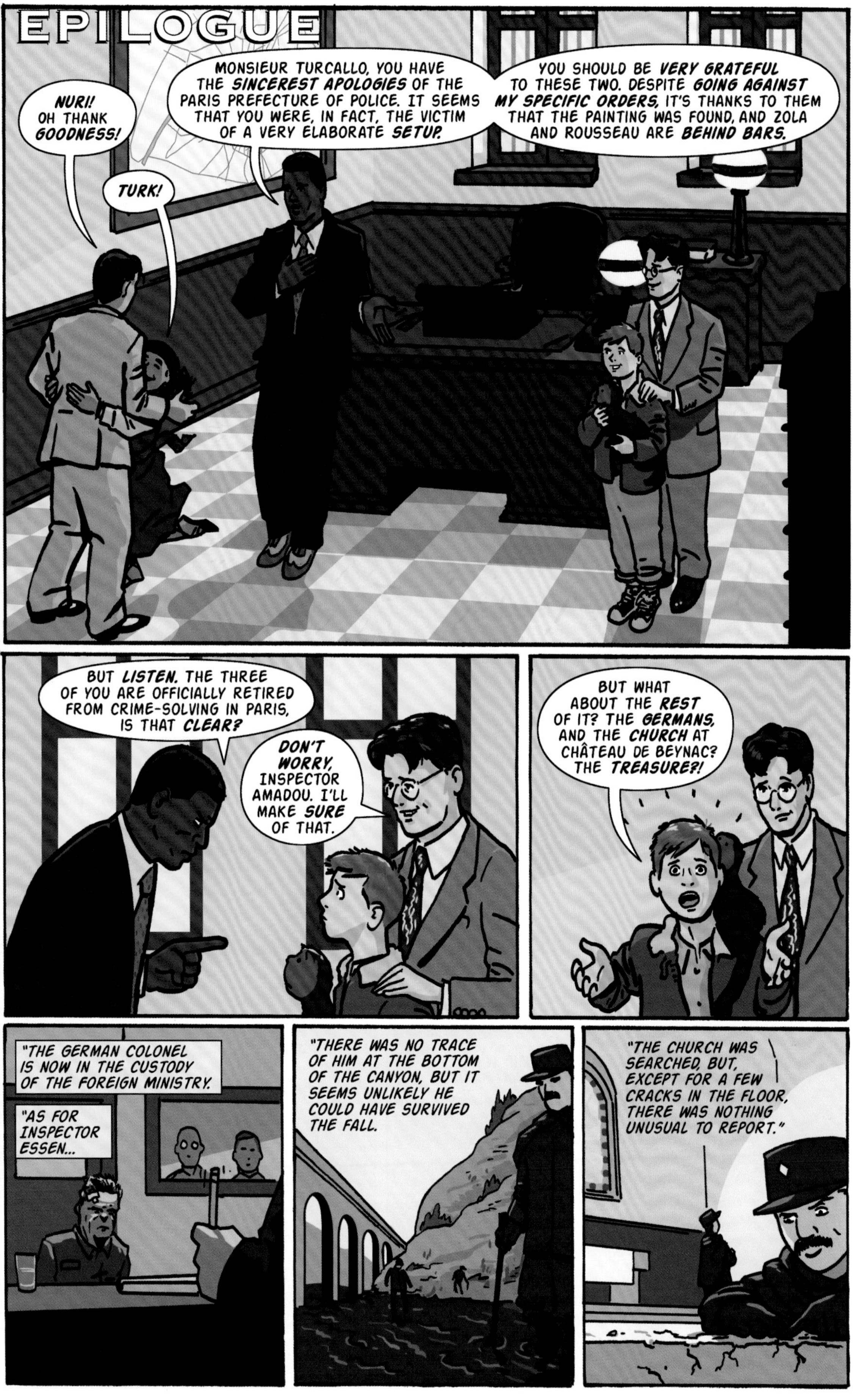
EPILOGUE
NURI! OH THANK GOODNESS!
TURK!
MONSIEUR TURCALLO, YOU HAVE THE SINCEREST APOLOGIES OF THE PARIS PREFECTURE OF POLICE. IT SEEMS THAT YOU WERE, IN FACT, THE VICTIM OF A VERY ELABORATE SETUP.
YOU SHOULD BE VERY GRATEFUL TO THESE TWO. DESPITE GOING AGAINST MY SPECIFIC ORDERS, IT'S THANKS TO THEM THAT THE PAINTING WAS FOUND, AND ZOLA AND ROUSSEAU ARE BEHIND BARS.
BUT LISTEN. THE THREE OF YOU ARE OFFICIALLY RETIRED FROM CRIME-SOLVING IN PARIS, IS THAT CLEAR?
DON'T WORRY, INSPECTOR AMADOU. I'LL MAKE SURE OF THAT.
BUT WHAT ABOUT THE REST OF IT? THE GERMANS, AND THE CHURCH AT CHÂTEAU DE BEYNAC? THE TREASURE?!
"THE GERMAN COLONEL IS NOW IN THE CUSTODY OF THE FOREIGN MINISTRY.
"AS FOR INSPECTOR ESSEN...
"THERE WAS NO TRACE OF HIM AT THE BOTTOM OF THE CANYON, BUT IT SEEMS UNLIKELY HE COULD HAVE SURVIVED THE FALL.
"THE CHURCH WAS SEARCHED, BUT, EXCEPT FOR A FEW CRACKS IN THE FLOOR, THERE WAS NOTHING UNUSUAL TO REPORT."

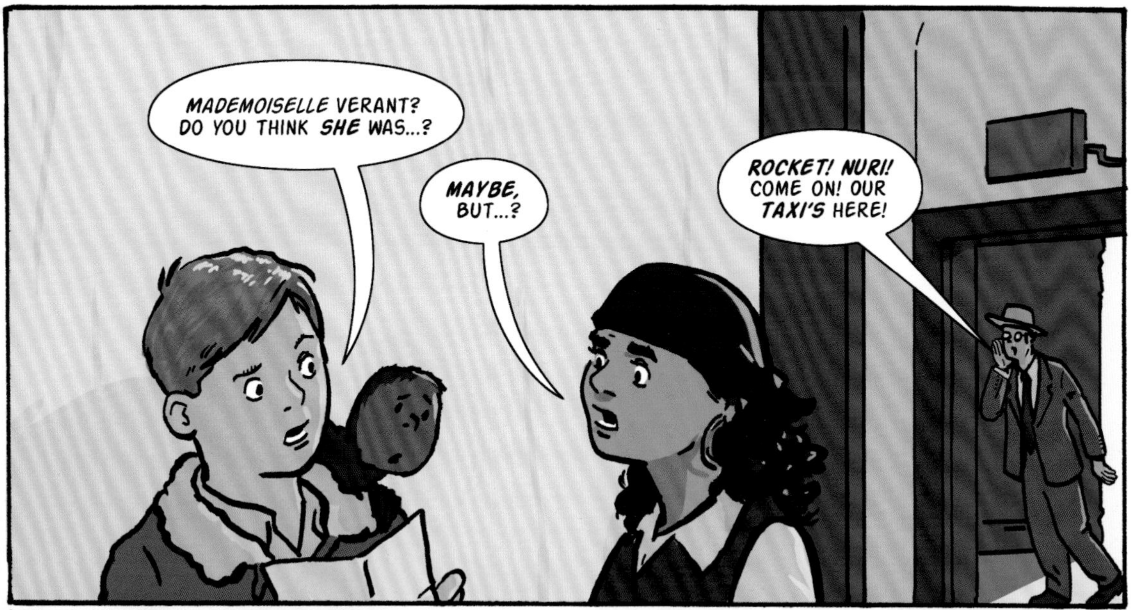
MADEMOISELLE VERANT? DO YOU THINK SHE WAS...?
MAYBE, BUT...?
ROCKET! NURI! COME ON! OUR TAXI'S HERE!

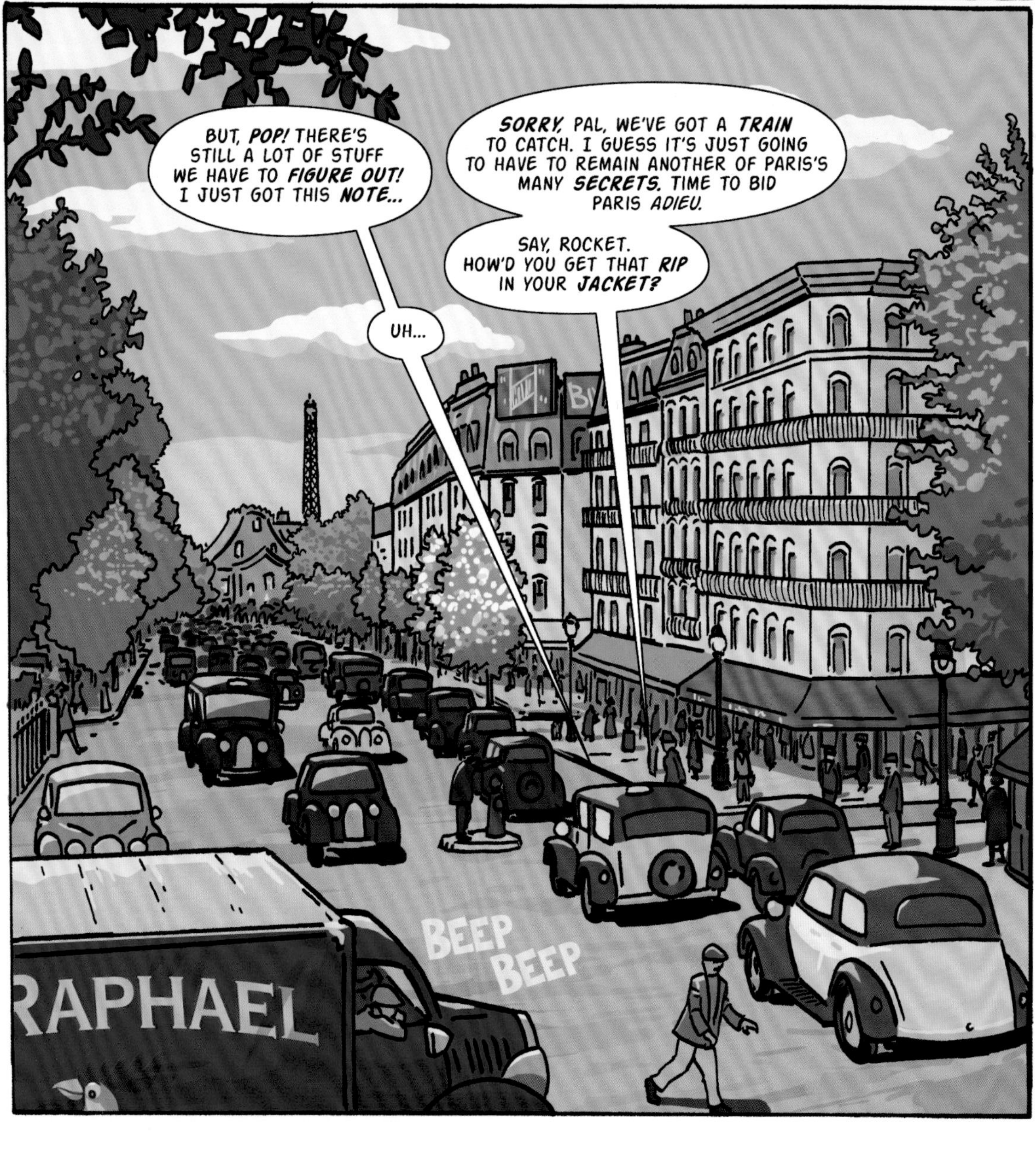
BUT, POP! THERE'S STILL A LOT OF STUFF WE HAVE TO FIGURE OUT! I JUST GOT THIS NOTE...
SORRY, PAL, WE'VE GOT A TRAIN TO CATCH. I GUESS IT'S JUST GOING TO HAVE TO REMAIN ANOTHER OF PARIS'S MANY SECRETS. TIME TO BID PARIS ADIEU.
SAY, ROCKET. HOW'D YOU GET THAT RIP IN YOUR JACKET?
UH...
BEEP BEEP
RAPHAEL

· Acknowledgements ·

I'm very grateful to the many people who have provided so much encouragement and support throughout the process of creating this book. I'm particularly thankful for those of you that read and enjoyed the first *Rocket Robinson* book and asked for a second. Of course, there's no way this project could have been completed without the generosity and support of my many Kickstarter backers. I am also indebted, once again, to the wonderful KATHY LYNCH for her editorial input and content expertise. My biggest thanks are for my loving and supportive family, especially my amazing wife, JENNIFER FARRINGTON. Once again, you made it all possible.

SEAN O'NEILL
Chicago, Illinois

Rocket Robinson™ and the Secret of the Saint

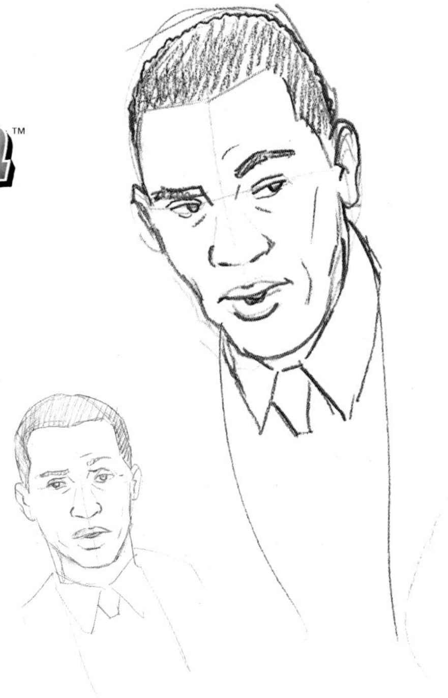

NOTES BY SEAN O'NEILL

A new book means new characters! While writing the script I did a lot of studies to get a sense of each new character's personality and mannerisms.

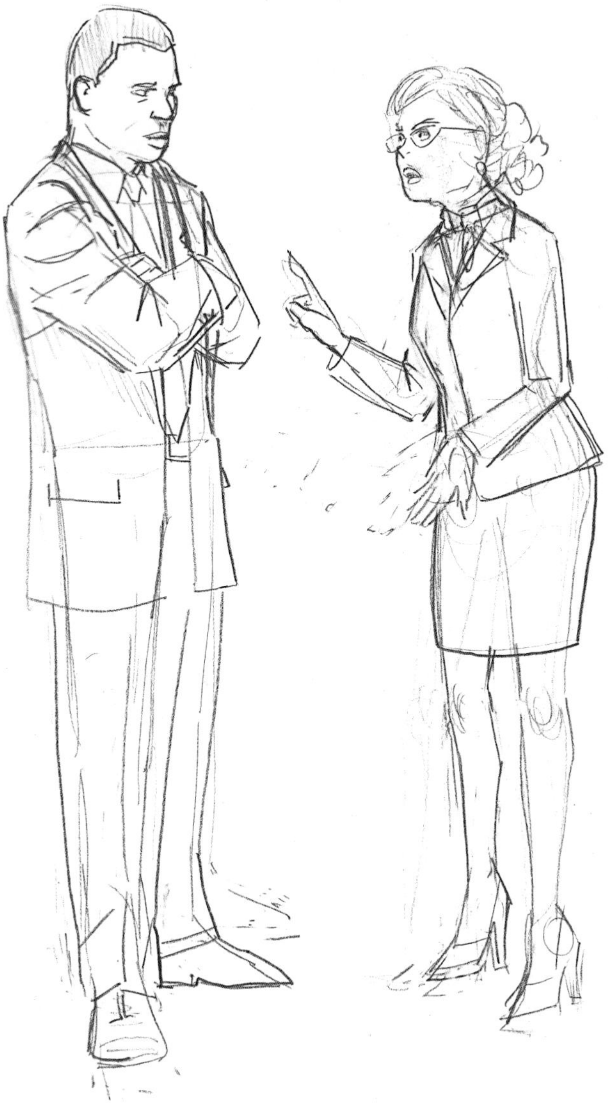

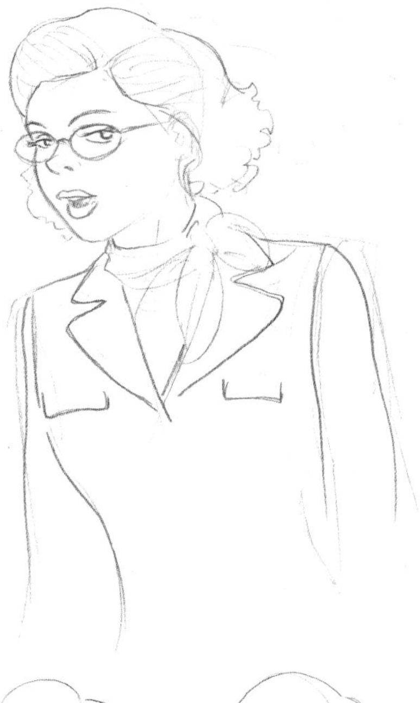

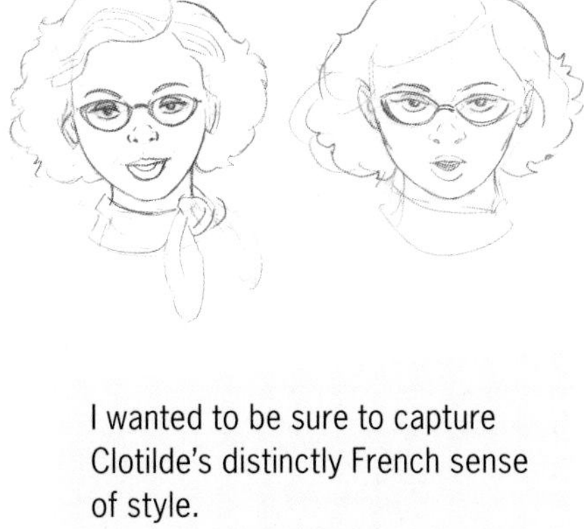

I wanted to be sure to capture Clotilde's distinctly French sense of style.

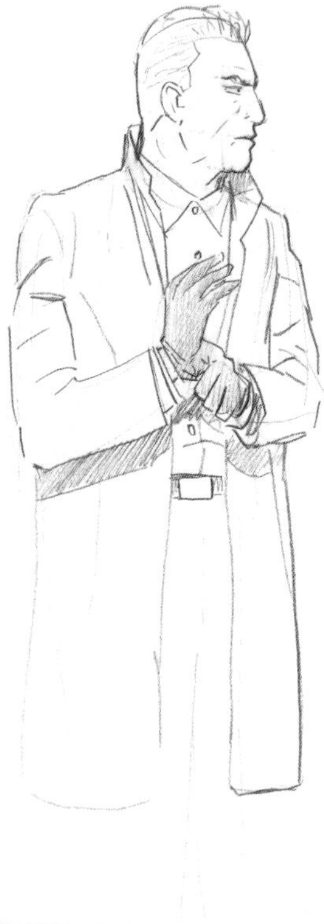

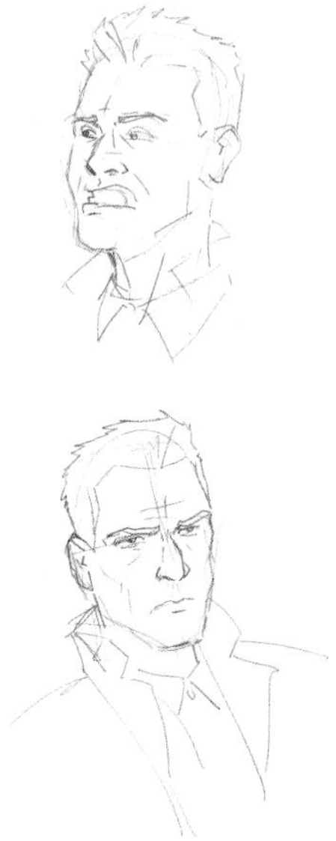

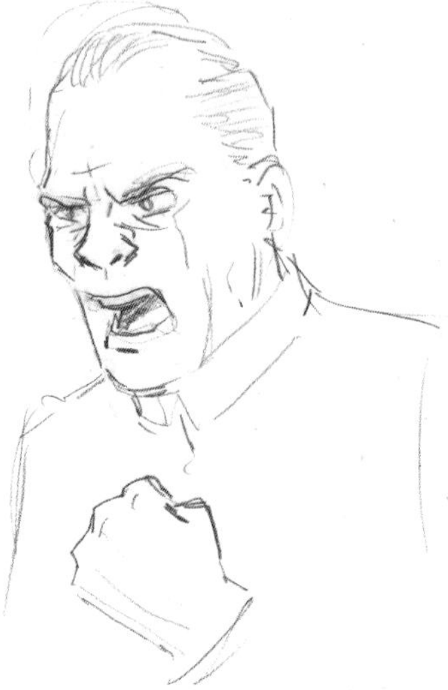

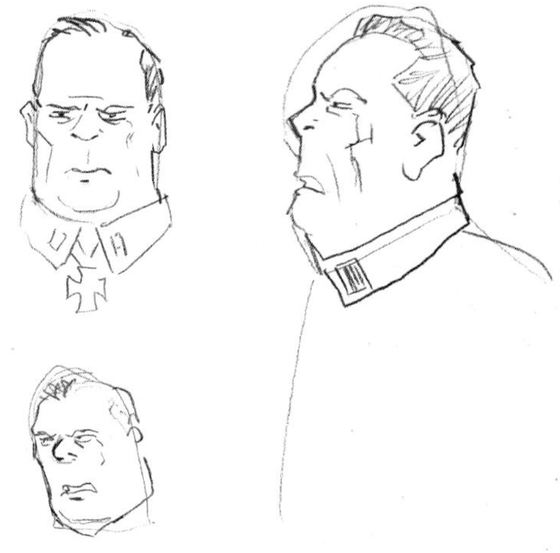

The villains of the story went through a lot of changes during the sketching process. I wanted to capture Col. Kreutz's obsessive intensity and Essen's cool, menacing efficiency.

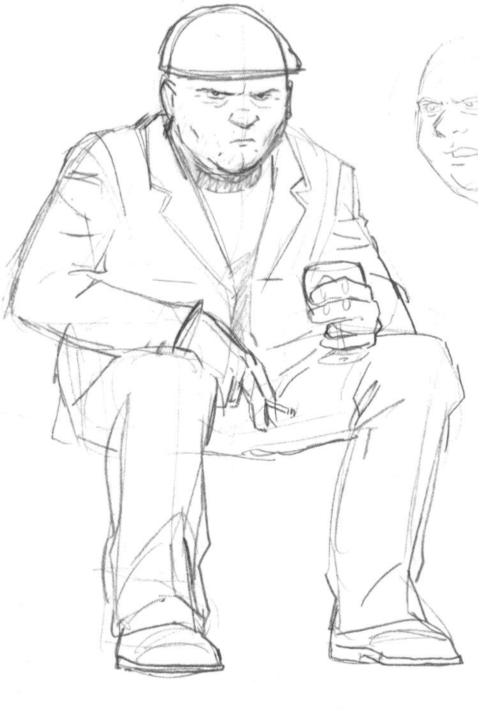

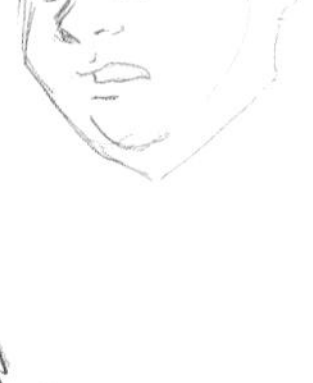

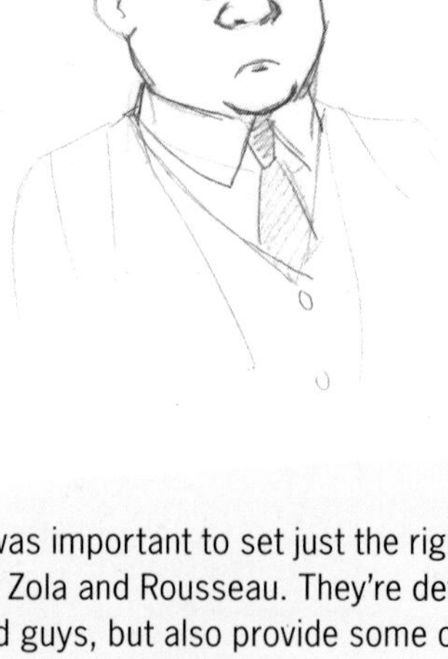

It was important to set just the right tone for Zola and Rousseau. They're definitely bad guys, but also provide some comic moments in the story.

This early sketch of the cover was done way back when I was just starting Book One. On the next page is a more refined version of what became the current cover.

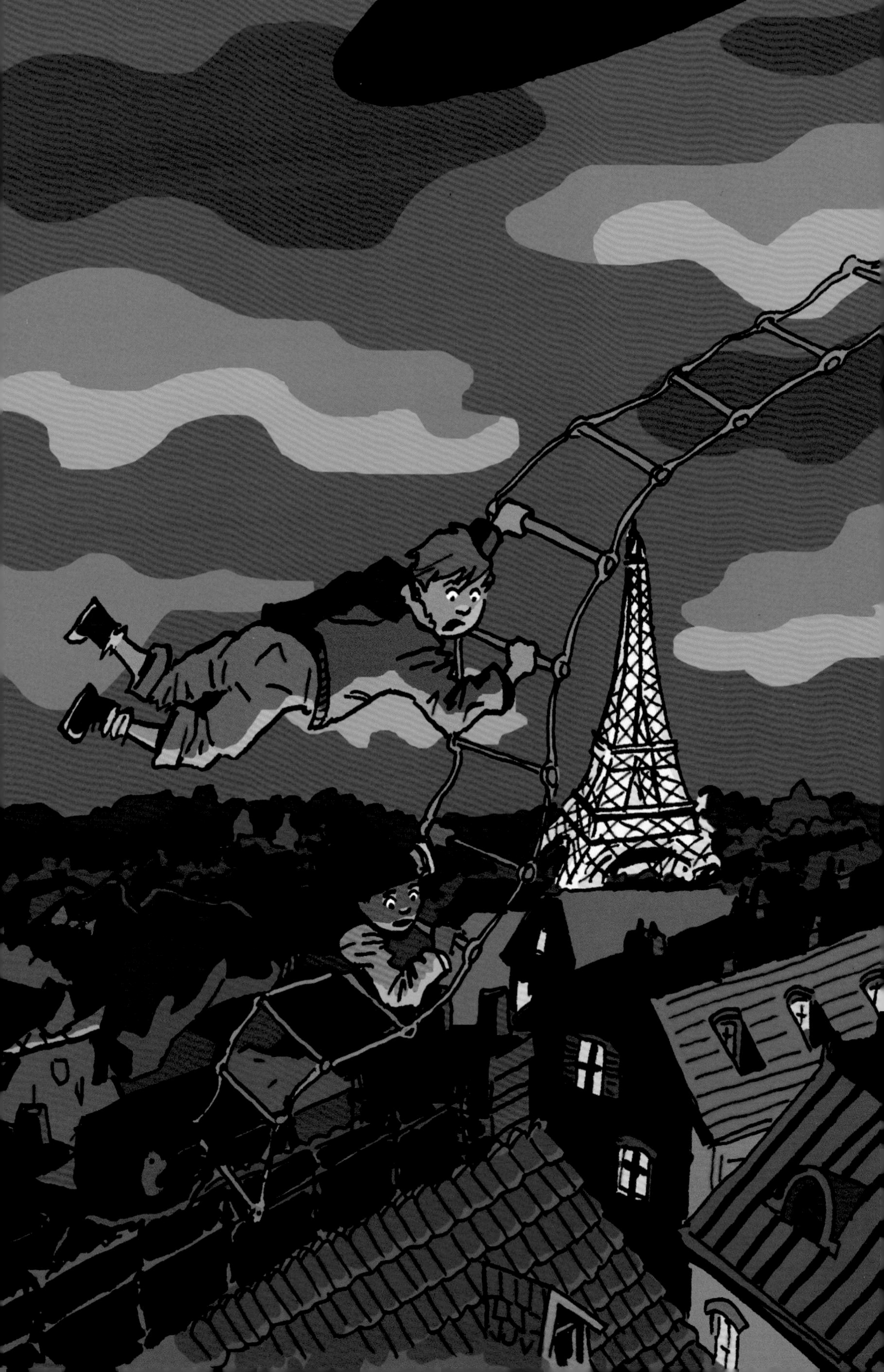

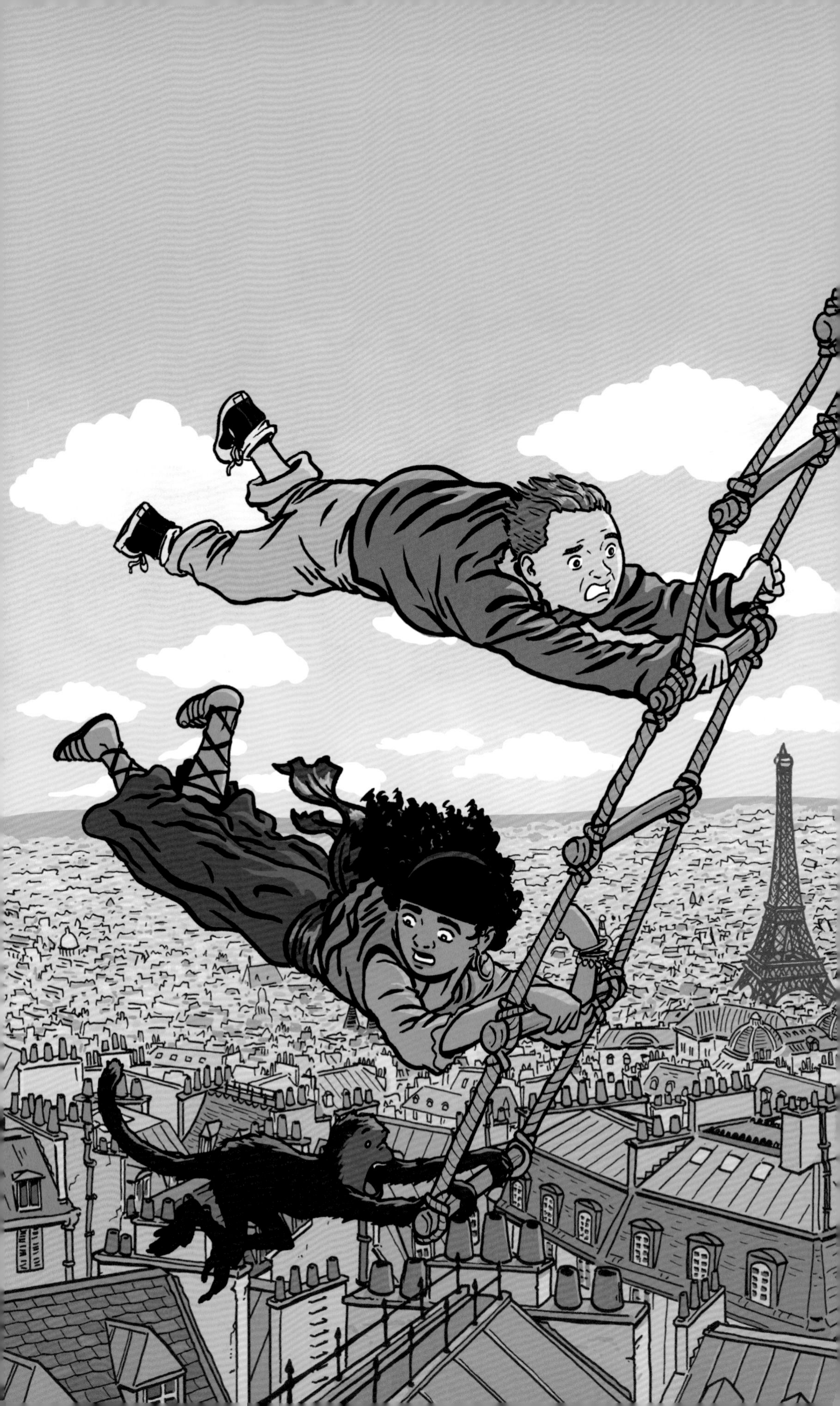

BOOKS THAT MIDDLE READERS WILL LOVE!

AVATAR: THE LAST AIRBENDER

Aang and friends' adventures continue right where the TV series left off, in these beautiful oversized hardcover collections, from *Airbender* creators Michael Dante DiMartino and Bryan Konietzko and Eisner and Harvey Award winner Gene Luen Yang!

The Promise ISBN 978-1-61655-074-5
The Search ISBN 978-1-61655-226-8
The Rift ISBN 978-1-61655-550-4
Smoke and Shadow ISBN 978-1-50670-013-7
North and South ISBN 978-1-50670-195-0
(Available October 2017)
$39.99 each

PLANTS VS. ZOMBIES

The hit video game continues its comic book invasion! Crazy Dave—the babbling-yet-brilliant inventor and top-notch neighborhood defender—helps his niece Patrice and young adventurer Nate Timely fend off a zombie invasion! Their only hope is a brave army of chomping, squashing, and pea-shooting plants!

Boxed Set #1: Lawnmageddon, Timepocalypse, Bully for You
ISBN 978-1-50670-043-4
Boxed Set #2: Grown Sweet Home, Garden Warfare, The Art of Plants vs. Zombies
ISBN 978-1-50670-232-2
Boxed Set #3: Petal to the Metal, Boom Boom Mushroom, Battle Extravagonzo
ISBN 978-1-50670-521-7 (Available October 2017)
$29.99 each

TREE MAIL

Mike Raicht, Brian Smith

Rudy—a determined frog—hopes to overcome the odds and land his dream job delivering mail to the other animals on Popomoko Island! Rudy always hops forward, no matter what obstacle seems to be in the way of his dreams!

ISBN 978-1-50670-096-0 **$12.99**

HOW TO TRAIN YOUR DRAGON: THE SERPENT'S HEIR

Picking up just after the events in *How to Train Your Dragon 2*, Hiccup, Astrid, and company are called upon to assist the people of an earthquake-plagued island. But their lives are imperiled by a madman and an incredible new dragon who even Toothless—the alpha dragon—may not be able to control!

ISBN 978-1-61655-931-1 **$10.99**

POPPY! AND THE LOST LAGOON

Matt Kindt, Brian Hurtt

At the age of ten, Poppy Pepperton is the greatest explorer since her grandfather Pappy! When a shrunken mummy head speaks, adventure calls Poppy and her sidekick/guardian, Colt Winchester, across the globe in search of an exotic fish—along the way discovering clues to what happened to Pappy all those years ago!

ISBN 978-1-61655-943-4 **$14.99**

SOUPY LEAVES HOME

Cecil Castellucci, Jose Pimienta

Two misfits with no place to call home take a train-hopping journey from the cold heartbreak of their eastern homes to the sunny promise of California in this Depression-era coming-of-age tale.

ISBN 978-1-61655-431-6 **$14.99**

DARKHORSE.COM

AVAILABLE AT YOUR LOCAL COMICS SHOP OR BOOKSTORE | TO FIND A COMICS SHOP IN YOUR AREA, VISIT COMICSHOPLOCATOR.COM

For more information or to order direct: On the web: DarkHorse.com •Email: mailorder@darkhorse.com •Phone: 1-800-862-0052 Mon.–Fri. 9 AM to 5 PM Pacific Time.
Avatar: The Last Airbender © Viacom International Inc. Plants vs. Zombies © Electronic Arts Inc. How to Train Your Dragon © DreamWorks Animation LLC. Tree Mail™ © Brian Smith and Noble Transmission Group, LLC.
Poppy!™ © Matt Kindt and Brian Hurtt. Soupy Leaves Home™ © Cecil Castellucci. Dark Horse Books® and the Dark Horse logo are registered trademarks of Dark Horse Comics, Inc. All rights reserved. (BL 6002 PI)

DARK HORSE BOOKS

MORE TITLES FOR MIDDLE READERS!

AW YEAH COMICS!
ACTION CAT
& ADVENTURE BUG
BY ART BALTAZAR & FRANCO

BIRD·BOY
VOLUME 1: THE SWORD OF MALI MANI
ANNE SZABLA

THE
COURAGEOUS
PRINCESS
BEYOND THE HUNDRED KINGDOMS
ROD ESPINOSA

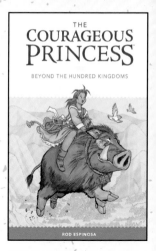

AW YEAH COMICS!

Art Baltazar, Franco, and more!

It's up to Action Cat and Adventure Bug to stop the bad guys! Follow these amazing superheroes created by Art Baltazar and Franco in this comic extravaganza with bonus stories from the Aw Yeah bullpen!

Volume 1: And . . . Action!
ISBN 978-1-61655-558-0
Volume 2: Time for . . . Adventure!
ISBN 978-1-61655-689-1
Volume 3: Make Way . . . for Awesome!
ISBN 978-1-50670-045-8
Action Cat & Adventure Bug
ISBN 978-1-50670-023-6
$12.99 each

BIRD BOY

Anne Szabla

Bali, a ten-year-old boy, is desperate to prove his worth to his northern tribe despite his small stature. Banned from the ceremony that would make him an adult in the eyes of his people, he takes matters into his own hands. To prove that he is capable of taking care of himself, he sets out into the forbidden forest and stumbles upon a legendary weapon.

Volume 1: The Sword of Mali Mani
ISBN 978-1-61655-930-4
Volume 2: The Liminal Wood
ISBN 978-1-61655-968-7
$9.99 each

THE COURAGEOUS PRINCESS

Rod Espinosa

Once upon a time, a greedy dragon kidnapped a beloved princess . . . But if you think she just waited around for some charming prince to rescue her, then you're in for a surprise! Princess Mabelrose has enough brains and bravery to fend for herself!

Volume 1: Beyond the Hundred Kingdoms
ISBN 978-1-61655-722-5
Volume 2: The Unremembered Lands
ISBN 978-1-61655-723-2
Volume 3: The Dragon Queen
ISBN 978-1-61655-724-9
$19.99 each

itty bitty
MASK
ART BALTAZAR & FRANCO

andi watson
Glister

SCARY
GODMOTHER
JILL THOMPSON

ITTY BITTY COMICS

Art Baltazar, Franco

Follow the adventures of your favorite Dark Horse heroes—now pintsized!

Itty Bitty Hellboy ISBN 978-1-61655-414-9 **$9.99**
Itty Bitty Hellboy: The Search for the Were-Jaguar!
ISBN 978-1-61655-801-7 **$12.99**
Itty Bitty Mask ISBN 978-1-61655-683-9 **$12.99**

GLISTER

Andi Watson

Strange things happen around Glister Butterworth. A young girl living on her family's English estate, Glister has unusual adventures every day, like the arrival of a teapot haunted by a demanding ghost, a crop of new relatives blooming on the family tree, a stubborn house that walks off its land in a huff, and a trip to Faerieland to find her missing mother.

ISBN 978-1-50670-319-0 **$14.99**

SCARY GODMOTHER

Jill Thompson

It's Halloween night and it's up to Scary Godmother to show one little girl just how much fun spooky can be! Hannah Marie with the help of Scary Godmother will stand up to her mean-spirited cousin Jimmy and her fear of monsters on her first Halloween adventure with the big kids.

ISBN 978-1-59582-589-6
Comic Book Stories ISBN 978-1-59582-723-4
$24.99 each